Kingdoms in the Marsh

ROBERT F. LACKEY

ROBERT F. LACKEY

Heron Oaks, Murrells Inlet, SC
Copyright © 2018 Robert F. Lackey

ISBN: 0692831355
ISBN-13:978-0692831359

Other books by Robert F. Lackey:
Pulaski's Canal – ISBN: 0692625267
Blood on the Chesapeake – ISBN 0692688676
Raven's Risk – ISBN 0692831320

As Pug Greenwood:
Bim and Them   ISBN: 0692569561
Tooey's Crossroads ISBN: 0692566198
Tooey's Crossroads II ISBN: 0692628134
On The Way To Alice ISBN: 069291417X

ROBERT F. LACKEY

ACKNOWLEDGEMENTS

*No book can make its way to print without the hard work of many people.
I wish to acknowledge the valuable assistance of stalwart beta readers and
thank each of them for their contributions.*

Judee Cooper of Edgewood, Maryland

Linda Cross of Avenue Maryland

Kathy Cullum of Havre de Grace, Maryland

Debra Gapa-Davidson of Grosse Ile, Michigan

Lori English of Las Cruces, New Mexico,

Jeanne Hawtin of Havre de Grace, Maryland

Diane Bassette Nelson of Interlaken, New York

Peggy O'Donnell of Port Republic, Maryland

Buddy Quade of Columbia, Maryland

Marian Stokel of Leonardtown, Maryland

Nancy Testerman of Havre de Grace, Maryland

Mike Webb of Newport News, Virginia,

who aided significantly in finalizing this manuscript.

FURTHER ACKNOWLEDGEMENTS

I offer my appreciation and recognition for the wonderful generosity of

The Susquehanna Museum at the Lock House, Havre de Grace, Maryland

The Havre de Grace Maritime Museum, Havre de Grace, Maryland

The Chesapeake Bay Maritime Museum and the St. Michaels Museum, St. Michaels, Maryland

Captain Jordan Smith and the crew of the Pride of Baltimore II, Baltimore, Maryland for sail and Atlantic Ocean sailing advice.

Mr. Robert McAlister, Director of the South Carolina Maritime Museum, Georgetown, South Carolina for historical information regarding shipping and harbor protocols in 19th century Georgetown, SC, and sailing conditions in an around Winyah Bay.

Mr.Keith Wilkie, acclaimed marine artist, for his generosity in permitting his painting "Three Egret Marsh" to be used as the foundation for this book's cover art.

And that exquisite gem at the head of the Chesapeake Bay:

Havre de Grace

ROBERT F. LACKEY

1

January 1844, the South Carolina Coast

Ben and Sonja Pulaski stood close together at the windward wheel of the schooner *Raven*. The ship held a strange mix of people brought with the Pulaskis and their crew. Twelve escaping slaves shared the decks, stolen from their Maryland owners by the Pulaskis under the pretense of selling them in South Carolina. Ben now called the slaves the "Solomons men," named for the Chesapeake Bay port where their owner had sent them on board. The Solomons men knew South Carolina was the heart of slave country, the home of the Charleston slave market, and it was not a place they wanted to be. It would be a long voyage for them all, testing their trust of each other, and of Ben.

Ben steered their ship into the mouth of Winyah Bay, making for the North Island Lighthouse, his first step in getting to Georgetown. Sandbars populating the bay and the ever moving channel would not allow him to sail further without risk of running aground. He would wait near the lighthouse for a steam tug to tow them up to Georgetown. Sonja raised her chin into the cold morning breeze that slipped across the deck and filled the sails, letting the wind play with her amber curls.

"So, you think Jeremiah will not cause us any trouble, Ben?"

"It doesn't matter, Sonja. I don't intend to deal with him again."

Sailing to South Carolina was part of Ben's deception as a slave trader, but it was cargoes of Georgetown rice and lumber that financed his crew and ship. Northern buyers called the sought after rice 'Carolina Gold' and were eager to buy it. The Pulaskis were not wealthy. The abolition society that used their service raised limited money, initially to purchase slaves in Charleston, but that was a fading effort. Other means became necessary to help slaves escape.

After Georgetown, they could run back to the Chesapeake Bay, not seeing the slave auction in Charleston on this trip. The Chesapeake was still in the South, still ringed by slavery, but connections were growing in those border states to aid escaping slaves. Some were calling it the Underground Railroad. A few Marylanders, like the Pulaskis, were awakening to the gnawing questions between old culture and morals. Once back in the upper Chesapeake, the Solomons men would be transferred near St. Michaels. From there, they would be taken into Pennsylvania by others who would help them disappear from slavery.

The motion of the ship settled among the moderate waves of the bay. Ben motioned to the first mate, his half-brother, Edward.

"Now that we're in calmer waters, Eddie, we need to knock down the temporary partitions in the hold. I don't know where the Solomons men will sleep, but we have to make room for the cargo."

A few of the escaping slaves stood nearby, watching their approach to land and listening to Ben. Among them was Simon Bond, Ben's longtime friend who had been swept up among the Solomons men when he tried to buy his wife.

"Simon, since that will take away the private space for you and Lettie, she can share the captain's cabin with Sonja. That's going to be the only place on board where women can have privacy until we get back to the Chesapeake."

"Lettie may not be a happy roommate for Sonja, Ben."

"They will have to adjust. Also, I need you to take charge of the Solomons men."

The paddle wheeler *Hannah* towed them up the bay and into the narrow Sampit River. Georgetown Harbor sat along the eastern bank of the dark river across from a low marsh island. The Sampit continued around the island forming a loop in the river at the northern edge of town. The exposed banks of low tide filled the air with the odor of soured pluff mud, old oysters and discarded fish. As the Raven's crew tied on to the dock, Ben sent Edward into town to the telegraph office.

Ben singled out another crewman. "Harry, I need you to go down to the hold and bring up a small barrel of rum." Ben pointed to the far end of the dock. "Take it to the Harbor Master's office. Hopefully, it will keep him friendly while we clear the wharf of all that stacked cargo long awaiting us."

As the men scattered to follow their instructions, Ben and Sonja left the *Raven* to join Edward in the town. Ben found Edward in a tavern not far from the ship.

"Were you able to send the telegram?" Ben asked.

"Just the way you told me, Ben. I used the phrase 'extra cargo.'"

"Good. Why don't you join Sonja and me for a warm meal, Eddie?"

"Oh, I don't want to intrude Ben..."

"Nonsense. I want you closer to me and my family, Eddie. There is still much we don't know about each other."

The three crossed from the waterfront to Front Street and found a well-decorated tavern on the next corner. As they approached, a lady and gentleman came out of the building. The gentleman tipped his hat to Sonja and smiled. Sonja returned his smile and turned to Ben.

"This place should be decent enough. Let's go in here."

Inside the well-lit tavern, warm air bathed their faces. The aromas of burning oak, roasted meat and fried fish blended with the smells of boiling coffee and fresh ale. Ben's stomach growled. The bartender pointed them to an empty table where he soon brought handwritten menus for their selection, a new experience for Sonja. While they waited, their conversation drifted from

3

discussing the voyage on to childhood experiences until the food arrived. They gave full attention to their meal in silence, only trading smiles between mouthfuls of venison and duck and sips of ale.

Several miles above Georgetown, along the Waccamaw River, the small paddlewheel steamboat *Lydia* plowed through the root stained waters. Her bow wave slapped the banks as she chugged past, making her best speed. Its owner, Jeremiah Williamson, stood on the foredeck with ice in his eyes, gritting his teeth and fingering the handles of his new pistols. Behind the small pilothouse, Ensign Cuttingham, the steamer's master, stood among five heavily armed men.

Jeremiah turned back toward the stern. "Cuttingham. You're sure it was Pulaski you saw?"

Cuttingham straightened. "Yes, sir."

A wide grin grew on Jeremiah's face. He pointed at the armed men quickly gathered from his plantation. "Kill anyone standing with Pulaski, but leave that bastard for me!"

The boson reduced throttle to make the turn into the Sampit River, heading for the Georgetown harbor. Cuttingham pointed out the *Raven* to Jeremiah as they neared it.

"Pass it," Jeremiah ordered. "Dock in front of the Harbor Master's office. He needs to know I am confronting a thief in his harbor. Might get him to impound that ship as well. I could use a good cargo ship."

Jeremiah stormed up the stairs to the Harbor Master's office, bumping shoulders with Harry on his way down.

Jeremiah glared at Harry. "Look where you're going, there, mister," then turned back toward his men. "Stay by the boat. Remember, not Pulaski. Do what you want with any others, but Pulaski is mine."

Ben heard a familiar voice call out in the dining

room.

"Captain," Harry called, zigzagging between the tables toward them, to the stares of the patrons. "We must go!"

"Why?" Ben and Sonja spoke as one.

Harry took in a deep breath, still breathing hard after his run. "There is a tall hateful man at the Harbor Master's office, with armed men and a uniformed man waiting for him by a small steamboat," Harry said. He focused on Ben. "He means you harm, Cap'n. He told his men 'do what you want with any others, but Pulaski is mine."

Ben turned to Sonja. "It must be Jeremiah Williamson."

Sonja gripped the table, eyeing Ben.

"Ben, you said we would not have any trouble with him."

Ben held his palms up.

"I said I did not intend to deal with him."

"Well, he obviously intends to deal with you," she said, then turned to Harry. "He has armed men?"

As Harry nodded to Sonja, Ben sighed and pushed his chair back from the table.

"We need to get back to the ship and keep him off it."

He fished a silver dollar from his pocket and dropped it on the table as the barkeeper was bringing them a fresh pot of coffee.

"That enough?" Ben asked the man over his shoulder.

"More than enough, sir," the barkeep said, but Ben was already out the door.

When they returned to the ship, the dock was clear, and the lumber crammed onto Raven's deck. Both the crew and Solomons men were breathing heavily and resting on the deck.

"It's all loaded, Ben," Simon told him. "We just finished."

"Already?"

"We had eleven men and a woman, Benjamin. All

with good reason to be away from this place."

"Well, now we have another reason to be away." Ben raised his voice so the others could hear. "Dangerous men are coming here, and we cannot stay a moment longer."

Ben glanced at the wind pennant flying over the Harbor Master's office. "The wind is right, Edward."

Recognizing the *Lydia* moored farther down the dock, Ben smiled. "Then let us be away," he said. "We have a westerly wind. Simon, get everyone on their feet. Edward, please have the mooring lines at the bow and amidships untied, but leave the stern tied for now. And, please have the jibs raised, just the jibs. We are going to sail out of here, now."

"Without a pilot or a steamer?"

"We'll have a steamer," Ben said.

Edward and Simon shared frowns. Ben ran to the captain's cabin, ignoring Lettie's shriek as he charged in while she stood naked, washing. He grabbed his pistol, and stuck it in his waist, then ran out of the cabin, tossing his apologies to Lettie over his shoulder. He ran back up to Front Street and turned north.

"God damn it," Jeremiah yelled at the Harbor Master. "The last time he was here, he cheated me. He bought a prized slave of mine for next to nothing using a cheap trick. I want his ship impounded, right now."

"I don't have a warrant or orders from the proper authority Mr. Williamson. I will not allow this office to be subverted for your private deeds."

Jeremiah stood, kicking over his chair, "You will not be the God damned Harbor Master long."

He burst out of the office, thumped down the stairs and returned to the *Lydia*, signaling the gunmen as he approached. "You men come with me." He pointed at the boat. "Cuttingham, you stay here and keep steam up in this thing."

Jeremiah peered along the dock, locating the masts of the *Raven* near the end, and marched toward it. The gunmen followed close behind.

Jeremiah spoke over his shoulder as he walked away, "Do not fire until I tell you."

They passed the alleyway without seeing Ben. He smiled as the group walked by, then dashed across the dock to the steamboat, leaping onto the *Lydia*. Cuttingham was directing the boson to toss additional logs into the fire box but turned at the sound of Ben's boot heel striking the deck. Ben shoved hard against Cuttingham's chest, propelling him off the deck and into the river. Cuttingham flailed his arms in the cold water, splashing, calling for help. Ben pulled out his pistol, placing the barrel against the temple of the boson.

"Toss that man a rescue float," Ben ordered.

The man obeyed then raised his hands as he turned back to face Ben.

"We are going for a little ride, Mister," Ben said to the boson.

"Yes, sir. Just say where."

"Back down the dock toward that ship that is starting to swing out."

The boson spun around and pulled the lever to let steam begin rotating the side paddles. The *Lydia* moved away from the dock with gaining speed. The gap started to narrow between the drifting bow of the *Raven* and the shore of the marsh island. Ben pulled the knotted rope to the steam whistle, giving it two blasts.

Jeremiah turned to see the *Lydia* pass, stopping to yell at it. "What the hell? Where are you going, Cuttingham?" Then he heard Cuttingham's screams from up the river. He ignored Cuttingham and gave his full attention to his steamer, locking eyes with Ben, who gave him a cold smile as he passed. Jeremiah's face flushed crimson and a snarl twisted into place.

Edward was on the bow of the *Raven* as it swings slowly away from the dock when the *Lydia's* whistle blew.

"Throw me your bowline," Ben yelled to Edward.

Edward grabbed the coiled line and threw it to the *Lydia*. Ben caught it and tied it to the stern cleat of the steamer.

"We gonna have a hell of a jolt when we get to the end of that line, Mistah," the boson said.

"Not if we do it right," Ben said. "Open the throttle all the way."

The boson shook his head and blew out his breath, then yanked back on the throttle.

"Cut the stern mooring," Ben yelled to the *Raven*, but Edward was already gone from the bow to see to it. One of the *Raven's* crew loosened the mainmast boom and swung it out over the river as others raised the mainsail. The gentle breeze began pushing the stern out into the river, shrinking the channel for the *Lydia*.

"Yes," Ben yelled, "Swing her ass out, too."

The *Lydia* drove into the collapsing space between the *Raven* and the marsh island. A gunshot echoed over the water, and the planking near Ben's boot exploded in ripped splinters. He dashed around to the far side of the pilot house and peeked back at the dock through the *Lydia's* windows. The boson ducked down as two more bullets splashed into the nearby water.

"Keep your eyes on the river, Mister," Ben said.

The boson dropped to his knees inside the pilot house, leaning his head out the other side and reaching back in with his left hand to steer the boat. As the gunmen's view of the *Lydia* narrowed, three more shots echoed off the marsh. Two bullets slapped into the nearby mud, and a final gash appeared on *Lydia's* stern before the *Raven* blocked the shooters' view.

The *Lydia* churned ahead of the *Raven's* bow just as the space closed behind her. The *Lydia* began snaking the tow line down river. The *Raven's* jib sails were adjusted to give her a little headway as she swung out into the river. Ben poked the boson with the barrel of his pistol. "Steer back closer to the dockside. I want to pull her bow around at an angle."

The boson smiled and nodded his head. "This won't be so bad after all, suh. We're just gonna dance her down the river."

As the *Raven* drifted toward the opposite shore, her stern swung out. Her bow and the steamer were moving closer to the same direction, only a few angles different. There was just a slight jolt of resistance as the steamer came to the end of the tow line, helping the *Raven's* bow swing into her new direction. The ship slowed as she took the weight of the *Raven*, the steam engine chugged to drive the paddles, and smoke thickened from the stack.

The steamer had moved out of sight from the dock with the *Raven* moving down the river behind her. The riflemen shifted their aim to the *Raven*, but with little damage to the ship.

"What's your name," Ben asked the boson.

"Achilles, suh."

"How would you like to go up north, Achilles?"

Achilles smiled. "Oh yes, suh. I would like that so much. Yes, suh."

Ben lowered the pistol, uncocked its hammer, and slid it into his belt. "Then take us down Winyah Bay until we run out of steam."

Achilles released a broad grin as he stood up. He tossed more wood into the fire box with one hand and steered into the deep channel with the other. The *Raven* obediently followed behind, like a mother hound trotting after her pup.

On board, the *Raven*, those still on deck hid at the bow, behind stacks of cured lumber sitting between them and Jeremiah's gunmen. The only damage to the ship was to the windows of the empty captain's cabin, while Sonja and Lettie sat safely forward of the brick stove in the galley.

As Ben and the *Lydia* towed *Raven* farther from Georgetown, Jeremiah fired his pistols into the growing space between them. The bullets dropped harmlessly into the wake of the ship. In a rage, Jeremiah threw his empty guns toward the *Raven*, where they fell wasted into the dark waters of the Sampit River. He stamped his feet, shook his fist and cursed. His voice bellowed over the water, faintly reaching Ben's ears above the hiss of the steam engine.

"God damn you, Pulaski! God damn you!"

Ben smiled.

Ben Pulaski leaned against the doorway of the pilot house on the steamboat *Lydia*. His hands rested in his coat pockets, and he hummed an old tune as he gazed beyond the bow. Achilles tossed the last few pieces of split wood into the firebox. Ben sniffed the freshening breeze, smelling the low tide mud from the marshes ringing the bay.

"Cap'n Ben, that was all of the wood. We ain't gonna make it out of Winyah Bay, but we can get pretty close to the North Island Lighthouse."

Ben nodded and shrugged his shoulders. "Well, Achilles, I guess that's the right thing to do. My first thought was just to abandon this boat in the ocean, but if I ever want to come back to Georgetown, it will be better to leave Jeremiah his little steamboat."

"You still thinkin I'm going north, Cap'n?"

"Aren't you?"

Achilles frowned. "I am if you're taking me. If you're not, I need to have a damned good story to tell Massah Williamson, why I pulled you and your ship away from him!'

Ben patted Achilles' shoulder. "You are invited to join the *Raven* and sail with us to the Chesapeake Bay, and then meet up with folks there who will get you into a free state. Is that to your satisfaction?"

Achilles kept his gaze beyond the bow with his chin held up. "That is to my satisfaction."

"Excellent. So then, please take us, and that wallowing ship behind us, over to yon lighthouse, Achilles!"

Minutes later the steamboat *Lydia* was at anchor, Ben and Achilles had boarded the *Raven*, and the

Raven's extended crew were scurrying around the lumber on deck, setting sails. A bold January wind popped the canvas sails out like full bellies. The *Raven* leaned away from the wind, dug her keel against the saltwater and dashed out of Winyah Bay into the Atlantic Ocean. Ben gripped the handles of the windward wheel, steering west. The twin wheel stood unmanned on the other side of the binnacle for the moment. Achilles stood nearby, enjoying the movement of the ship taking him away. She met the first Atlantic roller with a firm bow and charged over it through the spray. Achilles turned toward the stern and pointed.

"Cap'n," he called.

Far inside the bay, marked by rising black smoke in the distance, a steam tug churned southward. Her side wheels slapped the water hard, adding more foam to the bow wave.

"I'll bet her pressure valve is sputtering and hissing," Achilles said. "Most likely Massah Williamson is standing on her deck and sputtering worse than that."

"I don't imagine that man is happy with me," Ben said with a wide grin.

Achilles walked away as Sonja moved next to Ben, peering at the black smoke.

"Is it coming this way?" she asked.

"It's probably the *Hannah*," he said. "I didn't see any other steamers near the docks – except that little one I stole," he added with a smile. "*Hannah's* built for the bay and fresh water. Don't think she has enough hull to come out here."

Sonja lingered another moment. "You told me Anthony wants you to be in the rice shipping business. You also told me we need that business to pay for the ship because Anthony's group cannot."

"Yes..."

"How can we ever go back there?"

"Jeremiah is one man, and our cargo did not come from his plantation. We now have good business connections with two other plantations... and I think

12

with the Harbor Master, as well."

Sonja crossed her arms. "I'm afraid of that man, Ben. Afraid of what he will try to do to you if we go back."

"All will be well, Mrs. Pulaski," he said.

She sighed. "I am not so sure, but I have another question."

"Yes?"

"When can I take the wheel?"

The *Raven*'s deck sloped away from the wind, putting the downwind railing closer to the sea, where ocean foam splashed along the edge of the deck. She rocked forward as she conquered each long wave and took more spray over her bow. Ben moved slightly away from the wheel to allow Sonja room to step in but kept his feet braced apart and a firm grip on the wheel handles.

"Two hands and hold tight, Sonja."

"I know," she said, "I handled it well on the way to Annapolis, didn't I?"

"That was in the Chesapeake Bay; this is the Atlantic," Ben said.

He released the wheel, and the handles jumped half a turn before Sonja could take full control of them. Ben's hands reached out toward the wheel behind her, but he pulled them back. Sonja grinned at Ben from a reddened face, bracing her feet farther apart and leaning her shoulders to turn the wheel back to its position.

"Got it," she said through gritted teeth.

Ben stayed nearby, keeping exaggerated attention to the pennant at the top of the main mast. The wind gusted slightly, enough to lean the ship farther from the wind. Edward grabbed the twin wheel, the matched side by side tandem wheel that made the *Raven* unique and received a frown from Sonja.

"Yes," Ben said to her. "We'll need two crew members on the wheels in this wind."

"Should I have the crew shorten sail, Cap'n?" Edward asked.

"Not yet, Eddie, but I think you can have someone

loosen the preventer line a loop or two, and spill out just a little of the wind from the mainsail. We don't need all of this wind, just some of it."

Edward glanced around to give the instruction and found Simon already standing by the pin where the line was tied. Edward just smiled and nodded his head in agreement as Simon loosened the line, letting the boom swing out slightly and releasing a small amount of the pressure on the sail. The tilt of the deck lessened, but the strain at the wheel remained, and the *Raven* continued to gallop across the edge of wind. Sonja strained to keep control of the wheel with white-knuckled fists around the handles, and a stiff grin on her determined face.

Ben fixed Edward in his eyes, and when Edward met his, Ben directed them at Sonja. Edward nodded only slightly. Ben walked forward so Sonja could see him, checking the tie downs on the lumber and forcing himself to scan the ocean. He stiffened his back and clenched his hands on the nearby line, gazing out at nothing in particular. Sonja eyed the far horizon over the lumber and checked the compass heading. She glanced at her husband's back without turning her head.

"I've got this, Ben," she said in a whisper.

Edward glanced at Sonja from the corner of his eye and suppressed a smile.

Ben took in a deep breath and made his way to the forward ladderway, determined not to turn back at the wheel. Down in the cargo hold, the loss of human space was almost tragic. The area previously partitioned off was opened and lined with sleeping pads. One of the smaller Solomons men had managed to hang a hammock over the stove in the galley. The angle of the decks and the motion of the ship forbid a cooking fire, so the stove had been allowed to burn out.

"At least he will stay warm while the heat remains among the bricks," he said to himself.

The air was pasty with the taste of rice dust, accented with the smell of musty wood and sleeping men's bodies. Most of the central passageway was

14

covered by a line of rice barrels, leaving only a narrow aisle just barely broad enough for Ben. Where barrels could not be stacked double height, the crew had laid planks across their tops, and more bedding placed there. He turned and went forward again, climbing to the landing before the door to the crew's quarters. Like the captain's cabin, it was mostly below deck with its upper walls and roof a few feet above it. After a quick knock, he stuck his head in the little room. All six bunks were filled, including the one he would share in turn, which held Harry at that moment. Harry started to rise.

"No, Harry. Take your rest. We all have to share beds by shift. "

Ben closed the cabin door, meeting Simon coming down the ladderway.

"Did you find any loose lines around the rice barrels, Ben?"

"No. They all looked secure, Simon, but we sure didn't leave ourselves much room to sleep."

Simon turned his palms up. "It will do for now. It's no worse than what the Solomons men slept on at the plantation, and they know this is only temporary." He raised his eyebrows and offered a smile, "A fleeting moment while they dream of freedom."

Ben smiled and patted his shoulder. "Nicely said, 'Professor.'"

"Never did like that title," he said, and then smiled again.

"Well, you were educated far better than me, old friend."

"Ben, you know damned well, an educated slave is still a slave."

"And how many times are you going to tell me that?"

"'Til it finally sinks in, Benjamin Pulaski. You're a slow learner," he said, slapping Ben on his shoulder.

The ship yawed abruptly, pushing the two men to the side, but slowly returned to her course. Ben eyed the roof.

"She at the windward wheel?" Simon asked.

Ben kept his eyes on the underside of the deck beams. "Edward is on the twin."

Simon chuckled softly. "Aye aye, Cap'n."

Ben returned his eyes to Simon. "Lettie all right in the cabin?"

Simon nodded, saying "In luxury with the Captain's wife."

"Was...she treated badly at Grayrocks?"

A frown descended on Simon's face. "Treated badly? For a dog, no. For a grown woman, for any human? Hell yes."

Simon kept his eyes focused on Ben, his face expressionless.

"With her figure, Ben? You can imagine the kind of treatment she received. I wanted to kill every one of those bastards."

"How many?"

Simon exhaled, barely shaking his head. "Not this time, Ben, but only because I didn't get the chance. Her brother saw me in the woods. She came out to me, so I didn't have to go near the manor house."

"Did the plantation owner know you had returned to the area?"

Simon's face softened. "No, I don't think so. On our way down to Georgetown, I had plenty of time to speak with her brother and the others sent from Grayrocks. They knew I had killed the master's firstborn, but told me the old man survived and offered a lot of money to anyone who would kill me. They thought I was long dead until your crew pulled Lettie and me up onto the *Raven*."

"I was happy to see you, old friend – and surprised!"

Simon nodded. "We keep slipping into each other's lives, Ben. I guess it's fate."

Ben let out a muted laugh. "Is that good fate or bad fate, Simon?"

"Only the spirits know, Benjamin."

Simon raised his eyebrows and shrugged his shoulders, then stepped down into the hold. Ben smiled at his back and headed up the ladderway. On deck, Ben approached the windward wheel.

"Have you had enough for a while?" he asked Sonja.

She jutted out her jaw and shook her head 'no.' Her knitted cap was shoved into her coat pocket, and her hair blew forward in the wind. Her hands were white-knuckled, and the muscles in her lower forearms bulged under her skin, where she had her sleeves pushed back. Still, her grip was firm and her stance well braced. Ben pulled her cap from her pocket and fitted it onto her head, then pulled her coat sleeves down to her wrists and patted the back of her hand.

"Keep warm, Sailor Sonja."

Ben locked eyes with Edward, letting his expression ask the question. Edward only smiled back at him.

The wind blew steadily in their favor throughout day and into the darkness, when they shortened sail for the night. The daily routine set in, with the sails reset at dawn when they could see better ahead. The ocean was almost kind and the wind far less temperamental than their voyage coming down to South Carolina. Sonja joined the noontime position reading, learning to use the sextant to help plot their progress. Edward and Simon took turns directing the expanded crew for tending the sails. The Solomons men grew more confident with their new skills and more excited as their freedom neared with each nautical mile. Members of the crew and the Solomons men, who could cook, took turns working in the galley to prepare the single warm meal of the day each afternoon.

Three days later, the *Raven* kept the North Carolina barrier islands on her western horizon and rounded north, past Cape Hatteras. There the crew set her course for the last hundred miles reach to the mouth of the Chesapeake. The sun hid behind a sky full of gray tumbling clouds and the air smelled of rain. The air had grown colder and saturated with water from a recent storm that had rushed ahead of them, and then dashed out to sea far to the east. The water was still angry and white caps charged across the ocean's surface, slapping

17

into the side of the bow. They ran with the wind, their topsails taken below, the main and foresails partially reefed down to expose less canvas to the determined wind. As the *Raven* settled on her new bearings, Ben and Sonja stood between the ship's wheels talking to Edward and Simon, who were taking their turn steering.

"St. Michaels?" Edward asked.

Ben nodded his head, speaking over the wind thrumming through the rigging overhead.

"That's where we will meet the people who will take the Solomons men the rest of the way."

Edward shook his head. "In the same time it will take us to get there, we can be in Philadelphia and set those men on Pennsylvania soil. Why go to St. Michael's?"

"I can't do that, Eddie. I can't...we can't...this ship cannot be seen letting off freed blacks in Philadelphia! I am a slave trader."

"There aren't any slavers in Philadelphia, Ben."

"Eddie, You haven't seen how determined those people are to catch runaway slaves. I have! I was almost killed by one camped at the Pennsylvania Line. Don't you think they will know to watch there?"

"I never saw any."

"They look just like you, Edward," Simon added with a chuckle. "How could you spot a white man in a sea of white faces? But what stands out is a black face in a sea of white faces."

"Let the arrangement by good people do what they are committed to doing," Ben said.

Sonja drew her fingertips along the exposed shearling lining of her coat. "I would love to go back to St. Michaels," she said. "I want to tell Mrs. Lambdin what a wonderful coat she gave me. And I want a hot meal where I don't have to worry about a wave knocking it into my lap!"

Ben smiled and shared approving glances with Simon and Edward. "Yes! We all want that!"

A massive wave slammed against the side of the

bow and showered most of the deck with an ice-cold spray. Sonja snuggled deeper inside her sky blue Sou'wester, while the men stood around pretending they were sufficiently warm and uncaring of the spray.

Edward peered at Sonja. "I need to get one of those sheepskin coats... but maybe something brown or black..."

"Oh really," Sonja said. "You wouldn't wear a light blue coat?"

"Sonja, in this weather, I'd wear a pink corset if it kept the water out and me warm inside!"

"As would I," added Simon.

Ben refused to respond, fixing his gaze beyond the bow in determined silence, as chill bumps raced up his spine.

When the sun set over Norfolk and Hampton Virginia that evening, the *Raven* tacked onto a new course and ran across the wind through the mouth of the Chesapeake Bay, into Hampton Roads. The waves were shorter and the wind not as strong, but both still angry. Sailing north of Hampton, they changed course again, turning west. The *Raven* slipped deep into the mouth of the Back River, into kinder water and shielded from much of the wind.

As they dropped anchor in the welcome calm, the shoreline was merely a darker black line than the cloudy night sky. Edward stood under the lantern at amidships and pointed to the northern shore with the line he was coiling.

"Poquoson over there, Ben. Good people, some."

"Afraid we won't have time to visit, Eddie," Ben said.

"Wouldn't care to, Ben. The one person I'd like to see there lies underground next to her Mother and Father."

Ben turned to face Edward, "Someone close to you?"

"Close, but not close enough. She died with another man's ring on her finger, while he whored in Norfolk."

"Sorry I asked...I didn't know..."

"How could you know, Benjamin? We hadn't seen each other in thirty years, and you only accepted me as your half-brother a couple weeks ago."

Ben sighed, staring into the darkness. "Who was she?"

"I lived down this way for a while. She was the daughter of a sea captain. I was his second mate…"

He paused and leaned his hands on the rail, his eyes fixed toward the shore.

"She was already engaged to one of the town's gentry when we found each other. Even then she was already starting to die of the pox her betrothed had picked up in the taverns."

Ben stood near him, waiting for him to continue. Edward finished with the line in silence and went to the crew's quarters. As Edward moved toward the bow, Sonja approached Ben from the stern.

"What were you gentlemen talking about so glumly?" she asked as she stepped into the lantern light. Her light blue sou'wester was almost luminescent. Its thick fur lining nested snugly around her neck, blending with her curls, both highlighted by the yellow light.

Ben sighed but did not speak.

She raised her eyebrows in an unspoken question, but he shook his head and placed his hands on her shoulders.

"You have been magnificent, Mrs. Pulaski."

"Thank you, Captain," she answered with a serious frown, but could not resist an emerging smile. "I could feel so alive on this ship, but…" Her smile faded, and she turned away.

"But what?"

"But among the stains on this deck that haunt you, the one that haunts me came from a man whose hands were tied when you drove a knife into his heart."

"Roberto was a pirate. No less than the men who sailed this ship for Hoagg …and kidnapped you."

Sonja folded her arms and blew out her breath. They stood there in silence a long moment. A few clouds parted, allowing a bright three-quarter moon to gaze down on them. She turned her face to him. Her face was painted in silver light, soft and smooth. She was again the woman Ben had left behind with his sons, before he sailed away to China before she gave birth to Alisha, the daughter he never knew, ripped from her arms and drowned, before he came back, before Hoagg, before...before.

"I think I will always love you, Ben..." she said.

He opened his mouth, slow to put the words he searched for, to tell her how much he loved her as well.

"...But I cannot put out of my mind or my heart..." she continued, "the murder you committed even as I begged you to stop."

"It was an execution, Sonja. He would have killed us. He would have stolen our ship."

"The ship? Yes. Murder us? I am not as sure."

"They shot Joseph right in front of us! Didn't you see that? That is also one of the stains on this deck."

"Of course I did! But, Roberto did not shoot him, Ben. He said he only wanted the ship."

The blood pounded in Ben's ears. His chest tightened. Bright red flashes erupted at the edges of his vision.

"How can you say such a stupid thing, Sonja? Last year you shoved a marlin spike into a man's eye!" Ben pointed down at the deck. "His stain is here, too. How can you begrudge me my actions to a pirate two weeks ago?"

"I was kidnapped from our home and taken to this ship, and I was the only one with tied hands, then!"

"Roberto would have stranded us on Bermuda, Sonja! How would we have gotten back to our sons, to Havre de Grace? Our lives are tied to this ship! I don't understand you!"

She turned from him, speaking over her shoulder as she stormed away. "I was hoping you were beginning to."

Ben stared at her back as she stepped along the deck and into the shadows beyond the lantern. The clouds overhead closed together in front of the moon, turning off the silver light. He stood there, willing his heart to stop pounding, but it would not.

"Ben? Ben? Are you all right?" Harry asked a second time, his voice sounding far away.

Ben turned in surprise. "What? Oh...yes, I am fine."

"Are you sure?"

"I said so, did I not?"

"Yes, Cap'n. Reporting for night duty. You can have your bunk now..."

"Yes...yes, thank you, Harry. Sorry I snapped."

Harry buttoned up the collar of his wool coat and shrugged his shoulders. He was still staring at Ben in curiosity, pulling the hem of his knitted watch cap over his ears, when the first few snowflakes drifted down into the yellow lantern light. Harry held his glove out to catch one and frowned at the snowflake as it was joined by thousands of others, filling the air.

"Shit," he said through gritted teeth.

Ben walked away in silence.

3

Mounds of snow floated atop the thick undulating slush on the surface of the Miles River at St. Michaels. Even in a brisk wind with all winter sails raised, the *Raven* moved ponderously into the little harbor. Heavy snow continued to fall, draping a white blanket over the port and buildings. The water temperature of the Chesapeake Bay had not allowed ice to form below its blanket of snow, but the air temperature was a meaner creature and bestowed no such kindness. After a brief revelry among the extended crew, cavorting on deck with snowballs, they reluctantly complied with their harsh winter duties. Sailing up the bay, they spent their hours shoveling fast accumulating snow off the decks, and making precarious climbs up frozen rigging to knock the ice loose.

Wool coats under oiled slickers was the dress for the day, to keep bodies both dry and warm. Sonja was a spot of blue opal on a deck speckled with meandering black pearls. Small frosty clouds drifted in front of their faces when they spoke. Seagulls huddled on the shore, their hunger not yet more potent than their fear of flying into the snow soddened sky.

Sonja had lead helm at the upwind wheel, with Harry nonchalantly nearby if needed on the other. Edward stood behind her with his eyes flickering between the set of the sails and the shorelines. Most of the Solomons men were sent below, wrapped in their blankets, waiting for the word that they could rise and leave the ship in safety. Ben, Simon and Lettie stood at the bow, in front of the stacked lumber, chatting in hushed tones and peering at landmarks through openings in the falling snow. At the bow, Bartrum, one of the Solomons men drawn to sailing, leaned out at the bow tossing a weighted line into the water, then calling out the depth.

"By the mark, twenty," he said.

Simon crossed his arms over his chest. "Ben, I am still worried about sending the Solomons men ashore here."

Lettie kept her frown and put her hand on Ben's shoulder. "Please do not forget that my brother is among those men."

"I could not forget that, Lettie," Ben said. "But all these men will be protected, and not sent away unless I am assured we are dealing with men arranged by Anthony Renowitz."

"By the mark, fifteen," said Bartrum.

Ben spun around to address Edward. "Lower the sails and drop anchor! We are shoaling!"

Edward had already heard the depth when Ben and was directing men to perform both acts. Cephus bounded past Ben and released the bow anchor chain. As the ship's bow snugged down to the pull of the anchor, Cephus turned to Ben with a broad grin on his face.

"I may not be as fas anymo', but I sure know what's to do," Cephus said.

"Thank you, Cephus. A seasoned sailor is always welcome aboard a ship," Ben said.

Cephus stopped next to Ben, letting his smile fade. "Was I worth my weight, Cap'n Ben?"

Ben slapped him gently on his arm. "Yes. Yes, you are. I will be sorry to see you leave the ship."

"I'm thinkin I could go out some mo, if that's all right with you..."

"Cephus, that would be very all right with me. You're a strong member of the crew, and I would consider myself a lucky captain to have you, as long as..."

"Long as what, Cap'n?"

"Long as you don't try to burn my ship again." Ben allowed a broad smile to spread on his face and began to chuckle. His laughter was joined by Simon, Lettie, and

Bartrum nearby. All the Solomons men had heard the story of Cephus' attempt to set fire to the *Raven* when it was anchored in Spesutie Narrows the previous year. They also knew of his agony over losing his son to the pirates who once sailed the *Raven*.

Cephus gave a rueful smile and raised his hand in solemn commitment. "Never again, Cap'n. All I knew then was this was a slave ship."

"Alright then," Ben said. "You can put your mark in the log book as soon as we anchor in Havre de Grace."

Cephus smiled and returned to his other duties.

Bartrum stepped next to Ben as Cephus walked away.

"I'd like to stay as well, Cap'n Ben."

Ben frowned. "You don't want to go up to freedom with your fellows?"

"Someday, yes. But, if this is what you will be doing with this ship, I want to help. I peeked out at the slaves walking around the dock when we were in Georgetown. I always wished that someone with skin the color of mine would come to Grayrocks and set me free. I knew it would never come from old Massah Williamson, and knew it was just a dream..."

"Go on..."

"But when you told us you were going to take us north...well... I want to give that feeling to one of those boys down there."

Ben stuck out his hand. Bartrum hesitated a moment, then accepted it. As they shook hands, Ben said, "Welcome to the crew Bartrum."

Simon," Ben said, "Can you create a manumission paper for him?"

Bartrum joined Cephus and Harry, tying the snow-covered sails to the booms.

"Been meaning to ask you, Bartrum," Cephus said as he flipped a line over the bundled sail to Bartrum.

"What's that, Big Man?"

"What the hell kind of name is Bartrum?"

Bartrum finished tying the line and stepped under the boom to Cephus. Harry stood close, listening for the

25

answer. Edward joined them, his hands in his coat pockets.

"Massah Williamson bought me from Pine Bough plantation in Virginia, where I was born, I think. The wife of the Massa there had the family name of Bartrum before she married, and he named me as a wedding gift."

The men listening exchanged glances.

"Are you satisfied with that name?" asked Harry.

Bartrum smiled and shrugged his shoulders. "It's the only name I know me by." He glanced around at their faces. "Are you satisfied with me having it?"

"It's the only name we know you by," Cephus answered for them all.

Edward coiled a loose line and hung it on the railing near Ben. "Thought we could go easily into ten-foot waters, Ben, even with full holds."

"The note from Anthony warned me to anchor in water of fifteen feet or better when we came to St. Michaels."

"Keeps us pretty far from shore."

Ben nodded without speaking. Edward remained close waiting for an answer.

Ben sighed. "That's all it said, but I've learned that sneaky man has reasons for what he asks of us."

"You sailed with him, you said. When you sailed to China?" Edward asked

"I knew him even before that. He was a lieutenant, and I was a sergeant when I met him in Georgia. All that was years ago, Eddie."

Simon and Lettie walked to the forward ladderway. Simon spoke over his shoulder as he went. "Believe I smell coffee boiling down in the galley, and I'll make that paper while I'm down."

Ben and Edward made their way to the stern, checking the lumber lashings and met Sonja coming up on deck with a steaming cup in her gloved hands. Sonja shared her coffee with Ben, while Edward continued down to the galley.

"What do we do now, Ben?"

"I'm not sure, Sonja, to be honest. We were supposed to be here two weeks ago."

"Anthony's note, the note from the Argyle Corporation...did it give you any details?"

"You saw it too, Sonja. 'Anchor off St. Michaels in no less than fifteen feet.' There was nothing more."

"How long do we wait? What could that possibly mean?"

"I've thought a great deal about that very question since we left South Carolina...when we weren't fighting a storm...or pirates..."

She sipped her coffee and handed it back to him. The coffee steam joined the cold vapor of their breath.

"Maybe...maybe someone will see us out here. Sitting here could be our signal. No reasonable ship would stay out this far in this weather and then row to shore. I think we are meant to stay here."

Sonja shook her head. "Even the all-knowing Anthony Renowitz could not have foretold this weather a month ago."

"No. Of course, you are right," Ben said, "but he certainly knew it would be winter. We are out here for a reason. We are not meant to go to shore."

"I wish he had given us more information, Ben. He is so..."

"So...careful. There is risk to everyone involved in this act," he said.

The snowing thinned momentarily. Sonja peered along the docks of St. Michaels, then out to the northern shore of the river, and then farther up the Miles River.

"I don't see anyone coming our way," she said.

Ben smiled and handed the cup back to her. "Would you? In this weather? And then row ten men..."

"Nine. Bartrum is staying," she said.

"Eleven. Simon and Lettie are going with them," Ben said.

"Twelve. Achilles is going too."

"Oh, yes. Achilles. Twelve."

She sighed, and they both centered their attention up river for a long moment, losing the detail in the whiteout, the thin eggshell colored line merged between white sky and white water. Edward returned to the deck with fresh coffee. Ben and Sonja smiled at him as they made their way down to the galley, and warmth, and compressed bodies bundled in wool coats and oiled slickers wedged among the rice barrels, an opal sardine packed among the mackerel.

The next day the snow ended, and the sky was painted steel gray. Otherwise, nothing changed. Nothing happened. They kept the fire going in the galley; men, and women huddling near it in turns.

The following day, a few dark-clad people were seen standing on the dock. One even waved. Ben decided it was from curiosity, not a signal. Nothing happened.

The third day brought a bright sun in a clear sky. At mid-morning the air filled with the sounds of hissing steam, clanging iron and the slapping of large side wheels as a steamboat paraded by them. The *Raven* rocked at its anchor as the 180-foot steamer chugged up the center of the river and completed a tight circle, barely within the confines of the two shores. As soon as it completed the turn, the paddlewheels stopped, and the steamboat drifted toward them. Putting its side wheels in reverse, the ship stopped next to the *Raven*. The name on the sidewheel cover was 'COLUMBUS.'

A man yelled through a speaking trumpet from the pilothouse sitting two stories above them.

'Where in God's name have you been *Raven*?"

Sonja stood beside Ben, laughing. "So this is why we needed fifteen feet!"

Ben cupped his hands around his mouth and yelled back to the steamer captain. "Long story! Do you have time to come aboard and hear it?"

"Hell no! Give me your name."

"Pulaski! Who are you?"

"Holmes! What are you?"

Ben thought a moment. "Argyle Corporation has cargo on board!"

" 'Bout Goddamned time, Pulaski. Send'em over!"

Crewmen on the main deck slide a gangplank over the water between the two ships.

"Where are you going?" Ben yelled.

The steamer captain hesitated. "None of your damned business!" He kept the trumpet to his mouth, and then added, "They will be safe!"

An Amish man on the steamer stepped from the shadows to the edge of the gangplank and called out. "Captain Pulaski?"

"Yes?"

"Our mutual friend sends his regards. I will travel with your passengers the rest of the way."

"The rest of the way where?" Ben asked.

The Amish man smiled. "They will be safe, sir."

Ben motioned to Edward, who called the Solomons men up on deck. Ben shook each hand as they trotted across the gangplank. Simon and Lettie held on to each other near the edge of the plank. They shared a long passionate kiss, and with tears in Lettie's eyes, she crossed onto the steamer while Simon remained on the *Raven*. Simon faced Lettie then Ben, without speaking.

The steamer captain yelled out, "That it?"

Ben nodded his head, and the steamer crew swiftly pulled back the plank. The paddle wheel began to rotate and slap the water with increasing speed, pushing the steamer faster and faster into Eastern Bay.

"Bartrum. Cephus. Join me in the captain's cabin," Ben said on his way to the stern ladderway.

In the cabin, Ben withdrew the ship's logbook from the shelf above the desk at the side of the room. He opened it to his last entry, and then wrote in the date and listed the names of his two new crewmen on a clean page. Then he handed the pen to each man in turn for them to place an x by their names. To Ben's surprise, Bartrum wrote his name in a far better handwriting than his own scribble.

Simon stood at the door. "Are you not going to ask me to sign on?"

Ben smiled. "Wasn't sure of your plans after seeing Lettie go without you."

"Once we saw the steamer, we both felt the rest of the journey would be safe enough for Lettie and her brother. I told her I needed to stay and help you for a while."

Ben accepted the pen back from Bartrum and dipped it in the inkwell, then handed it to Simon. His penmanship for his signature was similar to Bartrum's.

On deck, the air was still winter cold, but the sky was bright blue, spotted high with tufts of cotton clouds and filled with seagulls diving for fish through exposed water.

Ben approached Edward. "Let's get the anchor up and head for Baltimore."

"Aye aye, Captain," Edward said.

Sonja pulled her knitted cap low on her head and stepped to one of the tandem wheels. Ben smiled and pointed to the other wheel. "Wind's going to come from that side," he said.

She stepped to the other wheel and spun it as the sails were raised and the *Raven*'s bow turned to follow the direction of the steamer. She stiffened an instant as Simon helped with the sails. Giving Ben a frown, she tilted her head toward Simon.

"Eleven," Ben said. "Simon is staying on board."

Sonja peaked her eyebrows then gave her full attention to the wheel.

In quick minutes, the *Raven* was out in the middle of the Chesapeake Bay, leaning away from a brisk wind and charging northward over the white caps.

Five hours later they passed Fort McHenry and sailed into Baltimore harbor. A dozen steamboats were tied along the western wharves near Light Street. Ben ran to the rail as they passed the Columbus. His face turned red, and he paced the deck until the *Raven* was secured in an open berth north of the steamboats. He jumped onto the dock and trotted back to the Columbus, dashing up its gangplank. He spotted Captain Holmes and confronted him.

"I could have brought them here, without waiting

three days!" Ben said.

Captain Holmes grabbed Ben forcefully by his arm and quickly glanced around. "Lower your Goddamned voice, Pulaski."

"Where are they?" Ben asked through gritted teeth.

"They are not here, you fool."

"Where?"

Holmes lowered his voice. "We offloaded on the bay to a steam tug going up the C&D Canal. They will be in Philadelphia tonight, and somewhere else tomorrow. Now get the hell off my ship!"

Ben let out his breath and apologized, but Holmes turned away and returned to his duties, speaking with a large burly man in a seaman's coat. Holmes nodded in Ben's direction. As the man headed toward Ben, Ben left the ship and returned to the *Raven*.

A man in a neat wool suit and white shirt stood on the deck with a leather satchel held by a gloved hand. His other hand held an envelope. Edward pointed at Ben when he came on board. The man approached Ben and handed him the envelope.

"I am with the Argyle Corporation," he said, then left the ship.

A work gang then came up the gangplank, led by an unshaven man clenching the last few inches of a thick cigar between his teeth, and holding a battered ledger.

"You Cap'n Pulaski?" he asked.

Ben slipped the envelope into his pocket and nodded to the man.

"We got lumber and rice to offload. You ready for that?"

"If you take the lumber first, then we can open the hatches and let you get at the rice below," Ben said.

"Jees. I never woulda thought of that, Cap'n," he said without expression.

Edward stepped next to Ben and spoke to the man with the ledger. "I'm the first mate. I will have booms rigged to swing out the lumber, and then hoist up the barrels. Your men can take it from there."

"Who sent you here?" Ben asked.

"The gentleman who just left." He indicated the lumber with a wave of his hand, taking the cigar out of his mouth and leaning forward to spit on the deck.

Ben snapped his hand to the handle of his knife and spoke calmly. "If you spit on this deck, I will cut... your... throat."

The man sneered at Ben, but stepped to the railing and spit into the harbor, then turned back to Ben, keeping his distance.

"The Argyle Corporation is receiving the cargo," the man said.

"Who is going to sign for it?" Ben asked.

"It's already signed for, Cap'n." The gang boss spoke slowly as if addressing a child. "That gentleman just gave you the receipt...sir."

Then the man turned his back to Ben and began giving his crew instructions.

Ben sat at his desk in the Captain's cabin. Sonja sat in the padded chair beside the door. Inside the envelope handed to him on deck were three other envelopes, numbered 1, 2 and 3.

"Anthony likes to control everything," Ben said.

He opened envelope 1. It contained the signed receipt for the cargo and identified the amount of the payment. With the receipt were two bank drafts. One draft was from a local dry goods company for the rice. The other was from a local lumber company. Both checks were fair prices for cargo shipped from South Carolina. Envelope 2 was a receipt for money paid to the firm of Lebeaux and Chambers, Property Brokers, for 'services rendered.' There was also a bank draft sufficient for the reimbursement and profit for James Williamson's ten slaves. Envelope 3 contained two unsigned handwritten notes. The first read only

March 20ᵗʰ, Georgetown, South Carolina

The second note read

Welcome home, Ben.
I am glad you and Sonja are safe. You will have to tell me about Bermuda when next we meet.

Ben handed all the contents to Sonja and relaxed in his chair sipping coffee as she read through them.

She raised her face to Ben when she had finished. "Then, you are to go back," she said.

"And you are not?" he asked.

"No."

Ben sighed and went up on deck.

The following day, Ben found a liquor dealer eager to pay almost any price for the Jamaican rum that Williamson had given him before the *Raven*'s previous voyage to Georgetown. Ben sold him all except two five-gallon barrels that he kept for the ship. The money he received for the rum he shared equally that night among himself, Sonja and the crew. At sunrise, they left Baltimore harbor for Havre de Grace and arrived well before sunset. Sonja was let off with her baggage at the pier, and then the *Raven* taken away from shore and anchored. Ben came ashore with Edward to visit James Williamson at the Tidewater Bank and Trust, leaving the rowboat with Edward for use by the crew.

The bell above the door to the bank jingled as Ben entered. James rose from his desk and walked briskly to the little gate near the teller windows. He extended his hand to Ben.

"Welcome back, Ben. I hope all went well."

Ben shook his hand then followed him back to his desk. James pulled open a drawer of the desk and withdrew two cut glass whiskey tumblers and a bottle. He poured a modest amount of whiskey into each glass and handed one to Ben, holding his own up in salute. Ben returned the salute and downed his whiskey, then pulled out the bank draft for James' slaves. James did not read at the draft but slipped it into the top drawer. He poured himself another drink and offered the bottle to Ben, who waved it away.

"I received a telegram from Lydia a few days ago – actually expected you here before now..."

"Storm at sea. Blew us to Bermuda," Ben said.

"Oh no," he said. "All is well I hope?"

"Well enough, James."

"So, as I said, I received a telegram from Lydia. She

says you cheated Uncle Jeremiah and abused the planters of Charleston at auction."

Ben locked his eyes on James. "Yes. Yes, to both charges."

James slapped his hand on the desktop and let out a friendly laugh. "Excellent! I knew you would be a suitable partner. Excellent!"

He held his glass up in another salute to Ben, "And to hell with Uncle Jeremiah!" He emptied his glass and asked, "Did he try to buy my slaves on the cheap?"

"He tried," Ben said.

"And at what price did you offer them to him?"

"Full market value."

James slapped the desk again in laughter, "I'll bet he was positively apoplectic!"

"He described his dissatisfaction and stormed from the room. Then had his steamboat ensign escort me off the plantation."

James continued to laugh. "I am so sorry you had to endure that, Benjamin, but I do wish I had been there to see that. He is such an egotistical ass. That's one of the many reasons my father ran him off from Grayrocks and helped him get started with his swampy Palmetto Haven."

James recovered and tapped his desk with his fingertip, just above his center drawer. "Do I owe you any of this draft?"

Ben shook his head no. "I already have my share," he said.

"Excellent. What can we do next?"

"Nothing more, for now, James. I have business at home to attend, and a property to re-settle, as you know."

James nodded his understanding since he had canceled the note on the property and given it to Ben in return for taking his sister Lydia to South Carolina.

"For now, I will take my leave and go home," Ben said. "Has the canal frozen?"

"Yes. Well, no. I hear it was starting to freeze, and the superintendent had it drained for the winter to avoid ice damage."

"Sounds like he knows his business," Ben said. "I do miss his predecessor, though. Will Boyd and I were good friends. We built my first barge together, the *Ugly Boat*..."

"Never met Mr. Boyd. He drowned before I arrived, but, the *Ugly Boat* I hear about regularly. Your son, Aaron, defends his boat with vigor at the Line."

Ben stood to leave. "The slave chasers have their jobs, but so do our canallers."

James stood to shake his hand, and then Ben left the bank. He walked down Oyster Street to the lane leading to the canal company barn. Memories of the little farm he and Sonja once had there flooded into his mind. But then the thoughts of his infant daughter drowning there in the icy river waters, her little body swept away in '39, burst into consciousness. He blocked it out, forced his mind to think of other things. Soon he was at the Canal Basin, then onto the towpath, that thin ribbon of cypress and soil arcing out into the shallows of the Susquehanna River.

The towpath defined the eastern edge of the canal basin and then tapered back in toward shore and defined the outer bank of the Susquehanna and Tidewater Canal. The canal was almost empty of water now, and the basin water muddy from lack of flow, holding only a couple of empty barges with nowhere to go until spring. Typically, water would enter the canal forty-three miles north and 230 feet higher, up in Wrightsville, Pennsylvania. It would flow through the canal's twenty-nine locks, stair-stepping downhill toward "the Line" and then slide the last fifteen miles in Maryland to Havre de Grace, refreshing the water in the basin where the barges usually waited for towing.

Five miles along the towpath, Ben stopped across from his farm, just below Lapidum. He stood there a moment, savoring the view. Two massive oaks stood guard on the grassy front slope that led down to the canal. A little wharf stood at the end of the slope with its feet in the canal. Ben's son Isaac had built the narrow two-plank dock on the bank in front of their home, when the only barge they owned was the *Ugly Boat*. Ben would tie up there when he came home. The log and frame house behind the trees had a full-width front porch where he and his family would sit together, watching the Great Blue Herons glide into the canal or out beyond the towpath to the Susquehanna River.

He turned to face out upon the river. It was docile now, pretending to be tame and subdued, but Ben knew the rage of what some called "The Bitch." Knew she could rise almost without warning and kill. The Bitch had shoved ice boulders as big as cabins up out of her banks while he was trapped in China, crushing their previous home near the basin and ripping his unmet newborn daughter from Sonja's arms. He shook his head to force the images farther back in his mind, then stepped down the bank of the towpath onto the muddy bottom of the canal bed, and crossed to his farm.

My farm, he thought. *Our farm. We have the papers for it and owe no one.*

He stopped at the iron pump beside the front porch to rinse the mud off his boots. Sonja came out wiping her hands with a blood-stained cloth.

"May I come in?" he asked.

"Of course," she said. "You can help me clean and bandage your younger son. He has been fighting at the Line again."

She turned back into the cabin, speaking over her shoulder, "How was the meeting with James?"

"He was satisfied with the money," Ben said as he mounted the steps to the porch. "But I felt like bathing after keeping my guise as a slave trader with him –"

Inside, Aaron was sitting in a chair in the front room, leaning his head back with a damp cloth held gingerly in place over his face by one hand of young Maggie Freidman. Her other hand held his.

"Miss Maggie, how are you today?" Ben asked her as he entered. She started to release Aaron's hand, but he snatched it back.

"I'm all right, Pa," Aaron's muffled voice came from under the cloth. "Just a bloody nose."

"It was awful!" Maggie added with the exuberance of a fifteen-year-old.

Ben gently pulled the cloth off Aaron's face and examined his bloodstained nose.

"Nothing split. Nothing out of alignment. Not broken," he said, then leaned over so Aaron could see him, and winked. "I think you'll live, young mister Pulaski," Ben said, patting his cheek and recovering his face and returning Maggie's hand to its place.

"Captain Pulaski," Aaron said from under the cloth.

Ben glanced up at Sonja standing nearby. She smiled and shook her head at his bravado.

"And where, pray tell, Captain Pulaski, is your damned boat?" Ben asked.

"Sitting on the bottom of the dry holding pond at York Furnace," he answered.

"How did you get home, son?"

Aaron raised his left foot and pointed to his boot.

"And in the snow!" Maggie added, stroking the side of his head.

Ben stepped into the kitchen and set a smoked ham on the counter. "From Forrest MacMallery," Ben said from the neat kitchen. "Everything seems to be in place, Mrs. Pulaski," he said.

"We still have good neighbors, Ben. Most things had already been brought back into the house while we were gone. Mac organized it. Oh, I met Catherine Price this afternoon, the new lockkeeper's wife."

"Thought he was a widower?"

"A widower with seven children and eager to have a new wife," she answered. "She was a friend of the family before he moved here. She seems to be a sweet woman. The children have taken to her."

Ben leaned close to Sonja and whispered to her. "No sweeter than Maggie, I'll bet. How close are they getting?"

"She turns sixteen in a few months, Ben. We need to

be ready for their announcement."

Ben sighed through a half smile and shook his head. "Surely not yet."

"We got a letter from Isaac," Sonja said and pointed to the mantel above the fireplace that warmed both the kitchen and the front room with openings on each side.

Ben snatched down the envelope and opened the pages inside. He smiled and mumbled random words as he sped through the letter. After consuming the last sentences, he held the sheets at his side with his eyes wide open. "He is being advanced to the next class! He passed all the first year tests in a challenge from his instructor, and now joins the second year cadets in Engineering and Mathematics!"

Sonja chuckled at his excitement. "Yes. I read that, Ben."

"I think this means he will graduate a year early!" He ticked off his fingers, counting. "He will be in their class of 1846!"

"I think so," she said calmly. "And hopefully with nothing more to do than build forts and parade around."

"He sent me a letter too, Pa," Aaron said from the doorway, his face wiped clean and still holding hands with Maggie. "He said he would be here in May, for...well.."

"For what?" Ben asked.

"Well..." Aaron and Maggie gazed into each other's eyes as Aaron spoke. "We, um..."

Sonja placed her hand on Ben's shoulder and leaned against him.

No. Not yet. Not yet, Aaron.

"I spoke with Mr. Freidman last night..." Aaron said, taking in a deep breath.

A tear ran down Sonja's cheek and into the edges of the faint smile she pushed onto her face. *Not so soon, Aaron. Please! Not so soon!*

"In April, Maggie will be sixteen, and I will be eighteen in May..."

Ben's breathing tightened in his chest. Sonja's fingernails dug into his shoulder, but they both forced anxious smiles onto their faces.

"We will be married then," Aaron said.

Not asking, Ben thought. *Telling us what will be.*

Sonja hugged Maggie and pulled Ben with her, and then she hugged Aaron while Ben shook his hand in a tight grip. Aaron's hand did not yield but held firm, matching Ben's grip.

"Well," Sonja's eyes met with Maggie's, "will you live with us or with the Freidman's?"

Aaron hesitated; sharing another glance with his fiancé, then shook his head. "Grandpa Jundt has offered us his house in York Furnace. He is going to North Carolina for a while."

"What?" Sonja asked in shock.

"He wants to visit his younger brothers. They have been writing each other."

Sonja eyes widened, her mouth slightly open, but saying nothing.

Ben stepped between Maggie and Aaron, and pulled them against him, squeezing them tight.

That night as Ben and Sonja laid together in bed; she rolled onto her side facing him and placed her hand on his chest. "Tomorrow, I am going to take one of our horses and ride up to see Papa."

Ben thought a moment. "Alright, we can leave early in the morning, if you want."

"I am going alone," she said. "I want some long moments alone with him."

"That's over twenty miles along the canal. You should not do that alone, Sonja."

"The canal is almost deserted, and I am not asking permission. I will take one of the pistols."

Ben rolled onto his side and faced away from her, as she gave him her back as well. They laid awake in silence, listening to the last of the fire crackling in the front room fireplace, and the sound of their thoughts screaming in their heads.

5

Ben stood on the porch as the dawn faded from gray to pale yellow over the trees on the Cecil County side of the river. The surface ice was spreading out from the shore. The remaining coots were meandering in the current, head down in search of fish. A fox on the far bank slouched through the thinned weeds, looking for an opportunity to grab one of the little black mud hens. His snout gave out small ragged puffs of vapor drifting away as he moved. Thin mist rising off the hindquarters of the horse tied to the porch below Ben rose in wispy strands. The shaggy farm horse nibbled in the bag of oats Sonja had tied over his muzzle, while she finished packing her bag. Ben stepped down to the ground and leisurely checked the strap buckles of the saddle.

"I did that right," Sonja said as she came out of the house and clomped down the steps in her boots. She was wearing the canvas trousers she wore on the *Raven*, and the blue sou'wester Mrs. Lambdin had given her.

Ben held up his hands in surrender. "Just a habit, Sonja, and something to do while you packed."

She hooked her bag straps over the pommel of the saddle and turned to Ben with a smile. "I didn't mean to snap, Ben. My heart is troubled by more and more things, and I need to talk to my Papa, and I need to do something on my own for a few days."

She turned her face up to his and offered her lips. They embraced and shared a long kiss, and then smiled within each other's arms.

"I love you, Sonja."

"I know. And I love you, Ben, as much as ever."

He sighed. "Be safe, please. Take no chances."

"No. Don't forget that I managed life alone for almost three years when I thought I was a widow."

"I know. I know," Ben whispered. "I can never completely make that up to you..."

"Nor should you. But I need...I need more... more room now."

Ben nodded and hugged her again, then let her go. She reached up and placed her hand gently on his cheek. He leaned his face into her hand and smiled. Then she stepped high to put her foot in the stirrup, bounced with her other foot and catapulted herself up into the saddle. She gave a smug smile down at Ben, leaned forward to slip slipped the feed bag off the horse and handed it to him. She kissed the air between them, then turned the horse toward the edge of their property. Ben stood there while she crossed the little bridge onto Stafford Lane, and pass out of view beyond the trees. Moments later he was still there, listening to the squeak of the iron pin as the locktender pushed the swing bridge out over the canal and the clomp of the iron horseshoes across the planks. Then her sounds were lost in the distance and the faint wind whispering through the bare oak trees above him.

Ben walked up the steps and back into the house, leaving the front door open to the fresh air, and meandered to the boys' room. Aaron was already out of the house. His bed was rumpled, and his last worn shirt dropped carelessly over the ladder back chair next to his bed. Isaac's side was still neat and empty, waiting for him to return. In the kitchen, Ben found the coffee pot still warm and a few stalwart coals still red in the iron stove. He took his coffee cup into the other bedroom on the far side of the front room. The two bedrooms had been added by the original cabin owner, giving it the vertical plank additions on either side of the hewn log center seen from the outside. He sat on their bed and placed his cup on the little table nearby, then pulled the old quilt from their earliest years onto his lap, and bundled it in his arms. Hearing voices outside, he pulled back the curtain as two men walked into his yard.

Ben grabbed his cup and stepped back out onto the

porch. "Morning Simon! Morning Bartrum!" he said.

They mounted the porch and shook hands. "We still have some coffee in the kitchen, gentlemen. Would you care for some?"

They followed Ben inside, Bartrum taking in all the details of the front room while Simon stepped close to Ben.

"Simon, be careful walking around Havre de Grace. Deputy Mattingly has a warrant for your arrest.

"Well, you know all black folks look alike..."

"Not you, and not to Mattingly." Ben shook his head. "I think Lyle has a real good idea what you look like, Simon."

Ben filled two cups with the last of the coffee and handed them out.

"Sonja not here?" Simon asked.

Ben shook his head. "No. She has gone to York Furnace for a while to visit with her father. He is planning to travel back to North Carolina for a while. She wants to spend time with him before he goes."

Simon nodded "Ben, you got anybody staying in the tack room?"

Ben gave a broad smile. "No, and those bunk beds are still in there, and the iron stove in there will keep you warm at night."

"Can Bartrum join me?"

"Of course! So can anyone else from the crew. It looks like I won't be taking the *Raven* out again until March, so I was planning to walk back into town and help folks decide where they would stay until then – or go until then."

Simon glanced at Bartrum. "We're fine on the ship a few days, Ben, but if we're staying around until March, we might be safer up here."

"I have my papers," Bartrum said.

Simon smiled. "Some of my best work, I do believe, Ben. I named him Thomas after the mule tender for old barge number 26."

Ben laughed at the name. Both he and Simon knew Thomas was the cover name for dozens of escaping slaves walked to Pennsylvania ahead of Barge 26.

What about you, Simon?' Ben asked.

Simon pulled faded crumple papers from his pocket and assumed a sloped shoulder posture with his other hand hanging loosely by his side. "I's Achilles, suh. Sold from Vaginny up to heah fo coal work."

Bartrum regarded Simon with an approving nod. "That'll do."

That afternoon Ben stood in the passageway in the hold of the *Raven*, discussing the plans among the crew.

"Harry and I can stay at your father's old house in Baltimore," Edward said.

"That was forfeited years ago, Edward. Your mother lost it after my Father died," Ben said.

"Ruined it, scavenged it, lost it and abandoned it. Same way she treated me," Edward said without emotion. "I bought it several years ago when it was almost dilapidated. Put on a new roof and fix what I can when I can."

Ben stared at Edward, with his mouth partially open, but saying nothing. Edward returned his attention, shrugging shoulders.

Ben's eyes were wide as he re-examined his half-brother. "I had no idea...does it stand empty all the time you are gone?"

Edward smiled. "Do you remember old Darby, the man who tended the bushes and backyard for our...your father? He used to sleep in the potters shed from time to time when he was drunk."

"Oh yes, I remember him..."

"I came across him not too long after I bought the property. He was in bad shape and needed a roof over his head. He lives in the house now and keeps it clean in his own way. Turned out to be an excellent cook since he gave up the whiskey."

Ben continued to stare at Edward.

"There is plenty of room there, and Harry will be welcome. So would you if you ever choose to visit the old place," Edward said.

Ben said nothing.

Edward turned away, speaking as he went. "I will check things on deck so we can button her up until March, Ben. Oh, and we will need another crew member if Sonja is not going with us then." Then he mounted the ladderway.

Cephus was still pushing his few belongings into his canvas bag as he approached Ben. "I'm going to the house, just to check on things, then I'll look in on Miss Hattie. I'll be at one place or another until we sail again, Cap'n. What are you going to do about Adam's place? He owned that outright, you know."

"No, I didn't know," Ben said.

"Adam had a will, Ben," Simon added. "Told me about it when I worked for him back when I first came to Havre de Grace. It's in that old place somewhere."

"Then we need to find it and get it to George Milton, Esquire."

"You need ta stay outta town, Simon," Cephus said. "That deputy wants to arrest you real bad."

Ben nodded. "That's good advice, Simon. Just tell me where I can find that will."

While Simon found a piece of paper to sketch the layout of Adam's Boatwright shop, Cephus took his bag up on deck.

Cephus rowed Edward and Harry to the docks and returned to the ship. Once the four men dropped the stern anchor, and the secured the hatches for winter, they returned to Havre de Grace. Ben and Cephus walked together toward Concord Cove as Simon and Bartrum headed north to the Pulaski farm.

⁂

Days later, as steel clock on Oyster Street struck three times in the distance, Ben walked up the outside steps to the second floor of the First National Bank on Washington Street. George Milton was alone in his office when Ben entered. They shook hands and Ben presented Adam's will. George glanced at it quickly.

"Well, Ben, he signed it in September of last year,

45

but there is no witness signature..."

Ben snatched the will back and yanked a pen from the inkwell on George's desk, and held the pen to sign the will. George grabbed Ben's wrist in a firm grip.

"Wait," George said, then he brought out another ink bottle and pen from a desk drawer and handed them to Ben. "This is closer to the ink Adam used to write his signature."

Ben signed the will and handed it back. George blew on it, sprinkled sand over it to help it dry and began to read it in detail.

"Who is Miss Hattie?"

"His best friend," Ben said. "A freed woman. She saved his life more than once with her heart remedies."

"Well, she can't own his shop. She's a black woman. Needs to be owned by a white person."

"Well, maybe I can..."

"No, Ben. You just signed it as a witness. You can't receive value from a will you witnessed, no more than I can as the lawyer processing it. We need to identify a white person as the owner, but who will let this Miss Hattie have free reign over it. "

"I know a woman..." Ben started to say.

"Can't be Sonja, either," George said.

"Mamie Stewart," Ben said.

George smiled. "I am sure she would do this. I will speak with her at dinner this evening."

"I think I should stop by there on my way and tell her about Adam," Ben said. "They appeared to be very comfortable with each other."

"I did not know Mamie knew Adam. Perhaps you could talk to her about Miss Hattie as well."

"No, George. That should be your conversation."

It was near four o'clock in the afternoon when Ben knocked on the door to the Pink House on Union Avenue. The original red oak planks that sheathed the outside of the house had faded over the several years since it was built, giving the house a decidedly pink hue, which gave rise to the landmark name for guiding friends around Havre de Grace. He reached up to knock again when he heard a gunshot from within the house. Ben twisted the doorknob and entered the house. Just off the foyer lay a woman on the floor in the parlor. Ben quickly searched around the edges of the room for a culprit, then checked the figure. The young woman had been struck hard in the face, unconscious but still breathing. She was the freed slave left behind by Lydia Binterfield when he took her to South Carolina.

"Sissy," he said to himself.

A second shot rang out. It came from below the floor. Ben and Sonja had stayed at the Pink House as boarders when they lost their farm, so Ben knew the entrance to the old foundation was from the outside. He dashed from the parlor through the dining room and out through the narrow back door in the kitchen. He jumped beyond the outside steps and turned to go down into the cellar when Mamie stumbled up the rock steps carrying a pistol in her hand. Smoke was coming out of the barrel. She could barely stand. Her face had been struck several times, and her dress was smeared with dirt and blood. Ben slipped the gun from her hand, took her in his arms and helped her into the house.

"I have shot a man, Benjamin."

"Who? Is he dead, Mamie?"

She turned her face up to Ben, struggling to focus. "I certainly hope so," she mumbled and reached for her pistol with a trembling hand. "If not, I believe I have more bullets..."

Ben stood in the open doorway to the cellar. Deputy Lyle Mattingly sat on the larger stone among the lower canted rock steps near the cellar floor, with his back toward Ben. He leaned forward with his elbows on his knees and pressed his handkerchief against the bloody scrape on his forehead.

"God damn, Ben! You shoulda told me about that big step down right under that main beam! Liked ta split my damned skull!"

"Didn't know about it, Lyle. I've never been down there."

"You said you had!"

"No, Lyle, I said I knew she had a cellar, and knew where the door to it was."

"Shit!"

"You need any help? Doc Harper is still up in the house with Mamie and Sissy."

Lyle peered into thin gray light by his feet. "Looks like I broke her lantern all to hell and spilt a couple cups of whale oil on the dirt down here." His crushed felt hat lay overturned in the oil puddle.

Ben lifted another lantern hanging from a nearby spike and shook it gently. "Here's another one. It's still got oil in it. Do you have matches?"

"Yeah," Lyle said.

Lyle turned reached up to accept the lantern ring, as Ben stepped down close enough to hand it to him. As Lyle turned, sunlight from outside illuminated the large patch of raw scraped skin on his forehead, blood still trickling down the side of his face. Ignoring his hat, Lyle took the lantern away from the whale oil puddle and struck a match in the darkness. The spreading yellow light slipped away from Ben's view as Lyle walked farther back into the recesses of the cellar.

Lyle's voice echoed among the rock walls and massive hewn beams. "This don't match the house very well."

Ben sat on the upper steps, well away from the beam Lyle had slammed with his head. "Cellar was built back in '15. It had been under one of the houses the Brits burned."

Lyle mumbled something as he went farther back, but Ben could not understand what he said.

"Mr. Stewart built this house over it in '35," Ben yelled.

Lyle mumbled several more comments as if he was having a conversation with someone, but Ben knew his only company down there was a dead man.

While Ben waited, he heard a woman scream in pain from within the house. He couldn't tell if it was from Mamie or Sissy but knew Doc Harper was doing what he could.

Ten minutes later, Lyle returned to the base of the steps. He blew out the lantern and set it on a nearby counter. He picked up his hat and mounted the steps, ducking his head awkwardly as he passed under the treacherous low beam. He kept his bent posture until he was entirely out of the stairwell and standing under the open sky. Oil dripped from his hat, hanging at his side from his hand.

"Who was it, Lyle?" Ben asked.

"Don't know. That would have been an odd thing for me to say a few years ago, but with all the people coming and going on the Canal, this town is full of strangers."

"At least we know he's not local."

Lyle eyed Ben a moment. "And you're sure you have never been down there before?"

Ben shook his head.

"He had this in his hand," Lyle said. "Just like the coin old Adam used to wear on a string around his neck."

Ben raised his eyebrows to Lyle but said nothing.

Lyle frowned at Ben and leaned toward him. "How

49

come every time I come across a man with his brains blown out, or a knife stuck in his gut, I wind up having a conversation with you?"

Ben's face tightened, and his lips pressed together, then he said, "All this happened as I was knocking on the door, Lyle. I just came into town from Lapidum."

"Mmm-mm," Lyle muttered and turned away toward the back door.

In Mamie's rooms on the first floor, Doctor Wallace Harper finished with Mamie and moved across the hall to the small room where Sissy laid on her bed, holding a damp cloth to her cheek. Mamie was sitting on a small settee near her four-poster bed and turned away as Deputy Mattingly tapped on her doorframe and entered. Ben followed him in.

Mamie's left eye was swollen shut, and the skin dark purple. Her other eye was turning black from having her broken nose forced back into shape. Her lips were swollen as well, and the edge of a large bruise peeked out of her loosened collar at the base of her neck. Her left arm rested in a sling from her shoulder, the hand wrapped in bandages.

"Mrs. Stewart," Lyle said, "Forgive my intrusion, but I've learned that much will be forgotten if not said right away. Please tell me what happened."

Mamie kept her attention toward a cut green glass bowl on the table in front of the settee, as she spoke. Lyle pulled out a pencil and a small notebook and scribbled on its pages. Ben stood by the door and said nothing; angry tears in his eyes over Mamie's condition.

"Sissy opened the door to a man who claimed to want boarding. Once in the house he attacked her and threw her on the floor under him. I heard her scream and ran into the parlor and hit him on the back of his head with a candelabrum. He rose up from her in a rage and attacked me, but I managed to convince him that he could get money from me if he would just leave..."

"Please go on," Lyle said.

"I told him I needed to get a key from the liquor

50

cabinet, so I could take him into the cellar where we keep our money. I keep William's pistol in that cabinet. The man smelled like he had already been drinking and grabbed a bottle of whiskey as I searched for a key. I quickly slipped the pistol into my pocket while he drank from the bottle."

"Yes?"

"When we went to the cellar door, he pushed me down the steps and tried to pull my dress up. As I struggled, he hit me several times, yelling things."

"What did he yell?"

"The usual slander I hear," she said.

"Tell me exactly, Mrs. Stewart."

She hesitated.

"I'm sorry, but you must tell me," he said

She took in a deep breath, jerking her right hand up to her face, then let out a ragged breath through trembling lips. "Indian Bitch. Indian Whore. Indian Slut. Nigger lover. Must I go on?"

Lyle sighed, not taking his attention from his notebook. "No, ma'am. What happened next?"

"I managed to push him off of me and ran back farther in the cellar. When he came at me again, I had the pistol out and shot him. In the chest or shoulder, I think. He fell to his knees, grabbing his shoulder and vomiting on the dirt..."

Lyle held his pencil above the next page in his notebook, studying her face, waiting for her to speak again.

"He looked up at me and begged me to let him go... I pointed the pistol at his forehead... and shot him again. "

Lyle's head popped up, and he stared hard at Mamie's face. Then he glanced at Ben and blew out his breath. As he inhaled, he turned back to Mamie.

"No, ma'am. That is not what happened. You shot that man in the chest, and he kept coming. He threatened to kill you. You closed your eyes and pulled the trigger again. That is what you told me. That is what you will tell everyone who must know what happened."

Ben spoke from the doorway. "That is exactly what I heard her say."

Lyle turned toward Ben and nodded his head, then turned back to Mamie.

"Mrs. Stewart. That is what you told me, is it not?" Lyle said.

Mamie rolled her eyes up at Lyle, then at Ben. Tears were slipping down her cheeks; she nodded her head, then looked down at her lap.

"Y..yes...that is what I said."

Mamie and Sissy were asleep as the day began to slip away finally and the first stars came out. Ben and Lyle stood on the back steps as men held out lanterns for others to carry up the body of the stranger on a stained leather stretcher. The undertaker led the way to his black wagon with a white bandage tied around his head. Fresh blood seeped through the cloth at the center of his forehead.

Ben turned to Lyle. "Didn't you warn them about that bottom step?"

Lyle grinned. He hesitated a moment then whispered, "Never have liked him."

Ben walked back into the house after Mattingly left and the backyard was finally empty of men and lanterns. In the parlor he found Mamie and Sissy sitting together on a settee. Mr. Heyden, the Austrian engineer who boarded at the pink house, sat in a nearby chair, a pistol lying in his lap.

"Ah, Herr Pulaski," Heyden said, rising from his chair. "The guard changes, yes?"

The women looked up with such faces of appreciation Ben could only smile and nod his head in acceptance. Heyden stood and stretched, stifling a yawn with the back of his hand.

"Oh dear, I beg your pardon, Mrs. Stewart."

Mamie gave him a faint smile through still swollen lips.

"Thank you, Mr. Heyden, for staying with us," Sissy

said with heavy eyelids.

"Are you really staying, Ben?" Mamie asked though it was difficult for Ben to understand her.

Ben hesitated, then answered. "Yes, of course. Please feel free to retire. I will be here if you need me."

Soon Ben found himself alone in the parlor, holding Mamie's pistol. He examined the cylinder and found two chambers empty. Ben had seen the Colt Patterson before but was curious about the model with its hidden trigger that only folded down when the hammer was cocked. It had a short barrel and scaled down handle, reworked for a smaller hand. On the side of the frame, it was scroll engraved with the words "For My Tigress." Ben smiled and walked to the ornate Chinese cabinet that Mamie used for liquor, remembering she told him she took it from the drawer as the dead man reached for a bottle. In the second drawer, he found powder, shot and loading patches. Within moments he had reloaded the two empty chambers.

He added a split log inside the iron stove keeping the parlor warm. On the table before the settee were two printed periodicals, The Saturday Evening Post and Godey's Lady's Book, both recent of December. He leafed through the Post, finding a short story written by the author Edgar Allen Poe. Ben had heard of the man but had never attempted to read a story. Since he had finally learned to read under Simon's tutelage while a prisoner in China, his only attempt to read anything other than shipping lists, was a few pages in the Bible. The title of the story was "The Black Cat." He held the paper closer to the nearby lantern light and sighed. He forced himself through the words of the first sentence, mumbling as he went.

"For the most wild, yet most homely narrative which I am about to pen, I neither expect nor solicit belief."

Ben huffed and mumbled to himself, "Why didn't he just say 'You're not going to believe this'?"

He shook his head, but then smiled as he easily read the words on the page. Silently, he continued to read, paragraph after paragraph. When he finished reading, he flipped pages back and forth, looking to see if that indeed was the end.

He blew out his breath and muttered, "The walking dead. Nonsense. The man is crazy..."

A hand landed on Ben's shoulder, and he jumped to his feet as chills ran up his spine. Mamie stepped back, laboring in saying "Sorry...did not mean to startle..."

"No. No. Not at all... I was just..."

Mamie noticed the magazine in his hand. She half smiled through her bruises. "Poe?"

"Yes," he said, dropping the periodical onto the table. "Can I get anything for you, Mamie?"

"No. Can't sleep. Hate being afraid."

She sat down on the settee and patted the cushion next to her. Ben glanced around the room then joined her. They sat in silence for a long moment, listening to the fire pop in the iron stove and the winter wind moaning outside. Mamie reached for his hand and pulled his arm over her shoulders, then leaned her head against him. Soon she was sound asleep. Ben pulled a crocheted coverlet from the back of the settee and spread it over her. He sat there staring at the flickers of yellow light lancing out from around the door of the iron stove, making their shadows jump and dance on the walls of the room.

Ben entered the front room of his house as the sun rose above the treetops on the hills across the river. Aaron sat at the kitchen table eating breakfast. The kitchen and front room held a thick layer of smoke tumbling slowly in a slice of sunlight streaming in through the doorway. Ben sniffed the air.

"Have a little trouble fixing breakfast?"

Aaron gave a soft chuckle. "Had to go pee and the ham burned."

Ben patted him on his back as he walked to the coffee pot on the iron stove. "I guess we're lucky the fire stopped with the ham," he said, then noticed the singed cloth on the countertop near the wash pan. "Or did it?"

"Mostly," Aaron said with his mouth still full. "When is Ma coming back?"

Ben sipped his coffee. "Good coffee, son."

"Thanks. When is Ma coming back?"

"The moment we see her."

Aaron eyed his father, but Ben only shrugged his shoulders. "She needs to spend time with him, especially since he's going to North Carolina for a while."

"Where were you last night, Pa?"

"A man attacked Mamie Stewart and Sissy..."

Aaron blinked and stopped chewing. He faced his father with eyes wide. "Were they hurt bad?"

"Bruised and swollen."

"Who did it? I hope the man got caught. They should hang him."

"He was a stranger. Mamie shot him. Killed him."

Aaron stared down at his plate for a moment, then shrugged his shoulders. He finished chewing then stood up, wiping his mouth with his shirt sleeve.

"Don't let your mother see you do that," Ben said with a smile, tussling Aaron's hair as he stood up from the table. "Where are you off to next?"

"Helping Mr. Freidman move tools and barrels around in his storeroom. You need me to do anything first?"

"No. Not much we can do for now, but watch the river freeze and wait for your mother to come home."

Aaron grabbed his coat and hat heading for the front door. "Saw three deer on the crest of the hill when I came out of the outhouse earlier," he said.

The center of the river did not freeze that winter, and the upper bay had only thin sheet ice. The lower bay had almost no ice at all. Still, Ben walked into Havre de Grace every two or three days to check on the *Raven*. On his first such walk, he stopped by the Pink House, finally remembering to bring up absentee ownership of Adam Tuttle's shop. Occasionally, he would row out to the *Raven* and walk her decks, check the holds for leaks, and check the captain's cabin and crew's quarters for rain damage, but *Raven* was a dry ship inside. Simon and Bartrum helped at McMallery's blacksmith shop, learning the skills of the craft. Aaron spent most of his winter days with the Freidmans, seeing a particular young lady most often, but under the watchful eye of her older brother Abraham.

January slipped into February in a slow winter routine. Snow came often, and it was wet and heavy, but the winter sun begrudged it lying on the ground and melted much of it quickly. It rarely accumulated above the knee. Twice a week the four men would gather together at the kitchen table to share a meal, then spend the evening talking in the front room. More than once they hunted together as a team, shooting more venison than they could eat or fit into the smokehouse. The big hog killed the previous autumn, salted and smoked in the first cold air, had not been eaten and still took up most of the hooks. Ben and Aaron would take the extra pork into Havre de Grace and trade it for fresh oysters and ducks.

March came gushing down the canal when all the feeder gates were opened up in Pennsylvania. Ben and Aaron rode with Dan Bartlett on barge number 26 as far as York Furnace, when his mule pulled it north. They spent the night with Pa Jundt and Sonja. Aaron continued to Wrightsville to get the *Wilhelmina*, while Ben and Sonja came down together on the *Ugly Boat*, leaving it at Lapidum for Aaron's return. No sooner had Sonja settled in at their home, than it was time for Ben to take Simon and Bartrum back aboard the *Raven* for the journey to Georgetown. Edward and Harry were already aboard, answering the warmer season and knowing it was good sailing weather.

"We may need to stop in Annapolis and St. Michaels to look for the new crewmen," Ben had said to when he boarded. However, before the *Raven* sailed away, Aaron came by in the *Ugly Boat* pulling the barge *Turtle*. He introduced the two Quaker brothers who had spent the winter in the *Wilhelmina* in Wrightsville.

"Pa, this is David and Matthew Booker. David is going to stay with me to work the mules for the *Ugly Boat* and the *Turtle*." After Ben and David shook hands, Aaron introduced Matthew. "Matthew sailed on a couple ships out of Philadelphia and wants to offer himself to you as a crewman. I told him you were one man short."

Ben took his hand asking him, "What did you sail and to where?

"Went on the ship *Comet* twice to Morocco, and once on the *Philadelphia Star* to England."

"The *Star*?" Ben asked, "Is Scott still her Captain?"

"Yes, sir. You know him?"

"Sailed under him to China in '39." Ben motioned to Simon to join him. "This youngster sailed on the *Star* under Scott!"

Simon rushed to shake his hand, "When, um, I'm Simon, Hello. When?"

"Matthew. Last Year," Matthew said. "You were in China with him?"

"Far too long and never again," Simon added. "But, Captain Scott was a good man. He wouldn't take the *Star* down the Pearl River unless he had his whole crew – all that lived."

"He says precious little about China, except that he was there and his ship was held prisoner because the local prince thought he was English," Matthew said.

Ben turned away and continued another conversation with Aaron and David.

"Is Jeremy going to join you this year, Aaron?"

"No. Pa, Abraham is going to captain the *Wilhelmina* and pull the *Juniata*..."

"Juniata? Another barge? Whose barge is that?"

"Ours," Aaron said, "I am buying it with my half of the profits from the Canal."

Ben gazed hard at Aaron. "When did you decide that?"

"Yesterday in Wrightsville. The owner is quitting the canal and sold it at a fair price. I had the money."

A smile slipped across Ben's face. "Well...well, alright 'Captain.' I will trust you to make it work."

"I will, Pa. When you come back, the *Wilhelmina* will be under sail like the *Ugly Boat*. Three days up and back from Wrightsville with coal, then three days down and back from Annapolis with dry goods, tools and household items. Mr. Freidman will take all we bring, that we don't already have on consignment at other places."

Ben's smile was even broader. "You've learned well."

Aaron raised his chin saying, "Yes I have." Then he and David made their way over the railing and down onto the *Ugly Boat*.

Matthew stood waiting for instructions. "So I am going with you?" he asked.

Ben cupped his hands over his mouth and yelled down to the *Ugly Boat*, "He's going with us!"

A sea bag sailed up over the railing and landed on the deck near Ben. Ben directed Matthew toward

Edward to get settled on the ship and discuss duties. "I'll have you sign in on the ship's log book in a few minutes," Ben said at his back as Edward took him in tow for a tour of the ship and to meet the others.

By noon the *Raven* was ready for her run down the Bay

On March 19th, the *Raven* sat under the North Island Lighthouse in Winyah Bay, waiting for the steamer *Hannah* to churn toward them from Georgetown, leaving a long black smudge in the clear sky above her. The steamer captain said very little as he accepted the *Raven*'s tow line and took her into the Sampit River. The lower end of the dock was open for the schooner and the surface stacked with lumber and barrels of rice, just as it had been on their last visit. The Harbor Master paced back and forth beside the cargo holding several papers. As soon as the *Raven*'s crew tied to the dock posts and slid out the gangplank, the Harbor Master quick stepped aboard.

"Here are your papers, Captain Pulaski, and the bills for your dock space and tow," he said

Ben shook his hand and accepted the papers. "No need to deliver them to me, Master. I was prepared to visit your office and pay my respects."

"Sir, you need to load your cargo and leave this town immediately."

"Surely you can't be upset with my actions of my last..."

"Sir, you are in danger. Jeremiah Williamson has prowled this harbor daily with gunmen in tow, waiting for your arrival. He intends to kill you."

Edward, Simon and the rest of the crew had gathered behind Ben, their arms folded uniformly across their chests.

Ben gritted his teeth and glanced about the harbor. "What does the sheriff think of that?"

"William Postell is a good man, Captain Pulaski, but he was not elected by this county so he could be killed over someone not even from here! You have been warned." The Harbor Master strode off the deck and back to his office.

Ben turned to the crew. "Edward, let's start loading the cargo. I will need Simon for a different task."

Edward nodded his understanding and Simon stepped next to Ben.

"Simon, please take one of the pistols from my cabin and stand on top of the cabin roof. Watch for anyone approaching the ship."

Simon glanced over Ben's shoulder. "They're here now, Ben."

Ben spun around and faced four black men standing on the gangplank. "What do you want?" Ben demanded.

"We're from Mansfield, Suh. We were told to help you load our rice."

Ben smiled. "Excellent." He pointed toward Edward. "Go to that man, and he will tell you what to do."

Edward and Harry were removing the covers from the hatches while Bartrum and Cephus were rigging a boom from the Main mast, aided by Matthew. Edward pointed the loaders back toward the rice barrels, where they retrieved hand trucks and began rolling rice barrels up on deck. As the first barrel was cinched to a boom on deck and swung out over the hatch, Edward sent two of the slaves from Mansfield with Harry down into the hold to begin storing. The hand trucks started a rhythmic trail back and forth between the deck and the dock. Ben glanced up from observing the rice barrels to check on Simon. Simon was pointing farther up the dock, where a single black man came trotting down to the *Raven*.

"Cap'n!" the man yelled from the end of the gangplank. "Harbor Massa need you to sign a paper in his office!"

Ben muttered to himself and followed the messenger up the dock toward the office. The messenger ran far ahead and turned at the next corner. He waved Ben on and pointed to the walkway between two of the buildings, then ran in that direction. Ben rounded the corner, moving quickly to keep up with the messenger. A blurred figure slammed into him joined by another. Hands grabbed his arms, pulling them behind him as he struggled. He opened his mouth to call out, but a rag was shoved into it. Another cloth was slapped over his mouth and tied behind his head. A sack was forced over his head. There was a sharp pain on the side of his head, just above his ear. His world went black, stealing all of his senses, and then there was nothing.

Ben awoke. His head throbbed. Hard knots pressed against the side of his head, his shoulder and his hip. Something scraped his tongue. His hands were tied behind his back. Slowly, he opened his eyes. The darkness of the room faded from black to gray to the lighter gray of old wooden planks. Streaks of faint yellow light drew lines across the walls and exposed beam above him. He coughed. The echoes in the room told him it was empty. He sat up on the plank floor, releasing the pressure on his shoulders and hips. The gag was gone. He coughed and spat out the palmetto bug that had crawled into his mouth. His eyes were thick with sleep and dust from the flour sack thrown over his head that now lay on the floor beside him. He fluttered his eyes, letting his tears wash them so he could see better. Green amber light waffled among the rafters and the underside of a tin roof.

Dock? He thought.

The air smelled of the swamp. Ben coughed again. There were footsteps on the planks outside the room. He heard the sound of a chain running through a hasp, then a door was thrown open, and the darkness exploded in bright sunshine, sending sparks in his vision and nausea across his abdomen. He retched onto the floor beside him. A voice mumbled from the doorway. More steps sounded on the planks outside the room, then into the room coming toward him. He rose up; trying to focus on the figure, but the pain of the light was too intense. Drenching water splashed on him, and a wooden bucket dropped nearby. Heavy footsteps came next to him.

"Welcome back, Captain Pulaski," the voice said.

Ben tilted his head. "Ensign Cuttingham," Ben said.

"Yes, Old Boy. And it is my pleasure to welcome you back with a dunking of your own."

Hands grabbed him and hustled him out of the shed. The bright sunshine was painful to his eyes, but he recognized the plantation dock of Palmetto Haven. Before he could say anything, he was shoved into the water by a boot against his spine.

He fought in a panic to keep his head up but sank immediately under the cold water. He held his breath as long as he could, struggling to get his hands free from their binding, but could not. As the air began to explode from his burning lungs and flashes of light streaked across his vision, bodies were in the water next to him, pulling his head above the water. Ben gasped and coughed, trying to take in more air before they could push him down again, but he was raised up, instead. Hands reached down from above and hauled him back onto the pier. He laid there coughing, gasping for more air.

"Well, that was enjoyable," Cuttingham said. "When you are dry, we will take you up to the plantation house for an audience with the master." Cuttingham kicked him in his side and walked away. Several hands grabbed Ben again and tossed him back into the storage shed. He began to shiver in the mild winter air. Minutes later, he forced himself to stand and started pacing the room to raise his body temperature.

Near sundown, four muscular slaves entered the shed and yanked Ben's clothes off. They dropped slaves' coarse work clothes and a dirty bundle on the floor, then left with his boots and clothes.

8

Edward and Harry continued to wander the streets and lanes of Georgetown's waterfront, searching for Ben, or someone who had seen him. The visit to the Harbor Master's Office had been useless. A man hurried down the street toward them and signaled for them to approach him.

"Are you the sailors looking for Captain Pulaski?" he asked them

"Yes. Do you know where he is?"

"You don't ask questions in this town, mister. I am the Sherriff, William Postell."

Harry and Edward both released a torrent of questions and worries, to which the Sheriff held up his hand to stop them.

"I am informed that he is the guest of one of our leading citizens. I suggest you visit the taverns on Front Street, then go to your ship until your captain returns."

As Harry and Edward continued to shower him with questions, the Sheriff smiled and walked away.

On the deck of the *Raven*, the rest of the crew and the Mansfield men sat near the stern sharing some of the ship's rum. "Are you not going to be in trouble with your master?" Edward asked the Mansfield men.

One man, who appeared to be their leader, smiled and shook his head 'no.' "We go up and down the river as the master needs. No overseer. No whips. We work the barge and bring the rice. We will go back in the morning."

Edward and Simon exchanged glances. "Not as bad as we expected," Simon answered the unspoken question.

One of the other slaves glanced around the nearby dock and commented in a hushed tone, "We are not free, but we are not as bad off as the blacks who work cane or cotton. The master does not willingly beat us."

"No," another added with a mirthless grin, "the marsh does."

Ben dressed in the rough woven fabric and then opened the bundle. Inside he found a baked yam, a piece of smoked ham and coarse bread made from ground corn. In the growing darkness, he stuffed his mouth with the food and washed it down with river water left behind in the bucket used earlier to drench him.

Later, a slave brought Ben's clothes back to him, washed and pressed, his boots cleaned and polished. "Cuttingham comin back for you shortly," he said.

Ben redressed, and as he slipped on his boots, Cuttingham unchained the door and walked in with a lantern. "Time to see the master, Pulaski." Cuttingham held a pistol in his other hand and motioned with it toward the door.

Mooring at the end of a mile-long entrance canal to the front of the Plantation, they walked a brick footpath toward the mansion. Whale oil lamps burned brightly from white columns along the latter part of the pathway, leading up to the front entrance. Massive ten-foot teak wood doors stood between gleaming brass lanterns windowed with cut glass. The doors slowly opened by white-gloved house servants standing at attention on each side. Inside, the foyer echoed within its marble chamber between floor stones and columns. Bright light reflected by the polished marble bathed the entrance from a massive brass chandelier overhead. It held dozens of candles, trimmed to duplicate heights.

They were led by another servant to the master's den. Woven Asian carpets covered the floor and a bright fire burned within a head-high marble fireplace, where Jeremiah stood sipping brandy. He dismissed Cuttingham with a silent flip of his hand. Jeremiah faced Ben, scrutinizing him.

"My initial intention was to watch you hang,

Pulaski. I still may, but I am toying with another thought. First though, what did you do with Achilles?"

Ben stared at him in silence.

"What did you do with my property, Pulaski?"

"Sold him," Ben said.

Jeremiah allowed a small smile on his face and sighed. "Well, at least you didn't set the bastard free. I give you credit for that."

Ben said nothing. His face was devoid of reaction.

"How much? How much did you get for him?"

Ben shifted his feet slightly. "Fair market value. The man knew how to operate a steam engine."

Jeremiah snickered and sipped at his brandy. "God damn you, Pulaski. Have you no end of gall? How much?"

Ben hesitated. "Eighteen hundred."

Jeremiah chuckled. "Good God. Where?"

"Louisiana."

Jeremiah nodded. "Swampland, like here. A steamboat will be priceless. Who to?"

Ben slowly shook his head. "Private sale."

"Answer me, God damn it! I'm deciding whether or not to kill you."

"You're a sore loser, Williamson."

"You stole from me!"

"I bettered you in a sale. And your nephew thought you had it coming."

"James is a shitless bastard. I'm not even sure his father actually sired him."

Ben said nothing.

"I'll give you a chance, Pulaski. See if you can better me with a pistol."

Ben raised his eyebrows. Jeremiah snapped his fingers, and the four slaves from the shed trotted into the room, two on each side of Ben. They grabbed his arms and held them at his side. Jeremiah stepped in front of Ben and threw his brandy into his face. Ben tried to blink the burning alcohol from his eyes. Jeremiah slapped his face.

"We are going to duel, Pulaski. I will meet you at

sunrise, on our canal walk. If you fail to honor the duel, I will have you hung and gutted like a pig."

Jeremiah nodded to his men, and they drug Ben out of the house and back to the shed on the dock, where they threw him into the room and locked it.

The Mansfield men were able to explain to Simon and Edward the route to Palmetto Haven. "We've been to that dock, but not up the canal to the house and not ever in the house," their leader said.

"How long would it take us to row there?" Simon asked.

One of the men rubbed his chin and sighed. "If you left right this minute, it would be sunup before you got there."

At sunrise, the steamboat *Lydia* sat at the Georgetown dock for Sheriff Postell to step aboard. The *Raven*'s crew watched it steam past. Edward walked down the gangplank to revisit the Harbor Master.

An hour later the *Lydia* turned up the entrance canal at Palmetto Haven. They stopped halfway up the canal at a small landing, surrounded by white wooden columns separated by white painted lattice holding bougainvillea vines. Nearby live oak trees were festooned with drifting Spanish moss, flipped playfully by the morning breeze. At the upper end of the clearing, Jeremiah stood sipping coffee near a covered table, served by a white-coated slave wearing white gloves. Next to him stood Lydia Binterfield, his niece. Next to her stood her grown daughter, Nadine. Both women were in full pastel dresses and matching velvet coats. At the lower end of the clearing stood Ben Pulaski, guarded on each side by two slaves dressed in black suits. In the center of the clearing stood a small oak table, holding a walnut box already opened to the sunshine and the air. The box was lined with red velvet and contained a matched pair of new Aston percussion dueling pistols.

Cuttingham escorted the sheriff to the center table. He indicated the set of pistols. "As I informed you yesterday evening, Mr. Postell, this is an affair of honor. Mr. Williamson has been slandered and cheated by the rascal, Captain Pulaski. Mr. Williamson has challenged Captain Pulaski to a duel to settle the matter and Captain Pulaski has accepted."

Sheriff Postell glanced in each direction. "Who are your seconds, gentlemen?" he asked.

"I will serve as Mr. Williamson's second," Cuttingham said and walked toward the upper end of the clearing. He pointed to the four men holding Ben. "His seconds are there."

Postell frowned and faced Ben. "Is this correct?"

Ben hesitated and then nodded in agreement. The men released their grips on his arms.

Postell sighed, then picked up the pistols and examined them. "Who loaded these weapons?"

"I did," said Jeremiah.

"Since you are the challenger, Mr. Williamson, the selection goes to the other party."

Postell took the pistols to Ben and held them in front of him. Ben selected one. The four men beside him stepped back. Ben gave them a thin smile. "Don't worry. Your bullets will come later." The men exchanged quick glances, then focused their attention on their master.

Postell returned to the center and motioned for the duelers to approach him. The women and the four men stepped farther toward the marsh.

"Gentlemen, you will stand back to back and then on my command walk ten paces and halt. On my command, and not before it, you will turn and fire. You will hold your ground until both pistols are discharged."

As both men nodded, Postell went on. "It is my duty to ask you both, is there any other statement or action that can be taken to avoid this duel?"

Neither man spoke.

"Cock your pistols," Postell said, and then counted slowly to ten. As the man stepped out, Postell moved back out of the line of fire toward the marsh. "Turn and fire," Postell said.

Williamson was the first to spin around. He fired

almost immediately. The cloth of Ben's jacket flipped open in a slit above the waist. Blood poured from his abdomen. He slapped his hand over the wound, buckling at his knees and drifting toward the ground. Williamson smiled triumphantly over the barrel of his gun. Ben groaned and forced himself upright and held his gun barrel up in front of himself. Jeremiah licked his lips and made a hesitating move toward the marsh.

Postell withdrew his own pistol from its holster and held it up for Williamson to see it. "You must stand your ground, sir," he ordered.

Ben lowered the barrel of his pistol toward Williamson. Blood poured between his fingers of his other hand; he gritted his teeth and leaned forward, lowering his gun.

"Do you yield, Captain Pulaski?" Postell asked.

"Hell no," Ben grunted. He straightened and took careful aim at Williamson's face. Williamson's lips trembled. Ben's pistol barrel sagged again, but then he pulled it back up aiming it at Williamson's head. Williamson emitted a faint whimper. A dark stain arose at his crotch, spread across the front of his pants and then descended down his leg. Ben smiled, then lowered his barrel slightly and fired. Williamson howled as the bullet tore into his leg. And he collapsed to the ground. Ben limped to Postell and handed him his pistol.

"I am still standing," he said, "and my challenger is lying on the ground whimpering. Do you see that?"

"Yes, Captain Pulaski."

Did you also see that I aimed at a part of his body that would not take his life?"

"Yes," Postell said.

"And you will relay that as you have just stated?"

"Yes."

Ben began to collapse. The crew of the *Raven* swarmed into the clearing from their rowboat. All the men were armed with pistols, swords, and knives. Friendly hands took Ben by his side and carried him to the boat. Edward held his gun loosely toward Postell but aimed at the ground.

"May I assume this affair has ended?" Edward asked.

"And you are?" asked Postell.

"Family," Edward said.

Postell bowed slightly and returned his pistol to his holster.

"Cuttingham!" Lydia called. "Tow them all back to Georgetown." She turned to the men who had held Ben. "Shadrach, go get May and tell her to bring everything she has up to the master's bedroom. Ahab, Moses, Joseph, carry the master up to his room. Nadine, go get the Overseer." As Lydia's orders were obeyed, Jeremiah slipped into unconsciousness, and she followed them toward the house.

Lydia glanced back over her shoulder toward Ben. *I hope you die*, she thought. She turned and walked away. *I hope you both die.*

Postell poked his finger into Cuttingham's side. "Go to Litchfield Manor. It's only a couple miles from here."

"I know where that is," Cuttingham said. "I have taken Master Williamson many times."

"Then go there, damn you! Dr. Tucker can help this man."

Minutes later they made the western turn into the branch of the river to Litchfield. Within the hours Ben was lying on the table in Doctor Daniel Tucker's treatment room.

"Yes.." Dr. Tucker went on as he sewed the rip in Ben's abdomen, "lost more than one slave or family member, waiting for a doctor to make his way up from Georgetown. Learned to do it all myself."

He snipped the silk thread for his last stitch and admired his work, and then poured half a pint of grain alcohol over the stitches. Ben gritted his teeth and hissed, arching his back in the fire that traced his wound.

"You are mighty lucky, mister."

Ben grunted. "I don't feel lucky."

"You are lucky! Another sixteenth of an inch and that bullet would have opened up your belly like pouring out a bowl of slippery squid. Your intestines would have been around your ankles, so you could admire them as you died!"

Then he poured the rest of the alcohol. As Ben moaned, he continued to talk.

"That's called an antiseptic. It'll stop the rot – unless you stick your nasty finger in there messing up my good work!"

He slapped Ben's shoulder. "Oh, quit being such a baby!" He turned to Cuttingham. "Say Jeremiah got his leg shot? Take me there!"

Edward stood up from his stool in the corner. "No, he won't! He has to take us back to our ship in Georgetown!"

Dr. Tucker dipped his hands into a pan of clear water and wiped them with a clean cloth.

"Fellah, if you take this man back to your ship, you might as well shoot him in the head and bury him out in the marsh, because you sure as hell will kill him. If you want to keep him alive, he will stay here tonight, and maybe tomorrow too, if you have any sense!"

Dr. Tucker motioned to Cuttingham. "Well, let's go check on Jeremiah!" He turned his head back toward Ben as he walked out of the room. "Let's see if your shot was worse than his. Stupid fools."

Two black women came into the treatment room with clean bandages and a robe for Ben. The older of the two addressed Edward. "There are sick beds in the next room. We'll watch over him tonight." Then she turned toward Simon, "You are both welcome to stay in there with him."

The younger woman held a small glass to Ben's lips. "Laudanum," she said. "It will ease the pain and help you sleep."

He drained the glass and screwed up his expression. "Tastes like bad whiskey," he said. After Ben laid down on the bed, he turned his face to Edward. "I'll be awake all night, Eddie. You and Simon find something to eat and a place to sleep."

Shortly, the younger woman came into the room and Ben was asleep. She whispered to Edward and Simon. "Margret has food set out in the kitchen. The rest of your people are already in there." They glanced at Ben. "I'll be in that chair in the corner," she said. "If he wakes and needs anything, I'll tend to him."

9

Three days after his duel with Jeremiah Williamson, Ben walked awkwardly around the deck of the *Raven*, using a staff to keep his balance. The lumber was well secured on deck. The larger consignment of rice required several of the barrels to be lashed on deck and covered with oiled canvas in an attempt to protect the rice. The previous day, when his crew had brought him back aboard from Litchfield Manor, he was introduced to their new passengers. Six escaping slaves had been placed in rice barrels fitted with obscured breathing holes. The six, four men, a woman and a boy, were tucked down in the hold until the ship sailed. A man had arrived on deck right after the six modified barrels and handed Edward an envelope from the Argyle Corporation. Papers inside detailed the lumber and rice cargo, and included an unsigned note,

April 10, Pooles Island Light, 15 feet.

Ben stood near the tandem wheels re-reading the note. He turned to Edward.

"We are to anchor off Pooles Island Light in 15 feet of water," Ben informed him.

"I suppose we are once again to enjoy the charm of Captain Holmes on the Columbus?"

"It could be anything, Eddie, but fifteen feet makes me think it will be someone in a big damned boat."

Simon came up on deck and approached Ben. He held a threadbare coat and overly worn hat from one of the 'rice barrel passengers,' as Ben called them.

"Simon, is this really necessary?"

He sighed and looked out along the dock. "Ben, we

need to educate the black people down here. They need to know there are ways to leave without that dangerous walk all the way to Spanish Florida. The bargemen from Mansfield will help me find a place to stay in the marsh."

"This is no place for you, Simon," Ben said. "They will not arrest you. They will hang you."

Simon nodded his head and took in a deep breath, letting it out slowly between his teeth. "Bartrum is going with me."

"What? I need a crew, Simon! We might get by with one man down, but two?"

"One of your 'rice barrel passengers' worked on a sailing barge taking rice from here to Charleston. He can help with the sails... and Edward can teach the others to help. He's an excellent first mate, Ben."

Ben continued to stare at Simon from sullen eyes above gritted teeth.

'We'll know when the *Raven* comes back, Ben. Leave Georgetown late in the day and anchor for the night near the North Island Lighthouse. We will come to you when we have more 'passengers.'"

Ben sighed. "And if you do not come."

"Then I do not come, Ben."

Simon strode to one of the hand trucks still on the deck and pushed it down the gangplank toward a nearby warehouse. Moments later, Bartrum took the other one and followed in Simon's direction.

Edward stepped next to Ben.

"You knew about this, Eddie?"

"Yes. I think it's a brave thing to do."

"I think it is...foolish."

The steamboat *Hannah* chugged alongside, slowing nearly to a stop. Harry tossed it the tow line from the bow. As the steamer moved ahead, the bow swung slowly out into the river channel. When the bow began to point down river, a dock hand slipped the stern line from its post and tossed it into the water. Cephus and Matthew pulled the dripping line up on deck and coiled it in its place. Ben spun the wheel to feel the bite of the rudder and steered the *Raven* into the center of the channel behind the steamer. Smoke from the steamboat drifted along the deck of the *Raven*. Ben frowned as he swatted the smoke away from his face.

Edward walked one of the rice barrel passengers around the deck of the ship as the *Raven* was towed down the bay toward North Island. He patiently pointed out and named each line and sail to an eager young man with a bright smile. Ben heard Edward call the man Hiram.

April 10. Off Pooles Island, The Chesapeake Bay.

The *Raven* had spent a quiet night near the squat lighthouse built similar to the Concord Point Lighthouse in Havre de Grace and finished in the same year. Both were sisters of the Turkey Point Lighthouse near the entrance to the Elk River and the Chesapeake and Delaware Canal.

The day moved slowly. A variety of Chesapeake Bay watercraft sailed or steamed up and down the main channel, going to or from Baltimore. After midday, the air was shattered by the steam whistle of an approaching steamboat heading north from farther down the bay.

The Columbus came alongside and reversed its side wheels to halt its progress. Captain Holmes leaned out of the pilot house with his speaking trumpet.

"How many?"

"Six!" Ben yelled through cupped hands.

Crewmen on the steamer looped lines bow and stern between the ships, while others slid the gangplank across to the *Raven*. The passengers trotted quickly onto the deck of the Columbus, where they were hustled toward the back of the steamer by a black orderly in a white coat. A man handed Edward a canvas pouch, then the gangplank was yanked back onto its deck and the lines flipped of their ties. Within seconds the side wheels were slapping the water, pushing the Columbus north and gaining speed. *Raven* rocked in its wake. Edward brought the pouch to Ben and opened it. Inside was another envelope containing a one-word unsigned note.

Annapolis

"We are away to Annapolis, Eddie," Ben said.

The winds were mild with the scent of the Bay and fish spawning. The afternoon was warm and the sun bright as they set sail for Annapolis. Before twilight, they had moored in Annapolis and slid out the *Raven*'s gangplank. No sooner had the gangway touched the cobblestones than a man arrived carrying a leather satchel. He delivered an envelope and informed Ben that a work gang would be on board at sunrise to offload the cargo. In addition to the usual consignment papers, receipts and bank drafts were more unsigned notes.

May 20th, Charlestown, South Carolina. Do not go ashore. Fly the Maryland Flag on the foremast and show a three-sided dirty patch on the mainsail. Wait three days, then Georgetown.

There was a second slip of paper.

I will see you at the Wedding!

Ben sighed and handed the notes to Edward. "Before we left for South Carolina, Aaron told me he was getting married in May. I hope it is earlier rather than later. And apparently, you will have an opportunity to meet the ghostly Mr. Renowitz."

Edward cleared his throat. "And...shall I, um may I... attend the wedding, Ben?"

Ben slapped the side of his arm. "You are his Uncle, are you not?"

"I am reluctant to say that, Benjamin. The last time I claimed that title, you threatened to shoot me."

Ben turned his eyes away. "Yes...well, Eddie, much
75

has happened since that day. Much that you have shown me. And much that I have learned.'"

He turned back to Edward. "I would be disappointed if you were not with us for the wedding."

Ben glanced among those on deck and raised his voice. "You are all invited to the wedding of my younger son, Aaron."

Cephus tilted his head as he coiled a line. "When is that, Cap'n?"

"Well, sometime in May, I think. Hopefully soon!"

The *Raven* anchored just off the Havre de Grace under a brilliant afternoon sky filled with seagulls and darting swifts. Beyond the deeper water, the *Ugly Boat* rode at anchor, rocking gently on the translucent amber ripples gliding over the Susquehanna Flats. The mast and sails had been laid down on the deck, signaling its preparation to enter the canal basin. Aaron stepped up on top of the cabin at the center of the boat and blew the conch horn that was the trademark call of canallers. He waved frantically to Ben, motioning him to the barge. Isaac joined him in his uniform, and they both shouted for him to hurry.

"They seem excited," Ben said to Edward. "I will have Matthew row me over there and send him back with a message."

Ben darted into his cabin and grabbed his sea bag, while the crew lowered the rowboat. Ben and Matthew stepped into the rowboat together. As they neared the barge, both sons yelled at him.

"It is tomorrow, Pa! I was starting to wonder if you would be back in time!"

Another young man stood on deck, ramrod straight in his uniform, with striking steel blue eyes. Noticing Ben's attention toward the visitor, Isaac introduced him.

"Pa, this is my roommate at the Point, Tom Jackson."

They shook hands as Aaron and Isaac showered Ben with descriptions of the activities exploding at Lapidum.

"It's tomorrow, Pa!" Aaron bellowed.

Ben's eyes flew wide. "Tomorrow?"

"Mr. Renowitz arranged a short furlough for us, Pa. Aaron just picked us up in Perryville, and we have to leave tomorrow night!"

"What?? You're just down for the night?"

"We must return immediately after the wedding, Mr. Pulaski," Tom said, standing almost at attention.

Isaac smiled. "The commandant sent Tom along to ensure I was punctual returning." He tapped the double lined chevron on Tom's sleeve. " 'Cadet Corporal' Jackson is in charge of me."

"We both had to forfeit two days of our summer furlough for this exception," Tom said solemnly.

"Yes. Yes," Isaac added, "We won't be able to leave the Point until two days after everyone else."

"We will be testing," Tom added.

"Who cares," yelled Aaron. "I am getting married tomorrow!!"

"So, I assume Ma is back home?" Ben asked.

"Yes, yes. I brought her back last week. What took you so long?"

Ben hesitated, absently placing his hand on his stomach. "Other business..." then noticed Matthew waiting patiently in the rowboat. "Matthew, please return to the *Raven* and tell Edward the crew should come up the canal to our home tomorrow morning at..." He lifted his eyebrows.

"...Oh, yes," Aaron said turning to Matthew, "the wedding is at 10 O'clock."

Matthew remained motionless. "How is my brother, Aaron?"

"Oh! He is fine! We're all fine! He is over at the basin. He will be there in the morning also. I am getting married tomorrow!"

They grinned at each other for a brief moment, then as soon as he met Ben's eyes for permission, Matthew pushed off with his oar and headed back to the *Raven*.

"Well, everyone grab a pole," Aaron ordered.

Ben made his way to the stern and sat next to the

tiller. "I will steer," he said.

Isaac noticed Ben's stiff movement. "Are you all right, Pa?"

"I had a little trouble in Georgetown, but I am getting better each day."

"What happened?"

Ben wiped the question from the air with his hand. "We can discuss it later."

Within minutes they had poled the barge through the outlet lock and into the canal basin. They pushed past the waiting barges and found open water near the towpath, where David waited with one of the Pulaski mules in harness for the tow north to Lapidum.

"Is my brother well?" David Booker asked.

Aaron answered, "He's fine! He will come in the morning!" then he tossed David the bowline to be looped onto the mule harness. The poles were laid in their places on the deck, and the barge began to glide over the mirror-still water as the mule ambled toward the canal entrance in the distance.

When they neared the Pulaski farm, the *Wilhelmina* was sitting at the little wharf, scrubbed fresher than he had ever seen it, and festooned with white ribbon bows.

"We'll stop here," Aaron informed them as they reached the lower edge of the front slope. "Stake it and tie it," he called out to David as he and Isaac slid the gangplank down onto the ground. Aaron reached into the storage locker near the stern and pulled out several three-foot stakes and a heavy mallet. He joined David, pounding the stakes into the ground and lashing the lines from the *Ugly Boat*.

"Just leave the mast and sail and poles where they are, for now. They can be stored better after tomorrow," Aaron said.

Ben admired the front slope with a smile as he walked carefully up toward his home. There was a tall vine arch, rising higher than a man's head, in the center of the lower slope not far from the canal. The vines were bundled within wrappings of white ribbons and decorated with white bows pinned between bunches of wisteria and lavender blooms. There was a white cloth draped over the top of the arch. The trunks of the great oaks that framed the front slope were decorated with white bows, as were the posts on the front porch, the corners of both front windows, and the doorway.

Sonja stood in the open doorway, wiping her hands with a cloth, and smiling at him. She stepped quickly down the front steps and swept along the slope to him. He met her in a warm embrace and shared a long kiss. She pressed herself firmly against him, but he withdrew and placed his hand across his abdomen. A question flickered across her face but was instantly replaced by a huge smile. And another kiss delivered leaning over his hand.

"I am so glad you made it in time, Ben. I was worried why you were so long."

"I didn't know it would be so soon, and the business in Georgetown was more trouble than I expected..."

"Aaron said it would be in May..."

"Yes, but May is a month long..."

She slapped him playfully on his arm. "An eager young man tells you he is going to get married in May, and you don't think it will be early in May?"

"Well..."

She looped her arm under his and guided him up the slope toward the house. "I have the most wonderful surprise..."

"What?"

"Guess who has come all the way from Philadelphia to see our son's wedding and to meet with the man she loves?"

Ben stopped and stared into her face. "Lettie!"

10

"Simon stayed in South Carolina," Ben said.

Sonja's mouth flew open, but she could not find any words to push back the moment.

"He intends to help all that he can down there, and decided he could only do that by sharing time with them, helping them to believe there was a way to escape, that didn't mean a perilous journey on foot to Spanish Florida."

"But...but...Lettie...," she shook her head, tears racing down her cheeks. "He will be hanged down there if he is caught."

"Bartrum went with him."

"No. Not sweet Bartrum. He is too young, too kind..."

"He is a brave man, Sonja, as is our friend Simon. Lettie will understand that."

"Not this, Ben. She will not understand this. They had escaped. She was to be free."

"And she is. So is he."

"That is not freedom," she said, tension rising in her voice. "That is walking into his death!"

"It is his freedom that allows him to do that..."

"You sound more and more like that troublemaker, Anthony."

He stepped back from her, turning toward the canal. "I'll get my bag off the *Ugly Boat*, Sonja, then we can talk more about all this in the house."

"No. I mean, of course, you can come in the house, but there is no room for you to sleep there tonight. My Father is in the boy's room, sharing it with Aaron. Lettie and I are in our room – oh, God, Ben, she will be heartbroken..."

"Then, let's go talk to her now. Waiting will not ease

her shock."

Lettie sat without expression. Her face turned toward the wall as Ben spoke with her. She swallowed and rolled her eyes up at the ceiling then shut them for a brief moment and sighed. She clasped her hands together in her lap and lowered her head, gently rubbing the knuckle of her index finger with her other thumb. There was a short scar just below her fingernail.

"Cut my finger on broken glass when I was six or seven," she said quietly, her voice barely more than a whisper. "Still had my Momma then. She wasn't sold away until a few years later. Momma rubbed fire ash into the cut. It never did get putrid, but the ash made the scar black."

She locked eyes with Ben. "Did you know that's why colored people have black scars? We rub fire ash into cuts to keep away the rot. Did you know that?"

"Yes, Lettie."

"But you don't rub ash in your cuts, do you? They stay red and angry for a long time, sometimes forever."

Sonja placed her hand on Lettie's shoulder.

"Lexus was Momma's brother. He was my uncle, but we were forbidden to use names like that. They sold Lexus and my momma down to Mississippi because they spoke up when Massah Williamson had me moved into the big house for a maid."

She crossed her fingers in front of them, making an X. "Lexus had black X's all over his back from the whip. Momma rubbed ash into them each time he got new ones." She focused her eyes on Sonja's. "When they sold Momma and Lexus, they looked for Simon to sell too, said he was too uppity, but they couldn't find him. He came to me that night and said someday he would come back for me."

She looked up at Ben. "He will come find me. Simon will come find me." Tears filled her eyes and traced down her cheeks. "Simon will come back for me."

Burl Jundt stood at the opened doorway. "I've met Simon, Miss Lettie. I believe he will."

Sonja and Lettie fell into conversation while Ben

and Burl stepped outside on the porch, where Aaron, Isaac, and Tom were talking together. Aaron had a small crockery jug in his hand and offered it to Ben.

"Rum, Pa. Canal men and Lapidum men have been coming by all day bringing jugs. They sip a little and then leave it for us. There are three other jugs sitting in the kitchen."

Ben accepted the jug saying, "I believe I could use a drink of that." Then offered it to Burl, who waved it away, then to Tom.

Isaac held his hand in front of the jug. "Tom doesn't drink, Pa."

"I never drink intoxicating liquors," Tom said, sitting perfectly straight on his stool, "But thank you for the kind offer, Mr. Pulaski."

Ben brought the jug back to his lips saying "You are most welcome, Mr. Jackson."

Aaron pulled the jug back and took a long drink. Isaac wagged his finger at his brother.

"Not too much, Aaron. I don't want you mumbling tomorrow morning. I want to hear a manly and committed 'I DO'!"

The group shared the laugh and chatted amiably until one by one most had drifted off. Burl had gone inside to bed, while Isaac and Tom had walked down to the *Ugly Boat*, which served as the men's quarters for the night. Ben told them he would join them later. Well after midnight only Ben and Aaron remained on the porch.

Aaron put his hand to his chest. "Is this what you felt when you married Ma?"

Ben smiled. "If you feel what I think you feel, yes."

"I hear married men talk about marriage like it was a prison sentence and their wives are jailers. I don't want that to happen to Maggie and me. Do you ever feel that way, Pa?"

"Sometimes I think I want to do...frivolous things... and your mother helps me to see what I need to see, rather than what I want to see," Ben said. "And there are times when I don't appreciate that help,"

Aaron grinned at his father.

"But after those times, when I honestly look at myself, I see a little boy begrudging grown-up rules." Ben scratched his beard and sighed. "I never feel I am in prison or that your mother is my jailer. And every time I come home to her, I feel the same in my heart that I felt the day she married me."

"That is the kind of marriage I want to have, Pa."

"It doesn't mean it will always be easy, though, son. If you are both strong people, you are going to butt heads, from time to time. You must admit when you are wrong. You must be considerate when you are right. You must keep your meanest thoughts to yourself because they cannot be pulled back inside your lips. And they can hurt for years."

"Is that what you have always done with Ma?" Aaron asked, but knew the answer.

"No, but I wish I had. I have given her scars on her heart that shouldn't be there. All I can do is warn you, and hope you make better decisions than I have."

They sat there together in silence for several minutes, then Aaron stood up and stretched. He leaned over and hugged Ben with all of his strength. Ben stood and pulled Aaron down against his shoulder and kissed the top of his head. Aaron turned and went into the cabin, closing the door gently behind him. Ben walked down the slope with his hands in his pockets, and up the gangplank onto the *Ugly Boat*. He stood on deck a moment, his eyes focused on the reflection of the moon and the stars on the surface of the river sliding by, then smiled.

Sunday, May 5th, 1844, Lapidum

The sky was painted perfect for the wedding day of Aaron Pulaski and Margaret Freidman. In the late morning, a constant stream of arrivals came by foot or horse on the towpath, by barge from both north and south, and by foot, horse and carriage coming across the little bridge from Stafford Road. No circus visiting

Harford County ever had a larger crowd. Tables stood end to end offering yards of local and shipped in foods. Every guest with a wife and every guest who was a woman thought to bring food. Well-traveled men who came without spouse knew to bring food. Many came directly from church services with their souls scrubbed and their stomachs empty. Ben wandered at the periphery of the growing crowd while Sonja swirled within the eye of the storm.

Ben had managed to greet Anthony and introduce him to Edward and Tom Jackson. Mac had helped arrange for a minister, and Delbert Freidman had arranged for a Rabbi. Just before the wedding ceremony began, Sonja flew into the crowd and plucked out Ben to join her near the front. Everyone stood. Aaron and Maggie's faces were beaming. The minister led the ceremony familiar to most people there, who chuckled softly as the groom and bride stumbled through their promises. The Rabbi blessed the union and read their signed wedding contract. Aaron gave Maggie her ring again, and then Aaron broke a small glass under his heel, followed by the phrase "Mazel tov!" yelled by the Freidmans, several guests and a beaming Sonja. Ben had not been coached for the moment, so he released a coarse "Huzzah!" and threw his hand in the air, imitating Sonja.

In a rush, the new Mr. and Mrs. Pulaski were escorted down to the waiting *Wilhelmina* where they took seats on the white painted storage locker near the tiller. A crowd of boisterous men charged from the Pulaski farm and stampeded over the swing bridge to the towpath. Three other men pushed the swing bridge back into its standby position with a loud thud, to allow the barge into the waiting lock and the lower gates were closed. As the lock filled with water from upstream, several different musical instruments played a cacophony of different tunes to the laughter and enjoyment of everyone. As soon as the lock filled, a dozen hands shoved the gates to the upper canal open, and the tow group surged forward on the towpath, yanking the barge north. With a mighty chorus of yells chanting "Curtains in the cabin, curtains in the cabin," the canallers charged along the towpath, pulling the barge faster than it had ever traveled by mules. The celebration continued all the way to the next lock, where winded and inebriated men fell in a pile as another man hitched mules to the tow rope, for the rest of the journey to York Furnace.

In the quiet left behind at the Pulaski farm, visitors eagerly ate the food set out for them, drank the apple cider and rum and whiskey, and plied the parents with congratulations. Ben had only seconds with Anthony to exchange pleasantries when his carriage was ready to trot away with Isaac and Tom as passengers. They crossed Dr. Archer's bridge into Port Deposit on their way to the train station in Perryville. Dan Bartlett had two mules harnessed to pull Number 26 and took on passengers heading to Wrightsville and Columbia. Ben and Sonja escorted Lettie to the barge and waved as Number 26 moved into the next section of the canal.

Hours later, as the sun began its slide behind the treetops on the western ridge; they walked into the front room of their home, tired and almost numb from the excitement. Everything that could be out of place was. Burl sat in a chair by the empty fireplace, half asleep. Ben was eager to climb out of his new suit and into his canvas trousers and old wool shirt. Sonja had purchased new shoes, and now regretted her selection, happy to take them off and let her feet breathe, before slipping them back into her usual shoes.

In their room, they fell into a practiced rhythm, moving instinctively aside without talking, as the other changed position in the room for one thing or another. As Ben pulled off his shirt, Sonja noticed his bandage.

"Ben! What happened?"

He half smiled. "I got into a duel with Jeremiah Williamson-"

"A duel?"

"He had me kidnapped from Georgetown and taken

to his plantation."

"You shot at each other?" She came close to him, touching the bandage wrapping around his abdomen. "You were shot?"

Ben pulled in his stomach and gingerly rolled down the bandage so Sonja could see the stitches.

"Oh, my God! How can you be walking around with a wound that big?" She squeezed his cheeks and pushed open his eyes. "You don't look pale..."

"It was just a shallow cut. The bullet went across my skin. It barely cut me open at all..."

"It cut you open? Doctor Harper should look at you!"

"Yes. I will have him look at it. The doctor who stitched me in Georgetown made sure it was clean. He told me to have the stitches removed by a physician when I was healed."

Sonja continued to examine his wound. "How could you not tell me about this last night?"

"There were other things to talk about..."

"And no moment to say, 'Oh, and by the way, dear, I've been shot.'?"

He put his hands on her shoulders. "I am all right. I am sorry to surprise you with this."

He leaned close to her to kiss her, but she placed her palm against his chest, holding her head back.

"That's why you stepped back last night when we kissed?"

"Yes."

"Mister Pulaski, when you turn away from a kiss offered by Mrs. Pulaski, you better damned well tell Mrs. Pulaski why!"

He raised his hand and opened his mouth to promise, but she covered his mouth with a kiss before he could speak. A long moment later they separated lips and drifted against each other's cheeks, keeping their arms around each other.

"Congratulations on the marriage of your son, Mrs. Pulaski."

"Thank you, Mr. Pulaski."

"Will you two go to sleep," Burl yelled from the front room as he went to his bed.

Sonja stood near the bow of the *Raven* enjoying the wind run its fingers through her hair, listening to her father's voice. Burl stood near, chatting about his brother's antics when they were children and frequently in mischief. Sonja knew only little of her uncles and hearing stories of their youth brought her closer to them in her mind because they reminded her of her own sons.

"I never knew Uncle Jim was such a hellion, Papa."

Burl chuckled and patted her shoulder. "He was the life of any gathering, daughter. Maybe better than I tell it... or worse. All I can do now is tell you what I think I remember." He chuckled again.

The waves grew larger as the *Raven* left the confines of the Chesapeake Bay and ventured from Hampton Roads out into the long rolling waves of the Atlantic.

"I am so glad you came with us, Papa."

"Been a long time since I was on a ship. I was just a kid then. Me and Lenz Pulaski dashed up the ratlines to the *Richard's* sails like monkeys, never thinking one day that his son and my daughter would be married. Hell, not even thinking of ever having children of our own. We were too busy just being children ourselves."

Sonja looped her arm under his and drew herself against him.

"Things all right between you two, now?" he asked her.

She sighed and turned her face to his. "I love him as much as ever, Papa, but I don't always understand him."

He patted her arm. "Maybe that's the way it's supposed to be. I didn't always understand your mother, and I guess she didn't always understand me. I just wish..."

She waited for another word, but he did not say

anything else. She knew where his thoughts were. "I know," she said.

As the rise and fall of the bow became more pronounced, they retreated to the stability near the wheels. Ben had the windward wheel, and Matthew stood loosely holding the handles of the other one. Ben absently brushed his hand over his abdomen, gingerly touching his wound, where Dr. Harper had removed the stitches before they left Havre de Grace.

Harry's first cousin Rodney had joined the crew, but they still needed a sixth crewman. With the mild weather, Ben was taking an unnecessary turn at the wheel to allow Burl and Sonja more time together at the bow. Burl had insisted on using an empty bunk in the crew's quarters, leaving the captain's cabin for Ben and Sonja.

Ben smiled at Sonja and Burl as they approached, then flipped his chin in the direction of the low lying dark clouds on the horizon.

"There's a storm out there," Ben said. "Looks like it's heading to the north, but we should be ready for rough seas as we go around Hatteras."

Burl frowned. All seamen on the east coast knew about the reputation of Cape Hatteras, even seamen who had not been to sea in over fifty years. He remembered well that the shoals around Cape Hatteras were littered with broken ships; an area called the 'Graveyard of the Atlantic.'

Later in the day, the *Raven* ran into torrential rain, where waves and wind increased dramatically, slapping the hull and sending sea washes charging across the decks. The wind direction was against the *Raven* and forced her to endure the rough water for three days, with only little progress south. Ben managed to find an inlet into Pamlico Sound just south of Hatteras Island and took the *Raven* into the mouth of the Pamlico River for a safe haven until the worst of the storm waters passed. The waves were still angry when they returned to the Atlantic two days later, but the sky was almost clear, and the wind crossed the stern quarter favorably, pushing them quickly south toward the mouth of the Cape Fear River.

On the western shore at the mouth of the river, they entered the little harbor of Smithville. The river steamer "Magnolia" would take Burl up to Wilmington, and then the railroad would be able to take him west all the way to Morganton. His youngest brother would meet him in Morganton.

Ben was already late for his rendezvous in Charleston and was eager to put the *Raven* back out to sea. Still, he kept his concerns to himself while Sonja and her father spent their last afternoon together.

"I've never been on a steamer, before," Burl said. "I am so looking forward to the experience. I will write and tell you all about it!"

Later, Sonja and Ben stood at the pier waving goodbye to Burl as the steamer belched black smoke and slapped the dark water with its side paddles, heading up the River. When Burl was no longer visible to the eyes, he gently nudged Sonja's waist and herded her back to the *Raven*.

"Can we not visit a restaurant here in Smithville?" she asked.

"Sonja, we should have been in Charleston yesterday."

She huffed out a breath but went quickly with him to the dock where the *Raven* waited. They quick-stepped onto the deck, where Ben was about to direct the gangplank be withdrawn, but Edward stepped close with a frown on his face.

"Harry is not back yet, Ben."

"Damn! I told you I wanted everyone close, so we could get away while there was still light."

"Yes and I told that same thing to Harry. And he told me he would be back in ten minutes."

Ben scratched his beard. "And how long has Harry been gone now?"

Edward tisked between his teeth. "Half an hour."

"Damn! Do you know where he went?"

Edward pointed to a nicely decorated tavern down the street from the dock. Ben sighed heavily and turned to Sonja. "How would you like to have dinner at that tavern?"

She frowned into his face. "Will there be yelling?"

"No. I promise," he said. Then he turned back to Edward. "One hour. Then I need everyone on deck ready to raise anchor and set sails. Understood?"

"Yes, Cap'n. Do you need me to go with you to collect Harry?"

"No. I will 'invite' him back to the ship as Sonja and I are seated for dinner."

The tavern held several couples at the tables around a generous sized room. The men at the bar appeared mostly clean. One, in particular, caught Ben's attention, and as soon as Sonja was seated, Ben made a beeline toward Harry."

"Ah Captain Pulaski, we were just about to visit the ship..."

"Harry, you were to be back on the ship well before now - who is we?"

Harry smiled and patted the shoulder of the man standing next to him. "This is Howard Cook, an old friend of mine. We sailed together on two different ships, the last one not too long before I signed on the *Raven*."

Howard held out his hand, "Captain. I hear you need a crewman."

Ben smiled as he accepted his hand. "I do, but why is that interesting to you?"

"I need a ship," Howard said.

Ben glanced at Harry and then focused his attention on Howard. "Why do you need a ship? You do not sound like you are from here. Have you been put off?"

"I am from Mississippi, sir, and I put myself off. The old ship I came here in is truly rotten. Not in a moral way, mind you, she leaks like a wet rag. I have no desire to sign on with Davy Jones."

Harry leaned forward. "He's an excellent seaman, Cap'n. I learned a great deal from him when I first went to sea, and even more when we shipped together two years ago. I will vouch for him."

Ben eyed Harry an instant then nodded to Howard. "If you will get your bag and let Harry show you where to toss it, I will be aboard in a few minutes to sign you on."

When Ben joined Sonja at the table, a bowl of steaming soup was already sitting in front of his chair, and Sonja was beaming a smile.

"She-crab soup, Ben," she said excitedly. "I have craved this. Lump crab meat and fresh vegetables. They also put in a seasoning the waiter called 'Cajun' something. It comes from New Orleans. It is delicious!"

Ben carefully sampled the soup and rewarded it with a smile. They ate in silence, enjoying the soup. As Sonja finished her bowl, Ben was draining his second. They almost ran to the ship, with Ben's hand against the small of Sonja's back and a pensive frown on her face. Sonja made straight for the cabin as they came on deck.

Ben signaled Edward. Harry and Howard yanked up the gangplank. Cephus began flipping dock lines back on board while Matthew and Rodney loosened the sail lines. Ben motioned for Howard to follow him and as he turned to face the stern, he came face to face with Sonja. She handed him his log book and held out a small ink bottle with a stubby pen in its opened top. Ben smiled at her, made his entry in the log book and held it on top of the compass binnacle for Howard to sign. As the crewmen walked away, Sonja leaned in close to Ben.

"Say thank you for the soup, Ben."

He allowed a faint smile. "Thank you for the soup – Ben," he said.

She narrowed her blue eyes. "You can be such an ass," she whispered.

He smiled without comment, and she went below deck.

It was May 23rd when the *Raven* finally made its way into Charleston harbor. Ben remained concerned he may have missed a vital connection. He was flying the Maryland flag from the foremast. Generally, he flew a pennant from the foremast to see the wind and had never flown the Maryland flag there. When he went to Bermuda, he flew the American Flag from the mainmast, but nothing other than a pennant from the foremast. A large dirty triangular patch had been added to the mainsail, not that the sail actually needed a patch. Ben was unsatisfied with the arrangement.

They anchored offshore, away from the docks. With the mainsail partially raised to show the patch, even with the lines loose to let out the wind from the canvas, the ship swung at anchor in every direction the wind chose. He sighed and tapped his fingertips on the binnacle. He was not comfortable with the arrangement at all.

No one came in the direction of the *Raven*. She was merely one more ship waiting for her turn at the dock, for the particular location she needed to offload or on load her cargo into or out of the right warehouse. It was not unusual. No one came. The sun went down, and no one came. He directed the crew to set up shifts to watch the deck, even though he was there most of the night, waiting for a rowboat or a small cargo barge coming toward them with a lantern to light the way.

At sunrise, the smell of coffee and fried ham drew him down into the galley, where Cephus had surprised them all with freshly baked biscuits. Even then, he only tarried long enough to scoop ham and biscuits into a cloth, grab a mug of coffee and return to the deck. He continued to pace the deck all day, walking dozens of miles up and down the wooden planks between bow and stern. Sonja brought him a plate of fried fish for supper.

"The crew had great luck fishing," she said. "They tossed their hooks well away from the wharf."

The sun began to set as May 24th vanished. Then May 25th went away with May 24th, and still, no one came out to the ship.

"Maybe I need to go ashore, Eddie," Ben said.

"The note said to stay on board, Ben."

"It also said to be here by May 20th."

"Maybe we should give it one more day," Edward suggested.

Ben shook his head in disagreement, but halted his motion, peering out toward the docks. A rowboat had cast off and was coming toward the *Raven*. As it drew closer, Ben recognized the portly red-faced man with balding head and wispy silver hair fluttering in the breeze.

"Chambers," Ben said to himself.

The two other forms in the boat were black men, one at the oars and the other sitting in the bow. Moments later the boat wobbled among the small wavelets patting the side of the *Raven*. Chambers said something to the oarsman and handed him an envelope. The oarsman stood without any difficulty and faced the *Raven*.

"Captain Pulaski, if you please," he said.

"I am Captain Pulaski," Ben said.

The man handed up the envelope, "This is for you, Cap'n..." then he directed his hand at the man in the bow, "and so is he. Bought and paid for."

Chambers sat in the boat eyeing Ben. "Waited five days for you, Pulaski!"

Ben said nothing to the man.

"I added the cost of housing and food that I was forced to provide this Nigra, waiting on you," Chambers said.

He handed something small to the oarsman, who unlocked the manacles on the man in the bow and returned the key to Chambers. Matthew dropped the rope ladder down to the rowboat, and the passenger scrambled up on deck. His clothes were soiled and tattered, a large necklace of bear claws and bright colored beads hung around his neck.

"Make sure I am paid for my additional cost, Pulaski," Chambers yelled as the rowboat began its trek back to the docks, against the wind.

"Matthew, take this man down to the galley. Get him something to eat...all that he can eat," Ben added, then patted the man on his back, getting a whiff of sour body aroma. "And find soap and some clothes."

94

The man stood erect and offered his hand to Ben. "I am Archibald Betterton, Captain..."

"Pulaski," Ben said. "I hope they didn't treat you too badly."

"Yes, at first, but as soon as they discovered that I was mentally deficient, unable to perform even the lowliest task, they endeavored to pass me off as a mute witch doctor."

Ben blinked his eyes and frowned at the man, waiting for more comments.

Archibald showed him a broad grin, then slipped off the necklace and tossed it overboard. "I worked hard to convince them of that, so my cost at the block would be more tolerable to a buyer, hoping Argyle might be there."

Ben studied the man, tilting his head, "What do you know of Argyle?"

"Call me Archie, Captain Pulaski. It was so ironic that I was taken. I am a senior member of the Argyle Corporation." He chuckled, shaking his head. "So ironic. Wrong place wrong time. Apparently, Philadelphia can be just as dangerous as Charleston for a lone black man these days."

12

Archie spent his daylight hours writing in a ledger Ben had discovered in the storeroom. Many of the pages had been removed for other uses, but a couple of dozen unsoiled pages remained, still sewn to the spine. Archie had attempted to aid the work of the crew, but had been proclaimed "all thumbs" by Edward, and given the run of the ship as a passenger. Ben suspected he was displaying the same skills that kept him from slave labors.

Two balmy days later The *Raven* was towed into Georgetown harbor by the *Hannah* and tied up at her customary spot near the lower end, where piles of lumber and stacks of rice barrels waited.

Once again, as soon as the gangplank touched the dock, a man came on deck with an envelope for Ben and left without a word. Ben slipped it into his pocket without another glance and began giving orders for loading the cargo. The four Mansfield men arrived with hand trucks to assist with moving the rice barrels. One of them bumped into Ben from behind, and then dropped to his knees, yelling his apologies.

"Sorry, Massah Cap'n! Don't hit me, Massah Cap'n!"

Ben was speechless. He stood opened mouthed, standing over the man.

"Yell at me," the man whispered.

Ben leaned over him, speaking in a soft voice, "What? What did you say?"

"Yell at me, please Cap'n Pulaski. Please, suh," he whispered.

Ben straightened, "Watch where you're going, there!" he yelled.

"Mister Bond says stay the night at the lighthouse when you leave," the man whispered

Ben leaned over him again, "I heard you." Then he

raised his voice again, "Get back to work, you!"

Moments later, Archie sauntered by Ben, using his thinned ledger as a fan. He chuckled softly. "You are a poor Master, Captain Pulaski. 'Get back to work, you'? Hardly sufficient."

"If you wish to participate in ship's activities, Mr. Betterton, we have much work to be done."

Archie returned to his perch near the bow, under the shade of a loosely folded jib sail. Sonja caught the interplay between Ben and the Mansfield slave and Archie, but kept to herself, sitting in a folding chair near the stern ladderway. Ben absently rubbed his abdomen, gently touching the scar forming under his shirt, and displayed a growing dark frown as he peered toward the stern. Sonja leaned forward, arching her eyebrows in question, but Ben's attention was elsewhere. His gaze drifted along the dock until he turned facing the gangplank.

Ensign Cuttingham marched up the gangplank, removed his hat and extended his hand, offering a small envelope to Ben. "Get the hell off my ship, Cuttingham!" Then he turned his head slightly, keeping his eyes on Cuttingham but calling out to his crew, "Edward, bring my pistol from the Captain's cabin. Now!"

Sonja stood as Edward dashed passed her and trotted down the ladderway to the cabin. Ben's blood pounded in his ears, muffling out the sound of the seagulls overhead and the breeze in the rigging.

"Captain Pulaski, I am ordered by Madam Lydia to deliver this invitation to you and your wife."

Colored flashes spotted the edge of Ben's vision. "If you are still on my deck when Edward hands me my pistol, I am going to kill you."

Cuttingham took a step back as Edward placed the handle of the pistol in Ben's hand. Ben snapped back the hammer and pointed the gun at Cuttingham's face, the end of the barrel only a few inches away.

"P-Please, sir...accept this invitation I am holding, and I will be gone."

Cuttingham's voice sounded far away. Ben focused

on the small sight at the end of the barrel, centering it in front of Cuttingham's left eye. He began to press his finger. He could feel the slight movement of the trigger.

Sonja held her breath and brought her fingers to her mouth.

Ben tensed his arm to brace against the pistol's recoil. A little bead of sweat drifted down Cuttingham's forehead from his hairline. Tears filled Cuttingham's left eye, and he struggled to blink away. Ben raised the end of the barrel just above the top of Cuttingham's head.

Cuttingham dashed off the deck.

Ben released his finger pressure on the trigger, lowered the pistol to his side. He took three deep breaths, slowly releasing them while the pounding in his head faded and his vision cleared.

"Edward," Ben called, "Kindly accept the envelope from that trash whimpering on the dock."

Sonja released her breath, dropping her hand onto the chair arm and sank back into her seat.

Edward returned to Ben and handed him a pressed velum envelope embossed with a palmetto tree. His name was written in a flowing handwriting. He walked to Sonja and gave her the envelope, then laid the pistol on the nearby roof to the captain's cabin. He rubbed his eyes while Sonja read the enclosed card.

"The pleasure of our company is requested this evening for dinner, Seven O'clock, Palmetto Haven, signed, Mrs. Lydia Binterfield."

Ben and Sonja stared at each other a long moment.

"No," Ben finally said.

Sonja glanced up at the sky and blew out her breath. "This is insane. They tried to kill you there."

"You will be perfectly safe, Captain," Cuttingham said near the end of the gangplank, being careful not to touch it with his foot.

"I doubt that, Cuttingham. What is Jeremiah planning?"

Cuttingham hesitated a long moment, biting his lower lip. He placed his hands behind his back. "The master has become... infirm. He stays in the guest house where he can remain on the ground floor. He no longer ventures out..."

"No," Ben said.

"The dinner is being given by Madam Lydia..."

"No."

"Papers have been signed, Captain Pulaski. Madam Lydia is mistress of Palmetto Haven. Mr. Williamson remains as her guest."

Sonja stood. "What?"

Ben eyed Sonja. "No."

Sonja walked to the upper edge of the gangplank. "Tell me more," she said.

Cuttingham glanced around at the others on the dock, hesitating to speak further. Sonja turned back toward Ben.

"Either I go down and talk to him on the dock, or he comes on board, and we can speak in private," she said.

Ben blew out his breath and motioned for Cuttingham to come back on deck. Cuttingham froze halfway across the gangplank as Ben picked up the pistol. With exaggerated movements, Ben slipped the gun into his belt and held his hands out from it.

"Madam Lydia has heard about your cargoes," Cuttingham said. "Palmetto Haven is one of the few rice plantations still producing indigo dye. She wants you to take her rice and indigo to the Baltimore markets."

"I have all I can take from Mansfield Plantation," Ben said. "And it is already milled. Why would I even consider doing business with her?"

"Why would she even consider doing business with us?" Sonja asked.

"There is great pressure to ship rice through Charleston. They take too much of the profit from the growers. The Federals charge outrageous tariffs for rice sent out of the country, so she needs another avenue. She heard about your business after the...uh...unfortunate disagreement with her uncle."

Ben touched the handle of his pistol and leaned toward Cuttingham. "It was far more than a disagreement, you bastard. You almost drowned me, and he had me kidnapped so he could kill me in a duel!"

"That is all true, but you bettered him. His leg is crushed and useless, and he has lost..." Cuttingham lowered his voice even more. "...his nerve. Palmetto Haven no longer belongs to him. It belongs to Mrs. Lydia Williamson Binterfield."

"We should go," Sonja said.

Ben snapped his head around to face her. "What?"

"We should go, Ben. If Lydia wants to do business with us, it might be worth the time to talk with her."

Ben shook his head no. He faced Cuttingham. "Where do important buyers stay in Georgetown?"

"They don't, Captain. They normally stay at one of the manor houses."

"What if the buyer wants to meet with more than one seller?"

"Well, there's Whitehurst's Inn..."

"Fine, tell her we will meet her there tomorrow evening."

"She will not like that, Captain."

"Good," Ben said. "Now get the hell off my ship."

Cuttingham was back on the *Raven* later that day with a red whelp across his right cheek. He brought Ben and Sonja another invitation for the next evening, addressed to Captain and Mrs. Pulaski, as well as a second envelope addressed to Sheriff and Mrs. Postell.

"She instructed me to show you the second envelope in hopes that you will be more comfortable at Palmetto Haven with William Postell present."

Ben nodded to Cuttingham. "Very well. You will take the four of us together tomorrow afternoon. If Postell is not on your steamboat, we will not go, do you understand me?"

Relief flashed across Cuttingham's face. He saluted then quick-stepped off the *Raven*.

Ben and the crew finished loading the rice and lumber, and then he released the crew to enjoy the town.

The man from Mansfield made no further attempt to speak with him, or even make eye contact. Ben and Sonja discovered the location of the Whitehurst Inn and enjoyed a long dinner together. That night as they laid together in the hanging bed on the *Raven*, Ben shared all the details of the duel, what he knew about Simon's efforts, and the message from the Mansfield man.

After morning coffee and biscuits, Sonja spent several hours in town among various shops. Ben met with the harbormaster and then searched for the man who delivered the envelopes for the Argyle Corporation. When he walked into the office of Robert Cardwell, Esquire, Mr. Cardwell was instantly uncomfortable.

"You should not be here, sir," he said.

"We are part of a shared activity, Mr. Cardwell. A perfectly legal activity and that is what I wish to discuss."

"Very well, Captain Pulaski, please have a seat."

"Are you the one who arranges my cargo?"

"Well, sir, if you mean...um..."

"Rice and lumber, Mr. Cardwell. Rice and lumber."

"Oh...yes...rice and lumber."

"Why Mansfield?"

"They provide rice already milled."

"What if I can get it from another source, here?"

"Oh...oh, yes certainly, that would be most acceptable. My participation is adjunctive, to assist your business. If you wish to make arrangements for other products and other suppliers, you are most free to do so. I only assist to help assure an arrangement that provides you with sufficient profit."

"What about indigo?"

"Not many local plantations still produce that, Captain Pulaski, many switched to cotton in those fields. And with rice having two harvests a year, most others abandoned indigo for their second harvest of rice. Simpler use of the field hands – no retraining."

"I can't fit any more barrels of rice in the hold of my ship, but I have learned this morning that indigo is shipped in small crates that will fit well in my remaining space below decks."

"Ah yes, certainly. A ten-pound crate of indigo blocks will sell easily for four hundred dollars."

"Four hundred dollars?"

"Or more. Of course, the Federal tariffs and the Charleston fees will cut heavily into that." He thought a moment. "Do you wish me to change your cargo arrangements?"

"Not now," Ben said. Then he rose and shook hands with Mr. Cardwell and left. When he returned to the ship, he found Sonja lying in bed with a bloody cloth held to her face. He ran to her side.

"What happened?" he asked.

"I don't know, Ben. I mean, I know, but I don't know why!"

Ben held her hand and slowly lifted the cloth from her face. Her nose was swollen and blood crusted around the nostrils. He went to the water basin and rinsed the cloth in fresh water then returned it to her.

"I came out of one of the shops on Broad Street and a muscular woman approached me. She came close and said my name. When I stopped to face her, she whispered something, so I leaned close to hear her. Then she punched me in the face so hard that I fell to the ground."

"What? Why? Do you know who she was?"

"No. I never saw the woman before, and she walked away while I was lying down. The shopkeeper heard me call out and came to help me up."

"He did not know her?"

"He hadn't seen her."

"I'll take a nap, Ben, and maybe feel better later. We can tell the Sheriff about that woman this evening."

"Are you sure you still want to go?"

"Of course, Ben. It was just some crazy woman, probably drunk."

In the early afternoon, the steamboat *Lydia* chugged passed the *Raven* and churned to the far end of the Georgetown dock. Ensign Cuttingham stepped onto the pier in a crisply starched white uniform and made his way past the shops and into a poorly kept house near the end of town. There he met with the muscular woman who had attacked Sonja.

As he gave her a silver dollar, he cautioned her, "No more by you. Find me another woman to hit her again, but you must stay away from her."

He turned to the man standing with her. "You know which one is Captain Pulaski. He is not to be touched, nor is the big black fellow on that ship. Any other man will do, but you only hit one man, and you only hit him once. No more, so make sure it is as hard as you can hit, then run away."

The muscular woman grinned, showing the many gaps between her teeth, and the blacked edges of those remaining.

"I will come back next week and pay again. Same as before. One dollar for each strike," Cuttingham said.

At 5 o'clock that afternoon, the steamboat *Lydia* chugged to a stop near the bow of the *Raven*. Sheriff and Mrs. Postell were already on board the little steamer as Ben and Sonja stepped on her decks. The women were introduced and provided clean places to sit.

Dinner at Palmetto Haven was lavish, with the slightest whim of the guests met with instant attention by the servants. It was evident that Lydia was now the plantation master. Jeremiah Williamson was neither present nor discussed. Lydia was overflowing with charm and showed great concern over Sonja's attack, begging the Sheriff to search out the attacker and put her in jail. After dinner, Lydia discussed her rice and indigo offering before all her guests, not shooing the women off to a distant corner, typical of manner house business. She offered her cargo on consignment with no risk to Ben, at a much lower cost to Ben than Mansfield could afford, and suggested Ben deposit her profit in her brother's bank in Havre de Grace, for Ben's convenience. The small indigo crates would almost double Ben's profit each trip.

Lydia escorted the guests herself to the impressive

dock in front of the manor house, telling them all that she relied much on Ensign Cuttingham. Waving them off, Lydia withdrew to the guest house to tell her Uncle good night, as she had told her guests she would. A much scarred black woman with skin the color of coal and a pronounced limp went with her. Lydia unlocked the front door and sent the slave into Jeremiah's room to remove and replace the feces and urine saturated gown and bedclothes. She went to the small pantry and retrieved his drinking cup. She poured in a few ounces of laudanum, a sprinkle of arsenic, and filled it the rest of the way with whiskey, then took it into Jeremiah's room.

"Make sure he drinks all of his medicine, Ruth," she said.

Next, she lit another whale oil lamp and carried it to a second bedroom in the guest house and unlocked its door. Just inside, she held the lamp high.

"How are we tonight," she asked with a musical lilt to her tone.

"W...w...water..." Bartrum begged.

She regarded him a moment and sighed. "Maybe tomorrow, dear. I don't think you're ready to be helpful," she said.

Seconds later she held the front door open for Ruth, then locked it behind them.

"I'll be glad when that bastard dies," Ruth said as they walked toward the main house. "He almost beat me to death when your father sent me here."

She took in a deep breath of the cooling night air. "But, isn't this fun, momma?" she said.

13

Harry and Matthew pretended to work on tangled sail lines until the light keeper finally lost interest. With her stern facing the lighthouse, the *Raven* rocked easily among the gentle waves of Winyah Bay, thirty yards down shore. The sun was setting over the western horizon of the Bay, where the land was only a narrow band of green turning to black as it fell into evening shadow. The weathered white paint of the lighthouse was iridescent in the last golden rays before the sun would turn to blood and slip away. Ben was satisfied the sun's glare on the walkway around the lantern lens would blind the curious keeper from the activities on *Raven*'s deck, and they could finally cease their charade.

Edward paced near Ben. "What now, Ben?"

Ben shrugged his shoulders. "We wait."

Edward sent Rodney down to the galley to flame the coals under the boiling pot, and feed in more wood to cook their supper. Gray smoke drifted up on deck from the galley smokestack and was whisked away by the evening breeze dashing over the island trees from the ocean beyond the dunes. The aroma of fresh fish, old potatoes and plenty of black pepper was soon floating in the air. White beans had soaked the entire day and were added to the fish stew. No salt was necessary, though, that end of the Bay was near enough to the mouth to give them plenty of seawater for broth. Darkness fell quickly, but Ben withheld having the ship's lanterns lit.

There was a thump against the ship's side. Harry and Matthew ran toward the sound, with Ben and Edward close behind. Ben thumbed up the blinder holding in the light from the small lantern in his hand. Light shined down into the rowboat bobbing in the water. Four black faces peered up. One smiled broadly.

"We have passengers for you *Raven*," Simon said.

Come aboard," answered Edward.

The men scrambled aboard where Cephus quickly led them down the forward ladderway.

Ben grabbed Simon by his broad shoulders. Simon shook hands with Ben and Edward.

"How are you faring among the slaves, Simon?" Ben asked.

"I'm not among them much, Ben. The Overseers don't interfere with their work, but they watch them carefully. The people manage to slip away to find me."

"How?" Edward asked.

"The word is spread, and they slip away at night."

"Let's go down in the cabin," Ben said.

In the cabin light, Ben could see dozens of scratches on Simon's arms and several ragged tears in his shirt.

"You do not look well, Simon."

Simon grinned and showed his arms. "Sagos. They are a prickly bush. They look like squat palm trees sprouting ferns, but their tips bite like thorns."

"Come back with us, Simon," Ben said. "There are other ways to take away slaves."

He shook his head, "No. They need to be shown by someone they can trust."

"They look smart enough to me..." Edward said.

Simon flashed a frown at Edward. "These are bright, intelligent people, Edward. I only mean to show them a better way to escape, and to help them realize that they 'can' escape."

Simon turned his face back to Ben. "They call themselves 'Gullah.' They are the ones who really know how to plant and tend the rice. The masters here are generally not as cruel as the cotton, sugar and tobacco plantations, but they are still slaves, and they die in these swamps."

Ben and Edward waited for Simon to speak. He shook his head and frowned. "These are proud people. It is my honor to meet with them, and the north will be better for their arrival..."

106

"I saw Lettie," Ben said.

"What? Where? Did she not go north?"

"Yes," Ben said, "But she only went as far as Wrightsville."

Simons shook his head, "Wrightsville? NO! She needs to go much farther. I will find her where ever she goes. She must go farther north!"

"She came to Aaron's wedding...hoping to see you."

Simon lowered his eyes. "Damn!"

"Come with us, Simon," Ben said again.

He was silent a moment, glancing around the cabin, rubbing the back of his head. "No...not yet. I can't, Ben."

"Why?" asked Edward.

"We are planning a yellow fever outbreak," Simon answered.

"What?"

"They have already started to get sick."

"What? Could you have it, Simon?" Edward asked as Ben studied Simon's face.

Simon grinned. "It is our plan. We are pretending. The masters are letting their people lay in sick houses. They are accustomed to some of their slaves dying every year from swamp fever. They have slave quarters set aside for those too sick to work."

Ben eyed Simon and grinned, "And you know the symptoms of yellow fever."

"Yes, I do, Ben. But, I'm not having the slaves tell their masters, though. We're telling them what yellow fever looks like; in pieces, so they can figure it out for us stupid blacks. Now, they have begun staying away from the quarters, sending instructions by way of messengers, hoping it will run its course among the blacks. Hoping they won't have to buy too many more to replace the dead."

"...and then they are told slaves have died..." Ben said.

"...and you bring them here..." Edward added. "But what happens when the dead are not buried."

"We will bury each one. A log to keep the dirt piled high on the grave."

Ben and Edward smiled at each other and then at Simon.

"How many?" Ben asked.

"Twenty, maybe thirty."

Ben slapped his hand on Simon's shoulder. "Excellent-" He glanced around the room, frowning. "We need to alert Anthony about that many – Shit! We need to get word to him about the three you brought tonight..."

"I hear you met with Mr. Cardwell, Ben," Simon said.

"How do you know that, Simon? Do you know that he is connected to Argyle?"

Simon chuckled again and shook his head, then blew out his breath. "Our telegraph, Ben. You've got to remember. We know almost everything that takes place among the white people. If they have a slave or a black servant, we know."

Ben fixed his eyes on Simon's. A smile spread across his face. "Cardwell already knows, doesn't he?"

"He knows that I was bringing a few tonight, and a hell of a lot more next month."

Ben's gaze of admiration was apparent, as was Edward's.

"How do you get word to him?" Edward asked.

"Black people come and go every minute of the day, Edward. Unless we act like we don't know where we're going, they don't notice us, no more than a passing horse under a landowner's saddle. I carry a paper that looks just like the one the Mansfield men carry when they load rice on this ship, so I just walk in the back door and say good morning."

"Do you need anything, Simon?" Ben asked.

"I need to get back on land," Simon told them. "I have a long damned walk. I don't want to travel through the woods in the daytime." He patted his pants pocket. "This paper only works for me in town."

They offered him food and other items from the ship, but Simon refused them.

108

"Nothing can be found that isn't supposed to be there," he said

"What about the rowboat, Simon?" Ben asked.

"It will be here in the trees for me to find so that I can come out to you...I will know when you've come back. Messages among the slaves..." He hesitated. "Next time, don't anchor so close to the lighthouse. Anchor north of it."

"I'll need to figure out a reason to do that," Ben said.

"Rum and lighthouse keepers," Simon told them. "When men visit the lighthouse, they anchor to the north of it, and they bring them rum. Make friends. They see everything."

Ben and Simon shook hands, and then Simon blew out the lantern in the cabin.

"Thanks, Ben. A moment in the dark will help me see better on deck."

"My hand is in front of you, Simon," Edward said, "Unless you've moved."

Simon took Edward's hand while the three men chuckled lightly, then they went up on deck. Simon rowed toward shore in the early moonlight. Ben waited until he could see Simon's form break the faint line of the island surf, then raised his voice in a shout.

"Where the hell is that lantern, Harry? Why haven't you lit it yet?"

"Sorry, Cap'n," Harry yelled, like he was in a storm, then ran to light the ship's lanterns.

Ben approached Harry and patted him on the back. "Just the right touch," he said. "Let's go to supper."

Alone in the Master's Bedroom of Palmetto Haven, Lydia read the revised 'Will and Testament of Jeremiah Williamson.' The Will had been updated soon after her arrival, before Jeremiah's ill-fated duel with Ben Pulaski. When she came to the changes re-written by the legal secretary, and approved by the attorney brought up from Charleston, she read them softly aloud, savoring the language.

'To my only loving relation, Mrs. Lydia Williamson Binterfield, a white woman, my niece and only daughter of my departed brother, James Bonaparte Williamson of Grayrocks Plantation in Saint Mary's County, Maryland, and of his departed wife, Agatha Bond Williamson, I do bequeath all of my lands, property, certificates of holding, monies and any debts owed to me or my properties, without reservations or restrictions.'

Lydia leaned back in her padded velvet chair and drank deeply from her brandy glass. As the liquor slipped down into her stomach and spread its warmth across her body, she sat up and eyed herself in the mirror. She slipped off her shiny black wig and set it on the only bare mannequin head among the lined array of curled wigs, all alike with only minor differences in the curl style. She brushed the rust-colored nap on her head, enjoying the cool air among the coarse curls. Then she took up a cut glass brandy decanter near her elbow and poured another ounce into her delicate crystal glass, and carefully returned the Will to its cedar box.

Beyond the box was a small stack of certificates detailing Jeremiah's holdings. The one on top was not the most valuable in monies, but one she had read and reread several times that evening. In scrolled letters printed boldly across the upper quarter of the certificate, was the title 'The Tidewater Bank and Trust Company' to which Jeremiah Williamson held twenty-five percent.

She spun around in her chair, lifting her bare feet up onto the nearby bed, exposing the length of her legs. She admired the youthful appearance of her legs and her smooth almond-colored skin, tapping with her toes on another document laying on the bed. She did not have to reread it. She had read it a thousand times after her husband's death. Had thought about it as his killer lie in her bed while she writhed in a sweaty frenzy over him. The other document was her husband's Will that left all his holdings to her, which included half ownership of the Tidewater Bank and Trust Company.

Lydia rose sipping her brandy, letting her silk robe fall to the floor and walked to the tall hinged glass doors opening onto the private veranda. She pushed open the doors and stepped naked into the warm spring air, ignoring the mosquitoes. Up in the night sky, she found the little dipper and allowed her eyes to follow its points to the North Star. Six hundred miles in that direction sat the small town at the head of the Chesapeake Bay, Havre de Grace, Maryland. The town where she had been a queen. The town from which her half-brother James exiled her, taking her bank and home because she was not a white person. She held her glass up to the North Star.

Soon, James, you bastard. Soon.

Someone tapped on the door. Lydia set her glass on a nearby stand and scooped up her robe on the way to the door. Knuckles rapped on the door again. Too loud for a servant. She flung it open with a scowl on her face, which immediately softened.

"Nadine. What's wrong?"

"It's Ruth, Lydia. She's drunk and talking too much. Saying the wrong things. I won't have it."

Lydia pulled her into the room and closed the door. "Don't call me by my first name, Nadine. I am your mother. That is how you should address me."

Nadine sneered, eyeing the brandy decanter and spoke over her shoulder as she headed for it. "I know I know. I am also your sister, and I know that too!"

She poured herself a brandy and swallowed it down, then poured another. She turned to face Lydia, pointing a finger from the hand holding the glass. "We share the same father. I know that too, Lydia."

Lydia compressed her lips into a thin line. "What is Ruth saying?"

"She called me her daughter."

Lydia sighed. "Were you alone?"

"No! One of the servants was in the hall, and the door to the dining room was open. Ruth was eating at that table!"

Lydia frowned. "Who was in the hall?"

"Sarah."

"I was beginning to like her," Lydia said. "Run get the Overseer. Get him yourself. Send him to me in the main parlor. Then go stay with your...with Ruth. Take her to your room. Give her all the whiskey she can drink, but keep her in your room the rest of the night."

Moments later, the Overseer rushed into the parlor, breathing heavily.

Lydia sat in Jeremiah's favorite leather chair, holding a brandy glass. "The Master has been insulted, and I won't tolerate that kind of behavior!"

"No, ma'am. Of course not, ma'am. Who was it? What would you have me do?"

"I would have you do your job unless you are of a mind to leave this plantation!"

The Overseer straightened, standing stiffly, squeezing his hands by his sides. He opened his mouth to speak.

"I am becoming increasingly concerned over the growing lack of respect among the house staff. You need to set an example for the others, for them and yourself!"

"Y-y-yes ma'am, who..."

"Sarah, the new dining room servant."

"S-Sarah? Her, ma'am?"

"Don't question me!" she snapped. "She is to be punished severely. I will not tolerate such behavior. If you can't -

"No ma'am, I mean yes ma'am. I know how to control niggers."

"Do it now. Don't hold back. She needs to be an example to the rest of them. Don't hold back. Use your strongest man, do you understand?"

"Yes, ma'am."

"Then get to it. I want the master to hear her

screams. He was horrified by her language. I want to hear her screams, and I want everyone in the quarter to hear them – No, wait. Have them stand and watch. Get everyone out of their shanties, except the ones in the fever hut. Have them line up and watch!"

14

As soon as the Overseer left the room, Lydia grabbed a full bottle of whiskey from the cabinet and trotted up the staircase to Nadine's room. Together they offered whiskey to Ruth until she could no longer stand without assistance.

"Poor momma," Lydia said while making eye contact with Nadine. "You have tolerated so much. We are so glad to be with you."

"Yes," Nadine added. "We love you, Momma." Nadine returned the glance to Lydia and rolled her eyes.

"We need to get you out in the fresh air Momma. And tomorrow we are going to tell everyone that you are our mother."

Ruth smiled and tried to pat each on their cheeks, her hand tapping loosely on nose or eyebrow. Nadine stared into Lydia's face with wide opened eyes.

"Come on, Momma, let's walk down by the canal where the air is cooler than this hot ol' house."

With difficulty, the two slender women escorted Ruth down the front steps and out into the night. Screams began to pierce the night air. Nadine jerked her head around, almost letting Ruth slip to the ground.

"Hold her up, God damn it. Everyone is in the quarters watching punishment. No one is out here."

Nadine tilted her head and nodded. "Come on, Momma. Let's us ladies take a stroll in the moonlight by the canal where the air is fresh."

As they walked along the little dock, where the steam tug usually moored, Lydia released Ruth and stepped back. Nadine struggled to keep Ruth standing and flashed Lydia a stern frown. Lydia only tilted her head toward the water. Nadine nodded in agreement, and let Ruth fall off the dock. Ruth struggled to keep her head above the water, splashing ineffectively with her hands, and she began to slide under the water. Lydia and Nadine turned to walk away, but as they stepped off the dock onto the pathway, Ruth stood up in the shallows, coughing and gasping for air.

"God damn it," Lydia hissed and pushed Nadine toward her

Without hesitation, Nadine stepped down into the shallows and pushed Ruth back under the water. Ruth's hands flailed at the surface and soon slowed. For a long moment, Nadine stood bent over Ruth, holding her down, until movement in the water had ceased. Nadine giggled.

"Here, child," Lydia said, and held out her hand to help her back up the slope to the path. Nadine smiled and wiped her nose with the back of her hand and giggled again.

"Watch your feet, honey," Lydia said.

Nadine took Lydia's hand, with her attention directed toward her feet, as she was told.

Lydia's movement was swift. She smashed a large rock onto the top of Nadine's head with all her strength. She split open Nadine's skull, spraying blood into the air. Nadine snapped backward. Her unseeing eyes rolled up toward Lydia. Lydia smashed the rock again, crushing her forehead. Nadine crumpled down into the black water, slipping under the surface. She joined her grandmother in the gentle current swirling with her blood. The flow would take them both down the canal during the night, releasing them into the Waccamaw River.

Lydia tossed the rock into the canal and glanced around the dock area. Still, no one else was nearby. No one to be an audience of the murders. Sarah's fading screams continued into the night air. Lydia wiped her hands with a white linen tablecloth covering a nearby serving table, kept available for arriving guests at Palmetto Haven. She hummed to herself as she returned to the house and made her way to the Master Bedroom, where she slept soundly until late the next morning.

Lydia ordered a substantial breakfast brought to her room that was served by trembling hands of the slave girl grateful to leave the room uncensored. Lydia called for her room servant to assist her dressing. Afterward, Lydia ordered her to burn the dress worn the evening before because of spilled wine. She sent the woman off with instructions to have Nadine join her in the parlor for lunch. Then Lydia took a leisurely stroll to the guest house. In Jeremiah's room, she found him cold and stiff. She threw open the window, letting in light and fresh air, and picked up a new novel recently delivered from England. Then she settled into a nearby chair and read the first three chapters. She stood and stretched, and yawned. Spotting a passing servant, she gripped the window frame and yelled to her.

"Oh NO! Help, Tabitha! Help! Go get Ruth and Nadine. Quickly! Quickly!"

As she waited, she read a few more pages in the novel. Tabitha dashed into the room.

"Ma'am, they can't find Ruth or Nadine anywhere! How can I help?"

Lydia embraced the girl tightly. "Oh, calamity, Tabitha! My sweet uncle has passed away in his sleep. Please go find the Overseer. We must prepare for his funeral."

She caught another servant passing the open window and ordered coffee to be brought, then returned to her novel. Soon the room was full of moaning servants, some who had served Jeremiah for decades. Lydia sighed heavily and returned the book to its shelf.

"Get him cleaned up," she ordered, "And bring down his best suit from the house."

The overseer arrived and stood before her with the brim of his hat hanging from his fingertips.

"Ah, Mr. Jefferson. Is there any news of my servant or my daughter?"

"No, ma'am. No sign of them yet."

"Where on earth could they be? Did you speak with Ensign Cuttingham? Perhaps he took them somewhere?"

"He hasn't seen them anywhere, ma'am, but we both have men combing the plantation...ma'am."

Lydia sighed. "I am getting worried about them. Please add more men to the search. Add some of the field hands and servants, if there are some you can trust."

The Overseer almost smiled. "After last night, ma'am, all of'em want to be trustworthy."

"Oh, yes. That. Such a shame. Such a waste. How does she fare today? Is she of use to us?"

"I'm afraid not, ma'am. She did not survive her punishment."

"Well...sometimes you have to throw out a tarnished apple to save the barrel. Is that not so?"

"Yes, ma'am. Like children, they are. Spare the rod and spoil the child."

"That is so, Mr. Jefferson, that is so. And speaking of a spoiled child, apparently, my Uncle left behind another chore for you. Kindly follow me to the rear of the house."

She unlocked the door and motioned for the Overseer to enter while she remained in the hallway.

"That one stole something from Nadine's room," she said, "My kindly Uncle was attempting to correct him through restriction rather than the rod but I do not believe he was successful. It was an experiment, I think."

"W-water...please," Bartrum whispered.

Mr. Jefferson stood over him and moved Bartrum's face side to side, examining him. "Don't recognize this one," the Overseer said.

"Do you not know your own flock," Lydia asked with an edge to her question.

"S-sometimes the master would make assignments and turn them over to the Gullah supervisors. This must be, uh, one of those."

"Well, it doesn't matter now. He cannot be trusted. Use him however you choose, Mr. Jefferson."

"He doesn't look like he can do much, ma'am, but with your approval, I'll put him to work in the fever house. He looks like he may be getting it anyway."

Lydia turned away, "As you prefer Mr. Jefferson. I

will rely on your judgment."

The man knelt down close to Bartrum. "If you give me any trouble at all, boy. I will hang you."

"Water...please...water," Bartrum pleaded

The overseer stepped out of the guest house and tapped two servants with the end loop of his whip. "Take that piece of shit out of the back room and down to the fever house."

Both servants held their eyes wide and hesitated. "Don't fear the yellow fever," he snarled, "fear me. And then come back up here to scrub and burn sage in this back room. It smells like a mule barn."

15

The *Raven* anchored near the Poole's Island Lighthouse in the Chesapeake Bay. They were joined by a southbound steam tugboat towing six coal barges.

"Get those darkies over here," the captain yelled, "before these barges slam up against my ass!"

The three terrified escaping slaves threw themselves over the gap onto the deck of the tug. Once safely on board, the tug captain increased steam and sped away toward Baltimore. The three men, wearing new clothes and boots, each man with a small pack over his shoulder holding food and a blanket, smiled and waved at the *Raven*'s crew.

"God speed," yelled Cephus, and was joined by the rest of his shipmates, wishing them luck and waving.

Ben patted Edward on the back. "Let's get this cargo to Annapolis."

The Argyle Corporation responded to Simon's directions with its usual efficiency, and the *Raven* dropped anchor off Havre de Grace forty-eight hours after sending their passengers over to the steam tug. None of the Pulaski barges sat anchored outside the entrance to the canal basin, and Ben could see no one he recognized on the Havre de Grace docks. He and Matthew took the ship's rowboat to shore. As soon as he climbed up onto the walkway of the pier, an assistant to the harbormaster approached him.

"Don't tell me I've got to pay a docking fee for the rowboat, Abigail!"

She chuckled and shook her head no. "Got a note for ya from Sonja," she said.

She walked away as Ben tore open the envelope and read the note. Ben mumbled through the message, then snapped his head up at Matthew

"We have to get back to the ship!"

Once on deck, Ben had Matthew tie the bowline to the rowboat on the rear railing.

"We have to go to Shad Island, Now," he told Edward.

It took a maddening hour to raise the anchor, re-set the sails, turn the ship around, and sail back down to Shad island, which they had passed only minutes before anchoring at Havre de Grace.

Edward leaned close to Ben. "What is it, Ben? What's happened?"

Ben handed him the note.

'Ben,

Come to Shad Island. I need you.

-Sonja'

"Where that crazy woman lives?" He asked Ben, but Ben did not answer.

They soon slipped along the secondary channel, fearful of the hateful shifting sandbars surrounding the island, and dropped anchor fifty yards from shore. There were two rowboats already sitting on the beach above the high tide line.

"One of'em looks like Hattie's," Cephus said. "Mind if I go along, Cap'n Ben?"

Ben was already pulling the rowboat closer by its bowline. Matthew held a boat hook on the boat to steady it as Ben, Edward and Cephus climbed down. Quickly, they touched the sand at the edge of the island, and Ben vaulted over the bow, trotting up to the house. The little blonde headed girl sat on the steps to the back of the house, crying into her hands. Ben passed her and found Hattie seated in the kitchen next to an opened window, smoking her pipe with her bare feet propped up in another chair. Ben's face was full of questions. Hattie's was expressionless with dark baggy eyes. Ben ran down the narrow hall and into the room where they had seen the old woman when he stopped there before. Sonja sat next to the bed, resting her head on her arms folded on the edge of the bed. The old woman was lying on her

120

back, the blanket was laid neatly over her body, her hands were wrapped onto her chest, and pennies were on her eyes.

Sonja heard them enter and raised her head. Tear tracks meandered down her cheeks. The skin under her eyes was swollen and dark.

"All I had was pennies, Ben," she said through trembling lips.

Ben dug two silver dollars from his pocket and handed them to her. Sonja took them and gently replaced the pennies with the silver dollars, then sniffed and nodded her head in approval.

Turning to Ben, "She told her everything, Ben," she said.

"Told who what?"

"Damn, Ben!" She jabbed her finger at the old woman. "She, Rachel," then she jabbed her finger in the air toward the back of the house, "told her daughter, Mos..."

"Told her what, Sonja?"

"That I am her mother...and her real name is not Mos...it is Alisha Pulaski! Our dead daughter."

Ben stepped back, his knees buckling. He settled hard onto the wooden chair in the corner of the room, staring at Sonja's face, thunder pounding in his ears.

"Good God in heaven," Edward mumbled from the doorway.

Ben stared at Sonja from his chair.

"I told you, that's what I believed, Ben," she said. "I told you that when we were here before."

"I just thought...thought it was misplaced hope...a fantasy."

"Of a distraught woman? Of a woman who could not let go of her dead daughter? Rachel told me when we were together on this island before. She told me."

"Not clearly, Sonja..."

"Well, it was clear earlier today. It was specific, and it was absolute! She found Alisha trapped among floating limbs washed up on the shore of this island, and she took her in...warmed the life back into her...saved her life!"

"Stole her from us," Ben said.

Sonja turned back to the body on the bed. "Yes."

"And what do we do now?" Ben asked.

Sonja turned back to Ben, her eyes wide open. "We take our child home."

Sonja and Ben walked back out into the kitchen. Hattie stood as they entered.

"We need to find a place to bury Rachel. The owner won't allow her to be buried on his island."

"How do you know that?" Ben asked.

Hattie frowned and jabbed her hands on her hips. "Cause I asked him when she was sick before."

"We should bury her in Lapidum, Ben," Sonja said. "A girl needs to know where her momma is buried, just like a momma needs to know where her child is buried."

Ben stared at the floor a long moment, and then sighed heavily. "Alright."

Ben and Cephus wrapped Rachel's body in canvas and loaded it onto Hattie's rowboat. Hattie sat in the boat with Cephus and rowed it out to the *Raven*. Ben, Sonja, and Alisha went back with Edward in the *Raven*'s rowboat. Rachel was hoisted onto the deck, and the *Raven* returned to Havre de Grace with two skiffs trailing behind. Aaron had still not returned to the canal basin. The outlet lockkeeper told Ben that Aaron had entered the canal two days previously and was likely in Wrightsville, or on his way down to York Furnace, twenty-five miles north. Ben arranged for a northbound barge to accept the body, and allow it to be taken off at Lapidum.

Hattie and Cephus had spread word of Rachel's death and her burial in Lapidum. Several people gathered at the canal basin to walk her to her grave. Sonja, Alisha and Hattie rode on the deck of the barge, while Ben and most of the *Raven*'s crew joined the little crowd, walking the towpath. Edward and Harry remained on the ship. A rider had trotted ahead to tell the lockkeeper at Lapidum about the funeral procession. Forest McMallery soon began hammering two iron bars into a cross for Rachel.

When the procession arrived at Lapidum, no one knew where Rachel would be buried. Ben worked his way forward as Rachel's body was moved to a mule wagon. He led them to the base of the hillside behind the Pulaski farm and pointed out a small clearing beyond the cornfield. Several men grabbed shovels Delbert Freidman had pulled out from his hardware store and placed in the wagon. One of the women in the group with a lilting voice began to sing a well-known hymn and was soon joined by others as the men dug the grave. Mac came forward with the iron cross and showed it to Ben, then to Alisha when Sonja pointed to her. Alisha touched it and smiled at Mac.

"Thank you," she whispered.

The Methodist minister from town had joined the group walking up the towpath and asked if he could lead the group in prayer. Another impromptu hymn arose from the group as Rachel's body was placed in the grave.

"It is both heartwarming and sad that we can so easily create a funeral," the minister said. "Heartwarming that we can readily draw together and help each other with the grief of death and parting. Sad that we know the ritual so well because we have shared in it so often." He knelt down and asked the little girl the name of the departed.

"Rachel," she said, "She was my momma until today." Then she pointed at Sonja. "Now she is, I guess." She began to cry as the minister quoted scripture to send Rachel to her heavenly father, and commit her body to the ground.

After the funeral, the few mourners from Havre de Grace moved back down the towpath, leaving the people who lived at Lapidum. They all knew of Sonja's lost child and shared the shock of her resurrection after being kept by the lonely woman on Shad Island. Sonja escorted Alisha to the house and showed her the room she would have, as Ben followed like a lost dog.

"Who sleeps in the other bed?" she asked, inspecting the room that until that moment had belonged to Aaron and Isaac.

"No one now," Sonja told her. "This room will be all yours now."

Alisha began to cry. Sonja knelt before her and placed her hands on her shoulders.

"I've never slept by myself before," Alisha sobbed. "I always sleep in the room with Momma."

Then the crying erupted in great sobs that shook her body, and tears flooded down her cheeks. She cried for an hour until her sobs came in stutters. Then she fell asleep in Sonja's arms, as Sonja rocked her in the old battered rocking chair. It was the rocker Sonja sat in when Alisha was still an infant, before the flood and the ice, before the catastrophic anguish of losing her. Sonja cried with her in silence, letting the tears flow down her cheeks, smelling the scent of the little girl's breath and feeling the miracle of her soft breathing in her mother's arms again.

Ben remained silent. Content to sit close by, saying nothing, remembering a white crochet baptismal gown he had buried in his grief at the base of a tree that for years he and Sonja had called Alisha's Tree. He was saddened over the years he had missed with her, grieving over a child he never knew, but living only a few miles away all those years. He leaned forward and placed his hand gently on her golden curls. Sonja turned her face to his with a light he had not seen since before he sailed away to China. He placed her hand over his.

That night Sonja slept in Isaac's bed with Alisha, and Ben slept only three feet away, in Aaron's bed.

———————————⟡———————————

Early in the afternoon of the following day, the *Ugly Boat* and the barge *Turtle* came to a stop at the little Pulaski dock on the edge of the canal. Aaron strolled up the slope between the great oaks to the steps of the porch as David Booker tended to the mules on the towpath. The front door of the house was open to the fresh air. Aaron wrapped his knuckles on the door frame as he came in.

124

"Ma! Pa! You here?"

Sonja was in the field behind the house, picking early tomatoes and did not hear him. Alisha came from Aaron's room after hearing his call.

"Who are you?" she asked with a frown.

"Who am I? Who are you, and what are you doing in my house?"

Before Alisha could speak, Sonja entered through the back door.

"We have a big surprise for you, Aaron," Sonja told him. She raised her hand toward the little girl. "Aaron...this is your sister...Alisha."

Aaron stood for a brief moment, with his mouth open. Then he grew a smile and peered at his mother through narrowed eyes. "No really, Ma. Who is she?"

"Look at her Aaron. Look closely. Don't you see her eyes, the same color as mine, and her hair the same color as mine?"

"Yes...but..." A frown settled on his forehead. "No...this is a poor joke...no..."

"Yes, son."

"My name is Mos," the little girl said. "My momma is dead, and now this lady says she's my momma."

Sonja smiled at Alisha. "Remember, Alisha, Rachel told you who you were."

"She was sick, then she died!" Alisha ran back into her room.

Aaron stared at his mother. Sonja took him by his hand and brought him to the kitchen table, where she sat him down and told him Alisha's story. When she had finished, she smiled broadly at him, reaching over and straightening the hair on his forehead. "She is your little sister come home."

He continued to sit in silence.

Ben came in from the barn as Sonja finished telling Aaron about Alisha.

"It is true, son," Ben said. "All this time she lived only a few miles away."

Aaron stood and walked out of the house and down the slope to the edge of the canal. Ben followed him and stood beside him, trying to decide what else to tell him, but nothing broke the silence.

"She went under, Pa. Alisha drowned. We looked for her. Isaac almost drowned himself, diving into the water between the chunks of ice. He almost died trying to find her."

"She was trapped in branches, Aaron. That's what Mrs. Tatum told your mother. She floated with the branches..."

Aaron would not turn his head but kept his eyes on the river beyond the towpath. "Is it really her, Pa? Are you sure."

"Yes. Not in the beginning, but now, yes. She is our Alisha."

Aaron turned to face him. "What is this Mos name?"

Ben smiled. "Mrs. Tatum named her after Moses being saved in the reeds. Mos is short for Moses. It's the only name she ever heard herself called."

"How long do you think that woman knew whose child she was?" Aaron asked.

"I think a long time, Aaron. I think it ate at her."

"But not enough to take the child to her rightful family."

"No. Not enough for that. Not enough to wipe away our grief."

Aaron marched up the slope and into the house. He stepped into Alisha's room and knelt by her bed, where she laid, and held out his hand to her.

"Shake hands with me," he said. As she placed her little hand in his, he laid his other hand over it. "I am your brother Aaron, and I am pleased to meet you, Moses Alisha."

She smiled at the combination of names he called her.

"You are going to be an aunt early next year," he told her.

Sonja dashed into the room with her eyes wide open, "What?"

126

16

Aaron sipped the fresh coffee his mother had brewed and continued his description of plans for the barge business.

"Yes. Yes. Yes," Sonja repeated impatiently. "Tell me more about Maggie!"

"That was all there was to tell, Ma. She doesn't show yet, but she has had morning sickness. Her mother visited with her and said she is fine. And Mrs. Freidman promises to share everything with you when she returns to Lapidum. And she will make arrangements with you to travel together to York Furnace when the time comes. And that is the same thing I have told three times before. Now, please, Ma, let me talk about the business with Pa."

Ben beamed with pride, only hearing parts of what Aaron was telling him, envisioning a grandchild on his knee in the coming year.

"We need more barges, and right now they are low in price. We can increase our loads by four or five times. And we need to move from sail to steam."

"Steam?" Ben said

"Yes, Pa. There is a steam engine for sale in Columbia. It is an older machine, designed to pump water out of the coal mines. They have a bigger one now and wish to sell the older one."

"And... you would put it in the *Ugly Boat*?"

"Yes. Exactly. Its smaller size is perfect for the *Ugly Boat*. We can use side wheels."

"You won't be able to get it into the canal, Aaron."

"No. We won't. We will only use it to take our barges to Annapolis, or Baltimore or Philadelphia – wherever prices are best. And we will do it for less than the commercial steam tugs."

"Now explain that to me, Aaron."

"Pa, we haul coal. We get it wholesale in Columbia. The commercial tugs have to buy it from the colliers at a higher price than we sell it in Annapolis. Our coal will cost us half as much."

"And the *Ugly Boat* sits useless, waiting for our barges to come back from Wrightsville? Or does it waste coal pulling one or two barges at a time back and forth to Annapolis?"

Aaron frowned and shook his head. "When it is not pulling our group of barges, all of them at once, it will pull other barges. We can underbid the commercial tugs and still make a profit over cost. We need to grow, Pa. We are each getting a new child."

"That's enough business," Sonja said as she placed a bowl of boiled potatoes in front of them. "I need one of you to slice the ham that I baked. Then I need you out of the kitchen so Alisha and I can set the table."

"No, Ma," Aaron protested. "I need to be going."

"What you need to do, young man is to tell David to unhook that mule and bring it over the swing bridge to our barn, then join us for dinner. Shame on you for making him wait over there so long."

Aaron exchanged a quick glance with Ben, who held his hands up in surrender and chuckled. "I'll cut the ham while you get David," he said.

As Aaron stood, he snapped his fingers. "Almost forgot, Pa. A man in Wrightsville handed this to me and asked me to give it to you. He handed Ben an envelope, with Ben's name written on the front.

Captain Benjamin Pulaski aboard the Schooner Raven

Sonja stood near Ben as he read the unsigned note.

June 20th, Georgetown, South Carolina. No cargo. Go to the courthouse. Do not be late.

Ben raised his chin from the note, meeting Sonja's eyes. "The *Raven* will have to sail again next week."

"I need to stay here with Alisha," She said. "We just buried Rachel, and I want her to have a chance to put flowers on the grave."

Ben nodded his head in understanding, and they were soon re-joined by Aaron with David in tow. Aaron introduced David to his returned sister, still calling her "Moses Alisha." During the meal, the young men chatted amiably and continuously about the many changes planned for the barge business. Sonja met Alisha's eyes. Alisha held a half smile on her face and a new sparkle in her eyes. Aaron noticed it as well, reaching out to tweak her nose gently and sharing a smile between them. Sonja drew in a deep breath, letting it out slowly, savoring the moment.

Welcome home, Alisha, she thought.

Late the next week the crew of the *Raven* made their way on board after five days pursuing their rests and delights. Ben arrived in a boat belonging to local merchants, bringing aboard food and other supplies for the voyage. Ben showed the latest note to Edward.

"No cargo, Ben?" Edward said after reading the note.

"I suspect we will need the space for 'other purposes', if Simon is successful."

Another boat came alongside the *Raven*. It required two men to row, one on each side. Tied on raised racks along the middle of the lighter were two long wooden shafts.

Edward examined the shafts and frowned. "Too small for booms. Too large for gaffs. What are they, Ben?"

"Please load them and tie them securely on deck. I will explain them later."

Edward assigned Rodney, Harry, and Howard to manhandle the shafts on board. They used a gaff pole as a cargo boom and attached a pulley at its end, but needed additional help to pull them aboard. As soon as the shafts were on board, the men in the long boat yelled out. The boat contained to see four piles of heavy cordage. Edward glanced at Ben with raised eyebrows.

"That is part of our supplies as well," Ben said

Questions spun around in Edward's mind as he directed the crew to complete the loading.

When all was ready, they raised anchors and set all sail in a light spring breeze. They hoisted topsails above the mainsail and foresail, trying to capture as much of the timid wind as they could with another line of sails higher up. The *Raven* coasted south from Havre de Grace, barely leaning away from the breeze. The wind pennant fluttered weakly from the top of the main mast.

This will be a slow passage, Ben thought. Within minutes, Shad Island slipped by in the shallows to the west of the main channel. *All that time she was right there. All the grief that we endured; that was killing Sonja... and that woman had our daughter, so close to us, yet lost. Damn her to Hell.*

"So, tell me about these shafts, Ben," Edward said.

Ben blew out his breath, and then turned to face his half-brother. "No matter how efficient Anthony and the Argyle people are, there is no way we will be able to do this quietly. If Simon was correct in his numbers, we will need at least two rowboats, two trips each."

"We'll just get the light keepers drunk with rum."

Ben shook his head no. "We cannot risk the *Raven* or our arrangements with Georgetown. We must be another ship."

Edward smiled. "A false mast?"

Ben nodded. "We will leave Winyah Bay as *Raven*, but return later in the night, or even the night after that, ship-rigged. It will be during the dark of the moon, and we will be forced to use at least some lanterns. We cannot escape being seen at North Point Island."

Reed Jefferson, Overseer for Palmetto Haven, stood safely away from the fever house. The yellow rag fluttered over the hut in the distance. Two burly slaves drug Bartrum to the doorway held their breath and pushed him inside. They trotted away quickly, trying not to breathe the vapors near the hut.

"Go rinse off in the canal," Jefferson ordered them, then muttered toward the hut, "whatever you did little man, you'll die there soon enough, or I'll find reason to hang you."

Inside the hut, Simon came out of the shadows in the rear and helped pick up his friend.

"Water..." Bartrum's words were barely a rasp, but still unnecessary. The gourd filled with fresh water was already coming to his lips.

The old woman assigned to the fever house let the water dribble into his mouth. Bartrum reached up to grab hungrily at the gourd.

"Not too much, and not too fast, young'un. Else you'll be pukin it all back up straight away."

Another elderly woman rinsed a rag in a wooden water bucket, then wrung it partially and placed it on Bartrum's forehead.

Simon placed his hand gently on Bartrum's chest. "You damned fool. I told you to stay away from those girls in the quarter."

Bartrum's dried lips spread as he drank, the skin cracking as he smiled.

The woman holding the gourd shook her head from side to side. "The overseer and his men keeps they eye on them girls and knows if anyone sniffin around'em. You lucky you ain't dead, young'un."

"Tried to save some of them," he whispered. "Woman master had me chained in the little house."

"Lydia?" Simon asked.

Bartrum nodded as he continued to sip from the gourd. "She knew I was off *Raven*."

Simon frowned in the shadows. "Damn it."

The *Raven* tied up in Georgetown the afternoon of June 19th. The following morning, Ben made his way to the courthouse and was approached by Robert Cardwell.

Cardwell spoke in a rushed whisper. "Mansfield

Plantation charges you for absconding with merchandise under false pretense, and failure to honor your debts."

"What? How could that happen? You people are to take care of all that."

Cardwell glanced around the empty foyer. "Please keep your voice down. Yes, we took care of everything, which is why you are here."

"What? Why? How..."

"We withheld payment..."

Ben grabbed the man's lapels with fire in his eyes.

"It will all be remedied in minutes, sir. Please let me go."

Ben released his grip but kept a stern glare at Cardwell.

Cardwell opened his mouth to speak, but a door to the courtroom opened, and the bailiff called out, "Pulaski."

"Just trust me," Cardwell said, and they both entered the courtroom.

In less than ten minutes, they were out of the courthouse.

"As I predicted, sir," Cardwell said, "All is well, and your reputation is intact, bolstered by a profound apology by the attorney for Mansfield Plantation, and a rare apology from his honor, the judge."

"Was it necessary for me to go through that?" Ben asked.

Cardwell sighed. "You needed a good reason to be here without cargo or other business. And now you are free to go, with an empty ship, sir."

Ben's shoulders relaxed. "Yes. Yes, of course. I was so angry. I missed your ploy."

Cardwell extended his hand. "Yes, well we both have other work to do. Until we meet again."

Ben accepted his hand, saying "Out of court."

Cardwell smiled and walked away saying, "The *Hannah* is waiting for you."

As Ben returned to the *Raven*, the steam tug *Hannah* was alongside ready to tow his ship back down the Sampit River to the Winyah Bay. The captain of the *Hannah* was surprised when the *Raven* signaled for him to toss out the tow line still a mile from the Lighthouse.

The *Raven* set sails in a brisk warm southern wind and dashed out into the Atlantic. Once out of sight from the lighthouse, Ben turned the *Raven* almost directly into the wind. He began a series of long tacks out to sea then back toward shore, skimming along the face of the wind, but traveling only a few miles up the coast. On the night of the second day at sea, he brought the *Raven* into a protected inlet open to the ocean at the north end of the island. The crew raised the false mizzen mast, centered between their two real masts, with gaff poles tied across it and loose canvas hanging from them like sails. Crewmen then climbed the rigging of the real masts and strung lines to the false mast to hold it in place.

"Any serious wind will knock it down," Edward said while examining the rigging, then turned to face Ben. "But from a distance, we are a strange ship, not known in these waters."

"We'll need to stay in deeper water," Ben added. "Anyone from the lighthouse seeing us close to land will identify us as shallow bottomed. We must make them think we are a deep ocean vessel."

"Hoist up the two cannons," Edward ordered.

"Remember..." Ben started.

"I know. I know," Edward answered. "Rags and gunpowder only."

"...and only if someone starts shooting at us."

Cephus brought up the cannon staffs from below, slow match cord was wrapped around the hook at the end. Cephus showed a toothy grin in the lantern light. "Haven't fired one of these since my old Massah took me to sea to shoot Brits."

"Did you hit anything?" Rodney asked.

"'Bout everything I shot at. Old man Smith said I'd been one of his best crewmen when he set me free in 18 and 18."

"Well Cephus," Ben said, patting his shoulder. "This

time we miss, right?"

"Yassuh."

"Gentlemen," Ben called out. "Raise anchor and let us go back into Winyah Bay."

At the mouth of the Palmetto Haven canal, the steamboat *Lydia* was returning late from Georgetown. One of the paddlewheels jammed to a stop, and the new boson leaned out from the deck to find the cause. An oak branch had been caught in the wheel housing a few days before, so the boson reached in to feel for another. He screamed for Cuttingham when he dislodged the obstruction, pulling up Nadine's pale, bloated body by her arm. Nadine was brought to the manor house. Lydia sent for the Overseer and calmly ordered him to question the servants and field hands, including those in the fever house.

17

Near midnight, the *Raven*'s bow anchor was lowered into eighteen feet of water, off shore from a wide sandy beach just inside Winyah Bay. The sky was overcast, blocking the meager light from the stars. They were a mile below the North Island Lighthouse, which they could easily see in the distance. The nose of the cape offered a narrow bay free from the Atlantic rollers and a smooth pull on the oars to shore. They quietly lowered the stern anchor to keep the ship parallel with the beach, and dropped rope ladders over the sides. The crew lowered the ship's rowboat to have it ready and lit her lanterns.

Ben was concerned that there were no prearranged signals, so he had to hope Simon and his people were watching. Ben had told the crew to leave their boots below deck to minimize noise. Both cannons were on the side of the ship facing the shore. The wooden wheels on the cannon carriages were slathered in fat grease from the galley to ensure there would be no squeaks if they had to be moved. Cephus had lit the slow match from a lantern flame. The long burning cord would be used to touch off the cannon if they had to be used. They waited a long hour, staring into the blackness of the island's tree line. The modest surf and shoreline were only a dark gray line between the blackness of the trees and the water. Another hour crawled away.

Edward heard the complaint of a heron as it rose from its nightly perch in the shallows, then it flew off to another spot where it would not be disturbed. He tapped Ben's shoulder and pointed toward the shore in the lantern light.

"I think they're coming," he whispered.

A dark form created a gap in the surf line, and a

rowboat came out to the ship.

Ben whispered to the men nearby, "Get ready to help them on deck, and get them below as quick as you can."

There was a muffled thump against the side of the ship. Harry held a lantern over the side, shining light into a rowboat holding only Simon. Ben dashed to Harry's side.

"Where are the others, Simon?" Ben asked in a hoarse whisper.

"Wasn't sure it was you," he said, "The three masts confused me."

Ben gave him a toothy grin. "That's what it is supposed to do."

Simon sat down in the boat and picked up the oar handles. "I'll go get the first load."

Ben turned to Rodney, "Take the other rowboat and follow him to shore."

Rodney scrambled down into the *Raven*'s rowboat and rowed after Simon. Moments later Ben heard men mumbling on shore. A dark break in the lighter line of sand on the beach gave him the indication of their return to the ship. Five men scrambled up the rope ladders from each rowboat. One of the first faces into the lantern light belonged to Bartrum.

"Welcome back!" Ben said as he helped the man over the railing. Ben leaned over the railing and spoke to Simon. "How many did you bring out?" He asked

"About thirty-five," Simon answered.

Ben whispered to Edward, "Now, by God, this is worthwhile."

Harry was near them. "Even one is worthwhile," he said

"True, but this is great," Ben said.

The wind increased slightly, pushing the *Raven* slightly closer to shore, but the anchor lines held without trouble. It took longer for the second trip.

"Twenty men," Ben said to himself, as the slaves were herded below deck, spotting two women. "Twenty people," he corrected himself

The wind had grown even stronger, and both Rodney and Simon were almost out of breath. Ben ordered Matthew and Howard to go after the next load and suggested Simon and Rodney come up.

"No," Simon answered, "but we can use two men rowing. Two boats will still bring eight more each trip."

It was a full twenty minutes before the group of eight came over the railing. Cephus rushed them below deck with the others.

"Twenty-eight," Ben whispered. "Do you need a rest," he asked down in the darkness, but the rowboats had already gone back. "One last trip," he said.

Before he could see the rowboats at the surf again, a gunshot flashed from the trees, followed by three more in ragged succession. Ben heard a man scream in pain and other men yelling obscenities. Flashes of gunfire spat frozen pictures of the instant and immediately gobbled by the dark. In the flash of another gun, Ben could see the front of the shooter, pointing down at a black man lying on the sand, his hands raised in a futile motion to stop the bullet. More flashes in the night, shooting stars of bright amber lilies. Then others followed, but these were brilliant yellow blooms with red centers.

"They're shooting at us!" Edward yelled. "We need to shoot back."

"We don't know who or where to shoot, Eddie."

More flashes erupted at the surf line as the guns fired. The boats were pushing off again. A form at the stern of the second rowboat fell into the water. Another weapon fired nearby, illuminating Simon holding up an oar, attacking the shooter. There were yells among the crowd, surging across the sand. More gun flashes spat into the darkness, lighting several men with oars charging them.

"Cephus!" Ben yelled, but Cephus was already at the cannon.

Edward and Harry helped to move the muzzles out over the water. Cephus touched the slow match to the first cannon. The night exploded in a ball of yellow and red light. The brightness seared eyes held wide open in the darkness, leaving its image on the brain of anyone looking. The explosion thundered over the water. Birds flew up into the night sky. Ears were slapped deaf for an instant, and then began ringing from the noise and the concussion of the boom. Men were frozen in mid-motion on the shore. A man in a straw planter's hat stood motionless on the beach during the explosion of light and sound as an oar slammed down on his head, splitting his skull.

In the following silence, the air exploded again. Blinded men, lost in the dark, felt their way ahead as they ran. Harry screamed at the shore. Jubilant at the terror generated among the pursuers by the cannon. Another gun fired from the tree line. There was a wet thud near Ben. He turned as Harry's back exploded in a crimson spray flinging the man down onto the deck.

"Load it again," Edward yelled at Cephus and dashed away.

Cephus sponged out the first barrels and began shoving in another bag of gunpowder. Edward returned with a small keg of nails, his eyes wide in fury.

Ben could see the two rowboats coming close to the ship.

"Put out the lanterns," he ordered.

The firing from the beach had stopped. Ben placed his hand on Edward's arm.

"No, Eddie. No more. We need to pull up the others and set sail."

Ben spoke to Cephus. "Fire that gunpowder toward the beach, and then strap down the cannon."

Cephus stood up at the rail, yelling in a perfect British accent, "Surrender or die!", and then he touched off the last explosion, screaming a war cry as it thundered over the water again.

Ben knelt beside Harry. Harry's blood filled the narrow grooves Ben had carved in the deck where an old friend had fallen. The blood spelled the name of Adam

138

Tuttle, gleaming in the yellow lantern light until it was extinguished. The last men came up over the railing and were helped down below deck. Ben and Cephus carried Harry's body down.

In the glimmer of the hold, the planking was splattered with blood. One man was bleeding profusely from a wound in his abdomen. Simon slipped the slender body of another man from his shoulder, already gray in death, and laid him next to Harry. Simon was bleeding from a bullet wound in his left forearm. The young man lying next to Harry was angelic in his pose.

"Poor Matthew," Ben whispered

Rodney stepped next to Ben. "This is not what I signed on for, Captain. If we make it back to the Chesapeake, I'm getting off." Then he walked away.

"We need to get the anchors up, men, and set sail," Edward said. "We need to be away from here before they have time to find their nerve again."

Ben stood and moved toward the forward ladderway. "Everyone who can move needs to be on deck."

<hr>

With the anchors up, the sails set, and the bowlines of the two rowboats tied off at the stern, the *Raven* edged forward. They moved along the shoreline trying to work the ship out into deeper water, but the wind tried to push her onto the beach. Gunfire came from the beach again, firing at the black form moving over the reflected stars on the surface of the water. Bullets thumped into the sides of the ship. As the *Raven* neared the nose of the cape, they caught enough wind coming down the Bay to push the ship away from shore. Ben took her out to sea over the horizon until he found sunrise and then turned the ship north where she could not be seen from land. The shaft that had pretended to be another mast was dismantled and thrown overboard.

"What happened, Simon?" Ben asked.

Simon shook his head. "I don't know, Ben. I thought we had gotten away without...I thought we were...I don't know. Something gave us away."

The wounded escaping slave died during the night. His name was written in ink on his canvas covering, '*Martin, A Free Man.*' Martin was buried at sea with Harry and Matthew. The name of the slave killed on the beach and left behind was not known. He had come from one of the outlying plantations with his only friend, Martin.

The next morning at Palmetto Haven, the graves of slaves who recently died of yellow fever were dug open, only to find the logs. The overseer ordered the two black women assigned to the fever house given one hundred lashes. He had their bodies hung from the live oaks at the entrance to the slave quarters. Similar actions occurred at other plantations along the river.

Ben sailed the *Raven* past the mouth of the Chesapeake Bay, and on to the Delaware Bay. He dropped anchor near Cape May, New Jersey, and then moved the *Raven* to the docks when he could find an opening there. Once at the docks, he left the ship to send a telegram to Anthony Renowitz in Philadelphia.

> HAVE DOCKED AT CAPE MAY,
> NEW JERSEY WITH MANY OF
> YOUR FRIENDS. YOU NEED TO
> ARRANGE FOR THE REST OF
> THEIR JOURNEY.
> - B. PULASKI.

Two days later a steamer arrived in Cape May without passengers. The ship steward presented himself to Ben and asked how many would be joining them for dinner.

"Thirty-three," Ben informed him.

The man opened his leather satchel, counted out thirty-three tickets and handed them to Ben. Bartrum decided to go with the other escaped slaves. Wearing new denim shirts, canvas trousers or skirts, and new brogans (some looped over their shoulders by their shoe strings), the newly freed people left the *Raven*. They walked in single file to the steamer *Herald*, under the uncontrolled stares of Cape May visitors.

Ben also received reservations for himself and his crew, except Cephus and Simon, for two nights at the new Atlantic Hotel in Cape May. The crewmen voted to remain on board unless the hotel would accept the entire crew as guests. No one from the *Raven* went to the hotel. At sundown, an enclosed trade wagon pulled up near the gangplank of the *Raven*. Two white men in white coats and chef's hats began unloading tables and chairs, followed by a tablecloth and several silver covered dishes. The crew gathered at the railing to watch the spectacle. Chefs set candelabras on the table and lit the candles. A private carriage drew close. The driver jumped down and assisted a passenger wearing a perfectly tailored black suit, leaning heavily on a silver-tipped cane. As the passenger limped to the table, Ben walked down the gangplank to meet him.

"The Abolition Society is spending lavishly, Anthony," Ben said.

Anthony Renowitz glanced over the tops of his spectacles. "They are not spending a penny tonight, my old friend. It's all they can do to assist with the slave purchases."

Anthony swept his hand along the impressive dinner setting. "This is through the generosity of Grandfather's estate, as are the tickets on the *Herald*."

Ben stepped close to Anthony and shook hands. Anthony leaned against Ben and threw his arm around his shoulder in a hug, then stepped back and adjusted his suit coat.

"Do you think he would approve?" Ben asked.

Anthony chuckled, "Probably rolling over in his grave, Ben. He must have brought thousands of your passenger's relatives into Boston and Charleston during his lifetime. Made him rich. Now I intend to spend it all setting as many free as possible."

Anthony offered his hand toward the dinner table, "May we eat? I'm starving."

Ben turned back toward the *Raven*, "Gentlemen, our dinner is ready – that includes Simon and Cephus."

Between mouthfuls of rare roast beef and boiled potatoes, chased with plentiful wine poured by attentive servers, lively conversations filled the air near the table.

"I suspect the Society did not pay for those steamer tickets," Simon said to Anthony.

"No. I see your arm is bandaged, old friend, I hope it is not too serious."

"A bullet, but quickly and expertly removed by Mr. Doughty here." Simon pointed to Cephus in the growing silence as the crew stared at him.

"Mr. Doughty?" asked Edward.

"Cephus Doughty," Cephus answered the continuing stares around the table. "Says so on my freedom papers...Massah Smith asked me if I wanted a last name when he signed me over. Said I could have Smith if I wanted. Told him 'no disrespect, suh, but I always admired First Mate Doughty.'"

Cephus smiled around the table. "He was on Massah's schooner in the war. He was from Bermuda, spoke like an Englishman. Used to yell 'Surrender or Die' when we fought the Brits. Treated me like a younger brother, so I took his name...He was done with it. He died in that war."

Anthony raised his wine glass in salute, "To Messers Doughty and Bond, with apologies from my Grandfather."

The men laughed and emptied their glasses.

Anthony pointed his finger at Simon. "In complete answer to your question, no, the Society did not buy the tickets. My family owns significant stock in the Baltimore Steam Packet Company. I requested use of the ship for a couple days, in place of dividends for this year. They were most happy to oblige."

Anthony leaned next to Ben. "We also own stock in the Columbia Coal Company, so the cost of the operation was not as dear as you might imagine."

At the end of dinner, cigars were presented around

142

the table by the servers who also lit them for the guests. Cephus grinned broadly and took additional time having his cigar lit, to the knowing smiles of the others at the table. Ben waved away the cigar offered to him and withdrew his pipe and tobacco pouch from his pocket.

The blue smoke collecting above the table slipped away as a gentle Bay breeze swept in, ruffling the edges of the tablecloth and fluttering the candle flames. The few remaining clouds crawled north, opening the sky filled with bright stars and a faint crescent moon. Seagulls argued with each other overhead.

"I think you should stay a while in Maryland, Ben," Anthony said, studying his cigar. "Rumors are flying around Charleston about a British anti-slave brig raiding South Carolina shores. Governor Hammond has formally complained to the British Embassy."

Ben smiled. "I don't think I would mind staying home, Anthony. Our Alisha is back..."

"What??" Anthony stared at him in disbelief.

18

After the funeral for Matthew Booker in Darlington, Ben and Simon visited with Matthew's father and his older brother David. The sky was clear with a brightness that no one in the Booker family felt that day. The Quaker meeting house had been quiet as was usual for their periods of meditation, but the oppressive air of summer was even heavier with their grief. Ben sat with Simon on the porch of their farmhouse, sipping fresh spring water, listening to Mr. Booker recount memories of Matthew.

The father pulled himself away from his recollections, and locked eyes with Ben. "Please tell me that he did not participate in the fighting."

"No sir," Ben answered. "He rowed from the ship into the surf, trying to rescue as many escaping slaves as he could."

"He climbed down into our rowboat with an eager smile on his face," Simon added.

The man said nothing else, nodding his head slightly, facing the trees, tears filling his eyes. "He was a good boy," he said in a hoarse whisper.

"He was a good man," Ben said.

"Yes. He was a good man, Mr. Pulaski. He fell doing God's work."

Simon and Ben walked together in silence back to lock number 5 on the canal. They stopped and shook hands near the holding pond on the upper side.

"Give my regards to Lettie," Ben said, "Do you have any idea where you will go from Wrightsville?"

"We have been talking about Canada, Ben. The way slave chasers go into the north, I don't think we'll feel safe in the United States."

"They are too bold, by far, and it saddens me."

Simon glanced up the canal. "A man can connect barges all the way to Lake Erie in New York from here."

Ben nodded his head in silence.

"You and Sonja – and Alisha..." He shook his head, "What an amazing gift for you and Sonja to experience. I am so glad to have met her..." He sighed. "So, the three of you can come visit us on the other side of that lake."

"Maybe. Maybe someday we will. And maybe someday Congress will pass a law making the free states safer..."

"Maybe," Simon muttered.

"Goodbye. Until we meet again, my friend."

They embraced and patted each other on the back, then went in different directions.

———

Ben and Edward were all that remained of the crew from the last voyage to South Carolina. Rodney left the day they returned to Havre de Grace, and Howard signed on to another ship soon after. Cephus had given his house near Spesutie to a young family and settled into Adam Tuttle's old Boatwright Shop on Concord Cove. He named it Doughty's Fixit Shop, but most of the town still called it Tuttle's. Hattie was there most days, and most nights according to local gossip.

Ben and Edward hired a fresh crew and spent the rest of the summer bringing store goods up from Norfolk, Hampton Roads and Richmond. They transferred the cargo among the little fleet of barges Aaron had gathered, and sent them north, selling all they could. Isaac joined the *Raven* in July for his summer furlough from West Point. Aaron had managed to find crews for three tandem barge pairs and doubled the mules pulling them. With the barges tied together stern-to-bow in pairs, only two men were needed to work each pair. The 'Pulaski Shipping Company' had grown to six barges, a seagoing schooner, and a steam tug. The *Ugly Boat* had transformed from a pitiful flat-nosed frumpy scow, occasionally pretending to be an even uglier sailboat, into an outright nautical nightmare.

The *Ugly Boat* resembled nothing else on the

surface of the Chesapeake Bay. No fish, fowl, wild animal, vessel or structure this side of destruction, resembled it. It was squat, fat and downright un-nautical. The side wheels in their housings resembled a gargantuan black woman with hip bustles, who had risen from the dead of the colonial past. Space previously occupied by the cabin had been wrenched out to make room for the steam engine, with large iron rocking arms on its bizarre top, driving the paddles. The stern cargo hold and half of the forward cargo hold now carried coal for its furnace, with the remaining space toward the bow now filled by the pilot house.

Edward had described it as, "A grasshopper on fire, kicking the hell out of a turtle."

Coal and coal dust constantly showered her decks and sides. Aaron surrendered from trying to keep the steamboat clean. He painted the whole thing black, except for large white letters on the pilot house, unnecessarily proclaiming it the "*Ugly Boat.*" With no mule to tend, David had inherited the job of fireman, to feed coal into the flaming mouth of the beast. On windless days, the coal smudge billowing up into the sky from the *Ugly Boat*'s smokestack could be seen five miles away. Aaron was as proud of that boat as Ben and Sonja were proud of their three children.

It had only been a few days since Alisha had begun to call Sonja 'Ma,' and Sonja still felt as if her feet drifted off the ground in her happiness. She had received a letter from her father in North Carolina, who was enjoying his time among his brothers and cousins in Burke County. He had been spending most of his nights with his brother Jim, but he rarely went a day or more without visiting or being visited by family or friends. He wrote her that the years since he left there were melting away, and he was becoming much closer to the people around him. He told her that the day he got her letter with the wonderful news about Alisha, the entire congregation came together in a service of thankfulness and praise. Afterward, he had placed flowers on the grave of his first

146

wife, Sonja's mother.

When Ben walked up to their porch in Lapidum, Sonja still had a smile on her face from reading the letter.

"Good day?" he asked.

"I have many of those, now." She reached out to hold his hand a moment, then he sat in the chair beside her, taking in the view down the slope between the great oaks. Out on the river, seagulls were squawking at each other in the sunshine as they dived for young shad, but then they dashed out of the way when a Bald Eagle swooped in to take a fat rockfish.

"Aaron says we need a bigger barn for more mules," Ben said. "He has the barn in York Furnace full of them, but says it will help the company to keep more down at this end of the canal."

Sonja nodded as she pulled fresh green beans from the basket next to her, snapping them into the bowl in her lap and pulling strings off. Ben slipped one away and began to chew on it, savoring the crisp snap when he bit it.

"Catherine Price says her mother is seeing signs of a cold winter coming," Sonja said.

"Who?"

"The lockkeeper's wife, Ben."

"Thought he was a widower."

Sonja turned in her seat and eyed him with a frown. "Benjamin Pulaski, I've told you plenty of times about her!"

He grinned. "I know who she is." Then he stood up and stepped next to her, bending over and kissing her on the lips.

"Rascal," she said, slapping at his leg as he walked into the house.

Ben's voice echoed from inside the house. "No way in hell can someone predict the winter before summer is even over. Where's Alisha?"

"She's playing with some of the Price girls," she yelled back. "Aaron came by on his way up."

Ben stepped back to the front doorway. "Any news

147

about Maggie?"

"Getting bigger every day. Mrs. Freidman said it's going to be a girl."

He struck a match to light his pipe.

"Benjamin! Please. Not in the house."

Ben frowned and stepped back onto the porch to blow the smoke from his mouth.

Isaac returned to West Point near the end of August, tanned from his summer on the *Raven*. Autumn came early with a heavy frost in mid-September. By the first of October, thin ice sheets were forming on the upper Bay. In November the canal was drained for the winter. Ben sailed the *Raven* through thickening ice to St. Michaels and arranged for it to be pulled out of the water there for a hull scraping. Aaron had followed in the *Ugly Boat*, then took Ben and the *Raven*'s crew to Annapolis, where Ben paid them off for the winter. Edward decided to stay in Annapolis as well.

"Think I'll look for a ship heading to the Caribbean this winter, Ben," he said.

Ice formed thick on the upper bay, and by the latter part of November, even the new steamboat traffic to Havre de Grace and Lapidum was halted. Aaron ran *Ugly Boat* onto the mud banks in Concord Cove to protect the hull from a winter freeze. There was talk in Havre de Grace of boats and ships being crushed by the ice in a deep freeze. In December, the train company began ferrying passengers in sleighs over the ice between Havre de Grace and Perryville.

On December 19th, Alisha Moses Tatum Pulaski, as her parents had unofficially renamed her, experienced her first birthday celebration. She was only six years old. Aaron and Maggie had invited both families to visit them in Burl's farmhouse in York Furnace and stay through Christmas. The house had been built for a large family. Burl had bought it for himself and his second wife, thinking his daughter's family would join them, so there was room for all the guests.

Sonja and Mary Freidman took over all the women chores in the house, urging Maggie to stay off her feet and enjoy a rest. The women worked together baking the birthday cake and trimming candles for it. Several presents, wrapped in linen cloth or butcher's paper, and tied with colorful ribbons, sat neatly on the dining room table.

"I never had a birthday before," Alisha told them. Throughout the morning, she repeatedly wandered around the table examining the presents. Next, she would check the hall clock, her eyes sparkling, waiting for the hands to point at two o'clock. Sonja peeked at her every chance she had, just to see her little girl do typical little girl things, after years of grieving over her.

Aaron came by and snatched the little girl up into his arms teasing with her, tussling her gold curls and tweaking her nose.

"And there will be more presents on Christmas, little Moses Alisha," he said.

She giggled and pretended a frown, "Alisha Moses, not Moses Alisha."

"Well, Alisha Moses, your Uncle Isaac should be here in a few days, and he will cut all your hair off," Aaron said with a grin.

"He will not," she told him.

"Aaron, don't tell her that," his mother said.

Aaron pretended to toss Alisha to her mother, then set her down gently as both of them squealed in unison. Outside, someone knocked hard on the door. Aaron went to open it.

"Isaac!" he yelled and stepped onto the front porch to hug his brother and pull him into the house.

"Isaac," Sonja yelled as she led the charge of people to greet him, barely ahead of Ben.

There was a four-way hug in the front room, then Ben yanked Alisha into the middle, and Aaron drew Maggie into the crowd. Delbert and Mary stood near beaming at the sight.

When they separated, Aaron turned to Mary saying, "We hug," then he drew them into a three-person hug, joined by Maggie.

Ben messed Isaac's hair. "See what you started." Then Ben patted his sleeve. "You have two stripes now."

"I am a cadet corporal, now, Pa," he said.

Aaron gave Isaac a sloppy salute. "Aye. Aye, Corporal."

Isaac gave him a mock frown. "That is not how you say it." Then he turned to Sonja, handing her an envelope. "Mrs. Calvert asked me to bring this up. It came just an hour ago."

Sonja slipped the envelope into her pocket and placed her arm around Isaac. "You are just skin and bones, Isaac. We need to feed you."

Isaac pushed out his chest and deepened his voice. "I am a healthy man of Iron, Madam, ready to lead my men into fierce battle."

Ben gave a smile that did not reach his eyes. *May God never let you have such a requirement, son*, he thought.

Sonja led Isaac into the kitchen where she picked up a plate and began piling it with biscuits and ham from breakfast. She placed him in a chair at the kitchen table and poured him a glass of milk, then sat there watching him eat. She pulled the envelope from her pocket and found a penciled telegraph paper, and sighed as she began to read it.

"I haven't had one of these since..."

Aaron turned, waiting for her to finish her comment. Sonja's face was deathly white

"What is it Ma? Ma?"

She bowed her head and sobbed her body jerking. Ben heard her and ran into the kitchen.

"What is it? What is it?" Ben waited for her to speak, then turned to Isaac.

Isaac's eyes were wide open, and he held his hands open in shock, as Sonja continued to cry. Sonja released the yellow penciled note to slip onto the floor as she covered her face with her hands, sobbing into them.

Ben picked up the note and read it.

'Dearest Niece, I have the terrible duty to inform you that your father, my cherished brother, has been taken unto the lord. His train wrecked two days ago, as it returned from Lenoir City in Caldwell County. – Yours in Jesus, Uncle Jim.'

19

Sonja struggled through Christmas, forcing herself to smile for Alisha, but relieved to return to Lapidum. Expecting to slip once again into the dark tunnel where her heart lingered during the terrible days after the ice flow tore infant Alisha from her arms, having Alisha with her kept Sonja in the light. Alisha brought her daily joy and excitement that an exuberant six year-old girl can find in the world. She ached daily over the loss of her father, but Alisha shared the wonderment of life through her little blue eyes and gave Sonja reasons to smile in spite of her loss.

New Year's Day brought 1845 and Ben's 45th birthday.

"Everyone celebrates your birthday, Pa," Alisha said.

Forrest McMallery, the blacksmith, fitted his mules with spiked horseshoes and used them to pull his work sled up and down the frozen Susquehanna, selling coal. It was a small shared business he had with Ben when the river froze. The coal locked in the Pulaski barges when the canal was drained, provided a continuing source of income as well as extra heat for those running low on split wood. Most customers would sign for the coal and promise to pay in the spring fishing season. Still, it provided Mac a productive activity when his forge was unused.

The winter coal business also provided Alisha an opportunity to ride along with "Uncle Mac" and her friend, Patty Price. Indeed, all the other men outside Alisha's family in Lapidum became her uncles and the women her aunts. Patty was Alisha's age, and they became almost inseparable. The Locktender's house in Lapidum was cramped for the little tribe of seven children. Catherine Price was happy to let Patty sleepover with the Pulaski's whenever she was invited, which was often.

Delbert Freidman had a small extension added to the side of his hardware store and opened Lapidum's first tavern. With the river frozen and no barge traffic, the hardened towpath became a highway for saddle and buggy traffic to and from Havre de Grace. Many stopped at the Lapidum Tavern. The little town of Stafford that had sprouted along the nearby banks of Deer Creek regularly sent its foundry workers to the tavern. From as far away as Darlington, halfway to the Mason and Dixon line, men would make the trek through the cold for some corn whiskey and a chance to get out of the house. Even the occasional Quaker man would glance around to see who was watching when they slipped off their wide-brimmed hats and stepped into the tavern 'for a little sip.' Most evenings, the popular new song 'Old Dan Tucker' would spring into the smoke-filled air of the alehouse, from voices that should not have been allowed to sing.

The temperature continued to plunge throughout January, reaching zero that year. Some industrious men from Lapidum had attempted to chop a hole in the river ice so they could do a little winter fishing, but the thickness of the ice outlasted their determination. Many people thought the ice was three to four feet thick. In Havre de Grace, the Baltimore and Philadelphia Railroad put tracks down the slope on each side of the river and connected them to tracks laid over the ice. Not wanting to risk an expensive locomotive, they used a mule team with Mac's special horseshoes to pull the train cars across the river to Perryville. After the first successful passage of empty cars, the railroad began allowing the passengers to stay in the cars all the way across. A waiting engine on the Cecil County side would pull the cars up and then on to Philadelphia.

Ben and Sonja wrapped Alisha in a buffalo fur and headed to York Furnace on February 1st, in a two-sleigh caravan, with the Freidmans following close behind.

Maggie was due in mid-February, and the two mothers insisted they be in the big farmhouse well before that. The family matriarchs and patriarchs, and one little golden-haired girl descended upon the Aaron and Maggie Pulaski household, prepared to hold the vigil until the grandchild was born.

When the Pulaski-Freidman caravan arrived in York Furnace, Emma Calvert, wife of the local locktender, was serving Maggie a steaming cup of beef broth. Emma and Sonja hugged each other in a long embrace, while Alisha gripped Sonja's skirt in a rare moment of shyness.

"So sorry to hear about Burl, Sonja," Emma said. "John told me just the other day."

Sonja only nodded and gave a weak smile.

"So glad you had the time with him last year. He just bubbled when he talked about that visit after you left. Hadn't seen him so happy in years." Emma said.

Sonja introduced Mary then Delbert. Emma wagged her finger at Delbert with a sparkle in her eyes.

"Heard about that Tavern of yours, Mr. Freidman," she said, chuckling.

"From twenty-four miles away? Surely its reputation is not sordid?"

"Not at all, Sir. Aaron told us about it. Good for Lapidum. I don't think the ironworkers hereabouts could get by without our local one."

John Calvert came out from the kitchen, wiping his hands. His sleeves were rolled up showing thick muscular arms, and an anchor tattoo on his right forearm.

"What's all the commotion," he said with a smile.

Sonja made introductions and hands were shaken again. John told Emma the wood box was refilled. Sonja leaned toward Mary.

"Emma has helped deliver almost every child born in York Furnace since they moved here."

Emma stood up from hugging Alisha. "Twenty-six here in York Furnace..." She gently tweaked Alisha's nose, "and one in Havre de Grace – one we thought lost, yet here she is." She tussled Alisha's hair.

Aaron came downstairs to meet everyone, then kissed the top of his wife's head.

"All the rooms are ready upstairs," Aaron said, "one each for the Freidmans, the Pulaskis-the 'other' Pulaskis" he emphasized with a grin, and then kneeling down to Alisha, "and one for Princess Peanut."

He snatched the little girl up and tossed her over his shoulder, careful to fold her skirt properly, then lead the fathers upstairs with the luggage, Alisha giggling away and messing Aaron's hair.

The ladies sat together in the large front room, taking places on the long sofa facing Maggie's settee. Her face was slightly pale with dark circles under her eyes. She drew the wool shawl tighter around her shoulders as the wind outside moaned to get in. Sonja rose and peeked into the new iron stove sitting in front of the enclosed fireplace. She grabbed a poker and jostled the burning wood and coal, making the flames burn brighter. The cast iron teapot on the stove top hissed slightly, giving up the last of its water vapor.

"Here," Emma said, "I'll get that." She took it into the kitchen and pumped fresh water into it, then returned the pot to the stove.

"I just can't seem to get warm this winter," Maggie said.

"Coldest on record, sweetie," Mary said to her daughter, reaching out to pat her hand. "We'll get you good and warm."

Ben and Sonja were given the room Burl had slept in, and to her surprise, each night she slept soundly, wrapped in childhood dreams of her father. Each morning she awoke feeling him near her, and with each passing day, her lingering grief began to fade.

The 15th of February arrived at last, but Maggie was no closer to labor than when the parents had come. The four men had gone hunting together and were outside preparing to butcher the large buck Aaron had shot. Emma was near them with a pan to catch the blood as soon as they cut its throat. When the pan was full, she took it in the back door to the kitchen to make broth. The mothers agreed that all the signs predicted the child would be a girl and were engaged with Maggie in a long conversation over names for the baby. After each mother explained her preference, Maggie announced that she would name the baby Sarah. It was a name she had decided upon years before when she first understood that someday she would have a child. Mary and Sonja both hugged her and agreed that would be a perfect name.

That night Sonja dreamed she was lying in a huge feather bed in the center of a spacious stone-walled room. There was a warm fireplace in the farthest wall, filled with golden flames. Near the fireplace, sat a woman in a rocking chair. Her face was turned to the fire and Sonja could not see it. Then a door opened, and Sonja's father walked into the room. He smiled at her as he walked by the bed, but did not stop. He walked to the woman in the rocker and helped her stand. The woman was Sonja's mother, holding an infant that did not cry. Burl put his arm around his wife and escorted her to the door. As they closed the door, Sonja's mother turned back to her and said: "We are well."

In the earliest dawn when the light was timid and gray, unsure that it was welcome in the house, intense voices drifted up the stairwell, and bare feet thumped on the wooden floors. Sonja rushed from her bed in her nightgown and flew down the stairs. She flew past Aaron and Delbert standing in the hallway downstairs. In the bedroom that Aaron and Maggie had converted from Burl's old den, a child's voice whimpered in pain. Mary was sitting on the edge of the bed, holding Maggie's hand while placing a wet rag on her forehead. Emma was on her knees at the foot of the bed examining Maggie.

"It's breach," Emma said.

Sonja held her hand out, hoping for something to do. She reached for Maggie's other hand, but she was gripping the bedclothes and could not let go.

"Roll her on her side," Emma ordered.

Maggie released a long low cry when they pulled her onto her side. Her face was twisted, and tears flowed from her pinched eyes. She gripped her lower lip between her teeth. Mary massaged her back and spoke soothing words to ears that could not hear them. Emma pushed hard against her womb from the sides and front. Sonja took her free hand and held it, kissing it, adding her words to Mary's.

Outside the closed door, Ben joined the men. Delbert and Ben traded worried frowns as Aaron paced up and down the short hallway before the bedroom. He would stop at each loop and listen at the door. John brought coffee from the kitchen, but no one else wanted to drink it. Maggie's scream pierced the air. Aaron rushed the door and opened it.

"No!" yelled Emma, "Stay out of the way. Boil water!"

Emma had Maggie rolled onto the other side, and forcefully pushed her hands onto Maggie's expanded belly, pressing one side toward Maggie's head, and pulling the other toward her feet. Trying to rotate the little form trapped inside the abdomen. Maggie screamed again. Long agonizing minutes crawled by. Maggie was turned again, and pushed on again, and turned again, and pushed on again. Her screams were less powerful. The rasp in her voice growing. The breath of exhaustion falling from her mouth. Her eyelids were half closed, the energy to keep them open sapped away.

The minutes turned into an hour. The first hour became two, then three. The sun outside rose above a household that paid it no attention. John tapped on the door, saying the single word, "Coffee."

Emma opened the door. Her hair had fallen in twisted stands down the side of her face. She wiped the sweat away and reached out for the three coffee cups, curling a strong finger through the loops, pulling them inside and closing the door. Emma placed the cups on a nightstand, and dropped onto a chair, resting her elbows on her knees, breathing deeply over the floor. Maggie

157

moaned again but managed to lie on her back for a brief moment. Sonja passed a cup to Mary, who blew out a breath then slowly lifted the cup to her lips. As Sonja sipped some of the coffee, Emma stood back up and twisted her shoulders and neck, and stepped wearily to the bed.

"Roll her on to her side," Emma whispered and crawled back up on the bed. She leaned forward and kissed Maggie on her hip. "We're not giving up on you young'un, and we're not giving up on Sarah."

Maggie opened her eyes halfway, turning her face to Emma and blew out her breath. Her words were slurred. "Push me again," she said.

The moans soon turned to screams, and the screams went on two more hours.

"She turned!" Emma said. She examined Maggie. "I can see her head. Thank you, God."

"Alright, Maggie," Emma said, "You've lollygagged enough..."

Maggie and her two mothers released ragged chuckles.

"Roll her on her back, and bring her knees up," she ordered. "Time to push, girl."

When the next contraction came, Maggie strained down with it, groaning with the pain, her face turning crimson. "Again," Emma ordered. After each push, Emma would examine the baby's progress. "It's crowning," she announced. "Again!" she ordered.

"Her head is out..." then Emma stopped herself. " Cord's wrapped around her," she muttered. "Push, Maggie Push! Push with all your strength! Push now, girl! Push!!"

With an agonizing wail, Maggie lifted her head, almost sitting upright on the bed. Her scarlet face contorted and tilted down, dedicating all of her being into pushing out her daughter.

"She's out!" Emma screamed.

Maggie collapsed back onto her pillow, falling unconscious. Mary and Sonja tended her, wiping the sweat away, stroking her face and arms, patting her hands, their eyes intensely focused on Emma's face.

Emma shook her head no. After cutting and tying off the cord, she wrapped the blue baby girl in a cloth and laid her on Maggie's chest.

"Rub her and pat her back," Emma told them. "I saw one come back after it got on its momma's belly."

Emma blew out her breath and examined Maggie.

"She's still bleeding," she said grabbing a nearby cloth and wedging it under Maggie. Emma's eyes filled with tears as the fresh cloth turn crimson. She locked eyes with Mary.

"She still breathing?" Emma asked.

"Sleeping like a baby," Mary said.

Sonja's eyes met Emma's.

"I need a blanket, Sonja," Emma said.

When Sonja handed her the blanket, Emma pulled the towel from under Maggie and let it fall to the floor with a wet slap. Sonja leaned over and noticed the blood-soaked cloth, and the pool of blood seeping onto the floor around it. Her lip quivered.

Maggie opened her eyes. The words were slow, dreamlike. "Is it a girl?"

Mary glanced at the cloth on the floor and patted her daughter's shoulder affectionately.

"Yes, sweetie. You have delivered a girl."

Maggie smiled and patted the tiny form laid on her chest. "Hello Sarah," she whispered but did not have the strength to lift her head to look at her.

Emma whispered to Sonja. "Go get Aaron. Tell him all he needs to know, but get him in here now."

20

May 1845, York Furnace, Pennsylvania

At the far end of an apple orchard on the Jundt farm, a neat little clearing bathed in sunshine overlooked the Susquehanna River. Two graves were nestled inside a low rock wall there. One had been there over a decade, but the other one was fresh with a new granite headstone. Above the dates, the new stone read:

MARGARET FREIDMAN PULASKI
JOINED FOR ETERNITY
WITH HER PRECIOUS DAUGHTER
SARAH

Aaron laid fresh flowers on the grave and rose off his knees. Back at the farmhouse, three nervous escaping slaves sat in the kitchen, their coffee and breakfast long finished. They had spent the time waiting for Aaron to return by cleaning the kitchen and washing the dishes. Helen Booker had told them repeatedly that it wasn't necessary because they were her guests. Aaron met David on the front porch.

"Are they ready to go on?" Aaron asked.

"Yes. They are anxious to...Aaron?"

"What is it, Dave?"

"I want to thank you again for letting us move in here. It is so big and has so many rooms! You could stay..."

"No, Dave. I can't ever sleep in that house again. It is perfect for you and Helen, and your children. And don't forget, you are earning it." Aaron lowered his voice. "It is the largest station on the underground railroad for this part of Pennsylvania."

"Oh, we would do this anyway."

"Yes, but don't be sorry you have a grand house to share with your passengers." Aaron smiled and slapped him on his arm.

They led the three passengers down to the holding pond above the canal lock. The *Turtle* and the *Wilhelmina* waited in tandem, tied nose to stern with the *Turtle* in front. The passengers were loaded onto the *Turtle*, where they had free run of the decks and cabin, at least until they passed another barge. They were happy to be out of the claustrophobic hiding space between the cabin and the hold in the *Wilhelmina*.

Aaron had the false cabinet propped open to air out the space. Dozens of terrified people had ridden in the space over the past three years, and it was rarely open to fresh air. David tapped the backside of the lead mule, harnessed in single file with its partner, letting them know it was time to walk north on the towpath again. The long tow rope unwound to the bow of the *Turtle*. David dodged mule scat dropping onto the towpath, satisfied not to be shoveling coal all day on the *Ugly Boat*, at least until they made it back to Havre de Grace in four days.

Aaron made his way to the stern of the *Wilhelmina* and pushed the tiller over just enough to guide the two barges into the center of the canal. The canal was at its highest. Spring rains had flushed it out and filled it to its overflow weirs. Holding the tiller with one hand, Aaron flipped open the storage locker where the conch shell was kept. The shell provided a horn to canallers, allowing them to let the next locktender know they were coming. In the bottom, next to the Conch shell and a pistol, were several empty whiskey bottles.

Aaron glanced around before tossing four of the empty bottles into the canal, watching them fill with water and sink. He reached in to pick up one of the full bottles and pulled out the cork with his teeth, spitting it into the canal. He would not need the cork anymore. The bottle would be empty before he reached the next lock. He tilted the bottle up to his lips and swallowed a few ounces. The slight dizziness from the whiskey he sought soon returned for the day. It was what he searched for each morning, and what put him to sleep in the barge cabin each night. Under his breath, he sang 'Old Dan Tucker,' missing the tune, and forgetting some of the words.

Ben sat on the front porch of the Pulaski house in Lapidum, sipping his third cup of coffee. He held a tattered copy of the Cecil Whig, left behind at the lockhouse by a wandering steamer passenger. Earlier, Ben had noticed Dan Bartlett on barge number 26, waiting for his turn into the lock, and had meandered down to chat with him. Jesse Price, the locktender, had shared the newspaper with Dan, who had passed it along to Ben. Ben turned his head toward the open doorway.

"Spanish Florida has become a state, Sonja," he yelled into the house.

"How many does that make now?"

"Twenty-seven. And they say in the paper that The Texas Republic might join us too."

She came to the doorway, wiping her hands. "Guess they'll be making a new flag for Florida's star. Wonder what kind of shape Congress will come up with for twenty-seven?"

Ben frowned. "They might as well wait until Texas comes in. It'll be an even twenty-eight then. Four rows of seven."

"Well, we probably won't see it for years."

Ben leaned his head back toward her, "I might see it flying at the new Naval Academy in Annapolis. The school is right near the harbor."

Sonja crossed her arms and sighed. "I wish Aaron had been accepted there. It was the first thing he acted like mattered, since..."

"He has his work," Ben said.

Sonja shrugged her shoulders and went back into the house.

The steam whistle screamed into the morning air

162

and echoed over the river. Ben jumped from his chair.

"Damn it to Hell," he yelled. "I hate that thing going off here in Lapidum!"

Sonja laughed from inside. "Twice a week now, Ben, and it still startles you."

Ben stood at the edge of the porch, taking in the view of the river from between his front oak trees. The spring fattened river had ripped bushes from the far shore and flung them into the current charging southward.

"Used to be quiet here. Now that... and...what's that damned hammering?"

Sonja returned to the doorway. "Delbert is adding rooms above his tavern for steamer passengers. You told me that, yourself. What is wrong with you today, Ben?"

He folded his arms and sighed. "Aaron. He won't go into his house or ours. Only sleeps on the *Wilhelmina*, if you can call it that. And he drinks far too much."

Sonja stood next to him and placed her hand on his arm. "An aching heart takes a long time to heal. Some never do." Then she forced herself back inside to her morning chores.

Down on the river, the steamboat blew its whistle again, and its stern wheel began to turn. It added its own power to the angry push of the Susquehanna, slapping past him. Running along the towpath between the river and the canal, Alisha dashed along waving at the steamboat and yelling.

"Alisha!" Ben yelled.

She slipped to a stop and turned toward Ben, a toothy grin emblazoned on her face, her hair jutting out in disarray at all directions. Her canvas britches spotted with mud, she gripped a fat frog in one hand, holding it up proudly for Ben to see.

"You get back here this minute!" Ben yelled, instantly regretting his command.

She flung herself gleefully into the canal and swam across to their property, then charged up the slope still holding the frog. Her hair was pasted to the sides of her head and her drenched clothes melded to her slender body as she mounted the steps in a spray of muddy droplets. She presented Ben the frog.

"Here Pa! You can have this one, and I'll catch me another."

Sonja appeared in the doorway, with her hand over her mouth, unable to contain her laughter. Ben's frown evaporated, and he scooped her up into a hug, holding her close as they squished into the house together.

Two days later, the steamer from Norfolk unloaded its passenger in Havre de Grace. Passengers filed along the wooden pier, extending out beyond the shallows near the Concord Point Lighthouse. Two stevedores struggled along the narrow walkway with a handcart precariously overloaded with luggage, followed behind by the complaining luggage owner.

"Don't you dare let that hat box fall," Lydia Binterfield warned them.

Near the edge of the main channel, not far from the passenger steamer, the *Raven* sat at anchor as the last of the supplies were stored below under the watchful eye of First Mate Edward Leonard. Ben was satisfied with the crew. All of them had previous experience on ships, some ships much larger than the *Raven*. He had recruited them carefully, adding telling questions about their character among the others exploring each man's expertise. The simple questions sounded unimportant but told him much about their values.

Good men with backbone, he thought. *Men who value what a man does more than his color.*

Late in the afternoon, Ben arrived on deck and reviewed the ship and the log book with Edward. They joined the rest of the crew for the evening meal. The new cook, Warren, prepared an excellent dinner, showing off his talents for the captain. One by one, Edward directed the conversation at the table to each man, in turn, allowing Ben the opportunity to exchange a few words. Alistair and Daniel had sailed together in large ships crossing the Atlantic, ships where a skilled black man like Daniel, was accepted. Wyatt had spent his youth and early manhood sailing the Chesapeake in sloops and schooners, mostly out of Annapolis, but had never cruised deep blue water.

"No, sir," Wyatt answered with a boyish smile, "but you know the Bay. It can get terribly angry, especially down at Hampton Roads."

"So you've sailed to Hampton?" Ben asked.

"Newport News, generally, on our way up the James to Hopewell. 'Least until the steamers took the work."

"Well," Ben said, "Steamer shipping is expensive. The wind is free, and it can take you anywhere."

"As long as it's there, Cap'n," Alistair said.

"Aye, as long as it's there, but it ain't always," Daniel added.

All the faces turned to Daniel when he spoke. A black man with a thick Massachusetts' accent with an Irish twang was a new experience for them.

"So, you're from Boston," Ben said.

"'Til I was thirteen. Me father had a store and expected me to work in it, but it choked me to be inside so much."

"Ya don't look Irish, Daniel," Warren said, compressing a smile.

Daniel glanced at him without expression. "Really? Why, back in the old country, all the Irish look just like me."

Alistair spit out his drink laughing, glancing around the table. "I have been waiting for one of you to ask him that." He slapped Daniel on his back. "There's even a song about him, 'Oh Danny Boy'!"

Wyatt let his mouth hang open and squinted at Alistair, "Naaah..."

Daniel chuckled. "Might as well get the story out of the way, else you'll hound me forever to get bits and pieces. Me father is a Lily white Irishman from County Donegal. Me mother is the beautiful granddaughter of a Senegalese Princess, with skin like polished ebony. Mother was working in her dress shop there when me father met her. His store was next door to her's. Still is.

165

And, no, I don't look the slightest bit like me father. "

"But his sister does," said Alistair, to smiles sweeping along the table.

"And I'll strangle the man among ye who pursues her," he said with a smile, but the smile did not reach his eyes.

"So, do we call you Dan, Danny?" asked Wyatt.

"Ya call me the way I introduced myself," he said.

"Very well, Daniel," Ben said. Then he glanced around the table. "Get your rest tonight. I want to raise anchor at first light in the morning."

Moments later, in the Captain's cabin, Ben handed a new note to Edward.

May 28th, Charleston Harbor. Flag and patch. June 1ˢᵗ, Georgetown. Lumber, rice, and indigo.

"Doesn't waste words, does he?" Edward said, handing the note back to Ben.

"Well, we know what he means. We've done it before. We'll anchor and wait."

"As you told me, Ben, the crew doesn't know."

"They don't need to know, Eddie, and we don't need the risk."

The *Raven* encountered two days of rough seas passing Cape Hatteras and dropped anchor in Charleston Harbor on May 27th. Ben allowed the crew their evening in the city and let them sleep well past dawn the next morning. After sunrise Edward had the mainsail partially raised, to expose the triangular patch, and left it hanging loose as if it were being dried. The Maryland flag draped motionless from the top of the mizzenmast. After another pleasing breakfast from Warren, the crew lounged around the deck or fished for supper. By noon, Ben asked the crew to stop fishing, since they had already pulled in far more than they could eat. Late in the afternoon, several spaces had opened along the wharves where a ship could dock to load cargo.

Ben paced the deck, uncomfortable still sitting at anchor when spaces were available in a harbor notorious for ships competing to have them.

"Lower the flag. Tighten the mainsail," he ordered. "We need to dock."

As the men began to move, Edward noticed a solitary man standing on the pier waving his hand, and brought it to Ben's attention. Ben took up his telescope.

"Chambers," Ben said. "We need to dock near the fat man, Eddie."

21

As soon as crewmen slid out the gangplank, Chambers disappeared into a nearby warehouse. Seconds later, he emerged pushing a small black man in shackles. Chambers remained on the lip of the ramp as he pushed the slave onto his knees on *Raven's* deck. The slave's face showed fresh whelps that ran from forehead to chin. Bloody streaks seeped across the back of his dirty shirt. Chambers yanked out two papers from his coat and handed them to Ben, for his signature. Both were bills of sale, already signed by Chambers. Ben took the documents into his cabin and signed them and returned one to Chambers. Chambers said nothing when he snatched the paper from Ben's hand. He pointed at the warehouse as he walked away. The door opened and four barrels marked "rice" were wheeled quickly onto the ship by two other slaves, who returned to the warehouse without uttering a sound. Edward examined the barrels and directed the crew to hand-carry them below and keep them upright.

"Air holes," he whispered to Ben.

Edward began to lift the passenger to his feet, but the man screamed "No!" and dashed to the far railing, grabbing belaying pins in his fists and falling back to his knees.

"Leave him there for now," Ben said. "Let's weigh anchor and set sails."

The crew eyed the passenger closely as they performed their tasks, glancing at Ben and Edward several times. As the ship made its way out of the harbor, passing Fort Sumter, Daniel approached Ben.

"What is this, Captain?" Daniel asked.

Ben faced him fully. "We just picked up a slave, from a broker," Ben said.

Daniel stood still, his eyes locked on Ben's.

"I hold a slave trading license," Ben said.

"Set me off this God damned ship," Daniel said.

Alistair and Wyatt stepped behind Daniel.

"Edward said nothing about carrying slaves," Alistair said.

Warren stepped next to Wyatt, frowning and folding his arms.

Edward stood beside Ben, with his hands on his hips. "What is the trouble, gentlemen?"

Daniel glanced at the men standing with him. Their faces showed agreement with him. "We can't crew on a ship carrying slaves."

Ben turned and walked away, pulling a small key from his pocket and unlocking the shackles of the man at the railing. The man's eyes were locked on Ben while he rubbed his wrists. Ben handed the handcuffs to the man and stood back as he threw the shackles overboard. Ben returned to the crew.

"If you don't sail this ship, how are we going to get him north?"

Daniel chuckled. "You're taking him north?"

"No." Ben said, "We are...If you can work this ship knowing that."

At the railing, the passenger removed his clothes and threw them overboard. Ben pointed at him.

"Edward, please take our passenger below and find him some clean clothes."

The passenger walked to the closest hatch cover where one of the ship's buckets sat holding fresh water and a ladle. He set the ladle aside and poured the water over himself. He held the bucket out toward the crew.

"More."

Daniel stepped over to take the bucket and dipped it into the fresh water barrel tied to the mainmast. The man drank deeply from the bucket before pouring it over himself, and then plunged it back into the barrel to refill it. "People in the barrels," he said over his shoulder.

"Thought so," Edward said as he headed for the forward ladderway. "I'll open them while one of you get a drying cloth and some clothes for..." He stopped and yelled at the passenger.

"What's your name?"

"William Stone."

"Welcome aboard, William Stone," Ben said. He turned to Warren. "He will need some salve for all those cuts on his back.

Inside the barrels below deck, Edward found three young boys and an elderly woman. The woman was unconscious, and at first, Edward thought she was dead. He called for Warren to help him pull her out of the barrel and lay her on the floor. While Edward had his head pressed to her chest listening for a heartbeat, she came to and slapped him. Warren grabbed the salve he came for and ran laughing up the ladderway. Edward sat back on his heels rubbing his cheek.

"Thought you were dead, old woman. I was just listening for a heartbeat."

"I'm so sorry, suh. I didn't know what I was doin'. I'm so..." She stared at her surroundings . "Where am I, suh?"

"You are on board the Schooner *Raven*."

She sat up, propping herself upright with her hands. "A ship? Oh...yes, Mr. Stone he was going to make it happen..." then she stared into Edwards' eyes. "You a abolitionist?"

He smiled, standing up and offering his hands to help her. "I've never been called that, and never called myself by that name, but...well...I guess I am."

She stood up slowly and brushed off her dress. "You do this befo?"

"Yes, ma'am."

"And you just now figgerin you a abolitionist?"

Edward laughed and offered her his arm. "Are you up to climbing some steps?"

"Young man, befo I passed out in that barrel I could have carried it. Reckon I can walk up some steps."

"By the way, ma'am, I am Edward Leonard."

"I'm Esther," she said.

On the other side of the ship, William Stone poured a last bucket full of water over himself.

"We all gotta get neked?" she asked.

"No ma'am" Edward chuckled. "Captain Benjamin Pulaski, it is my honor to present Miss Esther."

Ben stepped closer and extended his hand to her. "Welcome aboard Miss Esther. Our excited young guests have talked about you quite a bit."

They ran to her and surrounded her skirt with hugs.

"You boys been outta the barrels long?"

The boys chattered over each other, each telling her something different, but all of them telling her of amazing experiences.

"We's free," the tallest boy said. Ben estimated that he was seven or eight years old. The others were younger.

William was wrapped in a blanket as he walked by the group. "Happy that you made it," he said to them.

Esther reached out to place her hand on his shoulder. "Thank you fo what you did, Mr. Stone."

He turned away and walked to the forward ladderway. Warren followed him with the salve and his clothes.

Daniel stepped near Edward. "Those boys were destined for a debauchery house. I have heard of it. For men who like boys rather than girls."

Edward frowned and gritted his teeth, shaking his head. "That is so sick."

Daniel stuck his hands in his pockets. "If they didn't have slave boys, they'd probably take up with sheep. It's all bestial."

The smell of fried fish drifted across the deck, drawing the boys and Esther down into the galley. Ben called out to Edward from the wheel.

"Make sure Warren is careful with the frying pan. Remind him that we are at sea, and we -"

"don't fry food at sea," Edward finished the rule as he headed for the stern ladderway.

In the galley, Edward lifted a warning finger at Warren, but stopped in mid-motion, staring keenly at the stove.

"It's a great way to cook at sea," Warren said. "...without just boiling everything. Look here."

He pointed to the deep cast iron cooking pot.

"The lid is clamped in place from hooks on the bottom part. The bottom has handles that are hooked from the stove." He unclamped the lid with a potholder and pointed inside. "The pot has a rounded bottom that sits in the hole in the stove."

The aroma of fried fish filled the galley making Edward's stomach growl.

"Wait. Got to spoon the fish out. It's done. Oh...and look at the spoon." Warren held up the metal spoon in front of Edward. "It's got slots in it. Drains the grease back in the pot before you can dish it out! It's all pure genius!"

Edward tapped his fingertip on his lips and then scratched his chin. "Clamp it shut, Warren, don't put anything else in there. I think the captain has to decide if you can do that in calm seas, or maybe mild seas." He snatched a handful of the fish and popped it into his mouth, blowing heavily around the fish to cool it as he went back up on deck.

"I don't know anything about it," Ben admitted to Edward as he was relieved at the wheel. "Cephus always took care of the galley," he said over his shoulder going to the ladderway.

In the galley, Warren repeated his display and demonstration of the unique cooking pan.

"All right, Warren. As long as seas are mild. It looks safe enough for me, but you keep the cooking grease to a minimum, or our next meal will be with Davy Jones. No meal is worth risking lives." The platter of fried fish filled the air with its aroma. "Has everyone else eaten?" Ben asked.

"Except you, Cap'n. And Edward only had a little nibble while we were talking. That Mr. Stone, he ate like he hadn't in days. Ate twice what I could hold and he's smaller than me."

"Did he say anything about his experiences?"
"Only thing he said was 'more'!"

Before entering Winyah Bay, Ben had the empty rice barrels tossed overboard to make room for fresh cargo. When they sailed near the North Island Lighthouse, the light keeper waved and used his flash mirror to signal the steam tug *Hannah* in the distance.

Edward smiled as sun flashes bounced between the lighthouse and the distant horizon.

"Semaphore," Ben said. "These are truly modern times, Eddie. Wouldn't surprise me to find telegraph wires out here someday."

"Dots and dashes," Edward mumbled. "How can people be so trusting of what a man tells you when all he heard were dots and dashes?"

"You say something to me?" Wyatt asked from the railing as he tidied the mainsail line.

Edward smiled and shook his head no. "Let's get the boys and Esther settled down below." He turned toward the windward railing. "You'll need to go below as well, Mr. Stone."

They exchanged glances as he went below. Stone had only spoken a few words since he came on board in Charleston, mostly one-word answers or prompts.

The nearby trees along the other side of the channel were full of Blue Jays yelling at each other as the *Raven* settled at her accustomed space on the Georgetown dock. The Harbor Master and a man in a business suit came up the gangplank as it was set down.

"Didn't think you would come back here," The Harbor Master said to Ben

"No. Not after the ...er...trouble here."

Edward stepped back toward the far railing, fingering a belaying pin.

Ben slipped his hands into his pockets. "Really?" he said.

"Well...yes...the way your ship left...and the shooting..." the other man said.

"Yes, the shooting..." echoed the Harbor Master.

Ben glanced around the docks for the Sheriff or armed men.

Maybe the damned fake mast never fooled them, he thought. *Damn!*

He gritted his teeth and pressed his lips together.

"We really must apologize," the other man said. "I can see you're not happy..."

Ben stood without speaking.

"Yes," the other man continued. "That terrible misunderstanding with the unpaid...I mean delayed payment by the company..."

"And the duel with that bully, Williamson," the Harbor Master added. "We thought we had lost your business forever."

"Forever," the other man said, and extended his hand. "Oh, sir we have not met. I only spoke with your attorney. I am Ralph Beasley, the business attorney for Mansfield Plantation."

Ben relaxed, accepting his hand and indicated Edward, who was walking toward them again. "This is my...my brother, Edward, who serves as first mate on the *Raven.*

They all shook hands.

"I hope you harbor no ill will toward Mansfield," Ralph said.

"Not at all," Ben said. "It was a small misunderstanding. Certainly not worth the concern you obviously hold. We cannot be your largest customer."

"No, of course not, I mean, the amount of business is irrelevant, not that it isn't appreciated. But, it was the point of honor, and we were concerned you might take offense."

The Harbor Master cleared his throat. "Yes, since you had accepted Mr. Williamson's challenge, we were...um..."

"Unsure, regarding your willingness to engage in a...similar response...if we had inadvertently..." Ralph hesitated.

"Insulted your honor," the Harbor Master finished.

174

"But...um... there is a small issue with your order from Argyle," Ralph said.

Ben smiled with his eyebrows arched, tilting his head slightly.

"Mansfield no longer produces Indigo, but Palmetto Haven still does, so we took the liberty of obtaining it for you...and with no added fee, of course."

"Very well," Ben said, "I will be happy to accept delivery and 'promptly' pay the invoice."

Ralph chuckled, and then both men shook hands and left the ship.

Ben and Edward exchanged glances and sighed, each smiling at the sky.

William Stone dashed by them and ran down the gangplank, chasing after the visitors, holding one of Ben's pistols in his hands. When he reached the two men, he shoved the Harbor Master aside and pointed the gun at Ralph's face, screaming at him. Ben could not hear what was said. Ralph shook his head slowly from side to side, holding the palms of his hands up to William. William leaned forward and placed the end of the barrel against Ralph's forehead. The hammer fell, and then Ralph crumpled on the sidewalk.

Ben dashed onto the dock, followed by Edward close behind. Ben snatched the unloaded pistol from William's hand, and Edward grabbed him around his arms as William screamed out a long line of obscenities at Ralph's unconscious form. Alistair joined them and helped Edward gain control of William. Wyatt came next and grabbed Ralph's ankles.

"Take him back to the ship," Ben ordered. The Harbor Master was on his knees patting Ralph's face, trying to revive him "Where the hell did that maniac come from" he asked

"Well...I was just in Charleston..."

"Did you just buy him, Captain?"

Ralph regained consciousness and sat up, "Am I shot?"

His hands rushed around his face and head, and then dashed along his body and legs like running crabs.

"The pistol was not loaded," Ben said.

The Harbor Master helped Ralph to stand, and both men began slapping dust from their clothes.

Ralph pointed to the men carrying William back to the ship, still kicking and screaming. "I remember him, now. I sold him at auction less than a month ago, at the market here in Georgetown."

"And he was just in Charleston when you bought him?" the Harbor Master asked Ben.

22

"Just three days ago," Ben said.

"Southfield got fed up with him awfully quick," Ralph said. "Since the British raid, there has been a shortage of field hands, and we're getting the rotten apples now. Ones that don't behave." Ralph frowned. "Why didn't you chain him up?"

"He was calm and quiet, in the hold with the other slaves," Ben said. "I suppose he managed to get loose. I need to deal with this quickly. Will you be all right, Ralph?"

Ralph waved them on. "I've had enough excitement today, John," Ralph said to the Harbor Master. "I'm going to get a strong drink, and then I'm going home."

"Don't you want to see him punished, Ralph?"

"I don't want to ever look at him again, or think about today."

In Havre de Grace, the bell over the door to the Tidewater Bank and Trust jingled as Lydia walked in. She wore a brilliant indigo damask dress and matching hat tilted low on her forehead. The overcast morning made the lantern light in the bank appear bright, illuminating the satin of her dress and the sheen of the obsidian curls framing her face. She ignored the approaching teller and walked back to James' desk, seating herself as her half-brother stared in surprise. She slapped a bundle of papers on his desk. She gave him a broad smile, then leaned forward and picked up the oak name plaque that read 'James Williamson, President' and dropped it into the trashcan next to his desk.

"I am suing you, James. Slander for spreading the rumor about my bloodline. Embezzlement for giving away bank assets without board approval. Coercion for forcing me out of my own house, when I was in mourning over the loss of my beloved husband. And forgery for presenting ownership papers on the bank stating you held majority control when you had only twenty-five percent."

She smiled sweetly and brought her gloved fingertip to her lips. "And the icing on my cake, sweet, sweet brother. You are fired." She stood and smoothed her dress. "My attorney will visit with you shortly. I suggest you toddle over to whichever rock yours stays under, and let him know the good news."

She hummed as she walked out, her fingertips gently stroking the cheek of the young clerk holding the door open for her.

James reached into the trashcan and retrieved his name plaque.

Before noon the *Turtle* and *Wilhelmina* passed through the last lock in Pennsylvania, only yards away from the line separating free state and slave state. Frequently, the slave chasers gathered around barges going north, searching for runaways, stopping them while they were still in Maryland. Only rarely did they poke an unwelcomed nose into barges going south. Aaron did not pay attention to them. The gray sky had held back much of the sunlight that morning. Aaron had lit a lantern in the cabin, which was still burning. After the barges entered the lock, while waiting for the water level to drop down to match the outgoing gates, Aaron remembered the oil lamp and went to turn it off. While he was down, he noticed the false wall still propped open and moved to close it. With no curtains in the barge windows, a slaver sitting near the lock whittling a piece of wood had a clear view of the Aaron in the cabin. Aaron had trouble closing it due to an empty whiskey bottle blocking the way. The slaver craned his neck to see more and smiled.

Once in the lower holding pond, David tapped the mule to begin its walk to the next lock, a few miles farther south. The slaver trotted along the towpath until the Pulaski barges crossed into Maryland, then he whistled for the men loitering around the mule barn. He whistled several times, excitedly pointing at the barges. One of the slavers stopped David on the towpath, and another grabbed a boat hook and pulled the barges to the bank. Aaron unhooked his barge and yanked the boat hook from the man throwing it into the canal.

"You are not coming on my boat, Damn you!"

By then the whittler caught up with the barge and pointed at the cabin, speaking to the man who lost his boat hook, "They got a hidie-hole in there. One of the walls folds up. Looked big enough to stash somebody, George."

George pulled out his pistol and stepped onto the deck of the *Wilhelmina*. Aaron spun around and dashed to the storage box, but fell on the deck before he could get to it. George walked down the steps into the cabin.

"Which wall, Sammy?"

Sammy trotted down into the cabin and stood in the center. "I was on the other side, but it looked like a front wall when I seen it in the lock. That one."

George began banging and pushing on the wall Sammy had pointed out, but nothing moved. Sammy examined the other wall and spotted the broken glass in the corner. I musta got turned around, George. I heard that bottle break."

George banged and pushed on the back wall, and it sprung loose from its housing. He wedged his fingers into the narrow space at the edge of the wall, then pulled. To his surprise, the entire section of the wall was hinged at the top and swung up to the ceiling. Behind it was enough space for three adults to stand. Inside he found that the area extended outward to both sides of the barge, creating a compartment big enough to hide a dozen adults. Aaron thumped down the stairs and pointed his pistol at George. Before Aaron could react, George snatched it from his hand.

"You're drunk, boy. And you're stupid. You ever go north with a nigger in here?"

179

Aaron reached for his pistol, but George kept it out of his reach. "What do you put in here, farmer? You hide slaves in here…"

"Whiskey," Aaron said.

"You need a drink, Farmer?"

Aaron sighed heavily. "I keep whiskey in there. That's why the bottle." Aaron leaned forward and slapped the doorway frame. "No taxes. No duties. I don't tell the guv'mint, and I don't tell the canal company."

George thought a moment, then shrugged his shoulders. "Well, I ain't the guv'mint, and I don't give a shit about hidin whiskey. There ain't anyone in here for me to grab, this time, so I'm gettin off this coffin."

George and Sammy jumped to the towpath. "*Wilhelmina*," George read aloud from the plaque on the bow. "From now on, *Wilhelmina*," he said pointing his finger at Aaron, "we're stopping this floating turd every time it goes into Pennsylvania. We're going to charge you a bottle of whiskey each trip up, and if we ever find a nigger in your little secret place down there…we will burn this barge to ashes."

The two slavers turned and walked back to the mule barn.

That afternoon the *Turtle* and the *Wilhelmina* slipped into the Canal basin. The other four Pulaski barges had already been poled out of the basin and were anchored behind the *Ugly Boat*, waiting near the shallows. Aaron said they would move the *Turtle* and *Wilhelmina* through the outlet lock in the morning. David tried to convince Aaron to come out to the other barges and join them for dinner, but Aaron refused, and David went on without him. Aaron went down in the cabin to straighten the wall panel that had been warped out of shape when he tried to force it over the whiskey bottle.

"No matter," he said to himself, "It can't be used again. The bastards know about it, and they'll pass it around."

He stumbled up the stairs to the stern locker and

rummaged around for another bottle. He found two and brought them out, setting one on the deck beside him and opening the other, spitting the cork out into the basin. Held the bottle up in a toast.

"Well, I was partially truthful, George," he said to the bottle. "Before I started putting them in the storage locker, I kept them down there." He took a long drink, enjoying the sound of the air bubbles rising inside the bottle, then laid back on the locker. "But it took too much time to go get them." He patted the top of the locker beside him. "Here is better."

George and Sammy caught a ride on a company barge following behind Aaron's tandem, giving the canaller twenty-five cents for his trouble, intending to ride all the way to the basin. When they heard the tavern music at Lapidum, they got off there, but the tavern closed at 7 o'clock, and they had not drunk their fill and headed down the towpath to Havre de Grace.

Long after sunset, both bottles lay empty beside the storage locker, and Aaron was snoring heavily. George and Sammy walked along the edge of the canal basin, and when they walked past the *Wilhelmina*, George spotted it.

"Hey farmer," George said, but Aaron continued to snore.

George turned to Sammy, "Almost turns a man off from whiskey...naaah, let's get some drinks of our own."

"Wait a minute, George," Sammy said in a hoarse whisper. "Let's see if he has any down his hidie-hole. He'll just think he drank it all."

George giggled. "Now you're thinking Sammy-boy. Free whiskey is always the best kind."

They crept down into the cabin. George quickly opened the compartment, but could not see inside it. Sammy pulled a lantern from a wall near the stove and lit it. It burned brightly for a moment but then went out. Sammy shook the lantern.

"Empty," he said.

"Must be some more oil in here," George said.

They both moved about the cabin, using a match for

light, and found two nearly full cans under one of the bunk beds. George opened the whale oil can and told Sammy to open the lantern well, then stand back and strike a match so he could see to pour. When Sammy struck the match, the oil he had spilled on his fingers ignited, and he tossed the match away. Oil poured over the little table top, and it flashed into flames. Sammy dashed up the steps. George dropped the oil can and ran up behind him. They jumped onto the walk boards, then onto the towpath and ran north toward Lapidum.

A canaller, staying on his barge overnight, noticed the flames and ran to the lockhouse to pull the fire bell. Other men from barges and the mule stable ran out to fight the blaze. Water thrown from buckets did not stop the fire. The basin was crowded with wooden barges filled with coal. The swing bridge was shoved aside, and poles were grabbed by a dozen men who pushed the *Wilhelmina* through the outlet lock into the bay. Within a few hectic minutes, the *Wilhelmina* received her last strained push away from the basin and into the river current. None of the other barges had caught fire. She drifted over the Susquehanna Flats, a burning cauldron of dried wood and coal. Aaron dropped onto a bench near the lockhouse with a heavy sigh. The *Wilhelmina* lit up the bay as she drifted south on the current. Aaron hung his head. The other canallers working the Pulaski barges stood on the deck of the *Ugly Boat*, mesmerized by the fiery end to the *Wilhelmina*. They laid down the poles they had grabbed to fend her off, and one by one returned to their bunks.

That night in Georgetown, Ben sat at the table in the hold of the *Raven*, surrounded by his crew and his passengers. Their space was cramped. It was the only area left available below decks, where the rice barrels and indigo crates competed for it. Ben continued to ask William questions.

"What did you expect when you ran off the ship with that pistol?"

"I expected to kill Beasley."

"And what would become of the other people on my ship?"

"I didn't think about that."

As before, William only answered questions. He could not bring himself to tell the story of his kidnapping and enslavement.

Ben sighed. "William, you endangered everyone on this ship. That's why I intend for you to explain yourself in front of them."

He glared at Ben.

"Why so much hatred for that one man? Of all the men involved in your kidnapping, why him? Were there others you would kill, but you saw him first?" Ben asked. He sighed again and faced the others. "Maybe that's it. I can't say I blame him for the rage, just the risk he placed on us."

Ben stood and went on deck. He fished out his pipe and tobacco and leaned on the railing facing across the channel as he tamped the tobacco into his pipe. Miss Esther came next to him.

"That stuff'll kill you, Cap'n P'laski."

He smiled at her then shook his head no. "I know men in their eighties that have always smoked pipes."

"Know a lot of'em do ya?"

"Well, no, not really, but that doesn't mean..."

She patted him on his arm. "You really don't know, do you?"

"Well, I've never thought about counting the old men I know..."

"I ain't talking 'bout that. I'm talkin 'bout Mr. Stone."

Ben turned to her in the lantern light. "Talk to me about Mr. Stone."

"You know he risked his life to save them, boys."

"Yes, I heard."

"You got the what, but not the why," she said.

"Of course, I understand the why. I can't image a worse fate for any boy."

"You'd hate a man that did that to your boy child?"

"Of course I would," Ben said

"Hate him enough to kill him?"

"Oh, hell, yes. Esther."

"What if such a man did it to you?" she tapped Ben's chest. "Would you shoot him in the head, right there in front a God and everbody? No matter what?"

"Well, hell yes, I..."

She searched in Ben's eyes. "And would you want to stand up in public and tell everbody why you kilt him?"

Ben stared at her in silence.

"Leave Mr. Stone be, Cap'n, and take us all away from this evil place."

"This is not an evil place, Esther. There are many fine people here."

"Not for me or mine, or folks that look like me. We work mules, is all we are here."

23

Ben walked the deck, making a final check before releasing the mooring lines to the *Raven*.

One of the Mansfield men who had spoken to Ben in the past stepped cautiously to the edge of the dock and spoke with a muted voice.

"Did Mr. Bond and Mr. Bartrum get away?"

Ben glanced around quickly to ensure they were alone.

"Yes. Do you want to go with us?"

"Yassah, I do, but I gots family an cain't leave'em."

The slave abruptly turned and walked away when he spotted a white man approaching. The *Hannah* was making her turn up the channel in preparation of coming bow to bow to take the *Raven*'s tow line. Cuttingham approached on the dock wearing a butternut cotton suit and a wide planter's hat.

"I hope you found our indigo satisfactory, Captain Pulaski," he said.

Ben frowned at him and blew out his breath. "Yes. I know the Mansfield people got the indigo from your Master."

"You can get it cheaper from us directly, Pulaski."

"I doubt that, Ensign Cuttingham. They passed it on without fee."

"It's not Ensign anymore, Captain. That was just an appellation Jeremiah used so he could show off his pet Brit. No, the steamer is in the good hands of the boson and the crew. Oh, and we charged Mansfield far more than we charge our usual buyers."

Ben remained silent, refusing to ask the question Cuttingham begged.

"You can also get milled rice from us now. We have our own milling operation, now that I am manager of

Palmetto Haven."

Ben folded his arms but said nothing.

"I am sure you know that Jeremiah finally died of the wound you gave him," Cuttingham said. "Mrs. Lydia Binterfield now owns the plantation, and she has promoted me to Manager of Operations."

"My congratulations to the both of you," Ben said then motioned to Edward to have the mooring lines freed, and signaled to the *Hannah* to take the tow rope downstream."

"You can make your congratulations to Mrs. Binterfield in person, Captain. She has returned to Havre de Grace."

Ben spun around to face Cuttingham as the *Raven* slipped forward. Cuttingham smiled and tipped his hat, then turned away.

Following the instructions delivered in Georgetown, the *Raven* once again anchored off Poole's Island. She sat there an entire day and was finally joined by the steamboat Columbus early the following morning. As the usual scramble ensued among the steamboat crew, a Catholic Nun stepped to the edge of the main deck facing the *Raven*. The Captain of the Columbus leaned over from the railing and yelled to Ben.

"You heard the news about Andrew Jackson, Pulaski?"

"What news is that?" Ben asked

"Died," was the only curt answer.

Ben faced out over the water a brief moment, then back at the steamboat captain, "Sorry to hear that. I served under him at New Orleans and in Georgia."

"So I was told," the captain answered, then stepped back into the pilot house.

The three boys jumped to the steamer and into the spread arms of the Nun. Mr. Stone bowed to her but remained on the *Raven* as the ships separated.

"I thought you would go to the other ship, Mr. Stone," Ben said.

"You assumed, Captain Pulaski, but you never asked me."

"True. I assumed. So where do you go from here?"

"I am from Annapolis, sir. And that is the location of my family, my home, and my shop."

Ben raised his eyebrows and smiled. "Shall I also assume you expect me to carry you there?"

"If you would be so kind," Stone said and turned to face out over the bay.

"The captain of the steamer just told me that Andrew Jackson had died," Ben said

"Yes, I heard him yell it...How old were you when you served under him?"

"Fifteen. Turned that just before the Brits came. Had been a drummer boy, but got my musket that day. What kind of a shop do you have, Mr. Stone?"

"I am a gunsmith, sir."

Ben smiled, and his eyes twinkled. "Do you sell revolvers?"

Stone turned and gave up his first genuine smile. "The very best, Captain Pulaski. The very best."

"Are you familiar with the Colt Patterson? I handled one in Havre de Grace not long ago."

The smile broadened. "Yes. I sold one to a prosperous gentleman there. William Stewart. Had it engraved. Do you know him?"

"He passed away. No, the pistol belonged to his wife when I saw it. My wife and I were guests at the time."

"Very well, Captain Pulaski, I will be pleased to sell you a Colt Patterson, and at an excellent price, I promise." He continued to smile as he turned toward the wind and took in a deep breath. "It will be good to get back to business. Yes. It will be good."

Ben stared at him a long moment. "I have met you before, Mr. Stone."

Stone turned back to face him, "Where?"

"You modified my old flintlock pistols for percussion."

"I did that for many people, Captain, I do not remember you as a customer. I hope the pistol is still in good operating condition."

Ben chuckled. "You just tried to shoot Reed Beasley with it."

Stone closed his eyes and tilted his head. "I recall the trigger mechanism feeling well adjusted. And the cap hit the nipple well centered. Unfortunately, the owner had failed to load it."

"Which is why we are both here to discuss it, today, Mr. Stone."

"True enough," he said facing Ben directly, "but really, sir, an unloaded pistol is merely a club."

Ben smiled and directed the crew to raise anchor and set sails for Annapolis.

In Annapolis, after stevedores unloaded the cargo, Ben collected the receipts and bank drafts then visited Stone's gunsmith shop. The man's brother had watched over the store in his absence, reassured by the society that Stone would return. Mr. Stone came down the steps from his apartment upstairs after visiting his wife. Stone walked straight to Ben and extended his hand.

"Thank you, sir, for bringing me home, and all that was necessary to accomplish that."

"You are welcome, Mr. Stone," Ben said, shaking his hand.

Stone turned back up toward the top of the stairs where his wife stood, still wiping her eyes. Ben removed his hat and bowed to her, and then she withdrew.

"Now sir, let's see what my brother Wilbur has left of my stock," Stone said.

Wilbur gave a beaming smile to his brother and patted him on his back as Stone slipped behind the counter. He pulled out three velvet-lined oak boxes, each displaying a Colt Patterson.

Ben handled the one Stone presented to him first. Ben worked the hammer and cylinder motion several times, and then set it back in the box.

"I will buy all three," Ben said.

Stone hesitated. "I can sell you two of these, and at a

very good price, but I must withhold one from sale. It is to be given as a gift."

"Oh, well, I understand," Ben said.

Ben paid for the two pistols, and then Stone set the third box on top of them and slid them across the counter to Ben. Ben hesitated to move. Stone offered his hand again.

"Thank you, Captain Pulaski. I remain in your debt."

"Call me Ben, please."

"And you should call me 'Stony.' No one ever calls me William, except my mother."

On his way back to the *Raven*, Ben noticed the *Ugly Boat* sitting in the harbor. He stepped in the direction of a coal merchant warehouse, with its back over the Weems River, where he had delivered coal from his barges many times. In the rear, he found some of the Pulaski barges lined up, some empty and some waiting to be emptied. The coal crew working for the merchant, typically rented slaves, swung an iron boom and large bucket over the barges and then hefted the load up onto the packed dirt warehouse floor. Their uncovered backs were wet with sweat and sprinkled with black coal dust. A white man brought a bucket of water and ladle to the workers, and Ben recognized him as David Booker.

"David," he called. "Where's Aaron?"

David waved and smiled. He pointed back into the town, then held his hand to his mouth as if he were drinking from a bottle. Ben frowned and went back to the *Raven* to lock away his new pistols. Heading for the more popular taverns on Prince George Street, Ben met David on his way to retrieve the *Ugly Boat*.

"He's probably asleep in the pilot house, Mr. Pulaski," David told him, "There is a narrow bunk against the back wall that he sleeps on sometimes. I'll see that we all get back to the canal."

"Thank you, David." Ben hesitated. "It has been hard on him. More than a man should have to bear."

"We all understand. We'll take care of Aaron."

Ben went back to the ship and made preparations to

set sail, but the crew implored him to stay the night so that they could have an evening in Annapolis. As soon as he committed to the stay, and paid them their share of the cargo profits, Ben thought to capture some time with his son, but as he dashed to the end of the dock, the *Ugly Boat* was already gone.

David must have found him there. No sense interfering with his work.

Ben had evening dinner on the ship and went to bed early.

The next morning, the *Raven* dropped anchor just off Havre de Grace, not far from the waiting *Ugly Boat*. Ben shared the rowboat with Edward and Alistair and left them as he headed home for a day or two, eager to talk with Aaron. In the canal basin, Ben found David holding the reins to one of the Pulaski mules and talking to one of the young black boys who hung around the mule barn, looking for work. David came to an agreement with the boy and gave him the reins, then spotted Ben. They fell in together walking toward the line of barges waiting to go up the canal. When they came to the *Turtle*, Ben re-examined the other barges.

"The *Turtle* and *Wilhelmina* have always been paired since the *Ugly Boat* was converted to steam," Ben said. "Where is the *Wilhelmina*?"

They stepped onto the deck of the *Turtle* as the mule pulled it forward, guided by the little boy David had just hired. David moved to the tiller and sat on the storage box, inviting Ben to join him.

"There was a fire last night, Mr. Pulaski. The *Wilhelmina* and all her coal above the water line burned. Her spine is out there on the flats, still holding a couple tons, but it'll wash away soon."

"Was Aaron on it? Was he hurt?"

"Not on the outside, sir. He said all the profit from all six barges was lost. I think it was the last thing he could take."

Ben turned his face across the canal basin at the river beyond as they neared the entrance to the canal.

190

"How is he doing today?"

"None of us have seen him since he towed us to Annapolis. The *Ugly Boat* was empty this afternoon, and his overnight bag was gone. There were eight full bottles of whiskey sitting in the storage box under the bunk. All that it could hold."

The tree line slipped by as they moved upstream in the canal. A large Blue Heron squawked and flew away from the canal shallows, gliding out over the river to the far shore where it would not be disturbed. Ben examined his hands, rubbing some tar from one of his knuckles, and sighed.

At home in Lapidum, Ben shared the disturbing news with Sonja. Jesse Price had not seen Aaron from the lockhouse, neither on a barge nor coming across the swing bridge.

Sonja kept her attention on her hands in her lap. "Could he have gone on to York Furnace?"

"Shortest way would be up the canal or on the towpath," Ben said.

Sonja raised her eyes to meet Ben's. A frown grew on her forehead. "Where could he be?"

In Havre de Grace, James Williamson rapped the brass knocker against its plate on the front door of the Pink House on Union Avenue. Sissy answered the door and brought him inside with a warm hug.

"Miss Mamie," she called out in the echo of the foyer, "Mr. Williamson come to visit!"

"Well, actually..." James began.

Mamie entered the foyer and took him by the hand into the Parlor. "What brings you here, sir, and of course, you are always welcome."

"Miss Mamie, I am a vagabond in search of lodgings."

"Is there work going on in your Mansion?"

He smiled, "There is definitely a piece of work going on in that house, Mamie, but it is not of my choosing. Mrs. Binterfield has returned and evicted me."

"What?"

191

"I am beginning to regret that Mr. Briscoe was unable to complete his business with my sister..."

"What on earth has happened, James?"

In the lower Chesapeake Bay, the steamboat *Thomas Jefferson* was making its southern run between Richmond and Norfolk, after making good time on its northern leg to Richmond from Annapolis. In the lounge on the mezzanine, a young man lay asleep on one of the settees, snoring loudly and receiving hateful frowns from the ladies passing by with their gentlemen. The waiter was told by several others to escort the drunk to his room, but the man was a first class passenger and had refused. He had given the waiter a silver dollar to leave him alone. After more complaints, the waiter approached his white supervisor and laid the issue with him. The head waiter checked the passenger registry and found his name and room number on the list.

"Mr. Pulaski, we need to help you to your room, sir. You cannot sleep here," the head waiter said.

"Leave me alone," Aaron growled.

"I am sorry, sir, but I must insist you go to your room."

"Another drink," he demanded.

The supervisor glanced at the bartender who firmly shook his head, no.

"I am afraid we cannot do that, sir, but I will be happy to send a bottle to your room...and ice, sir. We offer ice on this ship."

Aaron struggled to his feet and allowed the man to escort him to his cabin and lay him on his bed. The attendant set the latch from the inside and pulled the door closed behind him. As he walked away, he heard the unsettling noise of a man retching.

"Maggie!" the drunken man cried out.

24

Isaac came home for his summer furlough and helped with the barges, working closely with David, and Abraham Freidman, Maggie's older brother. Ben had installed a partition dividing the boy's bedroom, and cut a second door for Alisha, creating a small bedroom of her own. Days and weeks passed without word from or about Aaron. Sonja stood on the front porch drying a dish. On the canal below, a barge gorged with coal drifted down the canal, silently riding the timid current and following its mule like a huge obedient dog.

Ben stepped next to Sonja. "If you rub that bowl much more, that stripe at the edge of the pottery will be gone."

She glanced at him with a vacant stare. "I can't stand the thought of missing another child."

"He's not a child, Sonja. He's a full grown man with an aching heart."

"Let him ache here where I can help him."

Ben placed his hand on her shoulder. "Some things can't be cured by a mother. Some things are never cured; they just have to be accepted."

She locked eyes with him, her deep blue eyes winter cold, and walked back into the kitchen. Ben sighed and made his way down the slope to the waiting *Turtle* and *Osprey*. Isaac was with Jeremy, far ahead on two of their other barges, if not already at Wrightsville. The *Osprey* was another Pennsylvania built barge, like the others he owned for the trip between Havre de Grace and Wrightsville. Her cabin took only ten feet in length between the two sizeable open-topped cargo holds. The paint was still shiny on the sloping boards, giving the cargo holds their removable roof. The deck was fresh and unstained, and the cabin smelled of new wood. He remembered what Adam Tuttle had said about boat decks.

> *'Let nature do its job, Benjamin. Let this deck become sprinkled with fish guts, and tar and seagull shit, like God, intended. No self-respecting workboat is going to stay perfectly clean. It ain't natural.'*

The little boy David had hired to help lead the *Turtle*'s mule worked full time with the Pulaski barges now. His name was Matthew, a healthy youngster willing to walk long hours, occasionally cheerful and occasionally melancholy, but dependable so far. Matthew readily accepted a second mule and a two-mule single-file harness, needed to pull tandem barges. So, Ben paid him the same pay as his other mule tenders. Ben stepped aboard the *Turtle*, tied bow-to-stern behind the *Osprey*, and whistled for Matthew to start the mules. As soon as the tow rope straightened out, he pulled the tiller to guide the barges to the right side of the canal.

Delbert Freidman waved from his hardware store as the barges moved upstream to the lock. Delbert was sitting in his chair on the porch, letting his arms and back rest after helping to unload the hardware and store goods from Ben's barges. Canal company barges went empty on their trip north to Wrightsville and came back down full of coal, the cargo that made the most money. Privately owned barges, like Ben's, tried to carry cargo in both directions whenever they could. His trips to Annapolis in the *Raven* always brought back store goods for his northbound barges. Farm tools, furniture, tableware, fabric and even cotton were readily accepted on consignment in the shops among the many small towns growing up along the canal. On some trips, his profit was greater northward than when he brought coal southward.

Two miles above lock number nine back at

Lapidum, Ben's barges met another tandem coming south, full of coal and low in the water. Canal etiquette arose from the assumption that southbound barges were always low in the water from heavy cargo and northbound ones were still high in the water from empty holds. This was rarely the case for the Pulaski barges, which were typically low in the water for both directions. Still, since their mules shared the same towpath and attention had to be paid to the tow ropes, a slow ballet had developed along the canal, assigning specific moves to mule, rope, and barges, depending upon their direction.

Ahead, a small boy of only six or seven years rode the oncoming mule team. The boy and Matthew traded loose waves. The southbound barge swung slightly to the left of center, while *Osprey* and *Turtle* drifted toward the right skimming the shallows. As the two mule teams met on the towpath, the little boy slowed his team, allowing his cable to sink low in the canal. Matthew slowed his pace to gather slack in his line and tossed his towrope over the little boy. The descending barge continued its slow glide toward the position of the little boy as Ben's barges easily slipped over his submerged line. The little boy played with a grass twig and gave them a lazy wave. Ben returned his wave and smiled at his good-natured gap-toothed grin. Then, on the left, the four barges began to pass each other. The loaded barge was only a foot and a half lower in the water. Ben read the numbers painted on the bows of the oncoming barges: 42 and 53. The company man sitting at his tiller nodded to Ben as they passed.

As soon as the *Turtle* passed the little boy, he nudged the mules with his bare feet. They trotted down the path until they had taken up the slack of the towrope and could feel the weight of the barges pull against their collars, and then slowed to a leisurely pace, towing the barges smoothly on their way.

Ben retrieved one of his new revolvers from the storage locker as he neared the Mason-Dixon Line. He had bought a holster from a leather smith in Stafford and strapped it around his waist. He was not used to wearing such an obvious threat in public but had decided that the times justified it. There was no trouble at the *Line*, as they crossed from Maryland into Pennsylvania's last canal lock. One slaver yelled out "You got a secret compartment, Pulaski?" while they were still on the Maryland side, but no one attempted to stop him. The rumors continued that he had once killed a couple of men there, and most slave catchers tended to leave Ben Pulaski alone.

It had been a personal argument between an unarmed Ben and a rowdy slave catcher, who decided to raise his rifle at Ben. Ben hit the man with a tiller handle as the gun went off. A bullet grazed Ben's head, and the slaver died of concussion the next night. The story had grown in the years since then, passed on to new slave catchers with increasing embellishments. It had become a blazing shootout including Pulaski and several other men, some fighting with knives, all of which never happened.

Ben stood so his pistol could be easily seen and hoped that would be all the use he ever needed of it there. Beyond the line, on the more extended Pennsylvania section of the canal, the barges came to York Furnace. Ben looked wistfully at the sloping trail that led up to the Jundt farm as he passed through the lock there. Helen and David Booker had moved into the big farmhouse and he did not want to intrude, but it was unsettling to pass without stopping anymore. They made good time on the canal that day and stayed for the night a few miles north of Shenk's Ferry. Ben and Matthew shared white bean stew for supper, one of the most common meals among canallers. It was hearty and filling and cooking it could be started before leaving the canal basin. It simmered long and slow on the little iron stove barges bolted to the bulkhead inside the cabin. As many as six people could sleep in the cramped cabin bunks.

The next morning Ben started coffee while Matthew had another bowl of white bean stew. Sonja always added strips of smoked ham and bits of chopped onion when she made it ready for trips, and Matthew had decided Ms. Sonja's bean stew was the best on the canal. They made it into the Wrightsville basin before noon and found all four of the other barges still in line for coal. Ben took the other two crews and Matthew to a local tavern for an early afternoon meal, sitting together at a table and bench set out back, since neither blacks nor Irish were accepted inside. Isaac had joined David on his barges but was happy to let David give the instructions while he talked endlessly about West Point. David and Abraham captained the other two tandem barges, with eight-year-old Jesse Price Jr. and a black boy from Stafford, Archie, working the mules. Matthew and Archie were instant friends but included Jesse in their chatty conversations.

"Any word about Aaron?" Abraham asked.

Ben only shook his head, no.

"Are you going to pilot the *Ugly Boat*, Mr. Pulaski?" asked David.

"Thought you or Isaac might do that since he is an engineer and you piloted it down from Annapolis," Ben said.

"Well, sir...I...um..."

"What is it, David?"

"Sir, I really don't like doing that...and...well, Abraham enjoys it."

Abraham sat there with a wide grin on his face. "I love steam engines, Mr. Pulaski. They are amazing! I could work with them forever!"

Isaac shared Abraham's enthusiasm.

"Your father told me yesterday, Abraham, that he wanted you to come into the store; to be ready to take over for him someday," Ben said.

Abraham let his shoulders sag. "I need to talk with him. Jeremy McMallery doesn't want to be a blacksmith like his father. He told me his father understood and was looking for a partner, then Jeremy could do something else..."

"I knew Jeremy didn't want to be a blacksmith,"

Isaac said. "But I thought he wanted to go to sea."

"And?" Ben asked.

Abraham shook his head. "That was last year, Isaac." then he turned to Ben "Jeremy is good with numbers, and lists, and ledgers, and would make a wonderful shopkeeper..."

"Mmm. So you want to run off to the railroad?" Ben asked, instantly saddened by his thought.

"No, sir. Steamboats! Steamboats can go anywhere there is water. Trains only go where there are tracks, and it takes years to lay new track. In a steamboat, a man could go anywhere!"

"And where do you want to go?" Isaac asked.

"Someday...to Greece, but that's someday. For now, I like working the canal... and the *Ugly Boat*." He raised his eyebrows facing Ben.

"Well, until Aaron comes back, I am happy to have you pilot the *Ugly Boat*; after your barges return to Havre de Grace...assuming your father does not object."

"I could captain his barges," Isaac said.

Abraham smiled at the idea. "Then I could also tow the other barges while you go to Wrightsville and back!"

The bridge across the Susquehanna River between Wrightsville and Columbia was a mile long; the longest covered bridge in the world. It had an outside deck where the mules would walk, still pulling their barges below. The line of barges crossing the Susquehanna current was only a few feet apart as they followed their tow ropes dangling from mule harnesses above. The tandem barges had to be separated and sent across as singletons.

Eighty barges moved like slugs on parade, the entire line moving slowly to the rhythm of three coal filling stations on the Columbia side. Once filled, the barges joined another line of slugs inching their way back to Wrightsville. The previous day one of the older barges caught fire, closing operations until all embers were put out and the barge carcass removed from the center chute. The backup of waiting barges going to Columbia finally began to thin. The massive log jam on the river moved into the canal basin until no more barges could be admitted. A small number of the barges there were filled and could finally float down the canal. Each barge and mule required a hundred and sixty feet of length in the canal, and tandems needed two hundred twenty feet before another barge could be allowed to enter the canal. All northbound traffic was halted. Those barges had to stake against the canal banks south of Wrightsville and wait until the basin had emptied. As darkness fell, all the Pulaski barges still lingered in the river for return entrance to the Wrightsville basin.

Once at the Canal Basin in Havre de Grace two days later, they sent the mules to board in the Canal Company mule barn. Ben had told the boys they had three days off but would be needed back then, and paid them up. Matthew headed off to buy fresh food for him and his mother, while the other two dashed back down the towpath to Lapidum. Together, the four men poled the barges through the outlet lock to the *Ugly Boat* anchored in the flats and began tying them together as two rows of three each. The morning sky over Havre de Grace was an angry collection of rolling black clouds, lightning, thunder and a deluge of fat raindrops, slapping the cabin roofs like angry drummers. They all gathered in the cabin of the *Osprey* until the storm passed northward.

When the clouds cleared, Ben took the rowboat over to the *Raven* to check for leaks. On board he found Edward coming out of the crew quarters.

"Is everything well, Eddie?" Ben asked.

"She's a dry ship, Ben."

"Are you staying on board?"

"Yes. If you don't mind Ben. I have a bed here and can row over to the town if I need company."

Ben smiled. "As you like. I'm happy to have someone to watch it. I'll be going to Annapolis this afternoon. You are welcome to join us."

"No thanks, Ben. I don't care to be behind all that smoke. Ben...I saw Aaron in Annapolis."

"Where? I was there and about to look for him when

I met David...and...well... we thought he might be sleeping it off in the pilot house, but he wasn't there."

"He was getting on a steamer to Norfolk, Ben."

"Norfolk?? Did you speak with him?"

"Only briefly, Ben...he...he was drunk."

Ben frowned and turned his attention over the Bay toward the Cecil County shore. "What did he say?"

"He said he was going away."

"Where?"

"He just said 'away,' then walked up the gangplank onto the steamer. He said to tell you and Sonja that he would be all right."

A small boat backed over the waves on the Susquehanna Flats. The man rowing was struggling against the rising wind, being blown back the way he had come. Ben faced into the wind, frowning.

"He said nothing else?"

"No, Ben. Nothing else."

25

Near the end of August Isaac returned to West Point for his final year. Although his engineering and mathematics skills had elevated him a year ahead of those who entered with him, he faced a grueling military education program. His days were longer than others, and the modicum of patience shown the other cadets did not fall on him. If he was to graduate the following June among the class of 1846, he had to prove himself in all areas. Some instructors still resented his advancement and were determined to see him fail. Only the fact that his father had fought alongside Andrew Jackson at New Orleans tempered their resentment.

No further word came from or about Aaron. When she let herself, Sonja would fall into almost disabling worry about him, but the pure joy of life that sprang from Alisha steadily pulled her up.

Ben recognized what a good hard working man was David Booker, but he came to depend more and more on Abraham Freidman. After Mac found a right partner for his blacksmith shop and allowed his son Jeremy to begin helping as a clerk, Delbert Freidman finally gave Abraham his blessing to run the steamboat full time. Abraham had been able to find trustworthy captains for the other two barge tandems, and the three boys remained with him as Mule tenders.

Ben sat on his front porch in the early morning, chatting with Abraham before they left for Havre de Grace.

"Mr. Pulaski, I hear Mr. Wurlitz is going to retire and go live with his son in Lancaster. He has two barges he would sell to us. He has offered his mules, too, but they're old, and I recommend we not buy them."

"What is he asking for the barges, Abraham?"

"Half what you paid for the *Osprey*, and...my father is offering to pay for half of that, if he can have half the profits from those two barges."

"Are they in good condition?"

'Yes sir, they are only five years old, and with his old mules, he almost never carried a full load in them. You can still see clean wood at the upper walls of his cargo holds."

"Alright, Abraham, I'll go speak with your father, before we leave." He stepped down the ladderway and stopped at the bottom, then turned facing Abraham. Ticking off the names with his fingers, he said, "We have the *Turtle*, the *Juniata* that I named; the *Alisha* that Sonja named; and the *Osprey*, *Daniel* and *Simon* that Aaron named. So what do you have in mind for these other two?"

Abraham hesitated a moment, then said "The *Sarah* and...the *Margaret*."

Ben put his chin down and smiled. "Yes. I like those...and so will Aaron when he comes home."

Delbert was already in his store re-arranging shovels and pitchforks with Jeremy when Ben walked in. Ben grabbed an enameled cup from the stove top and poured himself a little coffee. Delbert sent Jeremy into the back room for the older shovels and walked up to Ben.

"So... Abraham spoke to you about the barges."

Ben nodded his head, yes. "We each pay half for the barges?"

"Yes, Benjamin."

"We each pay half the crew pay and mule feed?"

"...Yes... that is satisfactory."

"...and half of all fees? Coal cargo? Outlet lock? Towing to market? "

"...And split the profit on those two barges."

Ben smiled and held out his hand. "Done."

"Ben, did Abraham tell you the names he had in mind for the barges?"

"Yes, I think they will be fine."

"I think little Maggie would have approved."

"I think so, too, Delbert."

⸻⸻⸙⸻⸻

In the front room of the Binterfield estate on Adams Street, Lydia Binterfield gave directions to her new clerk. She paced the front room that had served as an at-home office for James.

"Stop by Mr. Nettle's office to see if there is any news regarding our lawsuits. Then ride down to the...Lapidum property... with that notice. That is my property, and I am not letting the help give it away. Nail it to the post on the porch, do you hear me? Nail the other one on the Union Avenue property on your way back."

"Yes ma'am," he said.

She had instructed the printer to make two eviction notices, one each for the Pink House and the Pulaski Farm. Mr. Nettle had suggested she wait on the act until he had received a preliminary ruling from the reviewing judge, but he had no wish to force the point. Lydia turned her back toward the clerk as he left the room. Walking to the liquor cabinet, she flung the doors open and found...nothing. James was using it as a file cabinet.

"Damn you, James" she yelled. She walked to the doorway and clapped her hands. "Hey! You! Get in here!"

The maid ran into the foyer, "Yass'm. I'm Frita, ma'am. How can I help you?"

"You can find the God damned brandy, or whatever liquor James had in this house, and put it in the God damned liquor cabinet, where it belongs!"

She eyed the stacks of papers in the cabinet. "Yass'm. And what must I do with those papers, ma'am?"

"Burn them, Fri-ta, burn the damned things."

⸻⸻⸙⸻⸻

September began as a continuation of the hot summer. Anchored near the deep channel carved by the Susquehanna River current through the sand of the Susquehanna Flats, the crew of the *Raven* was finishing final adjustments to her supplies and ballast. The sky was partially cloudy, and the view down the Bay was hazy. The humidity pulled sweat from the body, and the air lay on the skin like a wool blanket. The wind pennant hung limp from the main mast. Seagulls drifted lazily over the masts looking for shad hiding near the hull, but only finding occasional morsels. Edward Leonard pulled his hat off his head, wiping his brow and the sweat-soaked headband inside the hat.

"I wish we would get a breeze, Ben. This is going to be a warm autumn if it stays like this."

"If you don't like the weather on the Chesapeake Bay..."

"Yes, yes, yes, I know, Ben," Edward said and walked to the bow, hoping for fresh air coming down with the River water.

Moments later the clouds drifted together coming from the north and turned from white to powdered grey. The Wind pennant slowly unfurled for a brief moment, then settled down beside the mast, then rose again and stayed in the air. The loose mainsail rustled in the breeze.

"Gentlemen," Ben announced, "I believe our wind has arrived."

Edward ordered the sails hoisted but held off raising the anchor until he thought the wind would increase. By the time the sails were set, and the anchors hooked onto their rests against the hull, the sails were full, and masts were leaning away from the wind. Ben spun the wheel on the windward side until he could feel the rudder bite with steerageway, and set his course down the main channel.

"Annapolis for Rum," Edward said. "It probably just got up here from Jamaica, and we're taking it back down to Charleston."

He had a wry smile on his face. Ben had shared the latest note with him earlier.

Annapolis for rum. Charleston, dock at the blue pennant.

In mid-September, the *Raven* crept into Charleston Harbor with ripped and tangled sails. The remnants of a hurricane had driven up the western side of the Atlantic Ocean slamming Cape Hatteras with hateful winds and heavy rain. They had been shoved north as far as Nova Scotia, and the southwesterly winds had remained for days afterward, pushing against them. They were forced to tack back and forth across its face, wasting hundreds of miles east and west to gain only dozens south. They sailed ungainly through the outer harbor. Some of the *Raven*'s lines had been snapped and only crudely re-tied, keeping them from running through the blocks and preventing the crew from trimming the sails efficiently. Unable to lower the foresail and mainsail, they had to spill the wind several times to slow the ship by repeatedly swinging out the booms. She resembled a dying bird slowly flapping its wings, as she neared the dock that flew a blue pennant. The ship shuddered to a stop, bumping the wharf hard when the mooring lines checked her motion too late.

The warehouse where the *Raven* docked was the same one that had sent out William Stone on their last trip to Charleston. A single door opened and a man wearing an opened vest and dirty white shirt walked toward the *Raven,* carrying a ledger. He stepped near the ship and called out in a loud voice.

"Gangplank!"

The crew moved slowly, exhausted from lack of sleep. They slid the gangplank out to the pier and stepped back.

"Give us a moment to rig the boom and sling," Edward said.

"Nah," the man said. "We got lots of slaves to do all that. Just show'em where the ladderways are."

He turned back toward the door and whistled through his teeth. The slaves began to file out, like sluggish ants, not moving any faster than the exhausted ship's crew. Some of the slaves appeared to be in far worse condition than the others.

The supervisor came on deck and examined the

locations of the ladderways. "We'll use'em both. Down the forward and up the stern. That way they'll move better." But they did not. Like ants, they trickled down the forward ladderway, and then slowly emerged at the stern. The supervisor stood by the gangplank and marked in his ledger as each 5-gallon cask came up and wound its way into the Warehouse.

The *Raven*'s crew lounged on the deck as the long line of slaves circled through the ship taking the cargo. Ben and Edward watched from the wheels, leaning against the compass binnacle between them.

"There must be forty of them," Edward said.

Ben shrugged his shoulders and frowned at the slow-moving line, paying attention to the details of the slaves. After several minutes, Ben stood up straight and moved quickly to the forward ladderway and disappeared down into the hold. The supervisor did not notice Ben's movement and kept his eyes on the ledger and the rum casks.

In the galley, Ben found three slaves, leaning against the stove, which had not been lit in several days. Ben opened a canvas bag half full of ship's biscuits.

"Here," Ben said, "That's all we have been eating, but I'll bet it's more than you have had."

As hands reached into the bag, a fourth slave lingered in the galley, welcomed by the first three. Then joined by a fifth, sixth, until finally ten men were huddled together in the galley munching dried biscuits. Ben glanced around the cargo holds and noticed that five casks remain.

Edward yelled down the stern ladderway. "Supervisor needs you to sign the ledger, Captain."

Ben smiled at the escaping slaves and trotted up onto the deck. The supervisor showed him the ledger with the entire cargo counted into the warehouse. Ben frowned and pointed over his shoulder with his thumb, starting to open his mouth. The supervisor shook his head no and tapped the ledger where Ben was to sign.

"There's nothing left down in that hold 'cept what's

supposed ta be there, Cap'n."

"Yes...yes...that's right," Ben said.

He signed the ledger, confirming delivery, then the supervisor flipped the pages to the back of the ledger. He withdrew an envelope and handed it to Ben. The supervisor spun on his heels and walked back into the warehouse, yelling at the slaves with all the malice could muster.

"Edward," Ben called. "Take the men down and feed them. Have Warren start a fire in the stove and make them a good meal."

"Alright. I could use some warm food myself..."

"And, Edward, make sure everyone eats his fill. Everyone, Edward."

Edward rubbed the back of his neck, "Of course, Captain. Everyone."

"And don't let anyone back up on deck until I come down there and see that they have eaten, do you hear me?"

"Yes..." He frowned at Ben, "Yes...of course, Ben..."

Ben went to his cabin to read the notes in the envelope. There was a satisfying bank draft for the cargo and an unsigned note.

City Market 5:00 PM Alone. Best Clothes.

Ben's best clothes were only sailor's canvas trousers and worn shirts, but he did have a blue coat and neckcloth Sonja had bought for him in St. Michaels for Aarons wedding. The thought made him pause a moment but forced himself out of the sadness and down into the hold to visit his passengers. Ben's stomach growled, but the food Warren was cooking would take too long if he waited on board to eat. At 4:00 he left the ship and headed toward the City Market. Ben knew which way to go from his earlier visit to the public slave market, but had forgotten that it was a long brick building with many stalls and numerous doors along its sides. He arrived at 4:30 and decided to sit on a bench along the walkway near one end. The spot appeared to have the most foot traffic and offered an excellent view of the public clock. He sat there, smoking his pipe as the people passed him.

Almost to Ben's surprise, a tall elderly black man in a black suit, white gloves and top hat was standing before him.

"Captain Pulaski, suh, if you will kindly follow me, I will take you to your dinner with Mr. Renowitz."

Ben's eyebrows rose up his forehead, expecting Anthony to be nearby, but could not find him in the crowd.

"Lead the way," Ben said.

After a brisk eight minute walk along Bay Street, they came to a two-story brick building having a brass plaque hanging above arched double doors. The plate was engraved with the name McCrady's Tavern. The servant led Ben upstairs through the main banquet room, then to a private anteroom near a small stage.

Inside was a modest table suitable for four, covered in white linen, holding a glass centerpiece with fresh magnolia flowers and ferns, and surrounded by half-empty stemmed glasses holding dark red wine. Three men were already sitting. Anthony Renowitz stood and extended his hand to Ben.

"Welcome, Ben. I am glad you could join us." He turned to the other guests. "Ben, I am pleased to introduce United States Congressman, the Honorable Mr. John Slidell, visiting here from his home state of Louisiana, and another Louisianan, Lieutenant Pierre Gustave Toutant-Beauregard of the United States Army, West Point Class of '38."

Ben reached out and shook hands with Slidell, who smiled stiffly and shook hands from his seat.

Ben offered his hand to the other man saying, "Lieutenant Beauregard,"

Beauregard stood to shake Ben's hand, "Your servant, Sir. Please, call me Gustave; I much prefer that

208

to Pierre."

Ben smiled. "My son is at West Point now, Lieutenant, due to graduate in the spring."

Beauregard and Slidell exchanged glances.

"So I am told, sir," Beauregard said. "He could be in for some excitement, Captain Pulaski."

Slidell nodded in small movements, the barest smile fading from his lips. Anthony's face was blank. His emotions buried deep as they frequently were, staring boldly into Ben's eyes.

26

The waiter entered pushing a cart with steaming covered dishes, another wine glass for Ben and a bottle of white wine.

Anthony spoke as he sat. "I know there are other duties demanded of our guests, Ben, so I took the liberty of ordering ahead. I want to make the most of our time."

Ben smiled as he took his seat while the waiter placed dishes in front of each guest, beginning with the Congressman and ending with Anthony. There was stilted conversation while the waiter finished his duties and withdrew with the cart, closing the door behind him. A short awkward silence bloomed within the room but soon evaporated.

"You have a schooner, with much latitude in its...employment," Slidell said flatly, but it was a question.

"I am the owner, well the primary owner and the other owners are partners in profit, but do not typically have a voice in its destination, routes or cargo," Ben said.

"And you are a licensed slave trader."

"...Yes...I am."

Anthony turned his attention to Slidell, signaling the others at the table to listen. Slidell spoke directly to Ben.

"You have heard that the Texas Republic is being welcomed into the country as another state? Last year President Polk tried to push admittance through Congress, but Mexico threatened to declare war over it – Hell, Texas has been independent for nine years, and the damned Mexicans still can't accept it, and the Republicans kept it from passing."

Ben nodded. "I had read an article about Texas in a newspaper."

Slidell ignored the comment. "Well, the President is going to get his votes this year. Texas will come in before the year is out, mark my words."

"And we will have our little war with Mexico," Beauregard said. "There are many of us in the Army who look forward to it! We will put them in their place for once and for all."

Ben glanced at Anthony, but his face still showed nothing. Both Slidell and Beauregard nodded to Anthony then abruptly stood. Slidell gave Ben a curt nod and left.

"And I need to start packing for my return to Louisiana," Beauregard said, holding his hand out to Ben. "A pleasure sir. Tell your son to request service in Louisiana. What is his name?"

"Isaac. Isaac Pulaski."

"Excellent, he already has a fort in Georgia named for him! And what is his specialty?"

"Engineering."

Beauregard slapped his hands together. "Excellent, so am I. The army has my division fortifying our forts near shore, especially New Orleans. I will look for him!"

The two men bolted from the room, leaving the door open with Ben and Anthony in silence. Still, none of the covers had been removed from the plates. Anthony showed Ben a smirk.

"I wanted them to meet you, and you to meet them," Anthony said.

Within seconds two more men came into the room, closing the door behind them. Anthony rose and indicated their seats.

"Dinner has just been served, gentlemen." Anthony said. "I took the liberty of ordering for us. Meals at McCrady's are always a treat." He motioned to Ben. "Captain Ben Pulaski, allow me to introduce Mr. Walter Cramden and Major Bartholomew Aikens, United States Army."

The two men shook hands briskly with Ben and took their seats, immediately removing the silver warming covers.

Cramden spoke as he ate. "We need more slaves in

Louisiana, Captain Pulaski. The Brits are giving us hell now that they are out of the trade. Any slave touching the West Indies or any of their other islands get confiscated and freed. That terrifies the trade. And the sugar production in Louisiana is exploding!"

Aikens chuckled at the phrase, and Cramden allowed a smile to escape.

"All this means that the price of slaves is about to double – or even triple."

Ben turned his attention from Cramden to Aikens to Renowitz. "So how can I play a part in all this?"

"Let us invest in your voyages, Captain. We will all become rich."

"Us?" Ben said.

"The three of us," Beauregard said. "Slaves and gunpowder. Both will become as gold in the coming days."

"Gunpowder?"

Aiken's eyes sparkled, and Cramden's grin grew broader. "A war will demand millions of pounds of it, tons of it. Government contracts will be bought and traded among vendors like another stock market, Captain."

Anthony finally spoke. "With a government contract, you will bring gunpowder to Norfolk, Charleston and New Orleans for staging to Mexico, maybe even be contracted to deliver it on the shores of Mexico itself..."

Ben's eyes widened.

"Think of the profits, Ben," Anthony said. "Slaves from Charleston to New Orleans, and gunpowder to the Navy and Army. All of it worth more each day. The profit on a single load could even double just during the time it will take you to reach your destination. We could all be richer than we ever dreamed."

Oh, Anthony! Ben thought. *What are you getting us into? What are you getting ME into?*

Anthony motioned toward Ben's cover dish. "We have some excellent red snapper here, Ben. Do not let it go to waste."

Anthony stuffed his mouth full of the fish and Carolina Gold rice. Ben sipped at his wine, his stomach growling, waiting for Anthony to explain the meeting further. It dawned on Ben that Anthony intended to feed himself before saying anything else, and allowing the guests time to leave before speaking the truth.

I hope it will be the truth, Anthony!

Ben fell on his dinner with a passion he did not feel, but a hunger he could no longer deny.

In Norfolk, Aaron settled onto his bunk bed in a large merchant ship bound for Cuba to collect sugar. He had signed on the afternoon before and spent the day storing supplies, cleaning the decks and coiling unutilized ropes. He managed to finish the bottle of rum hidden in his seabag and fell asleep early. He was one of several "waisters" on board, inexperienced seamen assigned to mindless manual labor, primarily in the middle or "waist" of the ship. He pulled the lines to hoist and lower the sails, pushed the windlass to raise the anchor. He hauled in heavy mooring lines and muscled the cargo booms to swing crates and bales from the shore onto the decks.

On the voyage south, Aaron made no attempt to speak with the other seamen other than the words necessary to complete his assigned task. He was neither offered nor sought responsibility. Although whiskey drinking on board during the voyage was discouraged, there was frequently someone who would sell him a bottle or a mug full of rum. His only notable interaction among the crew occurred when he caught another seaman rifling through his seabag. The ensuing fist fight left the other man unconscious for several hours. Later, Aaron was taught the painful lesson of the whip when he received ten lashes for fighting.

In Havana, Aaron was allowed off the ship for a single night, which he spent meandering among the taverns along San Pedro Boulevard. Walking by an alleyway, he was grabbed from behind, beaten and robbed. He awoke late morning in the alley, lying in the mud with a cut on the back of his head, bruises and whelps covered his face, his pockets were turned out and empty. He stumbled along the boulevard searching for his way back to the ship, only to find an empty mooring. The ship had sailed. He sat down at the dock, staring at the vacant berth, and stayed there until nightfall. He finally fell asleep leaning against one of the stone mooring bollards. During the night he was attacked and beaten again, but the robbers stopped when they discovered his pockets were empty.

Aaron regained consciousness lying on his back in a narrow stone room with the sun streaming in through a small window high in one wall. He felt a bandage on his head. He sat up, noticing his bloody knuckles had been washed. Examining the room, he found himself on a simple cot of woven hemp covered in a tattered blanket. Turning his head further, he was overwhelmed by nausea and vomiting.

It was dark when he awoke again. A faint yellow light fluttered outside the open doorway to his room. On a stone block beside his bed was a pottery bowl of broth. He placed his fingertip into the liquid and tasted it. Then he brought the bowl to his lips, slurping the soup.

"Do not drink the broth too quickly, Americaño," a voice echoed softly from the hallway.

"Thank you," Aaron tried to say, but only a rasping hiss rose from his throat.

He lie back down on the bed and slept again. When he woke, the sunlight was again streaming in through the small window high in the wall beyond his feet. The bowl was gone from the stone by his bed. He sat up on his cot and let his feet touch the floor. The floor where he had vomited had been cleaned. Aaron braced himself against the stone and the bed to help himself stand. Still unbalanced, he moved toward the doorway. There was no door or bars there. He stepped out into a narrow hall, lit by a single candle wedged into an iron sconce on the wall several feet away. A little boy sitting on the floor with his back against the opposite wall, looked up seeing him, then dashed away yelling, "Padre! Padre!"

The little boy returned quickly with a Catholic priest in tow.

"So, you are sober enough to leave, Gringo, or do you wish to vomit in my guest room again?"

Dizziness overcame Aaron. He turned in the doorway to return to his bed. The blood pounded in his head, and the room spun around him, and he collapsed to the floor.

"At least you do not vomit this time, Gringo," the priest said as he and the little boy helped Aaron onto the bed.

⁕

Anthony stepped down from the carriage stopped on the dock between the *Raven* and the warehouse. Ben stood on the *Raven* at the top of the gangplank with his hands in his pockets. Anthony limped with his cane, walking around the carriage and motioning Ben to follow him. Inside, it was slightly cooler but without details in the dim light, almost dark until Ben's eyes adjusted. The warehouse was cavernous, easily three stories high with no floors between the bricks they stood on and the oak beams spans of the roof. Ben could hear the echoes of their steps. The tap of Anthony's cane reverberated like faint gunshots in the distance. The far wall was lost in darkness many yards away, marked only by pricks of sunlight sneaking between some of the boards. The entire warehouse was empty.

Anthony turned to face Ben with a grin on his face.

"One of my little subterfuges, old friend." He pointed to a small doorway nearby, then walked through it with Ben following. They entered a small office, with a few empty shelves on one wall, a narrow table, and two chairs. High in the wall overhead was a small window allowing paltry sunlight to drift into the room. Anthony pulled out a chair and took a seat. Ben sat across from him.

Anthony grinned again. "And we have more subterfuges to create, Ben."

"What the Hell are you doing, Anthony? What the Hell are you getting me into?"

"It's your own damned fault, Ben."

Ben waited impatiently for more comments, but Anthony could never resist dramatic moments, and let the silence settle a brief moment.

"God damn it, Anthony..."

"The raid you arranged in Georgetown was magnificent Benjamin."

"It wasn't me; it was Simon. He brought those poor people through the swamps so I could pick them up on shore..."

"Oh, was it now? It was Simon who disguised the *Raven* with a false third mast? It was Simon who fired the cannon from the deck of the *Raven*? It was Simon who kept the *Raven's* escape operation going even under fire? Was that Simon, Benjamin Pulaski?"

"Men died, Anthony. That was no parlor game. That was no game of whist among gentlemen for coins. Men died!"

"Thirty-three slaves escaped to the north," Anthony said. "It was the largest group escape in history."

"It should have been more. Two escaping slaves died, Anthony, as did the young son of a Quaker farmer in Pennsylvania."

"And that Quaker boy...Matthew Booker..." Anthony added.

Ben was surprised Anthony knew the boy's name.

"...was doing 'God's work.' Those were the words the boy's father said to me, as I understand he also said to you. Benjamin, I do not consider the death of men a trivial thing."

"Then why create situations that kill people?"

"Don't speak so naively, Benjamin, for I know you are not!" Anthony's voice rose. "We stood together in that Georgia swamp, during the long night with our backs against the cypress trees...out of ammunition...bayonets only. You, me, and the other scared young soldiers of our troop."

216

Ben closed his eyes to the memory. He was seventeen then and terrified.

"Our survival, Ben," Anthony said, "was your order to 'Strike!' when you sensed an enemy near us. We lunged as one, not seeing a damned thing, but trusting you. I was the lieutenant. You were the sergeant. But they trusted you. I trusted you. "

"Enough of that, Anthony. I do not want to be responsible for people dying."

They sat in silence a long moment.

"Benjamin, I am told that the rice plantations of Georgetown lose twenty to thirty slaves, 'field hands' as they refer to them there, to fever each year."

Ben said nothing, slowly nodding yes to Anthony's comment.

"One of my accountants says," Anthony continued, "that thirty 'field hands' only represents 0.15 percent of the total property books among their 20,000 slaves. Said another way, each year 99.85 percent of those slaves live."

Ben stood, knocking over his chair, and left the room, speaking over his shoulder, "Go to Hell, Anthony."

Anthony sighed and tapped several drum rolls on the dusty tabletop with his fingertips.

Ben returned to the room and yanked up his chair from the floor, slammed its legs onto the bricks and sat in front of Anthony, scowling.

"Tell me about the gunpowder, Anthony. Tell me everything! If you hold back one piece of information and I learn of it, so help me, God, it will end our friendship."

Anthony smiled and pulled several folded documents from within his coat.

Sonja was standing on the Havre de Grace docks, holding Alisha's hand when Abraham came to untie the rowboat. Sonja and Alisha were dressed in matching tan jackets and canvas trousers. Abraham's eyes kept flashing to their trousers.

"Good morning, Mrs. Pulaski." He scanned the bay in a quick glance. "Is the *Raven* due back this morning?"

Sonja smiled. "No, Abraham, I am waiting for you."

"Me?"

"I want you to teach me how to run our Ugly steamboat."

"Well...um...I...I don't know..." Abraham stuttered.

"Do you think I cannot learn it? Cannot steer it?"

"Of course, um, I'm sure you can, ma'am..."

Alisha twisted her head back and forth watching them, smiling red-cheeked, enjoying the moment.

"But a woman should not do such a thing, is that what you think, young man?"

"No.No.No. Not at all, Mrs. Pulaski, it's just that...well, Mr. Pulaski..."

"That what? Do you think I need my husband's permission to operate a boat? A boat that belongs to a company of which I am a full partner? Is that what you think?"

Abraham blew out his breath. "I think if I let you get hurt, Mr. Pulaski would kill me!"

She released Alisha's hand and folded her arms, raising her chin. Alisha made the same movement, still smiling.

"Is the steamboat so dangerous that at any moment it would explode and kill you? And only your bravery allows you to go aboard?"

He smiled. "Almost anything could kill a

man...could kill a person...if it is not operated properly."

"And you do not know how to operate our steamboat...properly?"

"No. Of course, I operate it properly."

She smiled. "So, Abraham, teach me how to operate my steamboat properly, so I will not blow up, and my husband will not kill you."

He sighed and motioned for Sonja and Alisha to join him in the rowboat. He placed Alisha in the bow and held his hand out for Sonja.

As she stepped into the boat, Abraham asked, "Would you care to row, Mrs. Pulaski."

Sonja tilted her head and examined the oars with a frown. "Yes. Yes, I would. You sit there in the stern and..." she turned to Alisha and smiled, "and...I will row us to our steamer."

It was not the first time Sonja had pulled oars on a rowboat, but it was the first time in a few years. Abraham remained stone-faced when she missed a few of the initial strokes and splashed him with water, but soon they moved smoothly toward the *Ugly Boat* in a satisfactory rhythm of rowing.

"I hear we have added two more barges to out little fleet, Abraham."

"Yes, ma'am. The *Lapidum* and the *Adam Tuttle*."

"Did Ben name the last one?" she asked.

Abraham nodded 'yes'. "Mr. Pulaski brought a gold coin he said Mrs. Stewart gave him for that barge, and nailed it to its stern post."

Sonja pulled the oars in silence.

On board the *Ugly Boat*, Abraham asked them both. "Are you prepared to get dirty?"

Both Sonja and her smaller mirror-image nodded their heads emphatically while tight golden curls bounced next to their faces like metal springs, and two sets of sky blue eyes sparkled.

The four tandem barge captains stood on their decks, checking the security of lines binding the eight barges together as the *Ugly Boat* pulled them south down the Bay. Recognizing the new crewmen on the

Ugly Boat the four young men planted broad smiles on their faces and traded animated waves with Alisha.

Sonja kept her attention glued to Abraham's every move when she was not checking on Alisha. She had agreed to observe only on this first trip, although halfway down toward Annapolis, Abraham allowed her to pilot the boat for a few miles. She held herself erect at the wheel, showing Abraham her serious intention at her task, although her heart was pounding in excitement, and deep inside her a giggly little girl wanted to scream in pleasure. Alisha, however, had no such constraints, and her giggles filled the air with the steam and the smoke and the steam whistle's scream of pure joy.

Abraham slowed the paddles as they entered the mouth of the Severn River, and steered north.

"Three openings will be to the south, on our left," Abraham told Sonja.

He pointed out the mouth of Spa Creek and the entrance to Annapolis Harbor as they passed the point where workers were putting the finishing touches on the new Naval Academy, preparing for it's opening in the coming October. Next, he pointed out the opening to College Creek.

"St. John's College is up that way," he said

As they approached the third opening, he blew the steam whistle three times and stopped the paddles.

"This is Weems Creek," he said. "Three blows to let the collier know coal is coming, and signal the barge captains to get out the poles and start untying all the lines."

The barges drifted up against the stern of the *Ugly Boat* and bumped gently against the thick knotted hemp bumper guards hanging down.

"If you will kindly stay on board, I need to assist them."

Abraham pulled up the loose tow line and looped it around two short upright posts at the stern. With the first two barges snug against the steamboat, Abraham stepped down onto the deck of the barges and made his way to the farthest barge. There, he picked up one of the long poles and took a position near the edge. He slipped his pole into the water, adding his push to the others. Slowly, one of the two barges at the end moved away from the pack as the men on it pushed their poles against the creek bottom. They poled slowly up the stream until the barge slipped out of view behind a warehouse near the bank.

From the *Ugly Boat*, Sonja could not see what was happening and had to wait almost an hour before the barge moved back down the stream into view, sitting higher in the water. A stout line hung down from its upstream end and floated in the water behind them. Abraham excitedly pointed to the line and yelled something, but she could not hear him. The captains poled the empty barge back to the pack and tied it on at the end. They then pulled the wet line from the water and tied it to the end of the next barge. Abraham waved his hand to an unseen person in the warehouse upstream. The short whistle echoed off the creek, and the wet line popped out of the water, and the next barge moved upstream, trailing its own tow line behind it in the water. Abraham ran to the stern of the *Ugly Boat*, flapping his hand to attract Sonja.

"They have a mule steam engine," He said, sounding like a child at Christmas opening gifts.

"A what?"

"A mule steam engine, a steam windlass. A little steam engine that winds up the rope pulling the barges. We don't have to pole them in anymore!! One of their men will bring out the tow rope in a skiff to tie on the first barge. All we have to do is pull it back!"

He ran back to the group of men standing on the next barge watching the second one move up the creek and patting each other on the back. In half an hour the men began pulling on the rope left behind by the barge and brought it bobbing down the creek to them, where it was exchanged for a full one. Abraham directed the captains to begin tying the empty barges onto the stern of the *Ugly Boat*, in a slow rotation that took full barges up the stream and empty barges down the stream to be re-tied in the new empty pack. In four hours they were finished and paddled down the Severn River to the Annapolis Harbor.

Once in the harbor, Abraham piloted the steamer toward the southern bank in a broad swing to bring the barges behind him. The end of the main dock that jutted out like a pier. He stopped the paddles, allowing the barges to kiss up to the stern of the *Ugly Boat*, where two captains quickly wrapped the tow rope around the sternposts to shorten the length between them. Abraham added power to the paddles and slowly moved forward, checking his distance again and again as he brought the sides of the barges to the edge of the dock. He released steam and stopped the paddles again while captains looped lines around the dock bollards. The steamboat and train of barges were longer than the width of the pier there. The last barge was still sticking halfway out into the opening to the harbor, and the *Ugly Boat* was blocking a boat ramp on the other side.

The barge captains chuckled to each other and took off their hats to Abraham and bowing. Abraham smiled broadly and blew out a long breath.

He turned to Sonja with a half smile. "I've never docked eight barges before." He waved at the captains, answering their salutes. "The barge pack is sixty feet longer than usual."

Sonja's eyes went wide as she admired the docking maneuver Abraham had accomplished. She smiled at him and shook his hand.

"If the harbormaster sees this, he may not like it," Abraham said.

As soon as he had spoken, one of the captains yelled his name. "Abe! Harbormaster is coming!"

Abraham shrugged his shoulders and grinned. "We need to load other cargo that Mr. Pulaski has already arranged." Then he frowned and lowered his voice, repeating a statement she had heard from Ben numerous times. "An empty barge is a wasted barge."

"You need to add another barge, Abraham," Sonja said.

"More?" he asked with a frown.

"Nine barges, three long and three wide."

His eyes went wide, and his frown shifted to a smile. "Yes! That would make the pack shorter and yet carry even more coal!"

"Can the *Ugly Boat* pull nine?" Sonja asked.

"Yes, she can... The engine can..." he frowned, "Mmm, we might need to strengthen the paddles...Yes...we can do that!"

While Abraham respectfully received the admonishments and warnings from the Harbor Master, the captains directed the line of stevedores and store clerks bringing crates and barrels for the barges.

Sonja was still exuberant, but Alisha was asleep in her arms when she stepped from the *Sarah* onto the wall of the lock at Lapidum and carried her up to their house. The sun was setting over the ridge behind their farm, and the sky was turning gray. Several of the lower leaves in oak trees were already becoming brown, and the first star peeked between the leaves as she mounted the steps. There was a note tacked to the porch post, but she did not stop to read it and took Alisha into the kitchen and sat her in a chair while Sonja lit a lamp. Alisha whined a little as Sonja washed off the coal dust finger marks on her face and then Sonja took her to her room.

Sonja returned to the kitchen to take the washcloth to her face and hands and then went back out on to the porch to pull down the note. She walked wearily into the kitchen and sat at the table, resting her arms on her elbows and holding the note up to the light to read it.

By Order of the Tidewater Bank and
Trust Company, You are violating
Maryland Law by inhabiting a domicile
without permission from the owners,
nor paying rent to said owners. You are
required to vacate the premises

within ten days or suffer the legal
consequences of fines and or
imprisonment.
Signed,
Lydia W. Binterfield
President
Tidewater Bank & Trust Co.

Sonja went into her bedroom and retrieved the new oak box Ben had brought home for her and took it into the kitchen. Then she reached up onto the top shelf and brought down his bottle of rum and half filled a nearby coffee cup. She drank down the rum in three gulps, then sat at the table, opened the box and lifted out the Colt Patterson.

She sniffed back the alcohol vapors and gripped the handle. "I thought that woman was gone!"

Ben leaned on the stern rail of the *Raven*, enjoying the view of the ship's waves catching the last golden light from the setting sun. The voyage from Charleston had been without heavy wind or hateful weather. The ten passengers ambled about the deck, still nervous at the approach of a white man, and grouped in knots of threes and four. Ben had once envisioned moments of jubilation when escaping slaves hid away from slavery and sailed out to sea, but he had learned that was never enough. They would not feel free until they crossed into a place they knew was without slavery.

Warren was taking a turn at the wheel, a fresh air reward for his excellent meals on a day when another crew member cooked. Warren was the only one who enjoyed his cooking days, but the crew shared the duty to keep him happy. The crew had decided that an appreciated cook would prepare better meals than a soured cook, and would probably never poison them on purpose.

Edward approached Ben, smoking a cigar he had purchased in Charleston. He fingered the cigar in front of Ben, regarding its appearance.

"It's a Cuban cigar, Ben. They say it is the best tobacco because Cuban women roll them on their legs."

Ben smiled and turned to face him. "Sure smells different from Maryland tobacco. How much did it cost you?"

"Fifteen cents."

"Good Lord, Edward!" Ben said. "For fifteen cents you could buy a whole supper in a good Havre de Grace tavern." Then he chuckled, adding, "Of course, I can't say whether the biscuit dough would be rubbed on anyone's leg or not."

Ben laughed. Edward turned away, scratching behind his ear.

"Well," Edward said. "I like it."

He stuck his cigar between his teeth and raised his chin. Clasping his hands behind, he strutted primly toward the bow, thick puffs of cigar smoke slipping downwind from him and out to sea.

"Maybe the fish will like it," Ben muttered to himself.

At that moment a whale surfaced not far from the ship, giving out a great exhale, blowing air from its hole in a high spray that reached several feet in the air.

"Maybe not," Ben said, laughing out loud. Some of the passengers turned toward Ben's laughter, but Edward did not.

28

Mamie Stewart paced back and forth in the kitchen. The crumpled notice tacked to her front door still gripped in her hand. She stopped and re-read it.

"...without the permission of the owner?? I am the damned owner!"

"Was there something you needed, Mamie?" Sissy asked.

"No, I was talking to myself."

"More like you were cussin' at yourself."

"Here," Mamie said and handed her the notice. "It was tacked to our front door when I came back from the Post Office."

Sissy read the note slowly. "What is a d-o-m-i-c-i-c-l-e?"

"Domicile. It is a word for a house, used by lawyers and cheats."

"Vacate?" Sissy mumbled as she continued to read the notice. "Mrs. Binterfield is trying to kick you out of your own house?"

"I heard she was back. It didn't take her long to start causing trouble."

While they talked, James Williamson entered the Pink House and walked to the sound of their voices.

"Good afternoon, Ladies. I heard your voices and just came around to say hello on my way up to my room."

"Mr. Williamson," Mamie called to him. "Would you kindly look at this notice from your bank," she said handing him the paper.

"What notice...Oh no. What will she try next, to create havoc in this town?" He handed the note back to Mamie. "Mrs. Stewart, I assure you that this...idiocy did not come from my bank. My sister...my half-sister, has gone too far. I knew she was trying - "

Mamie straightened her back. "Trying what, James?"

James sighed. "She is bringing several lawsuits against me, trying to regain her property."

Sissy's eyes went wide, and she brought her hand up to her mouth. "Oh, Lord. No."

"I have two attorneys drafting responses to refute her claims," James said. "This may take several months to put down, though."

"In the meantime," Mamie started.

"In the meantime, she is not free to act. She must prove her case before a judge. Then there will be opportunities for redress..."

"Oh Lord," Sissy cried, "She can't take me back. She can't! My momma went to South Carolina with her, so I could be free. She can't take me back now!"

Mamie pulled her into a hug as Sissy cried. "I promise you, Sissy. I will get you north before I will stand by and let that witch drag you back. I promise."

Sissy stepped back. "The law is for white people. You can't promise me that. Slave catchers all the time going up into Pennsylvania and bringing back runaways."

"Then we will go to Canada, Sissy," Mamie said.

James folded his arms. "There may be something else we can do. Something that could stop this nonsense sooner rather than later." He pointed at Mamie. "Can you cancel dinner one night this week?"

"Why? Why would I do that?"

"I want you to plan a dinner for another guest and me, but you must pretend it will be for a full dining room."

Aaron was sweeping the floor in the chapel when the priest found him.

"Ahh, there you are, Aaron. There is an American ship in the harbor. The man who buys supplies for them says they are short-handed. You must go there and sign on to that ship."

"I want to stay here, Padre," Aaron said.

"Yes, my son, I am sure that feeling is real to you right now, but you must do something with your life. If you do not work, you will spend all your time crying for your Maggie."

"I want to stay here and sweep," Aaron said.

"No, you don't, but if you stay and sweep long enough, you will be unable to do anything else. Go back to your home. Take Maggie in your heart, but do something she would be proud you are doing. She did not marry a floor sweeper. Go! Sign on to that ship."

Two hours later, Aaron walked up the gangplank to the Merchant Ship *General Harrison*.

"I need men to climb the ratlines and set my sails," the first mate said.

"I can do anything on a ship you need done, sir," Aaron said.

The first mate spun the ledger around so Aaron could sign his name. In the left-hand column next to the space he was to sign, Aaron read the words 'Able-bodied Seaman'. He signed his name and handed the pen back to the First Mate.

"How are you called?"

"Aaron. Where do I find my bunk?"

"You won't be in it that much, Aaron," he said pointing a finger toward the bow. "But you follow Smitty there, and he'll show you where it's at."

Aaron picked up the small seabag given to him by the priest turned, tossed it over his shoulder and walked toward Smitty.

"Hey," the first mate called, "Don't you want to know where we're sailing?"

Aaron answered over his shoulder, "No."

Moments later another man came up the gangplank pushing a cart full of bulky canvas bags. "Mail," he said.

"Take it two decks down to the Boson near the main cargo hold. He'll lock it in the mail room. It'll get to San Francisco in about two weeks – unless we sink," the First Mate said with only half a smile.

228

An early autumn was in the air over the Susquehanna Flats when the *Raven* dropped anchor off Havre de Grace. Ben had still not shared with Edward all the details of Anthony's plan, but Edward did know they were gaining government shipping contracts. Ben left the crew assignments to Edward and made his way to the Canal Basin just in time to catch a ride on one of his new barges, the *Margaret*. The tandem barge in front was the *Sarah*. There had been no news of Aaron after Norfolk. David Booker was the barge captain, who brought him up to date on the happenings within the Pulaski Shipping Company.

"She's operating the *Ugly Boat*?" he said, then smiled as he shook his head in wonder. "She never fails to surprise me."

"Us, too, Mr. Pulaski. She is not like any other mother I know of."

"No, she is not," Ben said.

He continued to smile, smelling the air in deep breaths, and letting the world slide by while David handled the barge. David was still satisfied that he did not work the *Ugly Boat*, and even more so now that Helen was with child. Ben gave him a hearty handshake and several pats on the back over the news. Ben told him of his own experiences at the births of his sons.

"There is no experience like it," he said, "A father's proudest moment."

David turned away. "Pray God that Helen fares better than poor Maggie and Sarah."

"Most do," Ben added, then fell into the silence that had wrapped around David.

At Lapidum, Ben said his 'good-bye' and 'thank you' to David then made his way to his farm. He lingered next to the barn, taking in the view of his house and front slope, then up on the porch he stopped again to view the river, savoring the moment. The front door was snatched open, and Sonja charged out pointing a pistol at his face. Her face was a snarling scowl.

"What the God damn hell..." she said, then halted in

mid-step when she recognized Ben and thrust the pistol down by her side.

Ben was frozen in his position, in wide-mouthed surprise.

"Oh, Ben. I am so sorry, I thought...I thought you were someone sent by Lydia."

"So she is back after all, is she," he said, placing his hands on her shoulders. "I see she has already pushed you to the edge."

"Can I come out, Momma," Alisha called from her bedroom.

"Yes, honey," Sonja answered, and slipped the pistol into the pocket of her apron.

"Need to get you a holster," Ben said as he knelt in the doorway to greet Alisha.

"I am so sorry, Ben, I-"

Alisha squealed with delight, "Papa! Papa! Papa!" and threw herself into his arms.

Ben stood up, spinning them both around, kissing the small of her neck and making her giggle. He reached out with one hand and grasped Sonja's. "Come on girls," he said and took them into the front room, kicking the door closed with his heel.

Grinning into his daughter's face, Ben said, "Alisha, your momma has become a gunslinger."

He chuckled, trading smiles with Sonja. Sonja slapped him gently on his arm and pulled them both into the kitchen. When Alisha settled down, they had dinner together, then both Ben and Sonja knelt by Alisha's bed while she said her nightly prayers. Alisha lay under her covers, still awake playing a while longer with her dolls until the nightfall came. In the kitchen, Sonja handed Ben the notice.

He sighed. "That bitch. Will she never leave us alone? Has George Milton seen this?"

"Of course, Ben. I took it to him the next day. He said he had to review the documents James Williamson had signed to cancel our debt, and then he was going to meet with James."

That night they lay together with the moonlight shining through the knitted lace curtains, holding each other tightly, each shrouded in their separate worries. When she spoke, she did not bring up her own problems but described Alisha's latest activities and accomplishments. He remarked on the courage of his daughter and her mother and did not speak of gunpowder or Anthony's new plans for the *Raven*, and him.

In Washington City, Congressman John Slidell readied himself for bed, sipping brandy shipped to him from friends in New Orleans. The year was going exceptionally well. The votes for Texas admission had passed quickly back in March. It was all carried in the more important newspapers. He smiled that his mention of that news impressed the schooner captain.

Ah well, he thought. *Sometimes politics is more theater than negotiations.*

President Tyler had managed that even before President Polk took office. And now President Polk had offered to name him ambassador to Mexico. It was a hollow appointment, he knew. Mexico had already severed ties with the United States last year when word came that Texas was coming in. They even threatened to declare war over it then. It was doubtful they would receive him as Ambassador.

Still, winter in Mexico rather than Washington would be enjoyable. Wait until they hear we expect them to move the southern border of Texas down to the Rio Grande! And our illustrious President expects them to sell the northern half of their country to us! They will just have to choke it all down. Ambassador. Ambassador Slidell. It does have a beautiful ring to it!

In another part of the city, General Winfield Scott shared a late night meal in the White House with President James Polk, at the President's request.

"General, in light of the reluctance of the Mexican government to see the sense of establishing a common border at the Rio Grande, we may need to...mollify...their confused sense of sovereignty over lands that clearly should go to Texas."

"Yes, Mr. President. And how do you see that happening, sir?"

"Well, General, I have received suggestions from members of Congress that we should be prepared for Military intervention. Remember, Mexico threatened to declare war on us just last year when Texas admission was considered in the House. We cannot allow ourselves to be...intimidated by other countries. President Monroe showed us our obligation in this hemisphere."

"We are already strengthening some of our shore forts along the Atlantic, sir," Polk said. "A plan is already approved to continue that project with our southern shores along the Gulf of Mexico."

"It should be the Gulf of America, General. And maybe we can make it so, together, but for now, we must be prepared to move our Army where it is needed."

"We are already developing preliminary plans, sir."

"Maybe they should be more advanced than just preliminary, General."

"Yes, sir." He raised his wine glass. "To your health, sir."

Polk raised his glass. "To yours, General. And to a strong America, stretching from the Atlantic to the Pacific, without the damned British or Mexicans in our way."

"Y-yes, of course, sir. Atlantic to Pacific."

In Philadelphia, the three executives of the Argyle Corporation were relaxing in the library of the host member. Anthony outlined his current plan for the Schooner *Raven*.

"We are each putting forward all the funds we can. And we know the moderate Abolitionist Societies no longer see us as peers, but rogues."

One of the other two raised his brandy glass. "To the Rogues, then, gentlemen. To hell with the timid."

The others joined him. Anthony continued.

"My plan has multiple facets. We want to expand our rescue of slaves, minimize the continuing effort to buy them in Charleston, but include Charleston among the rescues, expand operations into New Orleans and shores of the deepest south, and keep the *Raven* self-supported."

"That is an ambitious plan, Anthony," one of the other two said.

"It isn't a plan at all," said the third. "It is a wish, a desire. I have heard no details."

"And you will not, cousin. The next steps will be far more dangerous than all the previous for the *Raven*, and for my friend Ben Pulaski."

"How much of it does he know?"

"All of it," Anthony said, "Except your names and your businesses here in Philadelphia."

His cousin blew out his breath and rolled his eyes. "Don't get yourself killed, cousin, or our illustrious Captain Pulaski on our 'revengeful *Raven*'. To your success."

The other two raised their glasses. Anthony set his down on the narrow table by his chair, the glass still half full. He rose, leaning on his cane.

"I suggest we not meet again," Anthony said. "Unless there is a critical need. I will assume full operational and financial responsibility for this project and will continue to operate under the title of the Argyle Corporation. I suggest you disconnect yourselves from it, as best you can."

"Oh cousin," he said, "You make me worry."

"With this project, cousin, I worry myself."

He shook their hands and left the room. Downstairs in the foyer, the butler helped him with his coat and hat. "Good to see you again, Mr. Renowitz."

"No. You did not see me again. I was not here."

Anthony locked eyes with the butler for a long moment.

"No, sir. I did not," the butler said. "I don't believe I have seen you here in a very long time."

Anthony patted him on his arm and smiled, then

left the house, walking quickly through the chilled falling rain to his waiting enclosed carriage.

29

Ben and Sonja finished a late breakfast in their home along the canal while the sun began its creep over the treetops across the river.

"Must be after seven," Ben said, squinting at the sun. "Can't remember the last time I slept so late."

"Edward is getting the *Raven* ready, Ben. Let him do his job."

Ben rose from the table and stretched. "Where is our little hurricane this morning?"

"She was up at dawn, excited to go up the canal with David. She and Patty Price will go together. They'll spend the night with Helen Booker at...at the York Furnace house and then come back late tomorrow."

Ben lost his smile. "Tell her I said 'goodbye'."

Sonja noticed his expression and reached up to touch his cheek with her fingertips. "She told you that before you got up, but you were snoring in a deep sleep. I told her I would tell you she said 'Bye.'"

He kissed her gently and sighed. "We Pulaskis are always on the go."

"Well this Pulaski is not happy she is being left at the dock again, while you go off a'sailing," she said with a pouty half smile, "even if it is just a two plank dock at the edge of our yard."

He held her in his arms. "Too many new parts to this trip, Sonja. Maybe not the best time to introduce Alisha to ocean sailing..."

...or loading barrels of gunpowder with a crew that has never shipped it before, he thought.

"Tell me again about those parts, Ben."

"Empty to Annapolis, crates and big barrels to Norfolk, those unloaded in Norfolk, then more crates and little barrels to Charleston, 'passengers' from

Charleston to Bermuda, and more little barrels to New Orleans. Then we wait a while for Anthony to cook up more mischief for me."

Sonja believed all the 'little barrels' were rum or corn whiskey.

She stepped back, showing a frown and crossing her arms. "The last part is the part I don't like."

"I agreed to let him direct our ship for his larger plans, as long as we make enough profit in the end," Ben said.

"But, to simply wait..."

"We rarely wait long, Sonja. Maybe a day or two..."

She fought to suppress her smile. "In New Orleans, though, Benjamin. I've heard about those Creole women of New Orleans. And you will be down there by yourself...unattached for the moment..."

Ben released his laughter and let it echo throughout the house, then drew her close in another hug. "I can only handle one gun-toting tigress in my life, Mrs. Pulaski. I have no reserve of energy to spare for another! Besides, my brother will keep me honest."

"Your brother? I suspect he is the worst sort of dandy with the women...And when did you begin to call Edward your brother?" She peered deeply into his eyes.

"I know I was reluctant to accept him when he came back into my life..."

She pushed his hands away and planted hers on her hips.

"Reluctant? Benjamin Pulaski, you pointed a gun at him!"

"Well..." He faced away for a short moment. "I held a hatred for my half-brother for many years. You know that. I was ashamed of the affair my father had with his mother. I resented him destroying my vision of my father, and stealing from us when Pa brought him into our house."

"But not anymore?"

He shrugged his shoulders. "We have shared

236

experiences as men. He has proved to be honorable and dependable...No. Not anymore. He is my brother and the First Mate on my ship."

She reached out and patted his arm softly. "Our ship."

He grinned. "Our ship."

"I just wished the trip would not be so long. You will miss Christmas here...If we are still here..."

"You will be here. George Milton says Lydia will not succeed in her lawsuit.

Sonja's frown told Ben she did not believe him.

<hr>

Just before noon, the crew of the *Raven* finally drug up the bow anchor and sailed south down the Chesapeake Bay, expecting to be in Annapolis in only a few hours. The brisk October sky was dotted by cotton ball clouds, pushed thin at their southern edges by the wind. They were anticipating an overnight stay in Annapolis, especially Edward, who had developed a fondness for a particular lady there. He had spent a great deal of time with her during the previous winter and hoped to rekindle their relationship. As the ship neared Turkey Point, at the mouth of the Elk River, Ben ordered Edward to steer into the River. He gave Ben several questioning expressions as he ordered sails trimmed while he spun the wheel to change their course. Ben remained stoic.

Once heading northeast, Ben directed Edward to keep the ship in the center of the river. Just minutes later, amid growing stares from the crew, the *Raven* drew near the mouth of the Bohemia River. In the open waters formed by the two rivers, Ben ordered all sails lowered and the anchor dropped. Then he motioned for the crew to gather around him.

"We are not going to Annapolis for rum or Norfolk for gunpowder. We are going to Wilmington, Delaware, by way of the Canal. We will pick up the gunpowder there."

"That'll be some tight sailing, Cap'n," Daniel said. "Only time I ever went through there, we had to be tugged."

Ben smiled, "And that is how we are going through it. A steam tug will be here shortly, to take us all the way to Wilmington. People from the gunpowder mill will load it for us."

Relief swept the faces of the crew. None had loaded gunpowder before, except Warren, who had been plagued with questions since the moment Ben had described their next cargo.

"We still have to take care of it, and we still have to unload half of it in Charleston. Once we have our new passengers, we will sail to New Orleans. You will have two days to spend your time exploring the city...then we go to Cuba," Ben said.

Men shared happy murmurings.

"Well at least we're still going to New Orleans," Alistair said.

Edward remained sullen but said nothing. A steam whistle blew its long high note as a steam tug slapped the water with its paddles, charging down the river toward them. It approached the *Raven* at full speed, then made an impressive circle around the ship. On the side of the tug, its name was displayed in carved letters on a polished oak sign. The cut of the letters was filled in with scarlet paint, *"Renowitz."* Standing beside the tug's captain, in the open doorway of the pilot house was Anthony Renowitz, displaying a toothy grin like a child who had just chucked a snowball at a playmate.

The tug halted near the bow of the *Raven* and two of the tug's crewmen attached a bundle of canvas to the cargo boom hook. Anthony stepped into the middle of the bundle. As the hook rose above him, a wooden ring drew up the cloth around him, like a bag rising from the deck, until he was cuddled up to his armpits inside the canvas bag. Anthony gripped two of the four lines that held the contraption to the hook as the boom raised him off the deck. The boom swung over to the *Raven*, showing a hard wooden plank attached at the bottom on which Anthony stood, and set him down near Ben. The

238

bag collapsed onto the deck around Anthony's ankles. He stepped out of it, tipping his hat toward the crew and bowing. Then with a broad smile, he extended his hand toward the bag, like a stage performer introducing a supporting actor.

Alistair leaned close to Wyatt and whispered. "Seen it before. Usually just for women and the infirm. Most men have too much pride to use it."

Wyatt shrugged his shoulders. "Better than slipping on a wet ladder rung and dropping into the Bay. Seen that, too."

They both chuckled but joined with the Captain in applauding his old friend.

Ben and Anthony shook hands then Anthony shook hands with each of the *Raven*'s crew.

"Forgive an old man for his peculiarities, but I'm not as agile as I once was."

He patted Alistair on his shoulder as he shook his hand, leaning close, "But my hearing is extraordinary," he said with a warm smile, then slapped his arm like a shipmate and chuckled. The bow cable was run out to the tug, and the *Raven* moved stately into the water that was once called Back Creek, but had become the mouth of the Chesapeake and Delaware Canal, the 'C&D.'

Anthony stood with Ben near the wheel. Edward stood behind the other wheel, while the rest of the crew watched the countryside slip by from the bow. Anthony drew Ben's attention and directed his eyes toward Edward. Ben nodded yes, then turned to Edward, "This will be for your ears as well, Eddie, but maybe not for the others."

Edward gave a quick smile and stepped next to Ben. Anthony raised his eyebrows at Ben in silent question, but Ben nodded, yes, again. Anthony shrugged his shoulders and began to speak.

"Slidell is to be named Ambassador to Mexico, or plenipotentiary – whatever the hell they call it- early next month. His goal there will be to convince the Mexican President to sell the U.S. everything from Texas

239

to California."

"Can that be done?" Ben asked.

"We bought Louisiana, didn't we?" Anthony responded.

"Thought the Mexicans hated us," Edward said.

Ben nodded to Edward, glad to see him willing to join the conversation and hoping it might take the sting of keeping their destination secret from him.

"They do," Anthony said. "Well, the Mexican government probably hates us, but Texas was founded with the help of Mexicans who joined them fighting Santa Anna. Still, they both will likely hate us later..."

"And how does all that matter for *Raven*?" Ben asked.

"Government contracts for gunpowder. Those already under contract will make fortunes when war breaks out, even as hundreds more sign up."

Ben's face remained expressionless, leaving it up to Anthony to decide how much of his intrigue he will share. Anthony regarded Edward a long moment, glanced at Ben, then sighed.

"Can I trust you, Edward?"

Edward frowned. "What has Ben told you about me?"

"Quite a bit, but I want to look into your eyes when you answer my question, and I want you to answer it right God damned now."

"I will never betray my family or my country, Anthony," Edward said, using Anthony's given name for the first time.

Anthony faced Edward in silence, his face neutral, examining Edward's eyes intently. He took in a deep breath and slowly blew it out, then took in another.

"Our government has complete faith that Mexico will refuse to sell the land. It will also refuse to accept an Ambassador from this country. Mexico will protest, threaten war again and threaten to re-take Texas."

"And what will the United States do?" Ben asked.

"Execute a plan it developed last year." Anthony eyed Ben, then Edward. "We will invade Mexico." Looking directly at Ben, he added, "Using the gunpowder you deliver to New Orleans...just like Jackson used the gunpowder your father delivered in '14."

Ben blew out his breath as at the landscape slipped by. How odd it is to be so close to shore with the sails furled. He thought. Yet moving as if we were running before the wind while we actually push against it.

***

Judge Jessup accepted the glass of brandy offered by James Williamson. They sat alone in the parlor, chatting amiably and listening to the crackle of the small fire burning in the Franklin stove nearby.

"I hope the dinner was satisfactory, your honor," James said.

"It was marvelous, James. Mamie has always had magic in her kitchen, and I suspect Sissy may share in that magic – though, I must admit, the magic was challenged the moment I realized the dinner party I had come to was in truth a private dinner with you."

"A private dinner that never occurred, your honor, since neither of us is here tonight," James said, raising his glass in salute, which was joined by the judge.

The judge took in a deep breath as he unbuttoned his vest and patted his stomach. "Now that my mind is prepared to listen properly, I ask that you repeat our arrangement, so that I hear it bluntly, without the distraction of surprise."

James smiled. "Your burdensome loan from the National bank, which was secured by your land holdings to cover your gambling debts, will be paid off by you, using money that I will deliver to you. As a well known sporting man, coming into a bank with a thick wad of bills will only generate envy, not suspicion."

"Yes. Go on, please, sir," Jessup said.

"You will find no merit in the lawsuit brought upon me by my half-sister, charging that I am illegally claiming majority ownership of the Tidewater Bank and

Trust Company."

Jessup nodded, yes.

"Kindly say the word, sir," James said.

"Yes. I will."

"You will find no merit in the lawsuit brought upon me by my half-sister, claiming partial ownership of the Tidewater Bank and Trust Company, nor any right to assume any executive position within the Tidewater Bank and Trust Company."

"Yes. I will."

"You will find no merit in the lawsuit brought upon me by my half-sister, charging me with misuse of corporate funds and property, contrary to any corporate bylaws."

"Yes, I will."

"You will find that unfounded rumors of her bloodline were based solely on the public utterance of a madman, now deceased. You will, in the future, rule favorably on any lawsuit brought by Mrs. Lydia Williamson Binterfield. You will refer to her as a white woman of impeccable reputation, against any knave uttering rumors attested to, or based on comments by, the murderer, Samuel Briscoe."

"Yes, I will, but to be quite 'honest' – no jest intended, James – why even bother supporting her charade? I was there that night when she was without her wig. I saw the rust-colored nappy hair..."

"I want to give her something she can consider of value, and it was an excellent idea from Mamie...Isn't that right, Mamie?"

Mamie stepped into the parlor, smiling. "Yes. I think Lydia would value that more than the Bank or her house...your house, James, if she could only have one but not the other two."

Judge Jessup stood up, his face turning crimson, gritting his teeth, glaring at James. "You have abused me, sir! If I were a younger man, it would be pistols at twenty paces!" He pointed his finger at Mamie, "You! You! You..." She stepped back away from the angry display directed at her.

James remained in his seat. "And I have no doubt you would have bested me on a field of honor, sir. But, Mamie shares in our secret, because you have saved her house for her."

"And you have manipulated me in front of a witness, Williamson!"

"A minor detail between co-conspirators, I assure you." James rose to his feet, still holding his brandy. "I only allowed Mamie to listen to our conversation to help relieve the tremendous angst she has endured, thinking Lydia was about to kick her out of her own house. She knows who her friends are, Judge, and we are among them."

Jessup took several deep breaths, then retrieved his brandy and gulped it down. He set the glass down and faced Mamie, bowing to her. "Your servant, Madam. Please forgive me for my rash behavior."

Mamie stepped before him and touched his cheek with her fingertips. "You have saved my home, Judge Jessup. You will always be my hero, sir, and will always be welcome to sample my kitchen magic," she said with a warm smile.

30

November 10, 1845.

Sonja cried in the front room of the Pulaski house in Lapidum. Mamie rose from her chair and came to her, embracing her, stroking her hair. "We are safe, sister," she whispered.

Alisha stood on the front porch at the doorway, hesitant to come in, still new to long periods of happiness and easily pulled back into dread. "Are you hurt Momma?" she asked.

Mamie turned to bestow a reassuring smile on the little girl who had come again into Sonja's life. Sonja threw her arms open, and Alisha rushed into them.

"No, Precious," Sonja answered inside their embrace. "Sometimes a woman can become so happy, that only tears can satisfy the moment." As she hugged her daughter, she reached out with one hand and grasped Mamie's. "Thank you, sister."

Mamie sat a long moment enjoying the scene of a mother and daughter wrapped in each other's arms. She closed her eyes and reached back to remember the feel of her mother when the world could be held at bay in her lap.

"So, I need to get back to my house. My lovely, lovely, house that is mine forever more, as is yours to you."

Sonja faced Mamie and sighed deeply, drying her eyes and smiled. "I was afraid that I had received too much happiness, Mamie, that fate would rip my home away in payment for Alisha."

Mamie chuckled. "Nonsense. There are no scales, only totals. Sometimes a beautiful flower sprouts from a cow patty. Enjoy your moment and don't get lost in the 'woods of coulds.'" She stood and stepped next to

Sonja and Alisha, stroking each and raising Alisha's chin with her fingertips. Locking her eyes with Alisha's, she said, "Just appreciate the flower's beauty...and watch where you step." She laughed and turned toward the door.

In Washington City, John Slidell made his way to the various offices of Congressional friends to say goodbye and wish them well, and thank them for their continued support of Texas annexation. The treaty with the nine-year-old Republic of Texas allowed the incoming new state to divide into five, if it chose, all of which would be slave states and push the balance of vote far into the southern advantage. He had resigned from his seat as Representative of Louisiana's First District to formally accept his appointment as Ambassador to Mexico from President Polk. His assignment was to convince the President of Mexico to accept a short list of what he knew the Mexican government would consider outrageous demands. He knew he would not succeed at that assignment, as did the President.

In Austin, Texas, plans were being expanded for the celebration of becoming the 28th star sewn onto the flag of the United States. Many were excited over the access to the United States economy as well as its Army. Rumors struck like lightning around the Republic carrying stories of a massive army growing in Mexico to retake Texas. The rumors were not all rumors. The Treaty of Velasco signed by Santa Anna defined the Texas southern border at the Rio Grande River and served as the basis for founding the Texas Republic in 1836. However, the treaty was rejected by the government in Mexico City. It only begrudgingly and temporarily tolerated a border at the Nueces River, 160 miles north of the Rio Grande, but continued to seek opportunities to re-take its territory. President Polk had promised the Texans he would move the U.S. Army into the region between the two rivers, once annexation was official.

At Fort Jessup in Louisiana, 25 miles from the

border of the Texas Republic and back in his home state, General Zachary Taylor listened impatiently to the oral reports of his senior staff. Supplies were slow in coming and what he had was dwindling faster than it could be replaced. The recruits were slow in coming. The transfer of Army units from other forts was delayed. The need for gunpowder was horrendously unsatisfied. He slapped his desktop.

"Damn it, Gentlemen. Light some fires! We are going to assemble an army worth leading, and it must be adequately manned and supplied. Now get back to your duties and throw some grease into the gears!"

Once alone in his office, he withdrew his copy of a Texas map. He sighed and held a magnifying glass over the small print along the Texas coast, then tapped a strip of land hard with his fingertip. After considering several locations, denoted by several different smudges on the map, he had decided on the spot with the darkest smudge. Corpus Christi. The body of Christ.

Ben hovered near his crew as they gently transferred the barrels of gunpowder to a waiting river barge near Drum Island. The low square boat offered plenty of deck space to set the barrels as the *Raven*'s cargo boom lowered them. The Charleston Harbor Master had sent word out with the pilot boat to instruct *Raven* not to tie up at the dock but move two miles up the Cooper River, away from the harbor. The water surface near the island was calm.

When they had unloaded half the cargo, the Army Lieutenant supervising the barge signed for it. Peacetime rank was slow to come, and the Lieutenant's beard held a few strands of gray.

"I understand this is only half your cargo, Captain," he said with a smile. "Where do you go next?"

Ben accepted his copy of the receipt. "After we dock at the harbor, we go to New Orleans."

The Lieutenant laughed. "It's a shame to waste our effort." He waved his hand over the barrels being covered with canvas by the barge crew. "More than likely a good bit of that will be going to New Orleans as well." He chuckled and shook his head. "Well, that's the Army for you. No use moving something once when you can move it twenty times and run the risk of moving it to the wrong place."

"Oh, Captain," the Lieutenant added. "I almost forgot to tell you. One, you can't moor at the Charleston wharf with gunpowder on board," he pointed down at his feet, "and two, you need to stay at anchor here. Your next cargo is being brought to you."

The *Raven* drifted slowly around her anchor for most of the day. The crew waited in foul moods, mumbling about the missed opportunity to spend time in Charleston.

"At least we go to New Orleans next," he said to them. "We will dock close to the city and stay two days there. I promise."

The sky was dimming from bright blue to sullen gray when a single-mast sloop sailed down the Cooper River and asked to come alongside.

"You Captain Pulaski?" the sloop captain asked. "We have your consignment property here."

Ben signed the receipt as nine slaves climbed aboard the *Raven*. Each had been given a thinned and tattered winter coat, and none had shoes.

"Take them below," Ben ordered.

"I'll need those manacles back," the sloop captain said as he climbed on deck near Ben. "I had to sign for them separate from the slaves. We got a shortage of 'em here. You got your own, right?"

Ben nodded that he did as he accepted the key and handed it to Edward, who then went below deck with it.

"Wouldn't want you to run out of these," Edward said a minute later as he handed them over.

The sloop captain laid them on the deck, separated them and counted. "Yep, nine," he said, then handed Ben an envelope. He began tossing the manacles one at a time to his crew before returning to his boat.

Back on his own deck, he turned toward Ben and touched the edge of his cap with his finger while the sloop's crew raised the mainsail.

Ben sighed as he opened the envelope.

Cuba, then New Orleans.
Dock under blue streamer.

Ben's shoulders sagged, and he blew out his breath. He clenched his teeth and turned to Edward. "Please raise anchor and set the sails. I will be back on deck in a few minutes."

Ben went down the stern ladderway to his cabin and sat in his chair behind his compact desk, resting his arms on the desktop and tapping his fingers on the wood.

Anthony, he thought *but did not allow himself to pursue a fitting statement.*

Someone tapped on the door. "What?" Ben snapped.

The cabin door flew open. Wyatt walked in awkwardly, a tattered coat sleeve wrapped under his chin against his neck. An angry black face rested its chin on Wyatt's shoulder and a matching hand held a knife tip against Wyatt's cheek.

Ben stood. "No need to hurt him," Ben said, "We are taking you..."

"You not taking me anywhere," the slave said. "I'm taking you!"

Ben held up his open hands. "You are going to freedom. That's why we are here. That man you have is part of my crew, and he has helped many people to freedom. We all have."

The man pointed the knife tip at Ben. "You a liar. I let this man go you hang me, or you put me back in chains. I'm freeing myself, or I gut this man like a pig."

Wyatt tried to speak, but the man tightened his hold around his neck.

248

"You shut up," the man ordered, then he motioned to Ben with his knife. "You git out here."

Ben moved to the door. The black man pointed down in the hold. "Git down there."

Edward, Warren, and Daniel stood with their arms raised, surrounded by the other slaves, all armed with knives. "You setting us free," the man with Wyatt said. He was obviously the leader of their rebellion.

"We are taking all of you to freedom," Ben said.

"You God damned right you are, Mistah," one of the group snarled.

Another slave came out of the kitchen holding a lit lantern. He spoke to the leader. "Let's see what they got in this boat."

"No!" Edward said. "Don't take that lantern near the barrels!"

A slave near Edward punched him in his mouth. "Shut up," he yelled, then turned to the man with the lantern. "Yeah, you look at dem barrels. They looks like whiskey barrels to me."

"That's gunpowder," Ben said. "You won't be free if you're all dead and you blow this ship to hell!"

The leader exchanged places behind Wyatt with another slave who flashed his own knife up to Wyatt's face. The leader carefully examined the barrels. "Blow out that lantern," he ordered, then pointed his knife at one of the other slaves, "Thomas, take one of those barrels up on deck." He turned to Ben, "You got any cannon on this boat?"

"Two," Ben said. "They're down in the belly for ballast."

The leader tilted his head and frowned, "I know boats. I sailed some before I got sold down here. Why are they down in the belly?"

"We only have half a load..."

"Why you didn't spread them out?"

"We needed to make room for you, so we could take you to freedom."

The leader grabbed Ben, spinning Ben in front of him and bringing his knife tip up beside Ben's eye.

"You move the wrong way, and I'll kill you. You believe me, 'Captain'?"

"Yes," Ben said.

"We're going on deck, and you're gonna prove what's in those barrels."

The leader walked Ben up the forward ladderway, the others shoving the crew up ahead of them, all walking in single file up the steps. As they stepped on deck, Thomas was nowhere to be seen.

"Thomas!" the leader called out, leaning forward to survey the deck.

The metallic click of a pistol sounded close to the leader's ear, and the end of a gun barrel poked hard against his temple.

"Let go of my captain," Alistair said, "and drop the fucking knife."

The leader dropped the knife and released his grip around Ben's neck. Then he shoved him onto the deck and swept the gun from Alistair's hand with his fist, driving the gun clattering along the deck. The leader opened his mouth in rage and leaned toward Alistair to attack, but Alistair shoved the barrel of another pistol into his mouth, scraping the skin at the back of his throat and cocking the hammer on the revolver.

Lord God, please have this gun loaded, Alistair thought.

Alistair grabbed the leader's collar and pulled him along, keeping the barrel in his mouth. Ben scrambled to pick up the fallen pistol while the rest of his crew filed out. As the slaves came up, Ben kept his gun trained on their faces as they stepped onto the deck, ensuring each man was aware of his situation. Daniel pulled a third pistol from Alistair's belt and pointed it at the slaves. As the last slave come into view of the others, he spun around and dashed down into the hold. It was the one who had held the lantern.

Warren jumped after him, "No you don't!"

In the hold, the slave ran into the galley and

250

pulled out the lantern. Warren propelled himself into the man, ducking his head down and ramming him in his stomach, driving him back into the galley, smashing him against the brick stove. The lantern was still lit and fell to the floor. The slave punched at it with his fist, trying to break the glass. Warren grabbed the coffee pot, still half full, but cold, and splashed it onto the lantern, putting out the flame. The slave tried to get up, but Warren slammed the coffee pot down on his head, knocking the man out, and denting the coffee pot.

He kicked the unconscious man. "That was a new coffee pot, you, you ...stupid!"

Ben had the slaves tied up, then released them one at a time to visit the head at the bow and be fed, under guard. It took two days on their way to Cuba to convince them they would be set free. Ben's most significant challenge was convincing their leader, Wallace, but he eventually believed Ben and his crew and helped convince the others. The man who had fought with Warren, James, remained sullen but committed to follow Wallace's lead, frequently touching the large lump on his head.

When they docked in Cuba, Ben made no mention of their gunpowder cargo. The ship in the next Berth was a Boston Whaler, trading whale oil for sugar. The first mate of the Whaler visited the *Raven* with a note, after which Ben and some of the crew escorted the slaves to the whaler, to the great and joyous relief of the *Raven*'s crew. Wallace stood at the railing of the whaler looking down at Ben for a moment. His face was without expression as he nodded to Ben, and then turned away. The joy among the Raven's crew lasted only seconds when Ben informed them that they must leave right away for New Orleans and must remain on the ship, except Warren, who was permitted a quick dash to purchase another coffee pot for the *Raven*. On their way to New Orleans, Ben arranged a solemn burial at sea for the dented coffee pot, but it failed to do much to raise morale. He was reluctant to make any promises regarding shore leave in New Orleans.

31

At last, they anchored in Lake Borgne near Fort Wood, with instructions to stay out of the long tail of the Mississippi River and Lake Pontchartrain. The green-amber water in the lake reminded Ben of the Susquehanna Flats. Ben laughed and pointed toward the northern shore as they entered the southern end of the Lake.

"My father ran his ship aground over there when I was a boy."

"How did that happen?" Edward asked.

"We were down here just before the British attacked, the winter of '14-'15. My father's ship, the *Osprey*, was rammed by a damaged gunboat, so he ran it ashore to save the gunpowder."

"Gunpowder?"

"Didn't our father tell you any of that?"

Edward shook his head 'no.' "You Pulaskis just can't stay away from trouble, can you?"

Ben smiled.

At least we are finally near New Orleans, Ben thought. *And I will give the crew shore leave for an entire week, to begin as soon as they finish unloading the gunpowder.*

Two days passed before the Army quartermaster was rowed out to their ship. The crew was still angry, and the fishing had been poor.

The quartermaster scrambled up the side of the *Raven* and saluted Ben.

"Second Lieutenant John M. Jones, sir. Acting Quartermaster for armament. I apologize for the delay in coming out, sir. I was just informed of my new duties this morning. Allow me to share what I know about this with you."

KINGDOMS IN THE MARSH

Ben sighed with disappointment when the quartermaster informed him General Zachary Taylor had commandeered the *Raven* for transport of gunpowder to the coast of Texas – at a site to be identified later. Furthermore, he was told, the *Raven* was to be loaded with all the gunpowder her holds would accept. A barge came out to the ship and transferred even more barrels than they had delivered in Charleston. Ben was then free to release his crew on shore leave. The ship would sit in an area that was being patrolled by the U.S. Navy, but still required one member on the ship at all times.

Ben released his crew, after setting up week-long rotations on board. He took the first rotation. Relief swept over their faces, and soon Ben was alone on the ship. He slept most of the first two days. The next five days were uneventful, interrupted only once when Lt. Jones came by to check on the ship. Ben was happy to see Edward come out at the end of the week. After a short conversation hearing some tales about antics of various crewmen, Ben slipped over the side and rowed to Fort Wood. At Fort Wood, the quartermaster invited Ben to join him for a meal. During the lunch, he learned that it would be at least three weeks before the Gunpowder would be sent to another location.

Jones gave a beaming smile when Ben told him of his son, Isaac, at West Point. "I was in the class of 41," he said. After the meal, Lt. Jones suggested Ben hire a river sloop from among the local Cajuns. "They are happy to take fellows into New Orleans over Lake Pontchartrain for a few pieces of silver. And if they should offer to take you to a cousin's house for a meal, do not miss the opportunity. The food here in Louisiana is amazing."

In New Orleans, Ben took a room in a hotel the first night, then the next day he found a room at a boarding house and sent a telegram to Anthony, then to Sonja. Anthony answered that very afternoon.

"You are on a federal contract. All costs are reimbursable. You should have stayed in the hotel! Enjoy! -A.R."

The stay in the boarding house was unsatisfying, but there was no problem with the house or the housekeeper. Since his imprisonment in China, Ben had never been away from Sonja for so long. Once he shared his address with Sonja, they began to exchange letters.

The housekeeper was an elderly lady who relied on her son to maintain the household and run errands. Erick was a pleasant man of quiet manner with modest expectations, who appeared happy to live there. His mother, Angela, reserved at first, but over the days revealed an outgoing personality. She had traveled well, and often spoke her mind, a trait not always appreciated by her departed sea captain husband, she informed Ben. Her friendliness warmed when she learned Ben had been a part of the Army defense of New Orleans in 1815.

"That rascal, Jackson," she cackled above sparkling gray eyes, her two bellies bouncing. "I tried my damnedest to get his attention, just to make my husband jealous, but he was absolutely in love with his wife. You didn't see that often...still don't, but I see it in you for your Sonja."

Ben spent Christmas Eve and Christmas day with Angela and Erick, sitting on the porch wearing a light coat in the mild winter, smoking his pipe, during the hours they were away at Mass.

On December 29th, the city celebrated the Annexation of Texas, and the new flag was raised over Fort Wood. Lt. Jones had sent for Ben and his crew with the news they were to sail the next morning. Ben scribbled a short letter to Sonja and left it for Erick to mail, before headed to Fort Wood.

"We are going to a place called Corpus Christie, Texas," Lt. Jones told Ben when he arrived.

"We?" Ben asked.

"Yes, Benjamin, I am assigned to General Taylor's army of occupation in Texas, where you can, at last, disgorge me and all that gunpowder in your ship, and run back to your family in Maryland."

At West Point, when the class of '46 returned from Christmas furlough, the cadets were informed that after graduation in June, many of them would likely be assigned to join the Army of occupation in Texas, to protect the country's new territory along the Rio Grande. The growing Mexican Army was common knowledge at the Point, though not as large as rumors suggested. The curriculum among military skills intensified as the instructors were driven to more considerable efforts to prepare their cadets for the reality of war.

In their room one evening in late January, Isaac Pulaski and Tom Jackson discussed their lessons regarding previous wars and battlefield tactics. Tom's blue eyes were intense when he referred to battles won by the charge.

"You've got to go at them, and don't let up until they are finished," he said with enthusiasm.

Then pulling himself back from his exuberance, he had them both kneel in a prayer for peace with Mexico. One of the other classmen, who rarely spoke to Isaac or Tom, George McClellan, passed the open door as they prayed. He stepped into the doorway.

"I hope you are praying to raise your grades, fellows. I hear you are at the bottom of the class," he declared, and then strutted away.

"Pompous ass," Isaac said.

Tom allowed a shy smile with his eyes sparkling and wagged his finger at Isaac in a rebuke he did not feel.

Ben delivered Lieutenant Jones to a newly constructed dock, crowded with supply ships and troop ships but still could not unload his cargo. The *Raven* was sent to an older dock, half a mile away when the temporary Harbor Master, a Navy Ensign, was informed of Ben's cargo. At the ammunition dock, Ben and another lieutenant signed papers delivering and accepting the gunpowder after a sergeant counted the barrels again on the pier. The Lieutenant had Ben wait while he flipped through several other lists and telegrams he had shoved into his ledger.

"Oh, yes. Here you are," the lieutenant said, "I knew I had seen that name before."

He handed Ben new orders to deliver more gunpowder from New Orleans to Corpus Christie, and any troops, if there was sufficient room.

January slipped into February, then March, then April as Ben and the crew sailed the *Raven* back and forth across the Gulf of Mexico, between Louisiana and Texas. Once the gunpowder was delivered, the *Raven* was ordered to carry other supplies and troops that could fit into the schooner. The *Raven* joined a rotating swirl of continued shipping. The crew had several days rest at each location, as the supply chain became more and more complicated, and the waits to unload and reload took longer to accomplish. The stacks of supplies grew larger in Corpus Christie, but it was not moving out to the army in the field quick enough. The *Raven* was then sent after disassembled supply wagons while other ships were sent for more horses.

In mid-April they had delivered their fourth cargo of wagons and lingered in Nueces Bay, awaiting the signal for their turn to approach the docks for loading. The bay was a forest of shipping masts. Ben had requested a meeting with the shipping master. He and the crew of the *Raven* needed to go home. They had been in the shipping cycle for over four months. Ben felt he had done enough for his country and his bank account. He had missed Christmas with his family, and Alisha had turned seven, the spring flooding was in full force along the Susquehanna. Sonja had visited the new Photography Studio in Havre de Grace and had sent him a beautiful glass photograph of herself and Alisha. It had miraculously survived the shipment from Maryland buried in a crate of sawdust, and as much as he adored the glass image, he longed to be home. He longed to hold Sonja and Alisha again.

Ben sat down in the Army Shipping Master's office, which now rated a Major in command.

"I'm sorry Captain Pulaski. The Mexican Army

just attacked across the Rio Grande and wiped out a company of American Dragoons. The Army is pursuing them. I refuse to release any ship until I have a better sense of what General Taylor needs next. You are a civilian and can leave whenever you like after you deliver the Army stores in your contract. But I warn you, sir, you will carry a black mark against you and any future contract with the United States Army, if you leave today."

The major blew out his breath and stood up, then walked to a cabinet in the corner of the room. He returned with two small glasses and a decanter of brandy. He spoke as he poured.

"I apologize for my outburst, Captain. The spritely *Raven* has been an excellent little supply ship, able to get into and out of harbors that would severely challenge the larger ships. We are almost awash in large cargo ships. I could afford to lose three of them rather than relinquish the advantages I have with the *Raven*."

He sat down and sipped his brandy.

"Please give me a couple more days, and if possible, I will offer you a supply request that will take you home for a couple months."

Ben sighed and finished his brandy. "Thank you, Major."

As he stood, so did the Major, who extended his hand. "Your given name is Benjamin, is it not?"

"Yes, Major."

"Call me Frederick, when we are alone, Benjamin." He walked Ben to the door, a smirk slipping onto his face. "We have a friend in common back east. An exasperating ne'er-do-well from an otherwise reputable Philadelphia family...Anthony Renowitz. " He winked at Ben and returned to his desk.

The merchant ship *General Harrison* faced a storm-filled passage around Cape Horn, sailing in icy gales most of the way, finally struggling out into the Pacific Ocean. The ship had lost one of her masts, and two of her crew had been swept overboard. Aaron had

257

been among the crewmen who saved the first mate from going overboard and then led the crew to help chop away tangled rigging that threatened to capsize the ship. The ship stayed in Argentina two months, repairing its damage and rigging a temporary mast to get them to San Francisco.

Once docked in San Francisco, the first mate and the Captain offered Aaron a Boson position if he would stay with the ship, but he declined.

"I think I will stay ashore here a while, then maybe ship out to the Orient someday. My father went there." He shrugged his shoulders. "I don't really know," Aaron said.

Aaron was surprised to find so many Americans in California, Mexico's northernmost territory. There was a Mexican government office in the town, but the rowdy local citizens were by far more American than Mexican. Aaron patted his money belt snug against his waist and kept a sense of his surroundings as he walked through the town. Staying on what appeared to be the main street; he entered a tavern for a drink and asked the bartender where he might find a competent gunsmith.

"My trigger is too sensitive," he said, patting his coat at his side as if he carried a pistol under it. His lesson in Cuba had made him a cautious traveler. The gunsmith shop sold a variety of old used guns that were for sale at modest prices. His attention was drawn to an oak box on the shelf behind the gunsmith, who smiled when he opened it before Aaron.

"That there is a Colt Patterson revolver, young man. You won't find nothing better if you can afford it."

They bargained a few minutes, then Aaron said he wasn't sure he could afford the pistol and left. Close by, Aaron found a hotel that appeared clean and safe where he took a room for the night. Once in his room, he locked the door, tossed his seabag on the bed, and withdrew enough money from his belt to buy the revolver. He held back ten dollars and shoved the rest in his pants pocket. The ten dollars he slipped into a coat pocket.

Moments later Aaron returned to the gunsmith shop and offered him ten dollars less than the smith was asking. Aaron placed the money on the counter but held his hand over it.

"And an extra flask of powder, double the balls that come with it, and more caps than balls."

The gunsmith eyed him a moment, then slowly shook his head. "I don't think I can do that," he said.

Aaron crumpled the money in his hand and stuck it back in his pocket, then turned toward the door. He had only taken three steps when the gunsmith agreed to the terms. Aaron paid another two dollars for a holster and belt. The holster laid across the front of his waist on his left, making it easy to reach with his right hand.

Aaron asked him where he could find a good meal, and the gunsmith happily gave him directions.

"But where do you go to eat?" Aaron asked, thinking perhaps he was being sent to a place that would overcharge him and share a portion of his bill with the gunsmith.

"I go there every day, young man. My wife cooks there."

Aaron enjoyed an excellent meal and excellent ale fermented in the basement of the tavern. As the sun began to set, he meandered down a boardwalk toward his hotel. He passed an open doorway with a woman standing in it, leaning against the frame smoking a cigar. Her lips were painted bright red, and her blouse was open enough to show off her ample cleavage. She reached out to touch him gently on his arm.

"Would you like to come in and join me for a cup of tea, young man?"

Aaron tipped his hat to her and started to walk on, saying "No Thank you, ma'am."

She reached and grabbed his arm playfully, pulling him toward her. "I am just so lonely, and I would love your company. What is your name, honey?"

"Aaron," he said, and slipped away from her

grip, stepping toward the corner of the building.

A man stepped out from the shadows and pulled out a long knife, pointing it at Aaron. "Let's you and me go have some tea with Isabelle...Aaron."

Holding his package in his left arm, Aaron stepped back into the street and yanked his new pistol from its holster. He pointed it at the man's face and cocked the hammer.

"I already told the lady, no thank you, perhaps you didn't hear me," Aaron said.

"No, sir. No, sir. Didn't hear you. My mistake. No, sir."

The man backed away, and Isabelle slipped back inside and closed the door. Aaron walked away with a sense of power and confidence he had not experienced before.

I need to get back to the *hotel, and load this thing,* he thought as he slipped the pistol back into its holster.

32

The *Raven* lingered another week in Corpus Christie Bay, waiting for orders. The barrier of Padre Island beyond them blocked the heavier waves and harsher winds. The warm April sky was cloudless and filled with arguing seagulls and lines of pelicans skimming the timid waves near the shore. Unused canvas sails were stretched between the rigging to provide shade over much of the deck. The heat and humidity felt like July on the Chesapeake.

Ben anchored close enough to the little town to allow his men to take the rowboat and go two at a time for daytime shore leave. The small town had originally sprouted around Kinney's Trading Post at a time when most of the customers were from Mexico's revolutionary army. With the flooding arrival of the American military, taverns and brothels had popped up like dandelions between the dry goods stores and the barber shops.

"Watch your back and stay together," Ben warned them.

Warren and Alistair were in town when an army Lieutenant was rowed out to the *Raven*. He saluted when he climbed on board, stiff in his high collared wool jacket.

"Lieutenant Grant, sir, Regimental Quartermaster," he said, "I have dispatches for you from the Shipping Master."

Sweat trickled down the side of his face from under his heavy forage cap hat. Ben noticed the tunic on the man in the rowboat was soaked with sweat and suggested to the Lt. Grant he might allow the man to come up into the shade. Daniel escorted the man to the bow and offered him some shaded water, while Ben and the Lieutenant moved to the stern, sitting in folding canvas chairs Ben had purchased in New Orleans.

"To business, sir," Grant began. "There is a new formulation of gunpowder, developed by a mill in Delaware. We are informed that the increase in power can either allow us to lessen the gunpowder for firearms and keep the range the same or use the current volume we have in paper cartridges to extend the range of the ball."

"How can we assist with that, Lieutenant?" Ben asked.

"You are requested to sail to Delaware, and obtain a small shipment of this new gunpowder and take it to Fort McHenry, in Maryland, for testing. After testing, you are to deliver the test result reports and a cargo of the new powder to me at this location."

Ben struggled to retain his smile. "I would be happy to do that, Lieutenant," he said.

Lieutenant Grant smiled. "I understand from the shipping master that you are from that area?"

"Yes. Very close by. When would you have the orders for that, and when would you like us to leave."

Grant reached inside his jacket and withdrew a small packet. Handing it to Ben, he said. "In answer to both questions, Captain...now."

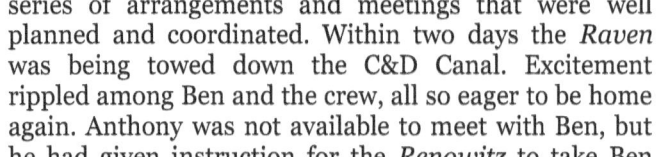

Ben's arrival in the Delaware Bay set in motion a series of arrangements and meetings that were well planned and coordinated. Within two days the *Raven* was being towed down the C&D Canal. Excitement rippled among Ben and the crew, all so eager to be home again. Anthony was not available to meet with Ben, but he had given instruction for the *Renowitz* to take Ben and his crew anywhere Ben required. Once back in the mouth of the Elk River, Ben released the *Renowitz* and sailed to Baltimore Harbor to deliver the four barrels to Fort McHenry.

"We had heard about this new powder," the major said. "Being mostly cannoneers here, we are looking forward to playing with it." He smiled and signed the papers Ben offered. "Come back in a month. We should have it well defined by then."

Ben returned to the ship and addressed Edward, "Let's get you to Annapolis." Then he turned to Wyatt, "What about you, Wyatt, is that where you want to spend the month?

After Annapolis, they sailed with a short crew to Havre de Grace. There, Ben released the other three crewmen after the ship was properly anchored and locked up. "Be back in a month," he reminded them, as they quick-stepped toward the train station, eager to be on their way, their pockets stuffed with pay.

Havre de Grace was in a buzz over the declaration of War with Mexico. Cargo shipments had expanded tremendously, and the little harbor was crammed with ships of all sizes, anything that could get through the channel of the upper Bay had come to pick up cargo floating down the canals. Trains from east and west were delivering supplies that could not find their way to Wilmington or Baltimore or Annapolis. Ben made his way through the crowds near the docks. Everyone moved in a rush. The canal company barn was empty of mules, horses, harnesses and people, except for Charles Briscoe, the blacksmith, working alone at his forge.

Ben stood in the middle of the barn and spun slowly around. "Where is everything, Charles?"

"Oh, Hello, Ben. Welcome back." He chuckled and dropped a red-hot horseshoe into a bucket of water, then spoke over the hissing, pointing around the barn with his tongs. "Everything is either rented, sold or stolen. We even had to hire a guard at night! Can you believe that? A guard for a mule barn. Ain't that something...?"

"Guess I'll walk to Lapidum," Ben said.

"Might as well, Ben. The basin is empty, too. Every barge is either gone up the canal or hauled out by steam tugs to Baltimore or Philadelphia. We got tugs waiting on barges these days!"

Ben waved to him and headed up the towpath toward Lapidum. An hour later he glanced across the canal to his home as he walked by it, yelling up the slope.

"Anybody home?" he yelled

As he came to the swing bridge over the canal lock and crossed it, Alisha bounded up the pathway and threw herself into his arms. Ben held her tightly as he walked, snuggling into the small of her neck as she giggled in delight, peeking over her shoulder at Jesse Price standing on his porch. Ben waved with one hand and carried his daughter to his little bridge over the creek at the edge of his property. Sonja was walking briskly from the house, wiping her hands with a cloth and showing him a beaming smile under sparkling eyes. She had a large swollen bruise on the left side of her jaw. Before he could ask anything, she wrapped her arms around both him and Alisha. The three of them stood there a long moment, just holding on, saying nothing, breathing deeply, enjoying the reunion, holding on.

"I got a letter from Aaron," Sonja said with her head leaning against his shoulder.

"Is he alright?" he said among her curls.

"Yes. He is in California."

"California??"

"Yes."

They leaned back when Alisha finally started to squirm. Alisha and Sonja took Ben by his hands and led him up to the house. The magnificent twin oaks were filled with lush green leaves, and the ground under them was covered in cast-off oak catkins. The green grass of their front slope was spotted with dozens of bright yellow dandelions. The canal had been flushed by the spring rains and slipped southward with a refreshed current. A soft breeze drifted off the river where hungry fish jumped out to gobble the insects at the surface.

Ben mounted the porch to their house and stopped in shock at the doorway, his mouth open. The walls in the front room had been painted white; the double fireplace that once opened into both the front room and the kitchen was bricked over. A black iron Franklin Fireplace squatted in front of the bricks.

Thickly padded chairs sat on either side of the iron fireplace. The one on Ben's side was covered in leather with small brass tacks lining the edges. The chair on Sonja's side displayed a Kelley green velvet covering, with the same brass tack trim.

Sonja reached over and pushed his mouth shut with her fingertip, while Alisha giggled. Sonja pulled him through the front room, into the kitchen.

A new iron water pump sat on the back counter overlooking a porcelain bowl cut into the counter. The shelves under the counter were enclosed in white painted cabinet doors, matching the walls. The iron stove Ben had carried in when he started their barge business was gone from the back wall, and the cabinets extended all the way to the side wall. In front of the enclosed fireplace sat a new iron stove with four lids and an oven on the side. Ben stepped to the counter to closely inspect the porcelain bowl and smiled.

"It drains outside," Alisha said proudly. "It is a sink."

Ben put his hands on Sonja's waist. "You are...amazing. This...is...fantastic."

She smiled, enjoying the moment.

"Where is the old wood stove? Did you sell it for a good price?"

Her smile continued. "No, I had it moved into the bunk room in the barn, when I had the wall boards battened. It's nice and cozy in there now. No more wind slipping in between the wall boards, either."

"But we had a little stove in there. It came out of one of the old barges. It was still good..."

Sonja planted her hands on her hips and tilted her head, her smile fading. "Do I have to explain each thing?"

He pulled her close. "No, sweetheart, I was just curious."

"Well, I had it moved to the new outhouse..."

"New...outhouse?"

"Yes. With enough room to boil water and bathe, in addition to the other usual reasons."

Ben smiled. "Is our bedroom still in the same place?"

Sonja placed her hand on Alisha's cheek. "Alisha, honey, Momma and Papa need to have a grown-up talk. Would you like to go play with Patty a while?"

Alisha answered by bolting out of the front door and charging down across the little bridge to the Price house. Sonja pulled Ben to their bedroom. The walls were painted light green, and the windows were dressed with dark green fabric. Sonja closed the curtains only seconds before Ben pulled her to him and kissed her, closing the door with his heel.

James Williamson walked casually from the steamer dock after seeing Lydia off. His meeting the previous week with all the lawyers and Lydia in front of Judge Jessup had been tumultuous. Lydia had taken the ruling poorly, releasing a barrage of deadly curses. He was glad she was at last out of his life. In celebration, he had given the day off...with pay...to his clerks. He unlocked the door to the bank and closed it behind him, then made his way to his desk. He sighed as he relaxed in his chair, pulling a decanter from a lower drawer and pouring a small glass of whiskey. He leaned back in his chair, with his feet propped up on the desk, sipping his whiskey and planning in his mind for his next actions, now that Lydia's distractions were out of the way.

The bell above the front door jingled as someone entered. James leaned around to see who had come in.

"I'm sorry, but we are closed for the afternoon," James said.

"I have a delivery for James Williamson," the voice said with a distinct southern accent.

"Very well, you can bring it back here if you would, please."

A tall, slender man came through the little gate carrying a box and approached the desk. James did not recognize the man.

"Are you Mr. James Williamson?" the man

266

asked, holding the box in both hands.

"Yes," James said, smiling as he leaned forward reaching for the box.

"I have a gift from your sister," the man said. Then he reached into the box, pulled out a pistol and fired it into the center of James' face, splattering the back wall in crimson blood and brain matter. The man placed the gun back in the box, stepped quickly past the desk and out through the back door. He walked briskly to the stallion tied near the horse trough, mounted it with ease, and trotted out of town.

Nancy Palmer peered out of the tavern door across the street from the bank, wiping her hands. "That sounded like a gunshot!"

Carl, the owner, and cook followed her to the door and leaned out beside her, letting his hand drift down her side, gently touching her hip. "It was probably nothing," he said

Nancy slapped his hand. "I know what a gunshot sounds like on this street, and it came from the bank!"

The testing at Fort McHenry progressed slowly. In early June, the major telegraphed Ben for additional powder. Ben arranged with Anthony for the powder to be delivered by towed barge from the DuPont Mill directly to Fort McHenry but under Ben's contract. Ben was allowed to stay in Lapidum during the transfer and was at their little farm on the canal when Isaac came home after graduation from West Point.

"I have orders for Texas," Isaac said after he reluctantly pulled away from hugs and kisses from his family. "I have to go to New Orleans first, then take transport to a place called Corpus Christie, which I believe is on the coast of Texas."

Ben sighed. "I think I can help with that, son."

The next day, while Sonja cooked every dish that Isaac had ever said he liked, Ben took a horse and rode into Havre de Grace to send a telegram. Before the end of the week, Isaac's orders had been amended, directing him to take any transport available directly to Point

Isabelle, Texas. A second telegram directed Ben to deliver the new gunpowder at Point Isabelle, as well.

"I will be able to take you, Son," Ben told him at supper.

"And we are going along," Sonja said. "We can at least have that time together, the four of us."

The following weeks evaporated in a whirlwind of conversations, gatherings with friends, packing, buying additional uniforms for Isaac, and new dresses for Sonja and Alisha. It also included repeated modest arguments as Ben reminded Sonja that he would be transporting gunpowder, which was dutifully ignored by his energized wife. They learned that the Tidewater Bank was to be closed and its assets sold, following the murder of James Williamson. His body was returned to Saint Mary's County for burial at his family estate, Grayrocks. Ben and Sonja were saddened over the death of James, but the actions of the Tidewater Bank and Trust Company finally, and at long last, no longer mattered to the Pulaskis. All of that washed over Isaac, Sonja and Alisha like a quick summer wave splashing on the beach, and then it was time to leave.

33

Ben and Delbert named Abraham general manager of Pulaski Canal Shipping, a recognition they agreed he had earned. He had established a successful routine for the barges along the Susquehanna and Tidewater Canal. He eliminated most of their empty time, providing a steady stream of store goods going north, as well as regularly picking up partial loads of flint in Stafford and pig iron in York Furnace. Emptied in Wrightsville, the Pulaski barges crossed to Columbia and then went south delivering thousands of tons of coal. Once through the Havre de Grace outlet lock, the Pulaski's *Ugly Boat* took them to Annapolis. While the bigger steamers competed to make tows to Baltimore or Philadelphia, Annapolis traffic was left almost unchallenged to Pulaski Shipping.

Abraham mastered moving the eye-popping pack of nine barges in and out of the Annapolis Harbor, to the satisfaction of the shopkeepers and the relief of the Harbor Master there. Ben was completely confident in Abraham and harbored no worries about the canal business while he prepared to sail once again to the Gulf of Mexico.

The *Raven* experienced a fairytale voyage from Havre de Grace to the Gulf of Mexico. The crew doted over Alisha and became an extended family for Sonja. Since Ben had accepted Edward as his brother, Sonja decided that he was, therefore, her brother-in-law. While on shore leave, Edward had become engaged to Belle Zagruda in Annapolis and was happy to share conversations about her with Sonja. The rest of the crew formed a circle of protective uncles around Alisha and congenial cousins to Sonja. With their sailing routines so practiced and well learned, Ben rarely had to act as a classic ship captain, leaving space in his mind and heart to be husband and father far more than he expected.

Like finding a diamond in the sand, during one of the many enjoyable conversations Sonja had with Isaac, he let slip that in addition to writing home to his Ma, he would also be writing to a young lady. With the persistence that only a mother could bring to bear, Sonja managed to pry out a few precious details about the young lady who would receive her son's letters.

Her name was Elizabeth, a shy girl with long chestnut curls, a sharp sense of humor and a comfortable understanding of engineering principles. She was not allowed to attend college to pursue a subject so coarse for a girl as engineering, but her twin brother was in just such a program at 'the Point,' and she consumed his books. Isaac had met her at a West Point social affair the previous autumn and had gained her permission to write. The only other piece of evidence Sonja could gain from Isaac's reluctant discussion of her was that she lived in New York, near the eastern shore of Lake Erie. All else about her remained a mystery to Sonja.

A hurricane far out in the Atlantic Ocean flung aggressive winds into the Gulf, and much to Sonja's disappointment, the *Raven*, was practically shoved toward the Texas coast all too quickly. They sailed through an inlet at the southern tip of the long Padre Island, a little more than a hundred miles south of Corpus Christie. Point Isabelle was fast becoming Port Isabelle, the site of an army fort anchoring the Rio Grande River for the United States, and the United States Army. Without fanfare or friendly introductions Second Lieutenant Isaac Pulaski, left the *Raven* while the gunpowder was being unloaded under the watchful eye of the Ordnance Officer.

Isaac was assigned to the Ordnance Corps, with his duties primarily involving moving cannon and caissons from one place to another, so someone else could fire them. It was disappointing to him, but it was his assignment, and he was determined to do it well.

Late in his first afternoon of duty, he stood on the catwalk behind a new brick wall of his post and fought the urge to wave as the *Raven* sailed away. Another officer approached him to provide a detailed tour of the fort. Isaac turned from the ocean and faced another new officer, whose deep-set blue eyes peered out at him in amusement.

"Thomas!" he yelled.

"Welcome, Isaac," Tom said, as they slapped each other's shoulders in greeting.

Ben received orders at Point Isabelle to report to Corpus Christie to pick up army passengers for a return trip to New Orleans. The wind was against them, and it took four days to claw a mere hundred miles north. When Ben arrived, he was informed he was to take wounded from the Battle of Palo Alto, fought in early May. The army had considered the logistics of sending wounded in a schooner, and many would still be on stretchers. The Army provided racks to install in the hold of the *Raven*, where the ends of the stretchers could be attached.

Ben had the hatch covers set aside so the loading booms from the dock could lower individual stretchers, each carrying a severely wounded soldier. Two hospital orderlies joined the *Raven* to watch over the 80 wounded soldiers being stacked in the holds like so much cordwood. Many of them moaned as they were moved. All of them had at least one limb amputated. A few had obviously become gangrenous in the moist heat, from the stench wafting off their stretchers. Sonja rushed Alisha to the captain's cabin.

The stretchers were stacked in three levels 18 inches apart, starting at 6 inches above the planking. Two sets of stacks were placed end-to-end, with an 18-inch gap between sets, and an 18-inch aisle between the rows. Two crates of bottled laudanum were brought on board, plus their food, and barrels of water, which would have to be strapped on the upper deck. The *Raven*'s crew watched it all in horror.

"Ben. Those men are going to suffocate down there," Edward said.

Ben stopped one of the loaders. "Shouldn't we spread them out more, so air can move around them?"

"Nope. You gotta take 80. That's the requirement for a schooner this size. That's the contract. Bigger ships can take a lot more, but it will still be 18, 18 and 18 down inside. Bigger ships also take longer." Then he lowered his voice and leaned close to Ben. "Some of these boys don't have much longer, Cap'n. The Army's giving them to you so you can get them to New Orleans as fast as you can."

Ben went to the Army office on the dock, and then returned shortly, calling his crew together on deck.

"These men need to get to a hospital in New Orleans. We're faster than the other sailing ships, and they don't have a steamboat available that can take them yet. We've got to do the best we can."

As soon as the receipts were signed, the crew hauled up the *Raven*'s anchors and set sail. Ben and Edward took turns at the wheel, keeping the *Raven* at the sharpest angle possible without risking the ship. The masts leaned far over, away from the wind, and the leeward deck rails ran through the foam on the tops of the waves. They had crewmen douse the sails with saltwater, to keep them stiff and squeeze out all the speed the wind could give them. Many of the wounded below became seasick, and the bilge flowed with vomit and urine, but the orderlies understood how crucial it was to have speed. The soldiers moaned and cried, and the orderlies gave water to those who could swallow.

Poor Alisha stayed in the cabin as her mother had ordered, crying for the wounded, already knowing death as her first mother died. Sonja put on her canvas trousers and pushed her way into the holds with buckets of fresh water, wiping brows, holding hands, whispering to the men who had been boys just last year. Ben ordered Alistair to pump seawater down into the hold, to flush it out. He ordered Warren to man the pump in the hold to empty the bilge. One of the orderlies helped him pump. Wyatt fashioned wind scoops with sail scraps and wooden mast hoops, to funnel some fresh air down into the hold. Everyone did all they could think of to relieve the suffering of the wounded soldiers.

The *Raven* dashed on and on toward New Orleans. Five hundred miles away. Eight knots an hour. Fifty-six hours to the mouth of the Mississippi River. A steam tug was supposed to be waiting for them there. Again water was flung on the sails. Every line to every sail at every opportunity was tightened, clawing a little more power from the wind. Demanding a little more push. Grabbing a bit more speed.

At twenty-four hours, the crew began to rotate finding a place to doze for a few minutes, while others watched the sails and compass. Into the night they pushed on, guided by the stars. The wind stiffened in the cooler night. The masts leaned farther away from the wind and the deck tilted, but they knew they were gaining speed. The crewmen found any place but a bed to sleep a few minutes. The crew's quarters had been jammed with supplies for the soldiers. None of the crew would give up.

Alisha slipped out from the cabin. She braved the maze in the hold to find ship's biscuits in the galley and passed them out to the crew and the orderlies. The angle of the deck was too great to chance a fire in the stove. Biscuit was their only food. Tepid water was the only drink.

On the afternoon of the second day, an angry gust of wind almost capsized the *Raven*. Tension lines were quickly loosened to spill the wind and save the ship. Within seconds the gust had passed. The lines were tightened again, and the *Raven* dashed on. The *Raven* could run no faster. She gave all she had. The sails stood out, filled with wind and hard as iron. The running rigging was as tight as violin strings, the pitch of the vibrations shrieked. She answered all that was asked of her. She dashed on toward the horizon. On and on, galloping over the waves, rushing, rushing.

Ben knew they were taking the ship to her limit. At any second, a spar or line or sail could surrender to the strain, and give way. Each crewman watched every inch of her, ready for the first hint of failure. Ben had the bilge flushed out again. Edward relieved him at the wheel. He went down to check the hold. He found Sonja bending over the pump handle, pushing with all her strength. They pumped together until the outflow went dry. She picked up the fresh water bucket and went back among the stretchers. Ben returned to the upper deck.

One of the worst wounded died. The orderlies slipped his body into a canvas bag and carried it up on deck. They looked to Ben for orders.

"Strap it to the railing. Let's try to get him closer to home.

The orderlies nodded in agreement and then returned to the men in the hold. The wind blew the stench of advanced gangrene across the deck. Ben and Wyatt moved the body to the bow, where the wind would blow the smell beyond the ship. That night another man died and was taken to the bow. The wind began to moderate. It was soon a soft breeze, unable to push the *Raven* further. The *Raven* lost way, then began to waddle in the calm sea.

Sonja tilted her head, standing in the narrow aisle between the stretchers, feeling the change in the ship's motion. "Oh, no," she whispered.

"Lower the rowboat," Ben ordered.

Ben climbed into the rowboat, his body slow to move. Without a word, Daniel climbed over the railing and joined him. Sitting together, each man took an oar and began to pull. The boat jerked when they reached the end of the line. They strained against the oars, pulling against the water. Slowly, the *Raven* inched forward. They braced their feet before them and leaned toward the bow with aching backs, pulling up on the oar with aching arms. The *Raven* gained the barest momentum. The ship moved a precious few yards farther along. A few yards closer to New Orleans, somewhere over the northeastern horizon.

After an hour they could no longer pull. The *Raven* drifted to them, and they were helped up onto the deck. Edward and Alistair climbed down into the rowboat. One of them grunted with the effort of the first pull. Ben turned toward the wheels. Sonja stood under a ship's lantern gripping the wheel, keeping them on course. The yellow lantern light illuminated her hair. Ben smiled at the sight and sat on the deck, then lay down with his head on the wooden planks, blood seeping from a blister on his hand, and dozed for a few precious minutes.

During the night, the wind returned from a different compass point, but it was useful. Warren and one of the orderlies were picked up from the rowboat as the *Raven*'s bow caught up with them. Alisha gave them cool water to drink. Ben helped the crew bring the boat back on deck, not wanting to lose a yard to its drag.

The morning of the third day came, showing the Louisiana coastline low on the horizon. A tapered smudge of black smoke in the distance marked a steam tug. It was not waiting on them. It was charging toward them. It came under full steam, billowing coal smoke into the air. It was coming for them. Spray jumped over its bow as it crested the waves. It was coming for them. Hurrying toward them. It was coming.

⁓

Two weeks later, the *Raven* returned to Corpus Christie with a cargo of shoes and belts. After unloading the wounded in New Orleans, Ben had taken the ship a short distance away from the dock and dropped anchor. They laid down wherever they were and slept. Two days passed before they were rested enough to move back to the pier for their next load. The Army had four thousand men on the march over rugged rocks and sand somewhere in the occupation zone. They would need more shoes. After unloading his cargo in Corpus Christie, Ben sailed the *Raven* down to Point Isabelle, hoping he and Sonja might visit a short while with Isaac. They were disappointed to learn that Isaac's unit had been ordered inland. He was on the march as well.

They returned to Corpus Christie and docked near civilian ships, away from the uproar of Army supplies and moaning wounded being loaded on steamers. Ben released the crew for three days, while he took his wife and daughter to a hotel that offered wonderful private bathing in large copper tubs. The ocean breeze blew into their third-floor room through the opened windows, pushing the lace curtains up into the room like floating clouds. Sonja and Ben smiled at the antics of their rambunctious daughter with her bundles of woven straw souvenirs and tried not to show their worries about Isaac, clawing at their hearts.

A servant tapped gently on the door to their suite. He bowed when Ben opened the door and handed him a thick envelope.

34

Ben gave the servant a nickel and then opened the envelope as he walked back to his stuffed chair. In the envelope, he found a folded note from the local Shipping Master.

I took the liberty of intercepting this letter from Isaac, while I forward the other from a mutual friend.

Sonja was already at his side peeking over his arm and reading the note with him. She snatched Isaac's envelope and dashed to the balcony to read it in the bright sunlight. Ben stepped out near her and opened the other envelope. Inside was a newspaper clipping and a folded unsigned note. The clipping displayed an advertisement from a South Carolina newspaper.

DONATE TO THE WAR EFFORT!
PATRIOTIC OWNERS!
Slaves required
To dig entrenchments
And Release our Boys
To their Noble Cause.
AVENGE THE MURDER
OF OUR DRAGOONS!!

The note said

No flags. New Orleans, quickly. Charleston, do not dock.

277

Cape May, where you please.
Aaron well in San Francisco,
Seen early June,

Ben sighed and turned his head toward Sonja. "Aaron was seen in San Francisco, early June. He was well then."

She smiled with her eyes wide, her eyebrows raised. "Anything else?"

"No," he said.

She returned to her short letter, re-reading it, her mouth forming words as she read, Alisha resting her chin on her Mother's shoulder, reading the letter with her. Alisha reached a hand down to the letter and pointed her finger at one of the written words.

"Monterrey," Sonja told her, then reached up to place her hand against Alisha's cheek, bringing her face against her mother's.

"It is a town in Mexico, where your brother Isaac has marched." Her eyes filled with tears as she turned her face to Ben.

"We need to sail to New Orleans," Ben said.

"Not more wounded. Please," Sonja pleaded softly.

"We go empty, then pick up some slaves, then up to Charleston..."

"And then?"

"More slaves, and then Cape May, New Jersey," Ben said. "I think you will like that town."

New Orleans was a pleasant destination on that voyage. There were people near the dock waving miniature American flags attached to sticks as Ben marched the slaves onto the deck of the *Raven*. A man at the beginning of the pier wearing a gaudy red, white and blue suit, held the people around him with rhetoric and song as the slaves filed down the dock to the ship.

"I hope that man is paid well for his risk and gets

away before they discover the lie," Edward said. "Is it all a ruse? Or will there actually be other ships to take slaves to Mexico?" he asked.

Ben smiled at him. "It is all a sham. There is no such demand for slaves. That's why we are leaving so quickly, and not showing our faces in the city."

"And why you had us drape sail cloth over the *Raven*'s name."

Ben smiled. "The Carney gets two dollars for each slave he loads."

"How many are there?"

"Count them as they come on board, Eddie."

Edward counted twelve, then the gangplank was withdrawn, and the crew of the *Raven* pushed away from the dock to follow the steam tug down the Mississippi River back to the Gulf. People on the docks continued to wave their little flags.

In Charleston Harbor, they spilled the air from their sails and drifted in the current a few hours. A steam tug came out from the dock, pulling a river barge behind it. Ten slaves sat cross-legged on the open deck. As soon as the *Raven*'s crew could hook on to the barge with boat hooks, the slaves were sent on board. After the experience with the uprising near Drum Island, Ben had Warren there to greet the slaves, whispering to each slave, letting them know.

"Hide below," he said. "We go north to freedom."

The crew was fully armed. Sonja and Alisha stayed below in the captain's cabin with the door barred until safety was assured.

The *Raven* turned back to the sea, while the slaves were fed and introduced to the others, all free to roam the hold, and promised permission to the upper deck as soon as they were out of sight from land. Beyond the harbor, their access to the deck soon ended as winds arose and the high waves rushed hard against the hull. Another storm raged out in the Atlantic, tossing the *Raven* off the peaks of the waves into the deep troughs between them. Most of the slaves were soon seasick, but some had been to sea before and were able to assist the crew. Ben had no option but to try to run ahead of the storm, taking the *Raven* far out over the ocean.

They ran for several days until the wind veered northeast enough to allow them an opportunity to steer northwest and claw out of the storm. The next day, with blue sky and clouds overhead and a good wind pushing them eastward, they were able to determine their position with the sextant.

On August 2nd, they sailed into Great Sound, within the hook of Bermuda. A pilot sloop ran out to meet them, flying the Union Jack ensign of Britain from her mast.

"Heave To," a man yelled from the bow of the sloop. "Prepare to be boarded in the name of the King!"

Ben ordered the sails lowered and assisted a British officer, and two royal marines come on deck.

"We are American," Ben said.

"Have you fever or slaves aboard?" the young officer asked. His voice was high. Sonja judged him to be fifteen or sixteen years old. Noticing Sonja sitting on the deck with Alisha nearby, he bowed to them and removed his hat. "Your servant, madam. Ensign Strutherington. My apologies for the delay."

"We have twenty freed slaves on Board, Ensign," Ben said.

"You have their papers, of course, Captain. Manumissions?"

"No," Ben said with a smile, "We recently stole them."

The *Raven* was escorted to the northern tip of the bay and ordered to anchor in the shallows near Kings Wharf at the Royal Navy Yard. A marine was placed on the *Raven*, while the slaves and the crew were kept on the ship, but not confined. Ben, Sonja and Alisha were rowed to shore and presented at Government House. The British were not inclined to accept Ben's claim of freeing the slaves and charged him with fabricating the story to keep his property from being confiscated, which they told him most definitely would be. Sonja asked the magistrate if he knew whether the Argyle Corporation had an office on Bermuda.

Three hours later, Ben, Sonja and Alisha were rowed out to the *Raven* in a British long boat by a squad of four British sailors. Sonja carried an unopened bottle of, an 'excellent claret' the magistrate had called it. Two clerks carrying ledgers joined them. One clerk was an employee of the Government House. The other was a clerk from the Argyle Corporation. They took the names and American origins of each slave, compared lists. The clerks returned to the longboat followed by the smiling marine, whom Alisha had told his red coat was cute and wished she had one like it.

The *Raven* docked at Cape May five days later and was soon joined by the *Columbus*. The captain of the *Columbus* congratulated Ben and Sonja and passed on a request from a mutual friend to linger in Cape May a few more days. The passenger ship which steamed off as soon as their new passengers were loaded, heading down the Delaware Bay, on her way to Nova Scotia. Ben released the crew to enjoy Cape May for the next three days. Edward managed to find a telegraph office, to send word to Belle.

Unknown to Ben and Sonja, two passengers had left the *Columbus* before it sailed away, and strolled along the pier to the gangplank of the *Raven*. The man and women, dressed in evening attire, stood there a moment near the ship, noting the worn condition of the *Raven*.

"Ahoy, the *Raven*," the man bellowed, but there was no response.

"Ahoy, the *Raven*," he shouted again.

Ben came up on deck, carrying a wine glass. He glanced down the gangplank a moment, then dashed along it, setting his glass on the railing as he flew down to the dock. He grabbed the man in a bear hug and extended a hand to the woman at the same time. He released the man, and then drew him into another embrace, slapping the man's back. He leaned back, letting the man go and turned his head toward the stern of the ship.

"Sonja," he yelled. "Come quick!"

The man laughed and put his hand on Ben's shoulder.

"It is good to see you, Old friend," Simon said.

Lettie added her hand to Simon's and smiled at Ben. She was well rounded with the coming child she carried.

Sonja screamed from the deck as she ran down the gangplank to them, engulfing them both in her arms and kisses. Alisha, awake from her afternoon nap, heard the yelling and came up on deck. She remembered Simon as one of Ben's friends, shaking his hand, and curtsied when she was introduced to Lettie.

As they chattered, walking up the gangplank, an enclosed delivery wagon drew up behind them on the pier. Two white-coated chefs stepped down and opened the back of the wagon. Ben pulled his visitors aside while the chefs withdrew and assembled the table and chairs. Simon smiled at Lettie and shook his head.

"Anthony is always the showoff," he said.

He and Ben chuckled, while Lettie and Sonja stared in wonder as the table was dressed and set on the deck, then the dinner placed and the wine glasses filled. They bowed and motioned to the chairs, assisting all three ladies from behind, then uncovering large pans filled with a variety of seafood, various cooked meats, and a colorful array of cooked vegetables. Another wine glass was placed by Alisha and filled with chilled milk.

The chefs remained for the meal until each of the guests could eat or drink no more. They removed everything they had brought, and then drove away. Alisha watched in amazement from the ship's rail.

Late in the evening, when everyone on deck had almost talked and laughed themselves hoarse, Simon and Lettie stood from their chairs on the deck. "We have a room at a hotel nearby, where our luggage was sent and must catch a steamer early in the morning."

282

"Can't you stay longer?" Sonja pleaded as Ben nodded his head in agreement next to her.

"It is not safe for us, outside of Canada," Simon said. "The slave catchers are bolder each day, and care less and less whether it is truly a runaway they have caught."

"Just as long as their skin is black," Lettie added, pressing her hand against her womb.

They hugged each other goodbye. Simon and Lettie walked down the gangplank onto the pier, passing a white couple strolling by the water. The white man tipped his hat to Lettie as they passed. Sonja sighed deeply and gripped Ben's arm as the couple walked away. Sonja pulled Alisha to her.

"Alisha, did you see that man tip his hat to Miss Lettie?" she asked

"Yes, Momma."

"That's how she should be treated everywhere."

Alisha shook her head no, "Not how it happens back home."

"Maybe someday," Sonja added, "Maybe someday."

Ben sighed and led them down to the cabin.

The next day, the steamboat *Renowitz* arrived late in the morning with Anthony on board. Since the crew of the *Raven* was still on shore leave for two more nights, Anthony had the Pulaskis moved to the Congress Hall Hotel as his guests, where he rented rooms for himself and them. The Pulaskis were escorted to a suite on the second floor having two separate bedrooms and facing the ocean.

Men in top hats carrying satchels came and went from Anthony's room like lines of ants, but he had promised dinner with them each night.

Sharing tender filet mignon, Anthony spoke quietly about the success of his endeavors, "...thanks in significant part to the *Raven* and the Pulaskis."

"Seventy-eight slaves are now free because of you," Anthony said. "You and Sonja should be very proud,"

"A few at a time, Anthony. We should be able to do better than that. I want the *Raven* to do better than that. And what of the other routes?" Ben asked

Anthony leaned forward, "You are sounding like an abolitionist, Benjamin."

Ben and Sonja glanced at each other.

"Never been called that," Ben muttered.

"Are you not?" Anthony asked. "Are you not finally that?"

"I want to free as many of those people as I can." Ben kept his eyes locked with Sonja's. "We want to do that, at least until the government changes it."

"Surely you see beyond that, Ben? If slavery doesn't end, all we are doing is rotating their stock. No, taking them north is less than half the battle."

Ben frowned and turned his attention to cutting his steak. "So, what of the other routes? What have they done?"

Anthony stared open-mouthed at Ben, then blew out his breath.

"Maybe upwards of three hundred, at least that we know of," he said, his smile returning and spreading between his wide side whiskers. He slipped another piece of bright red meat into his mouth, savoring the taste, and following it with red wine. "My gouty foot will pay the bill for this tomorrow, but tonight, I am enjoying it!"

"And how many are in bondage?" Ben asked.

Anthony's shoulders sagged. He sighed around his mouthful of meat. "We do what we can, Benjamin...hundreds of thousands, probably. No, not probably, the census counts them now...and the slaveholders, who claim they are not human, get 3/5 a citizen count for each one."

"What difference does it make?" Sonja asked.

Anthony wiped his mouth with a napkin. "The census drives the number of representatives we have in Congress. We only have two senators from each state, but the number of representative in Congress grows wherever the population grows." He turned back to Ben, "Over three million slaves in the 1840 census."

Anthony leaned back as a waiter refilled their glasses, and another brought fresh milk for Alisha.

"At around seventy thousand citizens per district," Anthony continued, "slaves alone account for around 30 seats in Congress. Between the whites of the slave states and the seats bought by the slave count, and the northern businessmen getting rich off cotton, sugar, and rice, pro-slavery laws are almost assured in every Congressional vote."

Alisha set her glass down and yawned, her eyes floating closed. Anthony glanced at her and chuckled softly.

"Alright. Apparently part of my audience has heard enough." He raised his finger to make a point. "Tomorrow night, the best seafood the ocean has to offer."

Alisha mumbled, "Fish again..."

Anthony chuckled and rubbed her head gently, "Whatever the little lady desires..."

Her eyes flew open, "Ice Cream!"

"Ice cream it is," he said and swiveled around, beckoning a waiter from the rear of the dining room.

"Not tonight," Sonja corrected. "Tomorrow...after a wholesome meal."

Alisha spoke to Anthony, "We ate just biscuits for three days when we took the sick men to Nawlens."

"Nawlens?" Anthony asked

"It's how they said it down there," Sonja answered with a smile.

As they parted for the evening, Ben and Anthony walked a short distance together.

"There is much I need to have done for the *Raven* before I take her to sea again," Ben said. "And I want us to be at home for letters from Isaac...maybe even another from Aaron."

"I understand," Anthony said, "I am afraid my little prank against Charleston and New Orleans may have stirred up far more anger than I anticipated..."

Ben chuckled, "You always did push your targets too far."

"Oh, I don't know..."

"Boson Hoagg was prepared to kill you long before our ship was held prisoner in China."

"Oh..."

"Pig manure in his snuff, Anthony?"

"Well, I admit, it should have been dried more..."

They both laughed.

35

The vision of the wounded soldiers they carried in such haste to New Orleans haunted Sonja's thoughts and her dreams. Sometimes it was Isaac lying in the claustrophobic hold of the *Raven*, jammed in between other moaning soldiers. He was crying for her, calling out for his Ma. His blood dripped like heavy raindrops onto the planks of the hold and ran in rivulets into the bilge. Other times he was lying in the sand of Mexico. His shoes were gone, and an arm or a leg ripped away, leaving only a bloody shredded stump where it had been. She awoke screaming his name, and Ben would hold her, wrapping his arms around her, telling her it was just a dream.

The year faded into a part of her memory that held nothing but fear and worry for her sons. They were both lost in the darkness, searching for her, calling out for her, but she was not there. Time slipped by. Moments passed that she could have spent talking with a friend, or harvesting tomatoes, or cucumbers, or later corn, but she sat on the porch while Ben and Alisha did that. Waiting for the next letter from Isaac, to tell her of his wounds, or of a message about Aaron, telling her he had died in California.

The blackness that settled into her soul when she thought Ben was dead, before he came back, returned and took up residence in her mind. It was like a vulture sitting on a branch above her dying body, waiting to feast on her flesh. There were brief moments of light, when Alisha came in with a new flower, or news of a favorite moment with Patty Price. Alisha had seen her other mother fade away, step at a time as the frail woman wasted, grew pale and withered. She refused to let Sonja slip down that path. Alisha spent her energies keeping her mother out of that darkness, bringing flowers or finding reasons to laugh until another letter would come. The letters always triggered the worst depressions. Sonja was terrified of the mail arriving and terrified of missing it.

The cold weather returned to Lapidum. Ben had left the *Raven* at St. Michaels, pulled out of the water, sitting on posts until after the winter. Her hull needed scraping after the time spent in the warm water. The storms had stretched and snapped her rigging. The winds had ripped at her sails. The salt water had leached the color from her paint and left her body peeling. Her appearance was the mirror image of Sonja's soul.

Ben once again joined the rhythm of the canal, while the *Raven* endured her pain and rebirth in St. Michaels, under the keen eye of Robert Lambdin and his men. Ben's barges passed boldly through *The Line*, the boundary between Pennsylvania and Maryland; between free state and slave state. Ben reacquainted himself with the slave catchers lingering on the Maryland side of *The Line*. He met them eye to eye, his hand on the handle of his knife or revolver, never hesitating to challenge their boldness with his own rage.

The Pulaski barges generally went unmolested by slave catchers at *The Line*. Still, there were some who were ready to shove their noses into the cabins, banging on the walls, searching for secret compartments that were not there. The Pulaski barges were captained by spirited men who openly resented their cargo to be molested, or their barges slowed. Confrontations became common and the slave catchers grew tired of them; they wanted the easy catches. The Pulaski barges were soon to be dreaded, to be passed without interference, to go through the lock at *The Line* without prejudice.

That is when Ben and Abraham knew it was time to modify one of the barges like the *Wilhelmina*. When the winter freeze swept over the canal, and the water was released back into the river, they selected the *Osprey*, the newest. This time there was to be no full wall that could be discovered. The *Osprey* was pulled against the little two-plank dock at the edge of the Pulaski property, so they could begin modifications with few prying eyes.

There they reworked the *Osprey's* support posts. Two posts were installed behind the rear wall, three feet apart. The center post was then cut away from under the deck and from the keel. The wall between the new posts was cut away, opening the hold to the cabin. Another bulkhead was built farther into the rear cargo hold, where the center post was reinstalled. Planks, carried in the bottom of the *Osprey's* hold for the last year, dented and blackened by the coal, were pulled up and nailed to the false center post, appearing exactly like the other walls within the hold. They installed a locker to act as a disguised door to the secret compartment.

Lockers were installed at the same location in all of the Pulaski barges. It was placed in the center of the rear wall, in front of the bulkhead post, separating the corner where the bunk beds were from the opposite corner where the little table sat. All barges were made the same, with a cabin in the center and holds for coal before it and after it. The bulkhead post in the center, before and after the cabin, reinforced the holds, supported the deck and prevented the coal in the holds from crashing through the wall into the cabin.

David Booker came down the towpath to help modify the barge. His new son, Matthew, born in Burl Jundt's house in York Furnace, and named for his lost brother, was healthy and growing well. The new locker in the cabin was attached to hinges which only showed inside the new compartment. Air vents were added that allowed fresh air into the compartment for openings in the top of the locker behind the scrollwork, unseen from anyone in the cabin. A mirror was installed in the hollow of a false ceiling beam over the cabin lantern fixed to the rear wall. The mirror reflected the lantern light into the compartment. Finally, fold-out seats were installed on the side walls, allowing the secret passenger places to sit. There were even hooks on the side walls to accept the rings of two hammocks. Urine from inside the compartment would flow into a shallow bilge under the cargo compartment, flushed out later. Ben and Abraham were satisfied with the modification and anxious to begin taking passengers into Pennsylvania the next spring.

"It isn't first class traveling, Mr. Pulaski," Abraham said, "but it will be safer and a little more tolerable than the *Wilhelmina*."

Sonja continued her vigil of the mail delivery, her anxiety rising each day. News of the battles in Mexico trickled into the local newspapers. Lists of returning wounded and those killed in action found their way into the newspaper as well. Sonja subscribed them to both the Cecil County Whig and the Republican, in hopes of missing nothing important. She frantically flipped through the pages of each new edition.

December pulled Sonja from her depression, and she focused her attention on preparation for Alisha's eighth birthday. Edward and his new wife visited, as did David and Helen with Matthew. Mamie visited with an armload of gifts that would have thrilled any child. On December 19th, Sonja baked a birthday cake for Alisha, covered in pink sugar icing and decorated with burning candles for Alisha to blow out. Alisha fell asleep in Sonja's arms that evening, and they both slept in her padded chair. Ben covered them with Alisha's favorite quilt, an old one with a tattered hem, one that had covered Ben and Sonja's bed long before Alisha was born.

Christmas came and went in a blur, although Sonja made every effort to make their little girl happy, the vacancies in Sonja's heart remained for her absent sons. Shortly after Christmas, a letter arrived from Isaac. It had been mailed well before Christmas, so Isaac wished them a merry Christmas and wished he could be home with them. Isaac had been a part of the fighting to take the city of Monterrey, but with hostilities over, the citizens did not appear as resentful as he expected. Volunteers had arrived from the United States, but their behavior was not as controlled as General Taylor expected. Isaac was in the same unit as Tom Jackson and spent most of his time with the cannons. Another month went by without further word from Aaron. Winter settled in hard along the Canal.

In February 1847, the newspapers reported a great Battle in the Mexican town of Buena Vista. The newspaper reported several hundreds of Mexican soldiers dead, but less than a hundred Americans. It was tortuous weeks before another letter arrived from Isaac. He was as yet unscathed but had participated in the battle with his cannon. At the time of the letter, Isaac's unit had returned to Monterrey, but they were to be transferred to the new units under General Winfield Scott. Isaac promised to write when he reached his new destination. Later that month, Ben received a letter from Anthony, saying a ship captain in San Francisco had seen Aaron. The message said Aaron had appeared to be healthy and in the presence of several other armed men.

No further letter arrived from Isaac for several weeks. In late March, the newspapers were filled with accounts of a Battle at Veracruz, a Mexican seaport town. Mexican casualties were reported heavy, but American casualties were reported as light. Again, Sonja had a vision of Isaac lying among the wounded in the hellish hold of the *Raven*, dashing to New Orleans before they died. She slept little for the next few weeks.

In early April, the newspapers reported the victory in Veracruz, now occupied by the American Army. Days later, Isaac's letter arrived. Sonja's hands trembled so severely, she ripped the letter, removing it from the envelope. She cried as she read the letter, holding the two pieces together to read the words that he was safe and was being detached from his unit to serve under a Captain named Lee for a period. Isaac wrote of his admiration for Captain Lee.

In April, the newspapers once again reported a tremendous battle, that time in a town called Cerro Gordo, not far from Veracruz. The reports claimed thousands of Mexican soldiers killed or captured and hundreds of American soldiers dead on the battlefield.

Weeks passed and no letter arrived from Isaac. Rumors circulated in Havre de Grace that the Army had begun to send young men in uniform to the homes of slain officers, to inform the family in person. The dread of official visits by the army swept among the mothers along the canal and in the towns. Weeks more passed, and still nothing from Isaac. Delbert's hardware had begun receiving mail as Lapidum's new Post Office.

Sonja paced the porch watching for the rider who brought the daily mail there. With the canal drained for the winter, Abraham functioned part-time as the postmaster for Lapidum. Ben had received word that the work on the *Raven* had not progressed well, due to other demands by the Navy in support of the war.

On a sunny afternoon, Sonja stood on the porch drying a dish when she spotted a man in an Army uniform walking down the towpath from Havre de Grace. She pulled herself back into the shadow of the porch, peeking from behind the edge of a post. He passed before the Pulaski home, heading toward Lapidum.

Maybe farther north? She thought.

Sonja then heard the swing bridge squeak as it turned at the lockhouse. She heard hard boots clomp on the planks. She peered down the narrow lane that ran across their upper yard to the little bridge across the creek to Stafford Road. She focused her eyes on the narrow opening between bushes and saplings at the mouth to their lane, where it kissed up against the Road. The soldier walked into view and turned toward their house.

Sonja dropped her cloth. With trembling hand, she set the dish in one of the wooden chairs beside her and backed toward the doorway.

"Ooooh," she said with a trembling in her voice. "Nooo, God, please, nooo. Turn away," she mumbled to the oncoming soldier."

He crossed their bridge and stepped onto the lane to their house. She placed her hand to her mouth

292

and stepped back into the house.

Ben was in their barn, repairing an old mule harness.

"B-B-en," she called. "Ben!"

Ben came out of the barn, facing up toward the porch, but Sonja was not there. He called back to her, but she did not come out, so he walked up to the porch.

He found her in the kitchen, standing against the counter, pale and trembling.

"He's coming to tell us Isaac is dead," she said.

"What? Who? What, Sonja?"

She pointed to the doorway as the young soldier mounted the steps to the porch. He stood at the open doorway, peering into the shadows, taking off his hat.

"Is this the Pulaski home?" he asked.

"NO! Go away," Sonja cried, "No, No, No!" The tears overflowed from her eyes.

36

Ben stepped to the doorway, squinting at the soldier, the sunlight bright behind him, and his face hidden in the shadow. "Who are you," Ben demanded.

The young officer stepped back. "Oh, I did not mean to intrude, sir, I only..."

"That is a West Point uniform," Ben said

"Yes, sir. Are you Mr. Pulaski?"

The cadet offered his hand to Ben. "Wallace Kincaid, sir. I am a friend of Isaac's."

Ben took his hand and brought him into the house. "I am pleased to meet you, young man. Have you heard from Isaac? Is he...safe?"

"We received a letter, that is my sister Harriet received a letter from him," Wallace said, removing his cap.

From the kitchen doorway, Sonja noticed his thick chestnut brown hair. "I am Mrs. Pulaski," she said holding out her hand to him.

Wallace accepted it in his fingertips and bowed to kiss the back. "Your servant, ma'am."

He smiled. "He is in Veracruz, overseeing incoming shipments of gunpowder and shot. He said if I was ever close to Havre de Grace, I should stop by his home to see you." Then he froze in mid-motion. "Oh, here..." He reached inside his tunic and withdrew two wrinkled envelopes. "I stopped at the post office in Havre de Grace to get directions to here. Isaac said it wasn't far, 'just down the towpath,' but I wasn't too sure what a towpath was..."

Sonja leaned close to accept the letters. The one on top was from Isaac. "Thank you...Wallace, is it?"

"Yes, ma'am. Wallace Kincaid."

"And your sister's name is Harriet?"

"Yes, ma'am."

Sonja smiled and pressed the letters to her heart. She offered him a seat. "Would you like some coffee or water?"

"Water would be wonderful, ma'am. I have had nothing but water from metal tanks since I left the Point. Some fresh well water would be a treat."

Ben escorted Sonja to her usual seat and stepped into the kitchen, working the pump until the water coming out was cool. He brought a glass full to Wallace, who gulped it down without stopping, closing his eyes as he swallowed. He sighed with satisfaction when he had finished. Ben returned to the kitchen and brought another glass full to the table near Wallace. Sonja opened the thickest envelope and quickly scanned the letter inside. It was a glorious three pages, but she set them aside for later.

"So, when did you last see Isaac, Wallace?" Sonja asked.

"Not since his graduation, I'm afraid. Harriet and I have shared his experiences only through his letters. But there are times when the mail is slow in arriving. Harriet becomes quite perplexed that the army does not give them the priority she desires, and then she worries. I only hope it doesn't end before I can graduate!"

Sonja nodded in understanding, her eyes sad, sharing the feelings of a girl only her son knows and trying to ignore the anxiousness of a little boy eager for war's horrors.

Wallace smiled. "And then it all catches up, and she gets three letters in one day."

"Ah yes," Sonja agreed. "That was my Easter present. Three wonderful letters, all at once!"

"So, what brings you down from New York, Wallace," Ben asked

"My uncle, sir. He is a member of Congress...he was...but passed away. He was buried in Washington City, and I was allowed furlough to attend the funeral."

"I am sorry for your loss," Ben said.

295

The clock on the wall chimed twice, drawing Wallace's attention.

"I am afraid I must be going, to catch my train." He gave Sonja a wry smile. "Isaac said it was just a few minutes' walk from the canal basin...it was quite a bit more than that, for me at least."

"We can take the horses," Ben suggested. "We have two friendly mares and a frisky gelding in the Barn. Let's saddle two of them, and we can go into Havre de Grace together, then I'll bring yours back."

Two hours later Ben returned to their little farm. Alisha was playing on the front slope with Patty. Jesse Price had built his girls a little playhouse from scrap lumber, but could not find enough room around the locktender's house to keep it for any length of time. Ben had offered the little level spot on their front slope, so the two fathers moved it to its new location. It drew the children like a magnet, to Sonja's great delight.

"Isaac is in a town called Chu-ru-bus-co," Sonja told Ben as he entered the house.

Ben frowned. "I had not heard of that place. I don't think it was in either of the newspapers we receive..."

She re-read a line in the letter, "not far from Con-tre-ras..."

"Oh yes. That was a huge battle. I was hoping Isaac was still in Veracruz and not in that. Was he hurt?" Ben did not repeat the report he had read in the Republican describing the large number of American soldiers who were lost in the battle. He bowed his head a moment, waiting for Sonja to read more.

"He says he is fine..." She laid the letter in her lap and turned to Ben. "But you know how stoic these Pulaski men can be..."

Ben smiled but did not turn his face to her. Then he picked up the map he had cut from the newspaper the previous month and tacked to a wide board. He held it in the sunlight and peered at it a long moment. "Ah, here it is." He grabbed up his pencil and made a mark on the map, then drew a line to it from Veracruz. He raised his eyebrows and turned toward Sonja. "The Army is not far from Mexico City. That is the capital of Mexico. The Whig says if we take Mexico City, they will surrender."

Sonja opened the second envelope. "Oh, Ben, this is for you. I didn't even look on the outside of the envelope."

Ben took the note from inside the envelope. It was unsigned. He sighed.

Sept 30. Georgetown. Usual Cargo. Three passengers.

The *Raven* sat pristinely on calm water fifty yards from the Havre de Grace docks. The blue sky was dotted with fat cotton clouds and noisy seagulls. A few ducks were muddling around the many ships, nibbling at trash and crumbs floating on the surface. There was a northerly breeze, bringing the smell of autumn down from the Susquehanna Valley and across the Susquehanna Flats. The dark green paint on the *Raven*'s hull was thick and shiny, making the white panel below her scuppers almost glow by comparison. The new red, white and blue wind pennant waved in the breeze from the mainmast. She appeared fresh and proud.

Ben's view of his ship was only through slots between the other vessels crammed into the harbor. In some places, ships tied two deep, with the harbormaster demanding the inner ship allow the outer one to drop their gangplank on his deck and walk through.

Crates and barrels stacked higgly-piggly without order, Ben thought. *Higher than a man's head, all around the docks and in the nearby street.*

Ben had to wend his way through a maze of cargo containers to gain access to his rowboat, which had been moved.

Had it not been painted with the name Raven on its stern, it might have disappeared altogether, he thought.

Ben climbed up on deck without fanfare. Edward was accompanied by his new wife who they would drop off in Annapolis on their way south. All the crew had returned. Slender little Warren had developed a bit of a paunch during his long summer absence, but Alistair, Wyatt, and Daniel appeared fit and well-rested. Ben motioned them to him. The crew circled around him, with Belle standing off toward the railing. Ben smiled and waved her close.

"You might as well hear it from me, Belle. Eddie will tell you all of it anyway." Everyone chuckled. "We are going to South Carolina, Georgetown...again. We will pick up a full cargo...and some guests."

"How many?" asked Alistair.

Ben shrugged his shoulders. "Perhaps three."

"You seem disappointed, Ben," Edward said.

"We bring one, or two, or three when there are three million down there."

"Three million slaves?" Belle asked. "Three million?"

Warren and Daniel scanned the area around the ship and leaned close to Belle. "Our voices carry over water, Mrs. Leonard," Daniel said, then lowering his voice to a whisper. "What we do is not only against the law, it can be dangerous. Abolitionists have been hung and their homes burned."

She brought her hand to her throat and stared wide-eyed at Edward. He patted her arm.

"We take proper precautions, dear."

She nodded in understanding, but the concern did not vanish from her face.

A man yelled from the docks and waved. He shouted a second time. The name "*Raven*" drifted over the water to the ship. Alistair tugged on Ben's sleeve and pointed at the man on the docks. Ben squinted his eyes in the sunshine.

"Mattingly...what the hell do you want?" he muttered to himself.

Mattingly yelled again and pointed in exaggerated motion to a small crate by his feet. Ben asked Warren to take the rowboat and bring the deputy

298

to the ship, but once the boat returned to the dock, Mattingly did not get into it. He only passed the box to Warren.

"This needs to go to Mrs. Binterfield," Warren said when he returned to the ship. "The deputy said it was personal effects of Mr. Binterfield that had been retained for the investigation of his murder." Warren reached behind and pulled something from his belt. "He said this was yours." Warren handed Ben his carved whale bone-handled knife.

Ben accepted the knife, turning it over in his hands, then held it up so Lyle could see that he had it. Mattingly waved and turned around.

"That's a beautiful knife," Belle said.

Ben smiled and nodded his head, then blew out his breath, tapping the knife's leather sheath against his palm as Mattingly walked away.

"It has quite a past," Ben said.

"Oh, really?"

"Yes. It was used in a murder, maybe several," Ben said, then slipped the sheath into his belt at his back. He tapped the little crate with his boot toe. "Warren, please stow this below."

⚬⟶◯◯⟵⚬

September 29th, 1847

The *Raven* rode at anchor below the glistening white lighthouse tower on North Island at the eastern shore of Winyah Bay. A gentle breeze blew across the mouth of the bay from the marsh a mile to the west, bringing the characteristic scent of 'Pluff Mud,' as the Georgetownians called it. Something in the slippery clay-like mud was enjoyable to rice. The combined flow of the five dark rivers and the tidal push back against them twice a day, created an amazing nursery for their rice when chaperoned by the Gullah.

The steam tug *Hannah* arrived after a short wait, to tow them into the little harbor. Rye whiskey was surpassing the demand for rum in the many southern states. They had picked up a cargo of rye whiskey in Annapolis, and the holds were crammed with one hundred twenty five-gallon casks. Ben considered his cargo profits. Between the profit on the whiskey and the northern demand for Carolina Gold rice, Ben would make an excellent profit on the voyage. The profit on that single trip would more than cover the cost of the *Raven*'s refit, but he would give it all away to have his sons back at home. It had been months without word about Aaron. He did not know if his younger son was dead or alive, and any day he could learn that his older one was dead as well. He shook his head and focused his attention on docking the ship.

While the cargo was unloaded and taken to a nearby warehouse, where local merchants would make purchases, Ben shouldered the crate and made his way to the Harbor Master's office.

"Always happy to see you, Captain Pulaski," the Harbor Master said. "It has been a while since you have visited us."

"Had to refit the *Raven*," he said. "She faced storms in both the Gulf and the Atlantic last year, and needed it."

"Well, sir, we are glad to have you back with us."

Ben smiled. "I need some assistance, sir. I have a small crate that needs to go to Palmetto Haven."

He smiled broadly, "Ah, something for the beautiful Mrs. Binterfield? I would be happy to assist in any way I could."

"It is the effects of her murdered husband..."

"Murdered? I never knew murder widowed her! All the more tragic! I sincerely hope the villain was captured."

Ben chuckled. "Lydia shot him in the head on a main street in Maryland."

The harbormaster blinked, wide-eyed. "I had never heard that! And you called her by her given name. You know her personally?"

"I brought her here from Havre de Grace, after Herbert's...murder. My home is just outside Havre de Grace."

300

"Oh, sir, there are so many questions I would ask you if you would consider allowing it. Maybe over a mug of ale?"

"Maybe sometime soon, but I would like to have this crate sent to her."

"I am sure you would wish to deliver it yourself."

'Well, no, n-"

"I insist. It would be my honor to send you up river with the *Hannah*..."

"That is kind of you Harbor Master, but I don't think the *Hannah* would float inside the Palmetto Haven canal..."

"Mmm, yes. Too shallow there for her..." the Harbormaster mumbled as he gazed out the windows onto the narrow harbor sitting in the bend of the Sampit River. "Ah! It' s there! The *Lydia* is docked just down the way." He dashed out of the office, yelling at the steamboat's boson to get his attention.

Ben sighed as the steamboat made the turn up the dark water of the narrow canal to the mansion. Spanish moss hung like funeral shrouds from the live oaks growing along the banks of the canal. In manicured spaces between the trees, marble statues of women holding grapes or flowers stared out at him with empty eyes. The manor house sat like an alabaster castle nestled among the trees at the bend in the canal. Ornamental white columns, supporting nothing marched along both edges of the brick pathway to the grand entrance.

A kingdom in the marsh, he thought.

In Lapidum, Sonja sat with Catherine Price on the Pulaski porch peeling apples.

"Poor Anna," Catherine said. "She was sitting on her porch, just like us, when the Army Lieutenant arrived to talk with her. Her brother was a captain under General Taylor down in Mexico. She told me last week when that man came to her, a cold chill ran up her spine, and a hole opened in her chest. She knew Walter was dead, even before the officer told her. Walter was her last kin."

The women became quiet, their eyes down at their laps, lost in their own visions.

"Do you have anyone in Mexico?" Sonja asked her.

"My cousin John, on my mother's side."

As they sat there, an Army officer rode up the towpath across the canal from the Pulaski property. He stopped a moment and appeared to study the slope in front of the Pulaski house, his face lost in the shadow of his military cap. His shoulders were bent, appearing tired after a long ride. He spurred his horse to move ahead. Sonja and Catherine listened to the iron shoes of the horse clomp across the swing bridge into Lapidum.

"I do hope he is not for me," Catherine said, but then breathed a sigh of relief as hoof beats sounded on the road. "Maybe someone in Stafford," she said.

They both peered at the end of the Pulaski's lane, the horse nudged into view and turned to cross the little wooden bridge.

"Oh my God," Catherine said and brought her hand up to her mouth. She stared at Sonja. "Oh my God," she said again through trembling lips.

Sonja shook her head. "No," she said through gritted teeth.

Catherine gazed at Sonja, her hand still over her mouth. Tears flooded Catherine's eyes.

"It is a cadet, coming to visit," Sonja told her.

Catherine shook her head. "He is an Army officer, Sonja. His uniform looks worn... and dusty."

Sonja stood, dropping the bowl of apple slices onto the porch. "No.," she said and went into the house. Catherine followed her.

Sonja stood at the kitchen counter, facing the back window. She kept her eyes focused down at the counter.

"This is filthy," she said.

She grabbed a cloth and dropped it into the wash sink. Boot heels came up the steps and onto the front porch. Sonja pumped the water. The steps entered through the open door. Sonja pumped and pumped again.

"No. No."

Catherine placed her hand on Sonja's back.

"No," Sonja said again.

Her heart thundered in her head.

"No." she heard herself say, but it was far away

A man's hand gently touched her shoulder. He said something, but she did not understand. It was lost in the pounding of her heart.

"No," she said.

The man spoke to her again, louder this time.

"Ma?"

She twirled around, the tears in her eyes filling her vision. She could not see him. She reached out to the blurred form and grabbed him with all her strength, pulling him to her.

"Isaac!" she cried.

Bibliography

Raven's Risk is an historical novel, and writers of novels take liberties with dates and incidents to blend them into the story. We are known to fold the actions of multiple historic incidents and people into a single character for continuity. Although no academic work is actually cited in this book, I would be neglecting due homage to my interesting sources of historical information, without sharing a bibliography with the reader. At least here, I can identify the original truths I 'massaged' in writing this story. I also offer my humble apologies to the historic researchers I so crudely burglarized.

Please visit my website rflackeybooks.com and select the page title "Pulaski's World" to see a complete list of books I read while developing this series.

ROBERT F. LACKEY lived in Havre de Grace, Maryland, for 23 years, spending many afternoons exploring the remnants of the Susquehanna and Tidewater Canal. He was a member of the Susquehanna Museum at the Lock House, and served a period as publisher for its newsletter. After moving to Havre de Grace from North Carolina in 1993, he fell in love with the little town sitting at the mouth of the Susquehanna River and head of the Chesapeake Bay. The area is rich in history and watershed culture reaching back to the beginning of the country. Among the many historic themes coexisting within the nearby sites and lanes, the Canal Era drew the author's attention first. Stepping outside technical writing to complete his first novel, *Pulaski's Canal,* Robert began a family story that has blossomed into a family saga. **Kingdoms in the Marsh** now joins the saga as the 4th installment of several sequels planned for the Pulaski family

"I wandered the trails and historic marker sites along the old Susquehanna and Tidewater Canal route, and it was easy for me to picture families centering their lives around the canal, the way community centers spring up along the interstates today. Of course I was drawn to the simpler times, barges only moved at three miles an hour, but my research identified not only the hard demands and historical challenges of that simpler life, but the richness of the world the people lived in then. Having access to the original gateway Lockhouse, still maintained by the local historical society, was an absolute thrill and it gave me my first backdrop.

Once the core characters of the story tumbled out of my imagination and onto the computer screen in front of me, they almost took on their own life. They frequently went in directions I had not planned in the

earlier part of the day, but evolved as the story evolved. Ben and Sonja, and their sons Isaac and Aaron, ARE the 19th century. Ben was born on the first second of January 1, 1800, Sonja in 1805. The Pulaski experience encompasses the national experiences of that century, but from the eyes of a Maryland family on the canals. Much as today's national news is perceived from the living rooms and household budgets of American families.

Now they are dear friends, and I look forward to keeping their story going through the 1800s. We will experience the changes that occurred in our country over the next two or three decades through them."

Robert is a member of the Historical Novel Society, the Surf Side Writer's group, and past president of the South Carolina Writer's Association. He is currently working on his fifth Pulaski novel, Brazen Deceit.

Robert currently lives with his patient wife, Sandi, in Murrells Inlet, South Carolina.

Coming in Autumn 2018
The next Pulaski adventure

The Pulaski saga continues with the 5th volume, into the years 1847-1849. Ben and Sonja face personal disasters and a painful separation. Ben's bold plan to free slaves from Washington DC, sends him into hiding in Leonardtown, Maryland.

Please visit Robert's website and Facebook(TM) page to learn about his current and future projects:
www.rflackeybooks.com
https://www.facebook.com/RFLackey.author

Books by Robert F. Lackey and his alter ego, Pug Greenwood, are available at his website, and through Amazon.com, BarnesandNoble.com, Booksamillion.com, and other internet book sellers. Kindle versions are available through Amazon.com.

Share your thoughts about this novel with Robert at
Rflackey.author@gmail.com